"Tomorrow is a powerful story that grabs your attention from the very first page! The gentle message of God's love flows throughout this book, and the character's struggles and triumphs will touch your heart. This beautifully written book will stay in your thoughts long after you finish it."

Sheri Martin,
Business Owner

"Be advised, it's very easy to get caught up in *Tomorrow*, Jeral Davis' unforgettable new novel about love, fame, and redemption. Clear your schedule before you pick it up, because once you start reading you won't want to put it down."

Marcus Folmar,
Screenwriter and Actor

"I am not an avid fiction reader. Yet, once I picked up Jeral Davis' debut novel, *Tomorrow*, I simply could not put it down. Once you delve into the lives of Ben and Juliana, it will be hard to turn way."

Judith Nelson,
Counseling Department Assistant

TOMORROW

TOMORROW

A NOVEL BY JERAL DAVIS

Tate Publishing & Enterprises

Published by Tate Publishing & Enterprises, LLC
127 E. Trade Center Terrace | Mustang, Oklahoma 73064 USA
1.888.361.9473 | www.tatepublishing.com

Tate Publishing is committed to excellence in the publishing industry. The company reflects the philosophy established by the founders, based on Psalm 68:11,
"The Lord gave the word and great was the company of those who published it."

Book design copyright © 2008 by Tate Publishing, LLC. All rights reserved.
Cover design by Lindsay B. Behrens
Interior design by Joey Garrett
Edited by Amanda Webb Soderberg

Published in the United States of America

ISBN: 978-1-60604-654-8
1. Fiction: Religious: Romance/Contemporary
2. Fiction: Action & Adventure
08.09.17

For Patricia, my mother, whose profound love deeply influenced my life. You planted the creative seed, and it finally blossomed.

This book is dedicated to every man, woman, and child infected with HIV and AIDS. I pray you never doubt that you were created for unfathomable purpose.

ACKNOWLEDGEMENTS

"It takes a village to raise a child." It certainly took an entire collective of family and friends to complete this novel. Without the following, the manuscript simply would have gathered dust and withered.

First, I want to thank Tate Publishing and the amazing staff in Mustang. Words cannot express my profound gratitude to them. They took a chance on this Coloradoan housewife and made a dream reality.

To Amanda, my editor, who was tough when required, humorous when I faltered, and exhortative when I doubted.

To my amazing family who prayed, encouraged, prodded, threatened, and made me realize it wasn't about me.

To my V.P. Family who always understood and allowed me to craft the tale of my imaginary friends. Trust me, your prayers were like gold.

To T.M. (my first read)—I will not be able spend another day without thinking of you. You never let me give up!

To Kiki, Biscuit, Jules, and Tampa Bay Lisa. You taught me to believe God.

To Marcus, who continuously inspired me to dig deeper.

To my children, who sacrificed time with me, dragged me to my computer, and plopped me in the chair.

To C.D.M.—I'll never forget our meeting at Carrabba's. You brought splendor and authenticity to this project. Keep laughing!

To Helen Hajiyianni and Cadre, both of whom worked tirelessly to encourage and educate.

To Christ, who first unraveled this intriguing tale in a night vision and penned it thereafter on my heart.

Finally, I am indebted to my beloved husband, Richard. You were ceaseless in your support, love, and patience. The sweat was also on your brow.

"Many are the plans in a man's heart, but it is the Lord's purpose that prevails"

Proverbs 19:21 (NIV).

CHAPTER ONE

Tomorrow never came.

Beside the Natal plum cart, Juliana dabbed her brow. Although only the third hour of the day, she feverishly patted the perspiration. She bit into the plum; her reward was a succulent eruption. Swiftly, she dabbed the sticky juice with a gauzy kerchief.

A breeze—heavy with guava, curry, and onions—swirled from the aisles of produce carts. Ambling down the market pathway, Juliana devoured the plum and tossed the tissue-veiled remains in her canvas bag. Standard practice decreed waste was trampled underfoot or by Continental radials. Juliana didn't judge those given to this custom, but her hand declined to further pollute. A group of white women, appareled in western tunics and vibrant capris, either rubbed or scrunched their noses. Juliana's nostrils had long grown accustomed to the raucous swell from the antiquated sewer system. The Boptang market maintained allure, novelty, and sustenance, but failed miserably at apt sanitation.

She meandered through the aromatic maze of homegrown produce, then suddenly halted. The sweet, chewy gems of candied figs, biscuits, and hertzog cookies caught her eye. Smirking, she handed over a few rand and stuffed the bundle in her violet canvas bag, company for the potatoes and wild spinach. A giggle erupted. She would be scolded for indulging Hanna, Lorato, and Kendrick.

After the late model cars had rumbled through in their morning rush, a frown darkened the youthful texture of her face. Maybe she had mistaken the time they planned to meet. She tightened the teal-hued kerchief around her mass of amber curls and headed toward the Toyota pickup.

Boptang whispered promises and conundrums as layered as the viscera of a rose. Unlike stateside, Boptang citizens welcomed visitors without prior notification and luxuriated in mealtimes satiated with proverbs woven by ancient sagas.

Juliana had also facilitated as a nurse's aid to homebound AIDS patients. Bandages were changed, salve caressed onto sores, and family members instructed how to administer care in her absence. In this secluded region of South Africa, the lofty position of the only child of the revered Pastor Quincy DeLauer vanished. It had not been her parents who placed the yoke upon her neck. A zealous faction of their congregation, assured their words bore exhortation, had attempted to constrict the harness. The daily pressure to march to the convoluted melody of a perfected life rescinded. In Boptang, Juliana could simply *be*.

Despite the abject poverty, implausible gender equality, and prowl of death, Juliana found Boptang the most blessed place in the world. Villagers possessed little, yet their devotion surpassed most in America. Residents reveled in indulgent worship. Here, Juliana surrendered with luscious abandon to her Savior without a thought of scrutiny.

A fierce wind rocked the durable pickup. Summers stateside paralleled winter in South Africa. July ushered brisk winds off the Indian Ocean glazing gold haze on the plains.

The front door to the third house on the right challenged the stern wind. It tittered, opening three-quarters, its hinges bewailing a sharp protest. She shut off the engine and jogged from the truck as her eyes canvassed the isolated area. Most Boptang parents benefited from the generous scholarships available to their children by the graciousness of her church, Living Water Fellowship. Thus, only the youngest crawled at their mother's feet or piled heaps of maize in the clay pots to be pounded for *papa*.

Mme Tboki called from her doorstep adjacent to the house Juliana was approaching, *"Dumela."*

Juliana replied apprehensively, "*Dumela mme.*"

Mme Tboki must have sensed alarm in Juliana's stance; the customarily reticent woman then asked, her tone taut, "*Kgotso, le phela jwang?*"

Before she could deem all was well, Juliana approached the door. The kitchen flowed into the seating area and the seating area toward the two bedrooms. Every item had been as she left it earlier before her market departure.

Juliana backed into the harsh wind and responded, "*Ke phela hantle, wena o phela jwang, mme?*" deeming all was well and inquired of the woman's health.

The scream sliced the gusty atmosphere swelling from the veld, the distance of two American blocks from the village. Juliana sprinted toward the waist-high grasses, her toned calves in adroit transport. To her right, two jet-black skulls thrashed above the dancing grass. Suddenly, she crouched as if a predator sniffing the scent of prey.

Another scream.

The men's pale shirts whipped against their chests and bellies as their fists landed unbroken blows upon the object of their fury. A scream soared from her belly, yet her throat refused liberation. Juliana raced forward, dread escalating with every stride. Her body impeded the next blow and one potent fist crushed her shoulder, the other caved in the flesh below her shoulder blade. The pain bit through her muscle as if energized by fire.

Black masks camouflaged their faces. Their eyes were baleful stones, calloused and unremitting. The one to her left reached for her. Her incalculable hours galloping upon treadmills and waging war with free weights permitted her squirm from his grip. Juliana propelled her body forward.

"Tomorrow!"

Juliana attempted to kneel beside her childhood friend and was yanked against the abuser to her right. His chest heaved against Juliana's back, his thighs lingered at the bulge of her rear. This nearness repelled her to nausea. No hints of humanity expelled from him; no heat, no helplessness of mortality. He was an aura of waste, desolation, and destruction.

"Stay out of this!" His putrid breath caused Juliana's stomach to tighten. He reeked of the cut-rate beer Umqombothi likely acquired from a local *shebeen*.

"Haven't you done enough?" the other vigilante accused. "Promising her passage to the States to consult so-called miracle doctors. It is too late."

Juliana looked at their hands. Tomorrow's blood streaked the rubber surface of their gloves. Savage swelling of her friend's eyes, lips, and jaw disfigured her broad, majestic features. Tomorrow's weeping cut Juliana like a machete through a baobab tree.

Juliana gulped in the dusty air, her lungs burning, not recognizing either of their voices. Although every inflection of their Sesotho dialect was flawless, the nuance of their tongue rang foreign.

"This is outrageous!" Juliana screamed and the pressure of his grip cut into her sculpted biceps. "She has done nothing wrong!"

"She has brought shame upon us and her ancestors."

"You know better than that."

"I know of nothing else."

His glare was a peculiar infusion of desperation and loathing. Juliana wanted to shout of the courage Tomorrow had shown after she discovered she had been infected. How she had waited for hours, baked by the sun's relentless heat, to receive check-ups and medication at the clinic thirty kilometers away. How at dawn, fatigued and troubled, she had regarded the welfare of her three young children crafting intricate and exhaustive plans despite the loom of sorrow. Yet, no matter the strain to render guilt, Tomorrow had refused to incriminate her adulterous husband. Juliana's chest heaved, these truths burning in her throat.

"Tell us how she was baked by the sun's relentless heat awaiting medication. Enlighten us how fatigued and troubled she was regarding the welfare of her three young children. Yes. Paint the picture."

Juliana shuddered at his intimate disclosure. "How?"

"It is imperative that we know."

"Then you know of Tiro's impertinent rationalization."

The ancient resolution of ingrained tradition smoldered in his eyes. "*Uena u, Juliana.* You are, Juliana. Your grandfather was welcomed here a half century ago by my ancestors. Your parents shipped plentiful resources to Boptang. You, daughter, have been nurtured and sheltered here. But, this is a matter of which you lack sovereignty to address."

The incessant racing of her heart abandoned every other vital organ to nourish its ventricles. *Uena u Juliana,* alerted Juliana that their phrasing was connected to Lesotho, which was over 300 kilometers away. Although she held no recollection of them, they knew of the DeLauers' history and her name.

She cried above the bellow of the wind, "Custom and tradition assert her husband is the only man who can sentence her to death. Tiro is not here. Therefore he could not have sanctioned such action. This is a grave injustice to who we are."

He retrieved something concealed in the swaying brush. The morning sun gleamed off the dark metal of the rifle. "It must be done."

"Let her go with me!"

The men glared.

Juliana panted as if her head had been forced beneath water. "*Please. At such a great distance, surely she can bring you no harm."

Silent, as still as a moonless night, she witnessed the struggle in his eyes. She stole a glance at Tomorrow. Her friend wiped at tears, then slowly stood. Tomorrow squared her shoulders and raised a trembling hand. Then she did something that disturbed Juliana with such intensity, her body rattled against the oppressor's grip.

Tomorrow smiled.

"No." Juliana whispered to Tomorrow, to the vigilantes, to God, and to every senseless death. Juliana saw in Tomorrow's eyes supreme peace. The type only emitted from bone-deep resolution of one's pending death.

"*Palesa.*" Tomorrow's vocal chords seemed strangled. "*Tshwarela. Ontibile.*"

Juliana shivered, the effect of her nickname crushing. "It's not time."

Tshwarela.

Forgive.

Ontibile.

God is watching over me.

Tomorrow affirmed that she was equipped for her end.

The base of the rifle smashed into Juliana's temple, and she was unconscious before her body reached the earth. The men turned to their intended victim and did not cease their aggression until the young wife and mother, her skull crushed, lay very still.

Although sunglasses protected his eyes, Ben still cupped a hand over the metallic bridge. South African weather was only spiteful in the summer when the winds raged over the Highveld and loosened sands of the mine-dumps, viciously whirling them in the air.

He had traveled ten kilometers west from Soweto to pay the farmer. Ben pressed the rand into the white farmer's palm, bitter. Diverting his hostility, Ben stared at colorful murals painted upon the towers of the Orlando Power Station in the distance. The man had taken advantage of the system. Streams trailed through the property, and he charged a fee to his surrounding black neighbors to supply water to their village tap. This resource had once been free to their ancestors, centuries before the installation of apartheid in 1948, "pass books," and the Bantu Authorities Act in 1951. Then those who resided on and worked the land were segregated into "homelands" and stripped of their political voice except within designated areas. The inhabitants became sojourners within their native land.

"Did you see that?" Bruce, his pervasive bodyguard, asked.

Ben followed his eye trail to the veld. As of late, the local media warned of vigilantes within the Gauteng district who stalked those infected with HIV. The belief was that these men beat their victims to death. They only attacked the unaccompanied in isolated areas. No one was immune to their form of rectitude, not even the elderly, and it conjured an edgy mood.

The farmer eyed Bruce as if he were a three-headed insect. Bruce towered well over six feet, was built wide, and wore his ebony scalp bald. Upon sight, many an overzealous fan had retreated straight away.

Ben asked the landowner, "Are there workers in that part of the veld?"

The cultivator, whose skin begged for sunscreen, turned to the area where Ben nodded. He faced Ben. "Nothing but grass for cattle to graze. Why?"

Ben looked to Bruce. Because of the necessity of immutable trust between them, they had developed a sense of symbiotic insight. Every look held a connotation only they understood.

"Follow my lead." Bruce's left hand on the shoulder holster concealed his revolver. Ben's bodyguard was a former marine turned FBI operative. During a precarious sting, Bruce Carter had thwarted the illicit activity. Several bullets had ripped into his right knee and thigh, tearing apart more than tissue and ligaments. Bruce had retired—being planted behind some desk would have been murder—with the highest number of accolades given by the Bureau to any agent. Bruce had been Ben's human shield for over a decade, beginning back when both men had barely entered their thirties.

The muzzle of a rifle poked above the stalks fifty yards to their right. The grass bowed as the masked men escaped over the incline and into the distance. Ben cursed; they were too far to legally subdue them. He and Bruce stooped in case the gunman decided to fire a shot. Ben mentally gathered details. *Two men, thin, swift as cheetahs, with black ski masks brandishing one rifle.*

"High caliber?" Ben questioned.

"A fifty based on the muzzle design."

Both Americans raced to the center of the field, shielding themselves from the dust by pulling up shirt collars.

"Strange. Why carry that type of weapon if it's never intended to be used? These lunatics use fists not bullets to conduct death."

"To induce both cooperation and fear," Bruce answered.

Near the center, the pasture bent into a Y-shape. Two bloodied women, abandoned like discarded rag dolls, were covered by the blinding sand. Bruce knelt and gently checked the pulse of the woman whose face was horribly disfigured. Grimly, he shook his head. The other woman, her temple discolored by a deep violet bruise, stirred. The men shared a look: *why had her life been spared?*

Ben knelt. "Try not to move."

She moaned, rubbing the menacing lump. Her eyes, the color of brown sugar laced with butter, centered on him with such ferocious meditation that he felt as if every unspoken secret, angst, and heartache of his being was exposed. This pensive stranger was butchering him, delicately, second by second. Ben ordered his eyes to divert, yet they rebelled, seemingly stupefied against her contemplation.

Bruce shifted; she slowly turned toward the movement. When she saw the woman to her left, she crawled to the woman's side.

She removed her teal kerchief and tawny curls tumbled free of restraint. The young woman wiped the dirt from the silent, broken face and rocked her cataleptic companion. She sang in Sesotho. Ben mentally arranged the words. "Oh, to carry you away. To hold you in my arms and carry you away."

Ben held out a hand the texture of bronzed calfskin. "It's not safe for you to remain here."

Her head jerked upward. "What do you know of it!"

"Let me help you take her to a safer place."

She blinked against the wind. "Help! You want to help me? I need nothing of the sort."

He inched his hand closer. "You do. I'll take her wherever you need her to be."

She stared at the flaccid body as the men waited. When she looked up, her eyes were filled with utter bewilderment. Ben imagined she must be wondering how it was bizarre to witness such heartless brutality and mercy within the same day. Slowly she nodded. Ben nodded to Bruce who jogged to the sedan and used his cell phone to contact the police. Ben waited in silence. The delay seemed to compile her pain beneath layers of desolation.

The authorities arrived and performed a concise investigation with gloved hands and masks. Afterward, they shrouded the body in tarp. The lead official eyed the temple-bruised woman who stood as if the harsh wind had been an abrasive against her marrow.

"Where to, then? Parker's?" the official asked, referring to the nearby mortuary.

"Yes," she whispered.

The farmer shot them a look of repugnance. The cultivator didn't appreciate that his veld had become a crime scene for a HIV-positive woman. He sputtered and cursed about the cost of cleanup.

Bruce held open the car door, and she crept in. Ben climbed into the front seat. She cleared her throat. "Parker's Mortuary. It's—"

"Yes, ma'am." Bruce's tone was passive, as if any remnant of control would shatter her. "I am familiar with the location."

Within the past month alone, Parker's had buried six Boptang residents, their lives taken by the disease spoken of in a hush.

Beneath the grainy dampness, which concealed nearly every inch of her athletic frame, Ben saw patches of skin the consistency of velvety caramel.

"Her name is Tomorrow," she stated, her pitch as fragile as dew encountering the scorch of the morning sun.

"That's captivating. Tomorrow."

She remained silent the remainder of their somber journey. Her companions weren't privy that a paramount aspect of Boptang's allure had died. Every visit, Tomorrow had enveloped Juliana, her embrace an assertion of inclusive acceptance.

Tomorrow would never come to her again.

CHAPTER TWO

Ben jumped. It took him several moments to realize he was on-board a jet headed to L.A. The nightmares, which had vanished for months, inexplicably returned during his stay in South Africa. Just before he was jolted into consciousness, he remembered the suffocating scent of his own blood hastily escaping his throat.

Bruce eyed him, their eyes speaking a confidential language. "The nightmare?"

Ben blinked then nodded, as if his head had been reattached that morning. The sun cast a breathtaking array of lilac and plum across the barren sky as it descended in the west. He fluffed the pillow, attempted to discover a comfortable position, found none, and bolted from his seat.

"I'm going to use the restroom."

The first-class lavatories were occupied, so he turned and walked down the aisle to business class. Ben walked through the galley, smiled at a flight attendant preparing a cocktail, and discovered an empty restroom. He turned on the faucet, washed his hands, splashed the tepid water on his face, and shut off the spout. He placed his palms on the miniscule countertop, shut his eyes, and breathed deeply.

July consisted of assisting orphanages, building and volunteering at a health care clinic, and conferencing HIV/AIDS symposiums. Ben's next film project wouldn't begin until August. The actor would board another jet, one bound for Denver where he would personify a cerebral detective tormented by his past. The detective element demanded research. The torment was as familiar as the back of his hand.

Maybe it was the reality that the question was as relentless as the answer was elusive. What part of the human psyche plotted and condoned the murder of an influential, beloved thirty-year-old schoolteacher? What basis propelled another human being to reason her death was of benefit to the community, their country, possibly the world? How could one so deeply loved, once infected, morph into an object of utter revulsion?

Maybe it was the hostile, political environment steeped in century-old sacred tradition that had beaten down a responsiveness toward compassion for those who had fallen. Maybe the utter senselessness of bigotry cut a deeper chasm than Ben had been able to witness standing on the outside, clothed in white skin, his blue eyes looking into those inflicted. Maybe its roots carried a poison so pervasive it didn't cease at simply distorting the intellect but made fraudulent the deepest regions of the heart. This insidious darkness that lurked in the souls of men caused him sleep deprivation. Regardless, Ben longed to remain in South Africa.

Normally, his return to L.A. would be marked by a sense of well-being—secure that he had amended someone's pain. But the burial of the young mother and the onerous product it had left upon her friend felt like sediment in the pit of his stomach. It had pierced the integument of his psyche, etching deep.

The fasten seat belt sign chimed. He unlatched the door and maneuvered around another passenger waiting on a turn for the bathroom. In the first row of business class, aisle seat, a mass of amber curls peeked above the blanket's edge. He blinked three times to substantiate there was no mistake. She squirmed. Ben imagined the blanket felt like bothersome whiskers against her silky, toffee-colored skin. Days before, that same skin and those satiny curls had been cloaked in flaxen earth, her composure isolated and barren.

Although he willed her, she didn't open her eyes.

"Sir." A flight attendant appeared. "It isn't safe for you to be out of your seat."

"I'm returning." Ben turned, his amble toward first class unhurried.

When the flight attendant moved out of sight, he reversed and studied the masterful, architectural flow of her exquisite features. She pumped her head against the pillow until it lay flat at the base of her neck. Restlessly, she opened her eyes. Ben stood only a few feet away, frozen to the aircraft floor. He wondered if it would be a flash in her eyes or a hand to her mouth that confirmed recognition.

Her eyes settled on him and the air in his chest seized. Her graceful brow frowned, and Ben thought those desolate moments they shared had sharpened in her memory. Suddenly, she yawned, then ducked beneath the blanket.

Ben returned to his seat, reaching for the only tangible factor he had of her. His hand dipped into his suit jacket and removed two items. The teal kerchief, left behind in the car, was concealed inside a compact hazardous waste bag he had obtained from the clinic. The carnelian patches of Boptang earth created an errant design against the cotton. In his other hand, Ben held the program from the young mother's memorial.

He eyed the black-and-white photo of Tomorrow. Her skin was flawless mahogany, her features regal and broad, and her stature as majestic as a mountain range. She was the type of woman to wile away the afternoon with, studying the gesture of her mouth and being lulled by the lilt of her voice. The program pronounced a husband and three children all under the age of eleven had survived her. Their photos formed a heart-shaped pattern around the obituary script. Yet none were present at the internment.

Tomorrow had taught primary school before the virus relegated her energy within the walls of her home. Most parents realized their children might steal away, so they hadn't refused their requests to attend the service. Tomorrow had birthed an incomparable hope in them. Ben had positioned himself in the rear of the cramped room. Other than Mr. Parker's two assistants', his had been the only white face in the multitude. In the forefront had been the woman he discovered at Tomorrow's side, whipped by the callous wind and malevolent humanity. Juliana DeLauer.

After the service, he had trailed the resilient mourners toward the gravesite, their voices a stabbing chorus of courage and expectancy.

That night after he and Bruce made their grisly discovery in the field, she had accepted the ride to a small *polata* within Boptang. A thick, morose language had permeated the cabin of the luxury sedan. Bruce rushed through every red light, acutely aware of the dangers had he stopped. Car jackers had lurked near streetlights, awaiting their next victim.

Just before dawn, they had pulled up to the jagged row of modest houses. Ben held up a hand to Bruce, hopped out of the car, and opened the door for Juliana instead. She limped beyond him in muted consumption. Ben felt shrouded in desperation and angst. He watched as she trudged toward the house to the far right then suddenly halted. Upon the doorstep were two leather suitcases. He and Bruce watched as disbelief sank her shoulders further into her chest. Her effort to lift the bags seemed to command strength she did not possess. Ben rushed from the car door and grabbed her personal belongings. She met his eye as if searching for an explanation. Ben desperately wished he could solve the puzzle instead of witnessing the perfidy claw at her soul. Her hands flew to her face, concealing the incredulity in her eyes.

Stepping, as if the disbelief had multiplied in her bones, she lurched to a home two doors down.

"*Mme Tboki*. It's Juliana. *Ako*. Please … "

After a moment, a woman in her forties unhooked the metal latch. She drew her bed clothing tighter when she saw Ben standing a few feet behind the distraught figure who had disturbed her sleep.

"Come," the woman said. When Juliana disappeared into the dark room, Mme Tboki beckoned to Ben. He dropped the belongings just beyond the threshold, stepped back, and stared as she shut the door.

Ben returned to Parker's and made full payment for all of Tomorrow's services. He demanded the mortician preserve his anonymity. The mortician eventually submitted. A man of his status and celebrity could create irreversible, resounding trouble if not obeyed.

He was alerted to the present by the hiss of Bruce's Pellegrino bottle. The actor studied the bubbles as they clung to the jagged edges of the ice chips. He returned his attention to a photo of Juliana and Tomorrow, somewhere in their teens, cheeks and chests pressed together. Glee was the word that surfaced in Ben's mind. They had shared uncompromised glee.

Ben returned the program and the sealed kerchief to his jacket and stretched his lengthy frame. His gaze was fixed on the dazzling sunset as his mind returned to Boptang.

"What are you thinking?" Bruce asked, neatly creasing the *New York Times* back into its original fold.

"She's onboard."

Bruce, ever the sharp-eyed professional, didn't even turn to look. "Business class, first row, aisle seat."

Ben gaped at him. "You saw her?"

"She boarded during the last call. I thought you did as well. I assumed it was the reason for your silence the past six hours."

Ben was irritated at the irony that he, a highly skilled actor, failed to summon appropriate words that would reach her. He removed his laptop from beneath the seat and e-mailed his manager, Grace Connors. His request was straightforward. He wanted to uncover the ambiguity of Juliana DeLauer, and the sooner the better.

Juliana exchanged one jet for another in L.A. She was oblivious that the man who found her, stunned and brokenhearted, was only two feet behind in the customs' line.

Ninety minutes later she landed and was whisked by the tram to baggage claim where she spotted her mother near the carousel. Dionne had never been the type of mother to wait at the curb; more than any other moment in their history, Juliana was profoundly grateful.

Instantly, Dionne discerned that her daughter could not give voice to her anguish. She touched Juliana's cheek. "You're home, Palesa. You're home."

Juliana found it impossible to smile at the nickname her mother had bestowed upon her only child. Palesa translated to flower in Sesotho. To Dionne, Juliana was the most precious bloom God ever created.

Juliana climbed into her mother's chili pepper red convertible and grasped her mother's hand. She leaned back against the leather headrest and closed her eyes. Dionne's potent voice permeated the cabin, serenading Juliana with gospel melodies. From Juliana's earliest memory, this action calmed her nerves with such persuasion no drug could compare.

The women drove beyond Pena Boulevard and merged onto the lengthy toll road of E-470 heading southwest to Parker. Thirty minutes later, the convertible pulled onto the spiraling driveway encased by soaring evergreens dusted with the pre-dawn glow. Her mother drove into the garage fit for six vehicles and lowered the door.

"Can you speak it, baby?" Her mother caressed Juliana's curls.

"Words seem vain."

Her mother opened the driver's door. "Come inside." Juliana stepped from the vehicle. "Head upstairs to your room. I'll bring in your bags."

Normally, Juliana would have protested. This day, she simply complied. She walked along the corridor with twelve-foot ceilings etched by crown molding, which opened to the massive kitchen equipped to create envy in any chef. Immediately, her nose detected the deep, nutty aroma of red bush tea brewing. The treasured scent nearly overwhelmed her.

She shuffled through the opulent dining room and brushed beyond the living room dressed with lavish custom furnishings where the birth of another sunrise flooded through massive windows.

Its graceful rays spotlighted portraits of the DeLauer trio—Juliana, her mother, and her deceased father. She trudged up the Brazilian cherry staircase to the second room on the right.

She flipped on the light. A supple golden glow illuminated her four-poster mahogany bed. Juliana flopped on the bedside bench adorned in silk the shade of eggplant and stared out the oversized French doors that opened to her private deck. Her bedroom faced the east, and the sun was just breaking through the blackberry sky. Juliana's eyes scanned the room, reacquainting her vision to the space she hadn't seen in six weeks.

Her bay windows were shielded by Hunter Douglas sheers that

ushered in or blocked sunlight by remote. Her mahogany dresser held three Mona Lavender plants potted in African Blackwood vases. She had first discovered the plants at the Kirstenbosch Botanical Gardens in Cape Town nearly thirteen years prior. She adored their vibrant lavender spikes, which never failed to blossom in early spring. The nightstands matched the same rich mahogany wood as her bed. Warmth, steeped with reminiscence, crossed her heart.

The frame seemed inadequate to encompass Quincy DeLauer's efflorescent personality. It held a candid shot taken by Juliana as he painted a vivid creation beneath the canopy of their backyard gazebo. Before. Before the cancer and subsequent radiation treatments sapped his force. Father and daughter were so identical in appearance and mannerisms to observe their interaction was to witness a mesmerizing concerto.

Where she refused to land her sight was the platinum frames on her left nightstand. It held metal casings of Tomorrow and her beloved children, Hanna, Lorato, and Kendrick. Juliana recognized it would take more than courage to ever study them again.

She leaned her head on the comforter and watched as her mother deposited her luggage near the customized closet.

"Hungry, Palesa?"

Juliana shook her head. "Thanks for hauling those up sixteen steps, Mom. They aren't exactly buoyant."

Her mother held up her arms and flexed her impressive biceps. Dionne continued flexing as she disappeared into Juliana's bathroom. A few seconds later, Juliana heard the rush of water in her Jacuzzi tub.

She entered her closet, where she undressed and draped a plum colored kimono around her body. When she exited, her mother no longer in the bathroom, Juliana shut off the water and dipped beneath the sudsy, lavender-scented foam.

Her mother reappeared carrying a steaming cup that she placed on the granite ledge encompassing the tub, so Juliana could retrieve it at will. Her mother rested on the ledge as well, eyeing the nasty bruises that marked her child's temple and shoulder.

"I can't remember what happened, Mom."

"None of it?"

"She was supposed to meet me at the market. But she never came."

Dionne waited, not wanting to usher more pain. Mme Tboki and her eldest daughter had traveled nearly an hour via a crammed *kombi*, or taxi, to the nearest Internet café. There she had sketched a lengthy e-mail detailing the vicious beating and eventual slaying in the veld.

After a few moments, Juliana said, "I remember the wind. I remember how it stung my eyes and covered my dress."

Again, her mother waited like a sentinel awaiting orders.

Juliana brushed her chin against the scented foam. "Mme Tboki said Tiro received an account while at the diamond mine in Jo'Burg. He insisted the children be removed from the home and my things set outside of the door. My welcome was revoked. I stayed with the Tboki's until the memorial and never once saw Tiro. I'm not certain he even attended. I wasn't allowed a chance to tell Hanna, Lorato, and Kendrick good-bye."

Dionne caressed Juliana's cheek. "Baby, I'm so sorry."

"The memorial was arranged through Parker's, but it seems as if I sleepwalked through the preparations."

"How so?"

"I have no idea how Tomorrow's body arrived there or who paid the expenses."

"There wasn't a record?"

"Mr. Parker was almost rude, only offering that the provisions had been paid in full by an anonymous donor. I sensed he was fearful somehow."

"Donor?"

"He almost seemed panicked that I wouldn't simply drop the matter. His agitation only increased that aggravating habit he has of writing numbers from the inside out. One by one, every single digit, inside out."

Dionne nodded, remembering the children she had helped bury after the 1976 uprising. Parker's had been in its infancy then, Parker himself barely graduated from university.

Dionne smoothed the natural curls on Juliana's head. "I suppose it's possible some of the village could have pooled and come up with the money. The percentage that refused to celebrate her death."

"That percentage would not have been able to carry the scale of memorial she had, Mom. It's certain expense was of no question."

Both women lost themselves in thought, seeking solution to the mystery. Juliana sipped the *rooibos*, Afrikaans for South African Red Bush tea, and moaned. The rich leaves had permeated the hot water, bathing her throat in a delicious combustion of sweet nuttiness.

"This is luscious. I smelled it as soon as I walked through the door."

"Nothing is too much for my Palesa."

"And you made it plain, instead of how they take it in Boptang with milk and sugar."

Juliana's resistance to battle the surge of pain failed. Dionne knelt closer and held her daughter's face in both hands.

Juliana fought the throb rising in her throat. "I am an element of them. The same substance of life that courses through their veins flows through mine. How could they shun me? How could they tell me I have no voice?"

Dionne shifted on the granite and held her child, undisturbed by the stain Juliana's soapy grasp created on her designer blouse.

"How could they suddenly deem me as an outsider? We've shared births and deaths, defeats and victories."

Dionne stroked her daughter's head. "Just let it out, baby."

"How could anyone reason that tradition was worth more than Tomorrow's life? She did not have to die!"

"Yes, baby. I know."

"Who received justice, Mom? Who? Tell me?"

Juliana released the acrimony she had suppressed for three days, the enormity discharging from her heart. Mother and daughter clung to one another long after the water cooled.

When Juliana was spent, her mother helped her pull on a nightgown and walked with her, shoulder-to-shoulder, to the bed. Although much anguish had been freed, Dionne saw evidence that more lingered in Juliana's eyes.

Juliana climbed into the bed; Dionne tucked the covers to Juliana's side and climbed upon the comforter. Juliana rested her head on her mother's lap. Dionne listened until Juliana's breathing grew louder than the whistling wind. Through the large bay windows, it swayed the heather and rustled through the evergreen-lined five-acre property.

Dionne stroked the top of Juliana's head, smiling slightly. Juliana adored heather, deeming the countryside a field of amethyst.

Dionne's eyes looked to the textured ceiling. "Lord, my baby's heart is torn apart. You said blessed are those that mourn, for they will be comforted. Comfort her, Lord. Restore her joy and peace."

Juliana stirred and Dionne caressed her cheek until she quieted. "I pray for Your presence and wisdom and judgment against the works of darkness in this situation. May all the veils be removed and spiritual eyes opened to see and know what is true."

Dionne didn't wipe away the tears that glided down her cheeks and clung to her chin. To wipe them away would diminish the immeasurable loss of Tomorrow. Her mind flashed to Tomorrow's children.

"Bring them to a place of comfort, peace, and understanding, Lord. Please protect them physically, emotionally, and mentally against all harm. Your ways are wonderful. Your assurance of joy and peace are promised. Thank You for being with us during this sorrowful time."

Words suddenly seemed wholly inadequate to portray the deepest stirrings in her heart. She held her only child close as if to convince that her presence was a formidable opponent against looming evil. She hummed quietly, her prayer drumming fearlessly beyond the regions of her heart.

"Amen."

CHAPTER THREE

Juliana's sandaled feet splashed through the gritty puddles on the LoDo streets of Denver. She pulled her magenta trench over her head and felt the cool rain splatter against her cheeks. Late August had produced drenching rain nearly every evening. Many Coloradoans opened their windows in welcome of the moist nocturnal breezes.

The vibrant trench weaved through the dense gauntlet of paparazzi that dominated the sidewalk entrance to Tanner's. Tanner's was notorious for both its exquisite food and alluring decor, yet patrons never had to wait in the rain. An intimidating line of bodies wrapped around the corner of the building. She grunted, then swayed to the front as if the lead model in a Milan fashion show. She hadn't shared a meal with Tricia since her return from South Africa in late July. Now that she finally surfaced from her four-week isolation, she had no intention of returning to her cocoon.

"William." She pulled the coat tighter so it framed her face. "Is the Queen of England a dining guest this evening?"

The head of security allowed her a slim grin. "Do you have reservations?'"

"My hunger is a perpetual reservation!"

He looked beyond her at the impending line of customers.

"Wills, have you not seen this face nearly every week for the past three years?"

"No reservation. No entry. No exceptions."

She diverted her attention to the flailing arms above William's towering head. "Juliana! Over here."

Juliana beamed. "Do you hear that? That is the sound of my reservation."

The retired Bronco linebacker-turned-restaurant-security-lead stepped to the side. Juliana stretched to her tiptoes and planted a glossy kiss on his right cheek.

When she was within arms' length, Tricia gripped her in a potent hug. If Juliana wasn't traveling for her writing position at provocative *Core*, or residing in Boptang, she and Tricia shared habitual companionship.

Tricia pulled away to study, her soft hands cradling Juliana's face. "Thanks for coming out, Jules. I've missed you like a stop sign misses the color red."

"I missed you, too, T. Thanks for being patient. Especially since your wedding is only three months away."

"Come inside before you catch pneumonia."

Tricia grabbed her left arm and escorted her through the aspiring, fashionable Friday evening crowd. Her feet squished inside her leather sandals, transforming her normal graceful gait into a cowboy swagger.

"T, there are paparazzi filling the whole block. What's going on?"

After Juliana checked her coat, Tricia escorted her beyond the merlot-colored leather booths of the bar to the opulent dining room where tables donned cognac-hued cloths. They ascended a flight of steps the color of brandy to the raised dining area. Tricia pointed to an open booth with unobstructed views of the entrance, the wraparound bar, and tinted glass balcony above. Juliana quickly scanned the patrons. This action assured Tricia her friend desired to participate in their customary sport.

"Think you can beat your world record?" Tricia teased behind the leather-trimmed menu. "Who has created such a stir at our favorite eatery?"

Juliana reached across the table, took a drink of Tricia's bottled water, then glanced at her watch. "It's seven-fifteen. My hunger has vaulted my brain juices."

Tricia shot her a puzzled look. "You're not biting tonight?"

Juliana rested her back against the seat. "Rain check?"

"I hope that wasn't a pun."

"Would it get me off the hook?"

Tricia conceded then observed that Juliana's grief lingered just beneath the surface like liquid about to boil. Tricia fought her desire to curse herself for being so insensitive.

"A letter arrived this morning from Jo'Burg," Juliana explained as she removed the silverware from the linen napkin then placed the cloth in her lap. "Hanna sent it to my mailbox at *Core*. She must have kept some of my feature articles and thought it best to send it to work."

Juliana reached inside her purse, removed an envelope, and passed it to Tricia. Tricia read the letter, her heart dipping into the insidious state of Tomorrow's children.

"Hanna's with fraternal grandparents in Soweto and Lorato in Pretoria with an aunt. Kendrick ran away from an uncle's house and hasn't been heard from since."

"I'm so sorry."

Juliana turned away.

"You wish you could be there."

Juliana faced Tricia, pointed an angered finger, then stopped to collect her composure. "What I wish is to collect them and bring them to live with me. That's what I wish. But, I have no custodial rights. Their father is still alive, although, according to Hanna, glaringly absent. If my inference is correct, he never took leave from his diamond mine post to attend Tomorrow's service. He endorsed orders, and the village honored his authority. I try to find consolation in the fact they are at least with relatives. Relatives who are much closer in the blood line than I am."

Tricia sipped her water and this time waited before she delved. "Have you remembered anything about ... ?"

Juliana didn't answer. Instead, she apprised that Mme Tboki had faxed an article written by Tomorrow's pupils memorializing her. Each student had written letters speaking of ways she had provided motivation to dream beyond the borders of Boptang. She had assured they were more prized than all the gold in Johannesburg as mysterious treasures to be discovered by the world. It had moved the editor so deeply, the publication dedicated an entire section to their earnest expressions.

Juliana searched the flawless, cosmetically enhanced face of the companion she had known since their junior year at Denver University, four years prior. Juliana figured it only a matter of time before some cosmetic empire discovered Tricia's exquisite mug. She imagined the corporation would navigate their prime negotiators toward Denver only to be rejected. Tricia's passion thrived in Vie, her flourishing day spas, and her fiancé, Winston Ong.

"I arrived at Tomorrow's bungalow after my morning market trip. Then I awoke in Mme Tboki's living area the following dawn."

Her expression shifted to something Tricia had only witnessed once. A home was burning while she visited relatives in Philadelphia as a child. A woman, held in the arms of a fireman, had screamed for her children. The childless mother had faced Tricia with a frantic, haunted look. She hated to see the same haunt on her friend's face. She shook off a shiver.

Juliana placed the silverware beside her plate, the gentle clink summoning Tricia to their dinner table. "Mme Tboki had to empty and refill her water basin twice because the dust covered my face, my throat, the back of my neck, my arms, and legs."

Juliana twirled the knife with her index finger. "I still can't bring myself to look at photos of her."

"Give it time."

Juliana sighed as if the air in her lungs was oppressive. "She'd smile when I'd tickle the children and their laughter swelled above the looming certainty of her illness. The last few weeks, the children prepared special lunches and watched her desperate struggle to keep the food down."

"Do you think you'll ever return?"

When Tricia saw Juliana's struggle to articulate the expressions from her soul, she assured, "You are not to blame."

Juliana shut her eyes, rubbing her temples. She wasn't sure if low blood sugar or the despondent letter had caused the throbbing. *It was pointless to pull Tricia into this pit,* she thought.

Suddenly, a boisterous roar drew their attention. It came from a lengthy table near the rear wall that was sectioned off with velvet rope. Two brawny men in dark suits stood guard. The grouping comprised of ten guys in khaki or denim with 70's-band t-shirts or political slogans. Two donned Raiders baseball caps. The professionally attired oddball amongst the set stood, shook a cloth napkin above his head, then draped it over his left arm. He gracefully captured a pitcher of beer in his right hand and proceeded to refill each glass.

Juliana smirked. "You've demonstrated remarkable restraint."

"I can't believe I'm sitting this close to Benjamin Powers!"

Juliana returned her attention to the rowdy men. "Why do you think he's serving the whole table drinks?"

Tricia released an exasperated sigh. "Did you not hear me? It's Benjamin Powers! I'm telling you, girl, his photos pale in comparison to up close and personal."

Stephanie, their favorite server, arrived and visibly relaxed. "I thought you two abandoned us for that new trendy place on Wazee."

"Never," Tricia promised.

"How are you two doing this evening?"

Tricia's grin threatened to rupture the seams of her jaw. "Positively glowing, thank you very much."

"Did you break the news to him yet?" Stephanie asked, holding menus near her chest. Tricia and Juliana had encapsulated every culinary item in their memory long ago.

"No." Tricia leaned her chin on her manicured hand and looked toward Benjamin Powers. "He has no idea Winston beat him to the punch."

"It's a shame really."

"Isn't it though?"

"Can we order, please?" Juliana broke up their banter.

Tricia ignored her. "I haven't seen you at the spa lately, Stephanie. I'm offering a autumn special for active women like yourself."

Tricia was the sole proprietor of two of the most luxurious excursions ever to be covered in stucco. Although Vie offered exceptional pampering spa services to the average Joe or Joanne, many celebrities and their spouses frequented the indulgent havens. The first location had opened in the Denver Tech Center situated near popular restaurants while the other took plot in Cherry Creek. Vie had been voted "Best Spa" in *Denver's* 5280 magazine a year after its inception. The second Tricia went public, Juliana vowed to purchase substantial stock.

"The crew from *Slow Bullet* arrived a few weeks ago and have kept us quite busy feeding them. Maybe I can make it in next week, that's when they're scheduled to wrap up."

"So you've spoken to them?" Tricia raised her perfectly arched chestnut brow and pouted her mauve lips colored by Bobbi Brown.

Juliana raised her hand. "Correction. She means have you spoken to *him*?"

"You wicked woman, you," she teased Tricia, whose grin only grew. "Yes. Very personable. He signs every autograph, smiles in every photo, and never fails to tip generously."

Juliana groaned. "I'll have the spinach salad as a start and the seared Ahi Tuna for my main course. Oh, and please tell Greg not to be so heavy-handed with the ginger."

Stephanie and Tricia stared at her. This time Stephanie remarked, "How often are you actually in the presence of a celebrity?"

"Especially one who has won two Oscars and a slew of People's Choice and Golden Globes?" Tricia educated.

"And don't forget he was also voted *People's* sexiest man alive for three consecutive years."

"I wonder ... " Juliana rubbed her chin with an index finger.

"What?" Tricia asked.

"Who was voted sexiest man dead?"

The Ben Powers Fan Club of two rolled their eyes. "I could ignore her for the remainder of the meal."

Stephanie shrugged. "It wouldn't influence her in the least."

Juliana grimaced. "Seriously, what does any of that mean?"

Tricia frowned. "We have to explain it?"

"He's a man, y'all. I don't care how many accolades he received, he has issues that plague him just like the rest of us."

"His recent divorce," Stephanie's eyes saddened. "Remember those photos of him leaving the divorce court?"

Tricia leaned forward. "He looked as if someone had ripped his heart out."

Juliana sipped the last of Tricia's water. "Can you bring us more water? I must be dehydrated."

"Dehydrated and heartless," Tricia remarked.

"I beg to differ. If I were heartless, I would have shut down this conversation long time ago. But I sat and suffered through your biography of Benjamin Powers."

"It's hard to believe anybody that gorgeous, wealthy, and influential ever has a bad day," Stephanie mused.

"As if any of those attributes exempt you from life," Juliana said.

"It sure would be nice if it did," Tricia commented.

Stephanie suggested, "Tricia, you should go and introduce yourself. He truly is a nice man."

"Uh-huh, Steph."

"Oh, go on. I wouldn't lead you astray."

"No." Tricia's upper and bottom lip formed a perfect O as she annunciated the word with fervent clarity.

"Tricia, here is the opportunity you've dreamed of, living and breathing only a few feet away, and you're going to pass it up?"

"It certainly looks that way."

"I don't believe what I'm hearing."

"What am I supposed to say that won't make me sound like a crazed fan?"

Stephanie folded her hands together, resembling a patronizing nun. "How about 'Hi! My name is Tricia Wilson. May I have your autograph?'"

Tricia contested. "You don't just approach a hugely popular, massively influential man like him."

"Why not?"

"Well." Tricia looked to Juliana, who shot her a look of challenge punctuated by pursed lips. "It simply isn't done."

Stephanie countered, "What do you have to lose?"

"My complete and utter dignity."

Juliana rolled her eyes. "Unbelievable!"

The memory of how they met crept to her mind. Their paths had collided the winter of their junior year at the University of Denver. They had converged on the dorm room floor of a jilted, mutual friend in intense consultation. Surrounded by pepperoni pizza, liters of Coke, tissue boxes, and love songs, they had consoled the brokenhearted junior. Long after their ditched pal had recovered, the immediate, undeniable click between the two prevailed.

Juliana was amused that Tricia's concept of casual dress was St. John denim. She even tugged her trash to the curb in full makeup, clad as if *Vogue* was scheduled to drop by for a photo shoot. Towering at six feet, Tricia carried her curvaceous figure as a prizefighter carries a championship belt. Juliana couldn't remember a time when some guy wasn't traipsing after her glitzy companion.

During the lean period when Tricia had met successive refusal toward the manifestation of her health spa, Juliana treated her to a weekend at the Broadmoor in Colorado Springs. As they had soaked in the magnificent scenery surrounding Cheyenne Lake, Juliana noticed the speckles decorating the froth on Tricia's latte. Tricia's coloring perfectly matched that of Madagascar cinnamon: subtle, warm, and sensual. During subsequent difficulties, Juliana had used the nickname created that weekend: Cinni.

"Cinni's scared." Juliana's tone was deliberately derisive.

"Oh, that's cute, Jules. I don't see you walking over there, Miss I-Am-Woman-Hear-Me-Bark."

"Is that a challenge?"

Tricia responded with a grunt and turned her attention to Stephanie. The twilight crowd swelled and the waitress sighed. "Let's bring this around to why you two really came. Miss Jaded here wants spinach salad with Ahi Tuna, light on the ginger. Tricia, the usual sirloin salad for you?"

"Perfect. Oh, and a stake to put directly through her heart, *s'il vous plait*."

"Right away." Stephanie playfully rolled her eyes at Juliana then departed.

"Imagine … "

"What am I imaging?"

"A woman of your success, intellect, and beauty is intimidated by him."

"I never said I was intimidated."

"You persevered for two years when nearly every bank in town turned down your request for a loan. You held your head high when they sniggered at your business plan."

Juliana looked at the linen cloth in her lap and the idea blossomed. Since Tomorrow's death, Juliana's zest had blatantly weakened. She had stood beside Tomorrow's grave; as the casket lowered into the earth, so had her relish to celebrate life.

Juliana slid to the edge of the booth. "Bark, huh?"

"Where are you going?" Tricia asked as Juliana stood from the booth. Tricia's frown transformed into shock. "You wouldn't dare!"

Before her better judgment could dissuade, she propelled her body toward the rowdy group. *What is there to lose?* she determined. Tricia's smile would be well worth it.

She walked to the velvet rope designed to segregate. Instantly, the two security guards descended.

"Excuse me."

When no one from the group replied, she stepped to the top stair and called out once more. She glanced briefly at Tricia, whose mouth had dropped to her chin.

Hulk One stated, "Ma'am, this is a private party. I'm going to have to ask you to return to your table."

At the head of the table, she believed, sat the film's director. He noticed her and withdrew his focus from the group. Juliana imagined his curio cabinet must have been burdened from the honors he won for his blockbuster action films, several of them bestowed by the NAACP Image Awards.

The object of her purpose sat to the director's immediate left, his back to her. The table broke into animated laughter over some comment he made.

"Now, ma'am. Otherwise, you will be escorted from the premises," Hulk Two advised.

The laughter calmed and immediate attention was directed at her. Benjamin Powers brought his glass to his mouth, turned toward the disruption, and stopped cold.

"Mr. Powers, I am Juliana DeLauer, and I would like to invite you for a cup of coffee."

Hulk One unlatched the security rope determined to keep his promise. Ben replaced the pilsner glass on the table. "A cup of coffee?"

The entire table shifted their gaze toward him. Juliana nodded as if a teacher responding to a simple mathematical equation. "Yes."

Some of the gang took swigs of beer, locked on the action. He grabbed an unsoiled napkin on the table. "Juliana DeLauer, may I use your pen?"

She felt the rush of blood to her face. "I ... I ... "

"Marcus, would you be so kind as to hand me that pen?"

The director complied by reaching into the casing that held the bill and withdrew a ballpoint. "*Miss* DeLauer, is it?"

"Yes."

"Have you completely thought this through?"

"What do you mean?"

"Your invite for coffee with this man. You could be ushering yourself into a fresh hell from which there is no escape."

The entire crew bellowed with laughter that helped dispel some of the nervous tension. The admired actor stood and moved to her. His height was shorter than she expected; in his films he appeared over six feet. The blue of his eyes created a cavity of nerves in her belly. Juliana felt as if she had witnessed those eyes somewhere before, somewhere far beyond this moment.

Powers' skin was vibrant, tanned, and looked ten years younger than his reported forty-two years. The platinum highlights of his spiky blonde cut were crafted with meticulous care.

His next move perplexed Juliana. He wrote the inner digits first, jotting them down from the inside out. He continued the process until all ten digits were written. He handed her the napkin.

Juliana stared at the tissue then looked him directly in the eye. They stood for a few moments gauging the other's next move. Only one other person had possessed the same annoying tendency.

"That is to my personal assistant. She can schedule a time for us to meet."

To the table, she stated, "Forgive me for the interruption." To Powers, "Thank you. Enjoy the remainder of your stay in Denver."

Juliana turned on her three-inch heels and deliberately strode as if she habitually invited celebrities to coffee.

It maddened her. Somehow, there was the sense he had looked at her with the same benevolence before, yet she couldn't place the occasion. It made no sense; she had never seen him *in person* before.

"You are completely crazy!" Tricia hissed, then crumbled into a warm giggle.

"Funny you should use those words."

"What?"

Juliana handed her the napkin. "Nothing."

Tricia's naturally large maple-colored eyes grew even larger. "This isn't just an autograph."

"Nope."

"There's a number."

Juliana nodded coolly. "Yep."

Tricia held the napkin to her chest and closed her eyes. "I have just witnessed the miraculous."

Juliana frowned. "God spoke this world into existence. God parted the Red Sea for the children of Israel. Obtaining Benjamin Powers' digits does not equate to the miraculous."

"I meant the fact those guards didn't haul you out by your elbows, Jimmy Choos flailing in the air."

The image caused the corners of Juliana's mouth to turn upward. It felt foreign, like an amnesia victim attempting to identify names with faces.

"Do you think this number is legitimate?"

Juliana shrugged. "He claims it's to his personal assistant. Call it and see."

Tricia scrunched her face. "What did you say to him?"

"I invited him for coffee."

"You are too much!"

"I get that a lot."

Tricia held up her left hand and wiggled her ring finger. "I cannot call him, my dear friend. I am very much attached."

"I suppose Winston would have quite a bit to say about that, wouldn't he?"

"Yes," she admired the two-and-a-half carat masterpiece. "Thus, this highly coveted piece of paper is all yours."

Juliana allowed the paper to rest between them. "I shall leave it lying in that very spot for someone who may actually be interested."

Tricia leaned forward. "You've always told me you don't believe in coincidence."

"I don't."

"He didn't have to include a number."

"It's to his personal assistant. No big deal."

"What did you expect? His unlisted home number?"

"Don't be ridiculous."

"It could become a very big deal. Very big indeed."

Juliana shrugged. Their order arrived, and Tricia blessed the fragrant meal. After they indulged in a few bites of the sumptuous cuisine, Tricia remarked, "Besides, how could you possibly know the end before the story has even been told? What have you got to lose? After all, he's just a man."

Thomas Elliott, *Core's* editor-in-chief, sipped the tea and relaxed in the atrium lobby of the Brown Palace Hotel.

"Now that I've answered all of your questions, I have a few of my own," Ben said.

"Fire away."

"Your staff writer, Juliana DeLauer."

Thomas' eyes narrowed. "Yes?"

"The manner in which you speak of her seems fonder than editor and staff writer."

"Why does this interest you, Benjamin?"

Ben looked at the luxurious rug at his feet. "I'm intrigued."

"And I'm protective."

Ben smirked. "I figured you might be."

Thomas sipped the masterfully brewed Darjeeling. "Maya and I met the DeLauers at a rally to abolish apartheid in Soweto during the early seventies. Maya was treating destitute patients in the village clinic while I photographed and published the acute misery apartheid had fashioned. The DeLauers covertly shipped in Bibles, assisted in planting crops, and constructed stone-upon-stone churches and schools. All four of us were beaten, jailed, and ostracized by those who deemed us 'too extreme for our own good.'"

"So you were there when the student uprising occurred?"

"Yes." Thomas examined his fingers, as if mentally aligning the shards of the tragedy. "We had been in the process of building a modest church in Soweto when the police turned their weapons on the marching school children and silenced hundreds of thunderous voices."

"I can't imagine the horror."

"We spent perilous weeks assisting the burials of the dead, proclaiming the validity of freedom, and shepherding those deeply rooted in the Black Consciousness Movement to safe havens. All until the South African government made it clear that if we remained, the price was high upon our heads."

"So when did you return?"

"Not until the summer of 1994 when the bloody system had been abolished and Nelson Mandela had been elected President of South Africa. Subsequently, we collaborated our time vacationing in one another's countries. A week before each Christmas, we deserted our London flat and skied in Vail with the DeLauers. They in turn crossed the Atlantic to retreat in London during spring break. Oh, the glorious times we spent ushering in the dawn, munching surullitos or koeksisters, hashing over the world's injustices."

"Do you still visit South Africa?"

"Every summer." Thomas paused to take another sip. "Except this summer. Maya was receiving specialized medical training in Boston."

Ben looked at his hands. "I was there."

Thomas' phone chimed. He read the display. "Excuse me. Yes, Novia."

Ben glanced at Bruce whose eyes exhibited caution. Ben needed to expel the secret to someone close to Juliana—someone who could assist his disclosure.

Thomas concluded the call. "She worries if I'm not home by nine."

"Thomas, did you know Tomorrow Lesaba?"

Thomas frowned. "Yes. Such a pity. Such an amazing woman. They still haven't apprehended her killers. Why do you ask?"

A woman approached and requested Ben's autograph for her granddaughters.

And several photos.

After she expressed excessive gratitude and departed, Thomas stood and extended his hand. "It's been a pleasure."

Ben bid him goodnight and sat staring at the custom-designed Axminister carpet. He refused to meet Bruce's eye for fear of what the man might convey.

As he stood to return to his room, he spotted Thomas by the entrance, cell phone to his ear, distress coloring his expression.

CHAPTER FOUR

Juliana stood and stretched her five-foot-seven frame from behind the confines of her office cubicle. She yawned then gasped. Her hands flew to her pelvis and she grasped the desk's edge. Inhaling through her nose, she counted nearly to twenty before the habitual pelvic pain subsided. When she erected, tears blurred the twinkling headlights of cars cruising Lincoln Avenue.

Juliana extracted the tiny blue pills from her purse designed to dull the pain. She inserted one on her tongue and sipped from the bottled water on her desktop. She bowed her back to discharge the piercing tension and dropped her head. Spiral curls spilled over her face, exposing the velvety dark patches on the back of her neck. She would never risk such exposure had she not been alone.

Her desk phone rang. "*Core*. Juliana DeLauer."

"Oh." The male accent was haggard, yet distinctively British. "Thank God you're still there."

"Thomas? What's going on?"

"I am at the Brown scrutinizing a flat rear tire and an even flatter spare."

"That is most unfortunate, boss."

"Are you able to do an old man a favor?"

She straightened her desk, gathered her belongings, and drove north on Lincoln to the posh hotel. She exited the car, tightening the collar of her red trench to ward off the evening chill, and handed the valet her keys. Entering through the revolving doors, her matching sandals clicked on the imported terrazzo marble. In the center of the nine-story ceiling, an immense crystal chandelier illuminated every nuance of the hand-woven rugs and onyx walls with gold leafing. The stained glass canopy ceiling entreated a languished study of the opaque summer sky.

She spotted Thomas sitting in one of the cozy resting areas chatting with a man whose back faced her. As she rounded the entrance to the area, an imposing man in black blocked her. Juliana blinked; his eyes promptly flashed from warning to munificence.

"I'm here for Mr. Elliott."

Thomas stood. "She's innocuous, unless you're blocking her entry to Nordstrom." He explained to the man who appeared to be one flowing muscle from the top of his shaved head to the tips of his size thirteen feet.

"Juliana," the sixty-year-old editor exclaimed. "My lifesaver."

She cringed at the false moniker. "You set?"

The man who shared the space with Thomas stood from the luxurious seat.

Juliana's jaw dropped. Seconds later, when she recovered, she tugged at her scarf. "Mr. Powers."

"Miss DeLauer."

Thomas crinkled his silver brows. "You've met?"

"Yes."

"At Tanner's a few nights ago," Juliana clarified.

"She approached my table and introduced herself."

"Is that so?" *Core's* editor folded his fleshly arms behind his back.

"I was dining with T."

Ben quizzed, "T?"

"My friend. Tricia."

"She held off two Kyoshi. Quite impressive."

"Pardon?"

"Kyoshi are those who've exceeded black belt status. They're a formidable bunch."

"Fascinating. Held them off, you say?"

"Never laid a finger on her. I think they were silently intimidated."

"Is there any question as to why?"

"Not anymore."

Juliana rolled her eyes. "T adores him, so I requested an autograph."

Ben raised an eyebrow. "For Tricia?"

"Her adoration for you is legendary."

Ben leaned closer to Thomas. "I get the feeling Tricia's adoration is not contagious."

Thomas squinted his eyes. "Umm."

"Pure genius," Ben commented.

"Come again?" Thomas frowned.

"Her method. I have never experienced anything like it."

Juliana sucked in a frayed breath. "I asked him to join me for a cup of coffee."

"Genius, you say!"

Ben winked at Thomas. "Very bold."

"They say many a glorious friendship has commenced over a cup of coffee. Personally, I prefer Darjeeling."

She cocked her head. "I was proving a point."

"By asking me to join you for coffee?"

She shot Ben a scolding look. "By requesting your autograph."

"Did my autograph accomplish your goal?"

"She was moved beyond words."

The gleam in her editor's eye caused Juliana to shift her weight from one foot to the other. "Ready?"

Juliana departed the circle and began her exit. From behind, she heard the editor's farewell. "It was a pleasure, Benjamin."

"You made it painless, Thomas."

Juliana stopped at the entrance, one hip extended in impatience. The two men made arrangements for their final meeting, then Benjamin turned to her. "I do not believe in coincidence."

"Is that so?"

Benjamin moved closer. "Perhaps I should ask for your number this time—"

"Oh, my word," Thomas interrupted. "I believe I have forgotten my satchel in the car. I left it there when I discovered the flat. Please, excuse me."

Juliana glared at Thomas, who merely squeezed her arm, then

waltzed through the door. She met Benjamin's gaze and again, the air caught in her throat. She tossed her head to one side.

"I believe in seizing the moment."

"That may not be a very good idea."

"No?"

"No."

He folded his arms across his chest and Juliana noticed the sculpted muscles beneath. "Why?"

"Several reasons."

"Name three."

"Why three?"

"It means you've at least put serious thought into snubbing me."

She squared her shoulders. "You don't know me from Adam."

Ben hesitated a moment. "Isn't that the point of meeting for coffee?"

"I could be a stalker."

He shrugged toward the door. "Not according to Thomas. He is quite enamored with you."

"You merely met him a few hours ago."

"Actually, we first met weeks ago when my publicist invited him to the set. We've enjoyed one another's company throughout my shoot. Maya even invited me over for *asopao*."

Juliana's mouth salivated at the mere suggestion that Thomas' wife had cooked the succulent Puerto Rican gumbo. "With chicken or shellfish?"

"Chicken." Ben grinned, his taste buds recalling the savory dish. "Their son, Robert, had visited from New York. I understand he's allergic to shrimp."

"Which means she also prepared his favorite empanadillas with marinated beef."

"I had a hard time fitting in my wardrobe the following day."

Juliana had been invited to share that evening with the Elliotts. Enticed by the lure of solitude, she had declined.

"Maya's culinary skills are dazzling."

"Undeniably. Did you know they had met on a double date?"

"Yes." Juliana rotated her wrist in a flourish. "Thomas had been originally chosen to date Maya's friend. He wasn't interested. As the evening progressed, both Thomas and Maya discovered their attraction was mutual. So, they ditched their designated dates."

"Bold."

"That's what occurs when you know what you want."

"Precisely." A smile began in his eyes and spread throughout his entire frame. Ben reached in his rear pocket and removed his billfold. He withdrew a business card engraved with his initials in elegant lettering. "Do you have a pen?" he asked.

She patted her slack's pockets then slid her purse to her forearm and searched the contents. No pen.

"Hold on." She reached behind Ben to a table that held pads of paper and pens with the hotel's insignia. Ben's bodyguard loomed like a gladiator ready for slaughter. She shivered, not from his imposing presence, but at the altruistic manner with which his eyes studied her.

She handed Ben the pen, and he jotted a number on the back.

"Is this his number this time?" Juliana teased, nodding at the bodyguard. She couldn't resist.

"What would the B.P. stand for?"

She eyed the bodyguard from head-to-toe. "Bullet Proof."

Benjamin lost himself in substantial laughter. "This is my private number." He handed her the business card with his scrolled initials. "Call me."

She spun on her crimson heel and headed toward the revolving door.

"Drive safely," Ben requested.

She raised a hand above her head and waved goodnight.

Thomas leaned against the valet podium, his breath creating alabaster arcs against the blue-black night. When he saw her, he stretched out his arms. "Ah, Juliana."

She handed her ticket to the valet. "When my car arrives, I may just run you over."

"You could. But what of our history? Soweto, Boptang, Jo'Burg. Our intertwined chronicles would be irrevocably altered."

"I'm perfectly willing to take that chance."

Juliana examined the traffic headed toward Seventeenth Street as they awaited the retrieval of her vehicle.

"Do I detect hostility?"

"You set me up."

He blinked. "What ever do you mean?"

"You knew I'd still be at the office."

"You rarely leave before nine."

"A flat tire, huh?"

"Yes. Right. Well, actually, two—"

"You could have called a cab."

Thomas rubbed his fleshly jaw. "I suppose you're right. But I needed to retrieve a few items from the office before I retired for the evening."

She tipped the valet and pulled from the curb. "So, tell me, Thomas, at what point did you decide to play matchmaker?"

He gripped the safety handle that hung just to the right of the visor. "Pardon?"

"Understand one thing here. I love Maya. But if I wound you, after I explained your actions, I'd think she'd concur."

He sighed. "Very well. Actors of his popularity tend to be so notoriously tedious, I savor the moment when I can flee their presence. But this man is distinctive. He's complex, direct, and deeply compassionate."

"He's an actor, Thomas! He could have been *acting* those traits. I have yet to meet an actor I would regard as extraordinary."

"We frighten people with our uncanny accuracy to judge character. Correct?"

She shrugged.

"After spending substantial time with him, I am left with the revelation that he is no foregone conclusion."

"Thomas, why would I need a star-studded complication added to my life?" Juliana placed a hand on her right side and gently massaged the tender area.

"You all right, kid?"

"Cramps." She deeply wished her pain were so simple.

"Have you taken your medication?"

"On the way to pick you up."

He waited until she ceased wincing. "Juliana, I want you to take a moment to answer this question."

She blew out a cumbrous breath. "I'm listening."

"Are you ruling those complications or are they ruling you?"

She made a hard left into *Core's* parking garage. He held tight to the safety handle and grinned. She inserted her parking card and drove beneath the striped sign.

"It's 9:30 on a Friday evening, Miss Juliana."

"My career is demanding, Thomas. You have intimate knowledge of my editor, so you know I speak the truth."

He shook his silvery head. "Not that demanding."

"Mom is on an evangelist crusade in Haiti and won't return until Tuesday. Tricia and Winston are at his parents for dinner. And my house, although replete with nearly every comfort, can feel very empty."

Thomas eyed her silently. "When was your last date?"

"I go out plenty of times."

"When?"

She pretended to recall. "Last Saturday."

"I'm not referring to your trip to the zoo with your Sunday school class."

She sneered. "Make your point."

"Sometimes we hide. We mask our true feelings behind that which brings us limited fulfillment too frightened to aspire for more."

"You sound as if I'm a hermit."

"You haven't asked for more in a very long time."

"It's complicated." A man would eventually require intimacy. Not merely physical, but he would want to discover what made her tick.

Then, the questions would begin: Why did she habitually don scarves or high collar blouses? Why was her preferred sleeve-length low to her wrists? Why did her medicine cabinet hold such peculiar prescriptions as Vanquia, Spirotone, and Clomid? No one thus far had interested her to the point of divulging any of those answers before.

Benjamin Powers possessed obsessive media attention. Juliana surmised he did not need a flawed companion. In Tinsel Town, he could easily discover or buy perfection.

And, more importantly, she did not need a man whose lifestyle attracted a glaring spotlight on her every move. She desired to live out a quiet existence without the relentless attendance of the press.

As the senior pastor's daughter of an internationally reputed ministry, she had weathered the heartrending accusations that her father had sexually molested someone. She had watched the 20,000-capacity sanctuary of Living Water Fellowship dwindle. With the incongruous accusation came an abrupt absence of friends. When Juliana needed the promise of companionship the most, only the Elliotts and Tricia had stood by her side. Far too many had been convinced by the circumstantial evidence and left the DeLauers to fend alone. She had endured the trial and her father's subsequent acquittal. A few months later, just after her college commencement, her father had died from colon cancer. She had experienced the trial of public opinion—been there, done that, and burned the t-shirt.

His snow-white brows lifted. "Yes, but complicated doesn't have to equate to lonely."

"So your answer is Benjamin Powers?"

"I didn't say he was the answer. People come into our lives for a purpose. Maybe you should try to discover what motivated you to ask for his number."

"I've explained that, Thomas. I was trying to make Tricia's day."

Her boss's eyes rolled and his lips crowded into one corner of his mouth. Juliana parked in a spot nearest the door. She shut off the ignition and stared at the dull gray wall.

"I'll not be a moment." Thomas exited the vehicle, and Juliana found the lights and chimes when he opened the door jarring.

Thomas rushed to the office door, inserted his identification key, and the elevator doors opened. In a place where she knew truth, yet refused to acknowledge its existence, the answer resided. It wasn't simply her career, the grief of her father's death two years prior, or that of Tomorrow's recent demise.

Juliana fully enjoyed the shroud celibacy offered. Her lackluster pursuit of a significant relationship veiled the reality that commitment would lead to proposal and proposal would stream into marriage. It would be at this point that the fairy tale ended since numerous experts disbelieved her womb was capable of producing children.

She touched the dark patches on her neck and stared out the windshield, seeing nothing.

Thomas returned, and Juliana drove south to his suburban colonial in Littleton. She diverted the conversation to the subject of her latest article. Denver was slated to host a multi-million dollar symposium on HIV/AIDS in November—a week before Tricia's wedding.

She pulled into his driveway.

"We would love to have you spend the night."

"Thank you. But I promised to assist at the church's food bank in the morning."

"Have you gone mad? Saturdays offer your sole morning to bury yourself deep beneath your covers until ten."

"I've shucked many of my responsibilities as of late. It's time I re-entered the race."

For several moments, he stared at her. He took her hand. "Perhaps tomorrow evening? Maya is cooking your favorite Caribbean meal."

"My favorite?" Juliana groaned.

"We'll salsa to Hector Lavoe until we're breathless."

She sighed. "Need me to bring anything?"

"That's my Juliana. Seven o'clock."

He kissed her cheek and exited the car.

Around 1:30 a.m., after the book she was reading dropped on her face the third time, she switched off her nightstand lamp. Behind the shadows of her eyelids, she felt a gentle stirring in her spirit.

She stood upon the edge of a cliff and a familiar, compelling voice beckoned. The canyon seemed centuries deep and the ridge across galaxies away. Still, the benevolent voice beckoned. The stirring seemed to impel her foot to step forward, into the atmosphere of the unknown.

Juliana arrived at ten to seven. The sun had descended behind the majestic range casting the metro area in a sensual, promising darkness.

"*Mi hija!*" Maya cried at the bouquet so wide it concealed Juliana's head and shoulders.

"These are in deep appreciation of the meal you prepared that I shall greedily devour."

After Juliana handed the floral mass to Maya and kicked off her Adidas, Maya planted a warm kiss on her temple. "You are most welcome."

Stepping over the brass threshold, Juliana was rushed back in time, the home redolent with the savory perfume of sofrito, a special seasoning blend native to Puerto Rican dishes.

Her parents had taken her along on their evangelistic crusades, but drew the line when it came to missing school. Juliana had resided with the Elliotts during those brief spurts while her parents traveled.

Maya had equipped every room with speakers where music engulfed. Friday evenings had been extraordinary. She and the Elliott clan, their sons Robert and Alan, had competed at board games—collapsing in laughter or dancing to Latin music with abandon. The delicious lure of those days stirred inside of Juliana as Hector Lavoe serenaded through the sound system.

"Maya, dinner smells so divine it has to be illegal." Juliana inhaled every spiced nuance. She removed her jacket and hung it in the hallway closet.

Maya took her hand and led Juliana in a cha-cha beyond the living room and study where Maya tracked her patients' health records. Down the corridor, the space opened to their roomy kitchen decorated with paprika walls, oxblood granite, and cabinets stained the color of cinnamon. Juliana felt the rousing.

Maya had stimulated Juliana's passion to express her affection for Latin dance. She had been a patient teacher assisting Juliana's mastery, yet she preferred salsa above all. Here, or in the confines of her bedroom, Juliana granted her body permission to release the fervor. In the asylum of slumber, Juliana's partner had always been faceless. She granted this stranger permission to grip her waist, caress her thigh, or bend her in endless arcs.

"So how did my goddaughter spend her Saturday?" Maya removed an intricately carved vase from a lower cabinet and arranged the bouquet, her hands fussing over the petals.

Juliana washed her hands in the sink then moved to the cutting board loaded with avocados, roma tomatoes, scallions, garlic bulbs, cilantro, and limes. Beside it was a mortar bowl and pestle to crush the ingredients to the desired texture. "I carted and shelved boxes of food for the church food bank. I haven't been there in so long, there were several unfamiliar faces."

Maya moved to the range, removed a spatula from the copper vase near the stovetop, and stirred something fragrant in a saucepan. Another gas burner supported a huge galvanized pot simmering the *arroz con pollo*—chicken and rice—another, the *sopon de pescado*, better known as fish soup. "I bet Pastor Michael was pleased to see you."

"He was. I haven't volunteered since my return from Boptang. There was much work to be done, so our conversation was limited. He's truly embraced his daunting responsibility."

"Thirty years old and shepherds thousands. You couldn't pay me enough."

Juliana eyed the alluring, bronze-skinned daughter of Puerto Rico. "Liar."

Maya looked at her goddaughter. "Surely, my ears deceive me."

"Maya, I would never disrespect you. What I meant was you're infamous for protesting wildly, arms flailing, then when God tells you to move, you don't hesitate."

"And your point, *mi hija?*"

"I'd imagine Pastor Michael must have experienced one of those moments. He made the choice to leave a congregation he adored in order to move to a city where he didn't know a soul to shepherd a grieving flock. No one in their right mind would take that on unless God spoke with pointed clarity and intent."

Maya considered this, gently stirring the sauce. Maya spoke little, yet when she did, her words were replete with methodical contemplation gathered from the edges of her mind. Juliana wondered what thoughts vied for attention during Maya's five-mile runs and wished every physician practiced such astute restraint.

"You have heard the rumors?"

Juliana nibbled a piece of cilantro and swayed her slim hips to the boisterous percussion and horn ensemble. "Of us becoming husband and wife?"

Maya placed the spatula on the granite counter and nodded.

Juliana shrugged. "No more than the gossip that I demand an allowance from the ministry to pay for my Nordstrom addiction."

"Well..." Maya tossed her lengthy, silken black waves and teased with a smirk.

Juliana still wondered how the long-legged, vociferous Britain ever captured the heart of this quiet, luminous Latina.

Thomas' eyes first took her in Puerto Rico.

He had been on assignment with a small publication interested in Caribbean health care.

She had plopped a box of medical supplies at his feet. He had attempted to charm with his crisp accent and flamboyant air.

She had turned on her heel. He had sought her out, but to no avail.

Two weeks later, he and his roommate embarked on a double date with a chatty flight attendant and a medical student.

She had walked through the door of the *fonda* and his elation soared... until it was explained the serene Latina was his roommate's date.

Maya Sanchez was her name. Thomas had attempted to impress by rambling in Spanish.

Once the plantains had arrived, Thomas feigned fatigue. Maya had joined him, purse in hand, explaining a strenuous test the following morning.

Neither his roommate nor the effusive attendant of the skies was ready to conclude the evening.

They had remained. Thomas and Maya had departed.

They had traipsed through the cobblestone streets illuminated by the creamy moon.

Maya had been in her last year of medical study. Thomas had been a struggling writer awaiting that big break.

A month later, he had worked up the nerve to ask her to become his eternal *novia*.

He had carried her to the States and his editor offered him a promotion. Thomas had increased his hours, funding her schooling to receive a medical license to practice in America.

He had shouted the loudest when she crossed the stage and received her certificate.

During her residency, and pregnancy with Robert, she urged him to take the managing editor's position at *Core*.

Within a year, they had celebrated the birth of their first son and *Core*'s surging circulation.

"Palesa?" Maya called. "What are your thoughts?"

"They're just silly rumors." Juliana squeezed the limejuice into the aromatic mixture encompassed in the mortar bowl passed down through six generations of the Sanchez family. Maya covered her hands with mitts dyed the color of nutmeg and opened one of the wall-mounted ovens. She carefully placed the hefty tray on the counter, and Juliana resisted the urge to peel back the foil and dive into the sumptuous enchiladas. Instead, Juliana picked up the avocados and sliced them, expertly plucking the pit from their center with a swift whack of the blade. Her hips pulsed in rhythmic trance to the horns, drums, and guitar.

"Do you think I should give them credence?"

Maya moved to the questioning woman, her walk the fluent language of grace. Maya was closing the distance, bringing with her those eyes that surveyed the furtive provinces of her Juliana's core. She smoothed the curls on Juliana's head. "That is not for me to say, dear heart."

"There is pressure and innuendo."

"That doesn't matter if it's not your truth."

"My truth? *Qué es la verdad?*"

"Is there a reaction when he's around?"

"He's my pastor." Juliana shrugged. "I watched him with Daddy during those last weeks. It wasn't just about him gleaning from his predecessor. Michael assured Daddy's vision, God's work, wouldn't die with him. He embraced Daddy's dream—consumed it."

Closer and closer Maya came, not consuming Juliana but enveloping her in precipitous acceptance. "Of course, I love him. Fiercely."

Maya removed the pestle from Juliana's hand, pushed the mortar bowl aside, and placed a warm hand over Juliana's heart. "As a woman, Palesa. Here?"

Juliana attempted to divert the candor of Maya's question, but failed. "He's everything a woman could desire. Great looking, compassionate, sincere, gallant, educated—"

"Yet?"

"Yet," Juliana fingered the bubbled surface of the pestle. "I'm just not sure, Maya. I've never allowed myself to even consider such things before."

"This pressure, is it self-inflicted?"

This time, Maya's candor caused Juliana to blush. She leaned her elbows on the counter and shielded her eyes. Maybe it was the pending arrival of her twenty-fifth birthday in January. Maybe it was Tricia's wedding in November that had alerted this alien notion within.

Maya caressed her back. "Give yourself time to realize whom God desires to have in your heart. I did. And, my goodness, he was nothing like anyone my *familia* would have chosen. Yet, my heart still leaps at the sound of his voice. *Si?*"

Juliana uncovered her eyes and looked at the astute beauty. *"Si."*

Just then, Thomas burst through the door leading from the garage. *"Novia!"*

"Si, my love."

"My arms ache to feel your exquisite contours."

Maya rushed to her husband who rewarded her with an engaging kiss.

"After three decades of marriage, aren't you considered too old for that?"

"Ah, Palesa, never." Thomas responded and kissed his wife once more. When they parted, he walked toward Juliana, stood by her side, and gave her hair a vigorous ruffle.

"You're incorrigible! How on earth did you ever become my father's best friend?"

"Lots of high-quality paint, blank canvases, and the wisdom to know when to remain silent."

"I could tell you I desire the latter, but that would be insolent."

They heaped the enchiladas, *sopon de pescado*, guacamole, and *arroz con pollo* onto vivid platters, placed the overflowing floral display on the dining table, and relished their uplifting company and the sumptuous meal.

"How are the boys?" Juliana asked, licking the traces of sauce of the enchiladas from her fork.

Robert and Alan both had graduated from NYU and, after their commencements, remained in New York. Robert, who just celebrated his thirty-first birthday, practiced emergency medicine at the NYU Medical Center; Alan, twenty-eight, had finally landed a supporting role in a favored Broadway production.

After they shared in the task of cleaning the dinner dishes, their bodies moved, unrestrained and joyous, to the energetic musical compositions. Satiated, the turmoil in South Africa momentarily distanced, Juliana collapsed on the sofa intending to merely shut her eyes for a brief moment. Near 3 a.m., she awoke to her own screams. She tossed aside the down cover and flipped on the lamp resting upon the side table. When Thomas and Maya arrived, covered in robes, they found Juliana shaking and sitting on the floor.

"I drove her to the HIV/AIDS clinic where others from the village saw us. I walked with her to the village well and forced her to hold her head up while others scowled as they gathered water. The more they shunned us, the louder I cried."

She paused, her chest heaving as if demons clutched her throat. "I knew better." She pounded her fists on her thighs and hissed. "I have known, since the first time I stepped foot on South African soil as a girl, women are forbidden to display such bravado."

Thomas knelt beside her. "It's not your fault, Juliana. It didn't matter if you were combative or still. The execution had already been set."

Maya took her hand. "It was also Tomorrow's strength that resounded."

Juliana said, "If you refuse to be silent, someone with more strength, more control, or power will command compliance."

"You are not to blame." Thomas asserted again.

Juliana pressed on, surprised that her self-loathing carried the strength to restrain her tears. "How can you be certain? You have lived in that world. You know very well what happens when you won't keep your mouth shut."

For several moments, neither could muster declarations to either object or affirm, uncertain their expressions would bring relevance.

"Do you know why getting Ben Powers' autograph was so important? It had nothing to do with his celebrity. I approached him because I was seeking relevance and purpose. I used it as an opportunity to make someone I loved happy."

Maya reclined beside Juliana on the carpeted floor. "So, you sought hope."

"Yes. Hope that the world hadn't become a chasm of desolation and egocentric obsession. I just can't make it form into any thing that makes sense. What purpose does it serve to murder a woman whose life was dedicated to edifying children?"

Thomas and Maya, enveloped by the shadows of their den, listened as Juliana maneuvered the tragic demise in lashing curves around her soul. "I seriously wonder if resurrecting hope warrants justification."

Maya gently touched her shoulder. "Did you receive the autograph?"

Juliana nodded.

"What did it do for Tricia?"

"She was ecstatic."

"That is who you've always been."

Juliana searched those luminous, dark eyes, waiting for deeper revelation.

Maya continued, "When you were born, your parents proclaimed you as their miracle child. You have brought them joy beyond measure. That is who you are, Juliana—an instrument to bring about joy."

Thomas cleared his throat, his hair a silver halo surrounding his muted features. "Despite the number of times your mother was summoned to the principal's office."

Juliana sighed. "You had to bring that up."

Thomas dropped to the leather sofa. "No matter how big the bully, you would race over, confront them, and demand they fight you instead. There were countless administrations of first aid and admonishing speeches. Which fell on deaf ears."

Maya rubbed Juliana's back. "Dionne would call me in near exasperation. Yet, she knew. She saw it long before she could give it a name. It is you."

Juliana rested her head on Maya's shoulder and allowed her warmth to calm her. Maya contended, "God is a magnificent healer. If He's allowed."

That night, Juliana made a haven of the bed cover and listened to the rain's serenade against the den window. Her throat threatened to shut as she released the words conceived from ruthless importune. "Tomorrow, forgive me."

CHAPTER FIVE

On Monday evening, she placed her thumbs in the belt loops of her silk trousers and drummed an erratic tune on her hipbones. The computer screen was filled with a showcase of research material comprised for her groundwork for November's symposium. Most of her colleagues would have shuttled the data to their home computers via e-mail or downloaded it to their cell phone.

Juliana printed the pertinent info and placed it inside a manila folder that rested on top of her briefcase. The texture of paper against her palms brought fixed gratification. The sensation felt steady, concrete, and secure.

She opened her wallet and removed the business card marked with the elegant numbering of Benjamin Powers. She twirled it through her fingers, then ripped it in two and tossed it in the wastebasket.

His picture graced hundreds of covers domestic and European. He faithfully attended every movie premiere, every talk show, sat for every interview to plug his projects. At the initial word of his marriage disintegration, there had been a hurricane of speculation as to why the couple had fallen apart. There were accusations of adultery, obsession with career, and a few jabbed at Powers' sexuality. Benjamin had kept silent and directed stern looks at any reporter or talk show host who dared head in that direction. This had fueled a savage hunger for the press to uncover every private detail of his life. Thus, the best place for the card was in the trash.

The staff writer adjusted the collar of her ruby calfskin trench and waited for the elevator. Yesterday, Juliana was jostled from her gratifying slumber by the snow truck's ambling beep through her subdivision. The Denver metro area had awakened to a snowstorm that blanketed the city with shimmering powder.

Suddenly, wild roars burst from the executive staff lounge down the hall. Because she never passed an opportunity to indulge her weakness to investigate, she turned the corner and headed down the dim corridor. Behind the frosted glass, Thomas and Ben Powers screamed at the 50" plasma TV. Their attention locked on a brutish boxing match.

"*Hola*, Miss Juliana!"

She looked to her left and saw the crew of cleaners arriving for their evening duty. The young writer returned to her position near the elevators. "*Hola!* Miguel."

"Are you going to watch?" Miguel, the head of the crew, performed a slew of boxing moves.

"That is very doubtful, Miguel."

"Too bad. Such a beautiful woman with such a soft heart should not spend her nights always working."

She watched as he proceeded down the hall, his words reverberating not only off the plastered walls but the ramparts of her heart. Were people merely casting their yearning on her, or was there truth in their aspiring expressions?

She swallowed the hard lump in her throat and then returned her attention in the direction of the lounge. Just as the elevator door opened, Thomas shouted her name. She slumped her shoulders and closed her eyes. His footsteps weighed heavily on the carpet as he ran toward her.

"What are you doing here?" she asked with a hand on her hip.

"I work here."

"Stop playing with me, Thomas. You know exactly what I mean."

"Ben and I just completed our final interview. We grabbed a bite of sushi and decided to retire to observe the match."

"Here?"

"Yes. Maya's day was taxed with arduous surgeries. I didn't want to disturb her domestic peace."

"Mr. Powers doesn't have a television in his hotel suite?"

"I didn't ask."

The elevator doors shut. Juliana jabbed the down button with her thumb. The doors reopened with a subtle swoosh. "Good evening, Thomas."

"Believe it or not, this had nothing to do with you."

"You've never lied to me before."

"And I'm not beginning tonight. You know the restaurant is next door. This seemed more convenient."

She gaped at him. Thomas was a man who didn't simply value seeking truth but also valued speaking it. It was the main reason she relished him as a boss. She allowed the elevator to descend without her.

"I am embarrassed at my audacity. I am sorry."

"I gave you my word that I have no intention on taking up the role of matchmaker. Whatever happens, if anything happens, will have nothing to do with me."

"I have snapped at more people this month then I have in my lifetime."

"We noticed that you weren't at church yesterday. Did Tricia tell you I treated our brood to lunch at Maggiano's afterward?"

"She did." Juliana fiddled with the strap of her briefcase. "I simply wasn't feeling up for a crowd. Not that I don't love Tricia, Winston, and Pastor Michael ... and Maya, of course ... but, you know ... "

Thomas touched her elbows. "We've ordered spider rolls."

"Spider rolls? You loathe them."

"Ben doesn't. Wait here and I'll go pack you a quick take-home parcel."

She leaned against the wall as he disappeared behind the conference room door. Sunday morning, she had pulled into her garage with an hour to spare to prepare for church. Hours later, she remained buried beneath her bedroom comforter. Even if her sleep hadn't been interrupted by the nightmare on the Elliotts' sofa, her desire to attend service was bleak. She had thought returning to her ministerial routine would have ushered anticipation and empowerment to heal. Yet, just the opposite had been true. She wanted to burrow deeper into isolation.

The disparaging faction at Living Water hadn't helped with their anonymous notes. Before Pastor DeLauer had died, their criticisms pertained to the length of her skirts either being too diminutive or too protracted. Lately, the unsigned notes stated her worship was glaringly uncultivated for a pastor's daughter. Her adulation should look dignified and proper. They understood deep adoration for the Savior, but Juliana's praise from her position in the pulpit was excessive. Undaunted, Juliana sat amongst the congregation, her worship as profound as ever. Then, the notes typified that her place was in the pulpit, beside the pastoral staff. They also added words of what they considered prudent advice.

"God has a plan for everything."

"His ways are higher than our ways."

"And we know that God causes all things to work together for good to those who love God, to those who are called according to His purpose."

"You shouldn't weep for those gone. They are in heaven, completely healed and restored."

And Juliana's favorite had been: "You will see them again some-day. So don't mourn, but rejoice. Certainly, they wouldn't want you to weep."

She concealed the fact that some days these aphorisms drove her to want to pound fist to wall. Presently, the restrictive concern of certain Living Water members felt like a straight jacket. When her father was alive, their words irked but hadn't cut like a scalpel to her spirit.

"Hello, again." Ben stepped from the conference room, Thomas by his side.

"Mr. Powers."

"Please, call me Ben."

Thomas handed her a plastic tray complete with sliced pickled ginger and wasabi paste. "Promise me you'll eat this tonight."

"How do you know I haven't already eaten?"

Thomas pushed his lips to the right corner of his mouth, his trademark indication of disbelief.

"Very well."

A vicious roar exuded from the TV. Both men cocked their heads to listen as the announcer confirmed a fighter was down for the count.

"Brilliant!" Thomas exclaimed, smacking Ben's back. "Excuse me, but my man is about to walk away with the belt."

They watched Thomas exit behind the glass door gleefully cheering at the screen.

Ben shook his head. "Do you follow boxing?"

"Only if forced."

His gentle laugh danced down the corridor. "My pick is getting his brains beat out. I now owe Thomas a monumental apology."

"Let me guess, his guy is a native Coloradoan?"

"Precisely."

"Your choice?"

"His father teaches drama at UCLA."

"Never had a chance."

He smiled lazily. "Meet me for coffee?"

"No."

Ben tossed his head back slightly. "No?"

"It's for the best."

"I don't believe in coincidence."

"Good for you."

He searched beyond the facade, attempting to reach into her. "You didn't approach my table for just an autograph."

"What?" She pressed the elevator button.

"Our meeting wasn't an accident."

"I think you're placing too much emphasis on a signature request."

"At the risk of completely offending you, aren't you curious as to why?"

"This may work on starlets and models or whoever else you date. My answer hasn't changed."

The elevator door opened. "Good night."

Ben failed to respond until the door shut. "*Tsamaya hantle*, Juliana. Go well."

––––––––––––––––––––

"Are you seated?"

"I'm driving."

"There's a buyer for the house. The bid is for the full asking price of $20 million."

Benjamin pulled into a parking lot, parked the rented Land Rover, and shut off the ignition. Not due on the set until that evening, he wanted to explore. He tightened the grip on his cell phone.

Across the street was a sprawling park occupied by pet owners tossing balls for their dogs and children racing in countless circles, giggling wildly. Only in Colorado could you experience snowfall and seventy-degree weather in the same week. Roughly twenty feet to the left, three men headed toward the bus stop awning, unzipping their jackets. A gardener meticulously sculpted the shrubs surrounding the perimeter. A teenager bounced down the sidewalk tapping the rhythm from his iPod earphones.

"Ben, you there?" his manager asked.

The actor nodded. "Yes. I suppose that is good news, Grace."

He and Eternity had spent five years etching their personal taste in every room. Their focus hadn't just been the texture of the carpet, the hue of the paint, or the design of the window treatments.

They had handcrafted the bend of their bedpost.

Had flown to Italy and observed the glass artisan hand blow their dizzying array of glassware.

Had trekked to Morocco for armoires, dressers, and tables.

Yet the last six months of their matrimony, their singular retreat no longer had promised refuge, but harbored memories too harsh to endure.

"I really thought this would top your week. I miscalculated."

He shook his head. "I am a bit surprised at my reaction as well. This moment has taken two years to arrive. Still, it feels as if something has been irrevocably sealed."

"I'm not trying to sound like a shrink here, but it's never easy to say goodbye, especially to something you worked so hard for."

A five-year-old girl raced toward a man who looked her twin by thirty years. Ben heard her jubilant squeals through the open sunroof as the man twirled her. "When is the closing?" Ben felt a weight press on his chest.

"Friday. You'll wrap your *Slow Bullet* shooting at three on Thursday, and your flight departs at six a.m. on Friday. I'll pick you up at LAX and drive you—"

"Grace."

"Yes?"

"That is all I can handle right now."

"I understand."

"I appreciate you calling. I'll see you on Friday."

Ben disconnected the call and leaned back into the soft leather. Beads of sweat formed on his forehead and ran into his eyes, despite the fresh breeze that rapped against the sunroof.

The Bel Air manor had been a creation that captured countless hours. Eternity had crafted a photography studio for him.

It had moved Ben to tears.

He had hung portraits of the emerald-eyed, raven-haired paradox on every wall.

In gratitude, as their bodies entwined in crazed affirmation of their love, they had vowed to make their marriage paramount.

Months later she had pulled away. Their interaction had grown constrained. When they had made love, his vigor to gratify seemed to aggravate her.

She had petitioned divorce.

He pleaded—she tossed furniture.

In a matter of months, their demise had consumed and it was over.

Even though he had vowed a lifetime.

Grace had packed the portraits into a corner of her basement storage room, impassive and gathering dust.

As they had exited the divorce courtroom, respective lawyers in tandem, she patted his shoulder and thanked him for being notably amiable.

It had taken every ounce of restraint not to lay her out cold.

He removed the keys from the ignition, stepped out of the truck, and shrugged on his navy suit jacket. He eyed the parking lot activity and was grateful no one recognized him. Bruce suggested he take security along, but he flatly refused. He craved solitude to seek answers that seemed ephemeral and mysterious. For this moment, especially in light of Grace's call, he simply wanted to revel in a quiet meal.

Juliana scanned the menu and sighed.

"Everything all right, Palesa?"

"Just the typical arduous deadlines, Maya."

"I swear my bladder has shrunk. Excuse me."

Juliana placed the menu on the table and twirled her water glass.

She was logical and methodical and bright. *So why does Ben Powers keep popping into my mind?* she wondered.

Ben opened the restaurant door and removed his sunglasses as his eyes adjusted to the dim wall sconces. He approached the hostess counter.

"Oh, my," she stumbled. "May I help you?"

Ben eyed the dense crowd. "Good afternoon. How long is the wait?"

She glanced at her color-coded pallet. "At least thirty minutes."

Ben turned and looked at those seated on the benches behind him. He counted fifteen.

"Thank you." He replaced his sunglasses.

As he exited, she called out. "Wait! Mr. Powers, I'm certain we can accommodate you sooner."

He approached her, leaned, and whispered. "Thank you. But that won't be necessary. After all, those people arrived long before I did. I appreciate the gesture."

He exited. As he stood contemplating his next move, his stomach growled. He looked to the left and right. His steps carried him to the bistro on the right.

"Will it be the usual, Miss DeLauer?" the server asked.

"You guessed it. The African."

Brad remarked, "Do you have any idea what Dr. Elliott would like?"

Juliana shook her head. "She should return shortly."

Ben stepped into the foyer. The walls were painted assorted shades of copper and held impressive photos of various world landmarks. The floor was a dark wood that gleamed beneath the brass chandeliers. Again, he stepped to the hostess stand.

"Welcome to Java Amore."

"Good afternoon. Is there a wait?"

"No sir. Right this way, please."

Ben followed the woman as she made a path beyond the brass and leather booths and linen-covered tables toward the rear. Several patrons pointed. Benjamin nodded, offering slight waves as they came to a series of closed doors.

"Here you are." The young woman opened a door and directed him to a private room.

As Maya exited the restroom, her phone buzzed. She detached it from her hip and read the text.

She leaned against the wall and grinned at the amorous message from Thomas. Maya attached it to her belt loop and looked at the couple approaching.

"Ben?"

"Maya?"

She embraced him. "Are you meeting someone?"

"No."

She touched his forearm. "Do you desire company or solitude?"

Ben reasoned a shared meal with her might revive him from his current funk. He followed Maya and the hostess into a room bathed in the same affable shades as the main area. It held a single table clothed in burgundy linen. Spanish guitars serenaded from the concealed acoustic system.

Ben stopped when he discovered Maya's dining companion. "Maya, this may not be such a great idea."

She approached the table. "Nonsense. Juliana, you wouldn't mind if Ben joined us?"

"Well, I mean, I suppose—"

"Excellent." Maya smiled.

Ben pulled out Maya's seat then removed his jacket, placing it on the back of the chair opposite Juliana.

The hostess uttered, "I would just like to say what a huge fan I am. I heard you were in Denver, but never, ever thought I'd actually meet you."

He smiled his most alluring smile. "Thank you. I'm sorry. I didn't catch your name."

"Ashley."

"Ashley, you must do one thing for me."

Her eyes widened in anticipation. "Certainly."

"Do not order any more snow."

She giggled. "Oh, all right. If you insist. Your server, Brad, will be with you shortly."

"Welcome to one of our favorite luxuries." Maya's pager beeped. She lifted it from her waistband. "Juliana, would you explain the menu to Ben while I return this call?"

Juliana and Ben watched as Maya dialed. Juliana placed a menu folded in three sections in the center of the table. "You have three options. Every meal consists of bite-sized portions with endless cups of select coffees, either regular or decaf, from the region you've chosen. There is the Parisian Indulgence, the African Delight, or the Peruvian Joy."

"I'm intrigued. Continue."

"The Parisian consists of espresso, smoked duck, foie gras on toasted bricohe, potato leek dip, and pastries made on site by an authentic Cordon Bleu-trained pastry chef. The African has coffee chosen from Kenya with an intricate array of Moroccan chicken bundles, baked mushrooms with Brazilian nut stuffing, carrot dip, and orange and chocolate parfait."

"My head is spinning."

"And the Peruvian has samples of salmon morando, pescado del Dia, ajide Gallina, tortilla rellena, alfajores, and maza mora morado."

"I understood salmon and tortilla out of that sentence."

He marveled that her chestnut eyes possessed such a commanding quality without the enrichment of age. Ben wondered how many men had met that confident stare and choked.

Maya concluded her call. "Bad news."

"What?" Juliana asked.

"One of my patients was just admitted to the ER." Maya gathered her items. "Palesa, rain check?"

"Okay."

Maya kissed Juliana's head and waved to Ben. They both looked at the door long after Maya exited.

"All right." He closed his eyes, blindly pointing his finger on a section of the menu. He opened his eyes and discovered he had chosen the Peruvian.

She closed the menu and rubbed the back of her neck.

Ben sipped from Maya's water glass. "I could make mine a take-out order."

"Don't be ridiculous."

"You look uncomfortable."

"I'm fine."

"There's really no point if—"

"Let's not make this a big deal. We can just sit here and enjoy the food."

Ben glanced around the room. "What was the highlight of your week?"

"It's only Tuesday."

"Nonetheless."

She clasped her hands. "Nothing, really."

Ben reached for his jacket. "It's plain that you'd rather dine alone."

"Ben, wait. I'm under stress at work and I'm being rude to you. I'm sorry."

"I can leave and put you out of your misery."

Her expression softened. "Last week, my Sunday school class and I reenacted Moses and the children of Israel crossing the Red Sea at our visit to a nursing home."

He halted his rapid exit.

"Well, Pharaoh was at our back and the Red Sea was ahead. We had no escape. Then, God spoke to me."

"Me?"

"Moses. God told me to touch my staff to the water, and suddenly, the waters parted. It was amazing! We crossed over in complete wonder of the awesome God we serve."

He looked to his hands and contemplated her apology. "So, Moses, how goes it in the Promised Land?"

She cringed. "Not great. We are wandering in the desert. The people are murmuring and complaining. There is talk they want me dead."

"Imagine."

She fidgeted with the scarf.

The door of their private space opened and Brad entered. As he repeated what Juliana had previously explained, his hands shook.

Benjamin met his nervous gaze with one of complete warmth. He pointed to Juliana. "She raved the Peruvian Joy is out-of-this-world. But she is half-crazed most of the time. What do you recommend because, frankly, I try never to heed the advice of lunatics?"

Juliana cocked her head to the side and perked her glossed lips. Brad's expression shifted into a playful grin. "Well, I agree with the lady. You can't beat the amazing baked salmon with purple potato, or the marinated and grilled fish with mango salsa, or the shredded breast of chicken spiced with turmeric, toasted almond, and aji sauce, which is a staple ingredient of Peruvian cuisine."

"I'm trusting you on this, Brad." Brad exited the door with a smile.

"Half-crazed, huh?"

"Miss DeLauer, you say that as if it's a bad thing. After all, consider my hometown."

She placed her delicate left hand on the back of her neck where the lavish scarf met the nape of her neck.

Ben drummed his fingers on the tablecloth. The jagged scar above his right brow, made nearly imperceptible by a skilled plastic surgeon, itched.

"Is this your first time to Denver?"

"Yes. Do you realize your state is very confused as what season it is in? Two days ago it snowed. Today, I'm sweating."

She shrugged. "It grows on you. In my trunk are snow boots, a wind-breaker, and shorts."

"Are you a native?"

"Yes." She sipped her water, replaced the glass on the tabletop, and twirled it. "Although I came very close to moving to San Fran."

"Why?"

"It was Stanford or Denver U. I chose DU."

"Let me guess. You are the only daughter, and the thought of you so far away was unbearable."

"Correction—an only child."

"Ah." He placed his elbows on the table. "Even more complicated."

"Things were changing rapidly in the ministry. I felt it unwise to attend an out-of-state school."

"Ministry?"

"My father was a pastor."

"Whoa." He released a low whistle. "Juliana DeLauer is a preacher's kid."

He pretended this was new information. Grace Connors, a virtuoso at satisfying his requests, had the inflammatory packet delivered to his trailer the first day of his Denver shooting. He could seamlessly recite her life story before the conclusion of the meal. Ben feigned surprise, ascertaining it was for his protection. He knew from past experience there was no such thing as being too careful.

"I am indeed."

Ben traced a water bead down the length of his goblet. "Do you ever feel as if you dwell under a microscope?"

She smiled, sarcastically. "More than twenty-four seven."

"I didn't experience that type of attention until I became an adult."

"My parents would have celebrated their thirty-eighth year in the ministry next month."

He squinted. "Would have?"

There was a lingering moment where she searched his eyes. The door opened, and Brad entered with the first course. He strategically placed every item on the table and poured steaming cups of fragrant decaf coffee, which caused the saliva to flow inside Ben's mouth. He nodded in thanks to Brad and the waiter departed.

Her eyes remained on him. "My father died of colon cancer two years ago."

"I'm sorry."

"You had no idea." She lowered her gaze and placed the cloth napkin on her lap, oblivious to the augmented, acrid taste of bile in his throat. "He is no longer in pain. And for that I am very pleased."

The nagging feeling of deceit, screaming that he was a fraud, taxed his appetite. Benjamin wanted to reach for her hand, yet wasn't certain of her reaction. According to Juliana's response on the jet from Jo'Burg, succeeding autograph request, and her lunch refusal, they seemed near strangers. She raised her head and revealed a melancholy smile. He began to regret his request for the packet in the first place. Juliana had been forthright with every response.

He already knew the answer, but still asked, "Did your mother take over the ministry?"

She sipped from the delicate cup. "No. But the board requested she remain a member to help them finalize their decision as to Daddy's successor. Once Pastor Michael was chosen, Mom resumed her evangelist crusades. She adores it, and I'm happy she's happy."

Perhaps to lessen his discomfort, Ben remarked, "Forgive me if this comes across as invasive, but, just now, you sounded lonely."

She didn't avert her eye. "Change may be good, but it is never easy."

They allowed silence to fall as they munched from their plates.

"Believe it or not, I used to sing in the children's choir and my older brothers played in the youth band."

"Do you still attend church?"

"Only when I'm home for the holidays. I find religion to be laboriously monotonous and unreliable."

When he graduated from Northwestern, his path to Hollywood left God, the church, and Crater, Idaho, behind. God seemed to have favorites, and Ben hadn't been one of them.

"I agree that religion never satisfies."

Ben frowned. "You do?"

"Religion consists of man-made regulations that do little more than restrict. However, a relationship with Christ is quite gratifying."

In order not to insult her, Ben studied the sultry, dark liquid in his cup.

"You believe that to be outlandish, don't you?"

His head shot up. "Obviously, I failed to mask my difference of opinion."

Juliana shrugged. "Far too many believe God is this remote, insensitive Being who isn't the least bit concerned about His creation. After all, doesn't the current state of the world reflect that? Yet, nothing could be farther from the truth. Everyday, He desires to have a passionate relationship with us."

Ben narrowed his eyes. "You sound like one of those Jesus Freaks from the 70's."

"As the song states 'there ain't no disguising the truth.'"

Ben rolled the spiced mango sauce on his tongue and reflected. "And when you're not proclaiming this from the rooftops?"

"I lead a team of volunteers to South Africa to support those affected by HIV or AIDS. We administer medical care to the homebound."

Ben noticed she didn't mention they also sponsored an orphanage in Jo'Burg and provided medical and financial aid to families unable to provide for themselves.

"If you weren't such a brilliant writer, is that what you would like to do fulltime?"

"How would you know my writing is brilliant?"

"My hotel has this month's issue of *Core* on my credenza. Your article stated it is estimated that 600,000 children have been orphaned as a result of AIDS."

She leaned forward. "It requires an immense amount of faith to not meet the end of the work week drowning in futility." She paused to smile. "My kids are so full of giggles and anticipation, I fly out of bed on Sundays. If I weren't writing about children, they'd have to be a part of my career somehow. Children have no issue with accepting love. If you're secure enough to release it, they are open enough to receive it."

Ben's mind rushed to the twins. Instantly, a smile lightened his face.

"What was that?"

"What do you mean?"

"That beaming."

"My cousin Sheila has two twin boys, four years of age, and they have this power to ignite my world. They've insisted on calling me Uncle Ben, and I've never resisted."

"Their acceptance is the purest form of love."

That statement unnerved Ben. It had the same quality as her eyes that day in the Boptang veld when she ripped at his masks and pretenses.

Ben verbally stepped out on the ledge, asking a question for which he didn't have the answer. "How often do you travel to South Africa?"

Her eyes dimmed. "With our ministry, nearly twice a year."

"There's this tone coating the outer edges of your voice."

"You are perceptive, Mr. Powers."

"Comes with my line of work. I'm required to tunnel deeper than most."

Her eyes traveled to candlelit sconces that cast tawny shadows on the amber walls. "Many agree it is repulsive for people to die from treatable diseases. Large-scale, private-sector programs and massive, private donations for the distribution of antiretroviral drugs propel the message that effective treatment is essentially a basic human right. Yet even though the destitute now have access to antiretroviral drugs, which was previously out of their reach due to the expense, still too many are dying at a staggering rate."

She sighed and reeled her emotions inward. "My mother's ancestors are from Boptang, South Africa. But my allegiance is also rooted in the obtuse nonsense of it all. Millions upon millions are dying. I am not all-powerful or arrogant enough to believe I can save the world. And I do not claim to have all the answers. But I am one whom God has quickened to be beneficial toward lasting change."

"You've been criticized."

One chestnut brow rose because his words formed a statement, not a question. "Often."

"There are scales of Americans impoverished and oppressed, afflicted in the same manner."

The smirk formed slowly, then faded. "My answer has never been fully accepted—possibly because some deem it desperately sophomoric. But God didn't press on my heart for any other area but South Africa. I have never ignored the need in my own backyard. I do participate in stateside areas. But my passion has been Boptang."

Ben's eyes wavered to his cup. Had he not witnessed her peril in the veld, he would have been convinced she was a set-up. Her impassioned expressions mirrored those of his soul. He had donated millions to research, education, medical training and assistance, and housing for the very same citizens.

Eternity had traveled beside him, but her heart was resistant. She had diligently attended seminars, assisted in the clinic administration, even donated some of her own salary. But she had wearied quickly.

Long before their departures, her eyes darkened as she had likened their efforts as an ant thrusting against a boulder.

There had been few constants in his forty-two-years. He had wanted to act, he wanted to donate his resources to those less fortunate, and he wanted to be a father. A lurking to share those suppressed words with Juliana surfaced. Especially in light of his clandestine prying. Still, he rebuffed it, for caution was supreme.

Their conversation flowed toward the completion of the remaining courses. When Brad entered with the bill, Ben took it.

"No, Ben. I planned on this being my treat."

He rolled his eyes and leaned forward. "If it were ever discovered I allowed a lady to pay for my meal, I would be disowned. So, please allow me to not delineate from the Powers' lineage."

"Thank you."

They gathered their belongings and started their exit. Before they made their way to the front door, Ben was stopped to sign autographs and pose for photos taken with cell phones. Juliana waited by the entrance.

"I apologize for keeping you waiting." He held the door open for her.

"It is to be expected, Mr. Powers."

He walked her to her car, and the breeze whipped her scarf creating a lop-sided halo around her head. Quickly, she tamed it with a brisk tug then removed her keys from her handbag. Ben scanned the parking lot and the surrounding sidewalk. Near the bus stop, roughly twenty feet away, stood the same three men he had spotted when he pulled into the lot.

Ben touched her forearm. "Thank you. The meal and company were amazing."

"I enjoyed it too."

There was an awkward pause as they searched for an appropriate farewell.

"Juliana?" A meticulously groomed young man stood at the restaurant's entrance waving.

"Pastor Michael!"

Benjamin watched as the handsome man excused himself from his elderly companions. He checked for traffic and sauntered over.

"How on earth did you break away?"

"It was not easy."

They embraced and Ben noticed that the man's hand lingered on her back. "Pastor Michael Cage, this is Benjamin Powers."

"Yes." The athletic man seemed to be barely out of his twenties. He offered his hand and Ben shook it heartily. "I believed you looked familiar. How are you?"

"Well. Thank you."

"Pastor Michael is my senior pastor."

Ben felt something utterly unexpected and confusing. He wondered if Juliana's heart was enchanted by the attractive cleric. Then he wondered why he wondered.

"She, her mother, and the church have made it a pleasure."

She shook her head and her curls swayed easily across her shoulders. "I won't be at Bible study tonight. Mom returns and we'll spend a quiet evening at home."

He smiled revealing teeth actors had paid thousands to obtain. "I understand." He turned to Ben. "I shouldn't keep my guests waiting. I hope you enjoy your stay. It was nice to have met you."

Ben nodded. "You as well, Pastor."

Pastor Michael kissed her cheek before rejoining his party at the entrance.

"I had no idea your senior pastor was so young."

"His task is monumental multiplied by infinity." Juliana unlocked her door. Ben held it open, his hand resting on the window.

"Ben! Who is the new lady?"

Benjamin looked in the direction of the shout. The three bus stop loiters now carried expensive photography equipment and were approaching.

"Get in!" He motioned to Juliana.

"She's kinda young isn't she?"

"By about twenty some odd years!"

They closed in. Juliana could tell one had earlier indulged in curry and garlic. Another approached so swiftly, he ended up shoving the car door and jamming her shoulder into the window seam.

"Go!" Ben pushed her into the driver's seat and slammed the door shut. Bulbs flashed incessantly.

"Looks like he plays both fields, fellas. This week it's little girls!"

Juliana shoved the car into reverse and safely departed the lot. He swiftly crossed the lot and disabled the alarm as more lurid accusations were tossed like venomous darts.

"Sheila know you're into pubescent boys, Ben?"

Ben opened the truck door, then halted. If he punched any of them as hard as they deserved, there would undoubtedly be jail time and an extravagant lawsuit. If he climbed into the truck expressionless and returned to his trailer, there wouldn't be the $100K photo of him losing his cool.

Benjamin climbed into the cabin and revved the engine. He checked the rearview mirror and placed the truck in reverse.

Their vulgarity had attracted attention. As Ben sped from the lot, he noticed Pastor Michael standing near the Java Amore entrance taking in every polemical second.

CHAPTER SIX

Soothing percussion from Brazilian drums enveloped. She twirled her ankles as the aromatic bath of sea kelp and Aloe Vera swished over her toes. The continuous jetted flow formed tingly bubbles against the soles of her feet. The workday complete, Juliana snuggled into Vie's cushy chair as she waited for her pedicurist.

Someone entered and closed the door. A swift smack landed on her exposed shin and she immediately straightened.

"Dish." Tricia demanded, placing her long-limbed body on the pedicurist's stool.

"Aren't you supposed to be in a marketing meeting?"

"We concluded early. Now, tell me all about lunch."

"I already did. My, we are cross."

Tricia cocked her head. "I'd hardly agree that emaciated call was adequate."

"I was shocked when Ben walked through the door. Maya invited him to stay then had to rush off to an emergency."

"Why was there tension in your voice?"

"In the parking lot, some photographers ambushed us. I had to speed away."

"That's crazy!"

"It reminded me of when Daddy was on trial. How I was hounded and screamed at outside of the courthouse."

"You okay?"

"It's not something I ever want to experience again." Juliana shook her head. "But he had the presence of mind to get me out of there. I had a call from him on my work voicemail by the time I reached the office."

"You still look a little shaken."

"It did not make for a pleasant memory."

Tricia sighed and rested her chin on her right knuckles. "Since they follow him everywhere, is that code for 'I don't ever want to see Ben again'?"

"Perhaps."

"Question: Paparazzi aside, did you enjoy yourself?"

"Much more than expected."

"So you liked being with him?"

"More than I imagined."

Tricia contemplated for a moment. "What has God said about it?"

The pedicurist arrived and set up her tools. Tricia amiably greeted her employee, then stood by Juliana's side.

"I didn't realize that was required after one coffee."

"Nope. You haven't asked. It's apparent by your response." Tricia touched Juliana's chin. "Are you more afraid of God's approval or opposition?"

Wednesday's daybreak had barely colored the nubilous sky as they embarked on their brisk walk. Juliana marveled at her mother, quickening the pace of their power walk with her ankles and wrists banded by weights. Her mother chattered about the miraculous acts God performed in her meetings. Juliana's spirit rejoiced, yet her flesh begged to be shrouded beneath bedcovers.

They faced the bottom of the steep hill that marked the midway point of their workout. Juliana stretched the length of her legs as they ascended the gravel path. A familiar throbbing gripped her right side. She filled her lungs with the damp morning air and pressed through the ache. Juliana caught up with her mother after she mounted the crest of the hill.

"So tell me, dear child of mine, what was the best part of your week?"

She shot Dionne a side-glance. "I had coffee with Benjamin Powers yesterday."

Dionne placed her hands on her hips. "You're not teasing me?"

"I met Tricia for dinner at Tanner's. He was there." Juliana gathered her breath, still battling the residual pain. "He's in town shooting a movie and was dining with his crew. I decided to make Tricia's day by introducing myself and asking him for his John Hancock."

"And apparently a cup of coffee."

"Yep."

Dionne squinted. "You're in pain?"

Juliana waved a hand. "It's the same old, same old."

"You had an appointment with Dr. Martin in May?"

"The screening came back negative, so it's the same hormonal churnings."

"The pain isn't sharp or residing in the same area?"

"Mom, stop worrying. I'd tell you if anything changed."

Dionne relaxed her shoulders. "I know my baby dazzled him. Did he dazzle you?"

Juliana scrunched her nose. "I enjoyed myself."

A jogger hit the top of the hill, waved, and continued down the steep path.

"So when do we see him again?"

"I'm not so sure we do."

"Juliana, you are not, nor have ever been, a game player. It is the reason I received calls from countless teachers who begged me for advice on how to tame your tongue. It was very difficult for adults to hear such unhindered truth from a child. I have never known you to back down from a challenge. So what about this man, and his situation, scares you?"

The women resumed their vigorous stride.

"There is something that resides within Benjamin Powers that pulls on me."

Dionne offered no advice. She merely marched beside her daughter and listened.

"I have never experienced the necessity to feel a man's love besides Daddy's. His love was unconditional, encompassing. What man could surpass that?"

Their pace quickened, resuming the brisk cadence of their hearts. Juliana relented. "Maybe it's Pastor Michael."

Juliana glanced at her mother, seeking a reaction. Dionne failed to offer one. "But, I feel it may very well be time to find out. And that terrifies me."

She had read books on grief. They talked of closure. Closure reeked of insult. It seemed too final.

No.

Closure was for destructive relationships or faulty business deals. Not for the treasured love between a father and daughter.

The evenings she hadn't pulled into the garage until well after midnight, he was there, waiting in the kitchen nook.

He'd glance over his half-moon glasses and grin.

He'd slice the fruit.

She'd sit and he'd push a few segments her way. They'd munch, carving the details of one another's day.

Juliana realized gone were the days of her father's tender touch, gentle teasing, or immutable love.

He would never smear another glob of paint on her nose, chide her to eat more fruit, or escort her down the aisle on her wedding day.

Dionne touched her daughter's arm. "But you must make certain of one thing."

"What's that?"

"You aren't seeking a substitute."

"A substitute?"

"As powerful as your father loved you, it still pales in comparison to how God adores you."

"I know." Juliana frowned. "Are you saying I've been blocking God's love by relishing in what Daddy gave me?"

Dionne looked into Juliana's eyes. "You had no doubt God would heal your daddy."

Juliana stopped. "Right."

Her mother's pace was so brisk, it took her time to slow, stop, and return. "And that He would heal Tomorrow?"

"Where are you going with this, Mom?"

"You're beginning to withdraw."

"Mom, we've spent hours together shopping, evenings at the symphony and catching movies."

"I'm not talking about with me, baby. I'm talking about your time with God."

"Is this because I missed some services and Bible studies?"

"You know as well as I do that attending church functions does not equate to spending time with the Father."

"So, what are you seeing? That I now doubt God's ability to keep His word?"

"That's what I'm asking."

Juliana cocked her head and bit down her anger. "It takes me time to process so I can articulate my feelings. I don't want to be misunderstood."

"I would never stand in judgment of how you feel, baby."

"It feels like you're judging me now. Because I don't grieve the way you grieve, I have failed in some way?"

"Never." Dionne held Juliana's shoulders. "I'm asking you to examine if those losses have created a wall that blocks out God."

Juliana tightened her jaw. She returned to their house in silence. She showered, dressed, and ate breakfast in the same sullen manner. At seven, she grabbed her purse and briefcase and headed to the garage. She opened the door and halted. No matter how much her mother's insinuations burned, she couldn't leave without saying goodbye.

"Mom, I'm gone!" she shouted, believing her mother to be upstairs in her bedroom in preparation for the day.

Dionne appeared around the corner of the kitchen wall. "*Tsamaya hantle.*" Go well.

Her mother's countenance, the poignant look in her eye, caused Juliana to rip in places reserved solely for Dionne. Juliana rushed forward. Her mother's grasp was as tight as a seal designed to ward off decay. When Juliana pulled away, her mother dabbed at her tears.

Dionne retrieved Juliana's purse and removed her makeup case. Tenderly, she repaired Juliana's makeup.

Juliana touched her mother's smeared cheek. "What about you?"

"Not my shade. I'm more of a pecan." She kissed Juliana's palm.

"You scared me."

"I know."

"You're right. Both deaths just seem so callously senseless. I know God is sovereign. But I am terrified to ask Him why. I may hate the answer. And if I hate the answer, will I begin to hate Him?"

"Even more reason you shouldn't bury your feelings."

Juliana shook her head. "No amount of supposition will bring either of them back."

"It's not meant to, baby. It's meant to restore your faith and draw you closer to the Father."

Juliana sighed. "I'd better get to work."

"Tell me something?"

"Yes?" Juliana placed the purse strap on her shoulder.

"Tell me what you liked most about Benjamin Powers?"

Juliana gazed out the massive window at the rolling acres of wildflowers. "His eyes. Those eyes tell you exactly what is in his soul. And that he's not only had to carry his pain, but that of someone else. Someone he loves deeply."

Dionne took Juliana's hand. "When do we invite him for dinner?"

Juliana erupted. "What!"

"Don't react as if I've spoken something peculiar. I love to cook. The man probably likes to eat. Invite him for dinner."

"He ends shooting sometime this week. I don't know if he can even come."

"Won't know unless you ask."

"Just like that?"

"Just like that."

"What do you mean he's in the hospital?"

Ben lowered the water bottle and leaned against the trailer door.

The first assistant director nodded, perturbed. "Due to the afternoon shooting schedule, Matthew got up early this morning and drove his family to Manitou Springs to ride the Cog Train."

"Cog Train?"

"It takes you to the top of Pike's Peak. Well, they arrive at the summit and there's some snow. The kids begin a snowball fight. In the midst of the frivolity, Matthew slips and breaks his leg."

"Man." Ben sighed, imagining Marcus's manic state. They had already lost one day's shooting due to the snowstorm.

"So, we've scripted the broken leg into the film so we can maintain schedule and end shooting in two days."

"Where was he admitted?'"

"He's being transported to Sky Ridge in Lonetree early this afternoon. It's out south, near Park Meadows Mall."

"Keep your chin up, Sandy."

"Don't have much choice. According to your stop date, you have to be done by Thursday afternoon."

"Pressing business in L.A. Friday morning."

"Right. You're not required back on the set until ten tonight."

"Is Marcus–"

"I'd recommend you stay clear. Go enjoy. It's supposed to be eighty degrees."

Ben shut the trailer door and returned to his laptop. A day's loss of principal shooting with major actors would cost the studio hundreds of thousands of dollars. Ben did not envy his friend, Marcus, the director. He and Eternity owned a production company and had experienced the same agonizing, pricey setbacks—thus the clause in many lead actors' contracts to not participate in activities that could cause injury and delay shooting.

Bruce lounged on the sofa near the door, reading *The Shack*.

Ben typed "Denver City Guide." "Anything in particular you wanted to see during your visit, Bruce? It appears we have time."

Just as Bruce opened his mouth, Ben's cell phone chimed. "Powers."

"Ben, hi. It's Juliana."

Benjamin straightened at the charge her voice created in him. "Juliana."

"Did I catch you at a bad time?"

"Not at all."

"Listen, my mother insists on cooking much more food than I could ever consume. Are you available for dinner?"

He grinned. "Yes. What time should I arrive?"

"Six." Juliana gave him directions. "Ben?"

"Yes."

"I apologize for not returning your call. I was a bit jarred."

"I'm sorry that was something you had to experience. I had no intention on saying such a hasty goodbye."

"I appreciate that. "

"I wish I could assure you it won't occur again."

"Actually, it already has."

"What do you mean?"

"Paparazzi were stationed near my subdivision guard shack this morning as I left for work."

Ben slammed a hand on his forehead and leaned back in the chair. Bruce looked up from his book. "Somehow, I don't believe your sense of humor is so perverse as to make that up."

"Not this woman."

Ben moved his hand from his forehead to the tabletop and smacked it so hard his palm throbbed. "I don't know what to say."

"Say you'll be here at six."

He did and flipped the phone shut. Bruce replaced the bookmark within the pages, closed his book, ducked slightly to accommodate his height, and joined Ben at the table.

"They've found her."

"You must have known it was only a matter of time." Bruce nodded in the direction of the tabloid photo faxed before breakfast from Ben's assistant. It encapsulated their brisk exit from Java Amore. They now had a name and residence for Juliana, and it caused Ben to seethe. "You're remembering?"

Ben didn't, couldn't verbalize the thoughts that raced through his head. Bruce found it unnecessary; he read every image in the distressed stare.

Ben shook his head, clearing from his memory the sweetness of Aiko. The paparazzi steal everything.

"You weren't to blame," Bruce said with such simplicity and directness Ben flinched.

"I've never agreed with you on that one."

"She didn't feel any pain."

Ben placed rigid fingers on the faint brow scar and rubbed. "So you've said."

"The coroner's report confirmed it. Her neck broke on impact."

"That's what the statement reported."

"It took me three seconds to reach the car and only five more to pull you from the wreckage."

"You should have saved her first!" Ben shouted and immediately regretted it. They had spoken dozens of times of that night. But this was the first instance Ben laid blame at his mesomorphic bodyguard's feet. "I didn't mean that."

"Yes, you did."

Ben met the frank stare of his guardian. "Oh, man."

"You say it with your eyes every time we have to outrun the paparazzi."

"What an astronomical ingrate I am."

"I had a choice to make."

"I know."

"And no amount of training prepares you for that moment. You get one chance and you need to make certain it's the correct one."

"I'm sorry, Bruce. I had no right to accuse you."

"When I looked in, she stared back at me, yet she didn't. Do you understand? Her eyes looked but registered nothing."

Ben anxiously wanted to divert his attention, yet was convinced it would sever more than eye contact if he did. "There's no excuse for what I've done."

"I pray for you, Ben. Often. Do you know what I pray?"

Ben, dumbfounded and fearful he would utter more stupidity, shook his head.

"I pray you'll never face whom to rescue and whom to let perish."

Ben called to him, but Bruce exited the trailer. He picked up the tabloid article of Juliana fleeing Java Amore and shredded it, tearing, ripping, and crumbling it into the trash when he realized the wail of paper had matched that of his soul.

CHAPTER SEVEN

The drive to visit Matthew had been morose. Ben searched for the words, but none readily surfaced. The rented Land Rover returned to the studio lot, where Ben and Bruce exited, and Ben entered his trailer alone. Two hours later, the SUV departed the studio lot, heading east on Speer. The set of three cars carrying paparazzi followed the Rover as it continued, eventually exiting onto I-25 and heading south.

"You can say it."

"What?"

"Call me a jenny, a burro, a jack—"

Bruce shook his shaven head. "What point would that make?"

"It would be correct, and it would make me feel much better."

Bruce studied the rush hour traffic. "So it's about you feeling better?"

"Yes. No! We have to get this right, Bruce. It's killing me."

Bruce contemplated Ben's apology for nearly ten minutes. Finally, he said, "Jenny denotes that you are not just a donkey, but a female donkey."

"Seriously?"

"Yes."

Ben ogled out the tinted windows and caught glimpses of the mountains through the downtown skyline. He turned to his constant companion. "Very well. I deserve it."

"You're right, Jenny, you do."

Juliana lived in the southeast part of town, a few miles near Franktown. As they cruised the length of Parker Road, the town brought back memories of Crater, Idaho. The string of local tractor businesses, feed stores, equestrian ranches, with the prominence of nationwide grocery chains, Home Depot, Lowe's, and a Wal-Mart. It was peaceful country with a hint of new millennium.

Ben shut the folder couried by FedEx the first morning of his shoot for *Slow Bullet*. Bruce glanced at him, curious, yet respectful of his client's privacy.

"She's been through more than I ever imagined, Bruce." Ben patted the surface of the folder obtained by Grace. "She's only twenty-four and has lived through insidious accusations and a trial, lost her father, watched as thousands of church members departed, and witnessed her friend be beaten to death."

"How did her father die?"

"Colon cancer. But I can't help but wonder if the allegations of sexual molestation pushed him to a brink he didn't have the strength to defy. And the enormous drain it must have taken to endure the trial."

Bruce kept his eyes on the traffic, but Ben could see the cogs spinning. After awhile he asked, "What was the jury's verdict?"

"Pastor DeLauer was acquitted, and the boy, fifteen at the time, dropped out of sight."

They turned left into her subdivision, checked in with the security guard at the front gate, and ignored the stream of paparazzi lining the area at the turn-in. The community harbored mansions ranging from palatial to colossal. Each property resided on rolling acres of vibrant lavender with private tennis courts, pools, or lavish courtyards. Juliana's property began at the entrance of her street and seemed to cover several acres. Off to the right sat what Ben assumed was the guesthouse, a mini image of the main residence with sandstone stucco, pillars, and massive evergreens. As Bruce drove the Rover up the extensive drive, Ben chuckled.

"Well, it's a relief she isn't interested in me for my bank account."

Bruce parked the under the portico, stepped out, and took precautions. Ben admired the matching flagstone, the wrap around decks, and large windows. When Bruce was satisfied, he opened Ben's door. The actor stepped out of the SUV, shrugged on his suit jacket, then gathered the gifts for the DeLauer women. Juliana answered the door with a generous smile.

"Welcome."

Ben waved playfully from behind the monumental floral arrangement. He stepped inside the Travertine marble foyer with hand-laid inserts, double-sided staircase, and cherry wood crown molding.

Ben nodded to Bruce. "Juliana, I don't believe you two have been formally introduced. Bruce Carter, this is Juliana DeLauer."

"Hello."

Bruce nodded. "Good evening. Do you mind if I look around to become familiar with your home?"

"Help yourself."

Juliana closed the impressive double doors. "Those flowers are exquisite."

"I hope Mrs. DeLauer will be impressed."

"She will be more than impressed. Orchids are her favorite. We'll be by the pool. Shall I?"

"Thank you."

Juliana held the bouquet as Ben removed his cell phone and Juliana's wrapped box from the inside pocket then handed her his jacket. She passed him the flowers before hanging the jacket in the hall closet. Clipping his cell to his belt loop, he tucked Juliana's gift in the crushed tissue encasing the dramatic spray. They turned left down a wide corridor that led to the dining room. On the fireplace mantle was a large portrait of Juliana and whom Ben perceived to be her parents. Juliana bore her father's curly, thick hair, toffee-colored skin, and refined features to the point of eerie precision.

Ben inhaled sensuously. "I haven't smelled anything this luscious since Christmas."

"Keep saying things like that and she'll adopt you."

They entered a gourmet kitchen that rivaled those he had eaten in with the world's top chefs.

"Mom," Juliana called to a woman who had just taken rolls out of the oven. "Ben is here."

Juliana's mother placed the baking sheet on the Viking range and faced them. "Mr. Powers! Welcome!"

"Ben, this is my mother, Dionne DeLauer."

Ben closed the expanse between them and embraced Juliana's mother. Even in a throng of people, her exotic features would create a stir. Her complexion was the hue of rich mahogany. Her body narrowed to a slim waist that flowed into ample hips.

"You have no idea how much I've been looking forward to this evening."

"Wonderful, Ben! I hope you brought your appetite."

"Absolutely." Ben withdrew Juliana's present and handed Dionne the flowers. "These are for you."

She placed a hand to her chest. "These are stunning! What a sweet thing to do. Thank you." She rushed to a cabinet and removed a crystal vase.

"Mom, do you need any help?"

"No, baby. You two head out to the pool."

They walked down a hallway with deep crown molding and ten-foot doors. They exited through the last door on the left, passed the pool, and took their seats underneath a large umbrella attached to the patio table. Ben delighted in the gurgling of the waterfall from behind that spilled into the sparkling liquid turquoise of the pool. He switched his cell to vibrate.

"Your home is magnificent. Have you lived here all your life?"

"We moved here about four years ago. It was an answer to prayer; like God's way of keeping us sane and expectant. Tea?"

"Please."

Juliana poured and added a sprig of mint. "Mom grew up in Georgia. It is unheard of to drink tea sans mint."

"I love her style. How was work?"

"Grueling. Deadlines are my life. How about you?"

Ben sipped. "Man, that is good. What is that flavor? Cinnamon?"

"She will be thrilled your taste buds are refined enough to notice."

"Let's see." He took another drink. "Ah, yes, my co-star broke his leg."

"What?"

Ben snapped his fingers. "What is the name of the train that takes you to the top of Pike's Peak?"

"The Cog Train."

"Yes! Well, he was so distracted by his kid's snowball fight that he slipped and broke his leg."

"What does this mean for the shooting schedule?"

"I'm done by tomorrow afternoon due to business in L.A. Thus, we'll more than likely shoot ten pages."

"Ten pages?"

"A normal schedule is to film five to six pages a day. We probably won't end until dawn."

Juliana crinkled her nose and sipped her tea. "Tonight?"

"I'm due back on the set at ten."

"Ouch."

"Precisely."

"Well, have you enjoyed your stay in Colorado?"

Ben pressed his back against the plush cushion. "Very much. Bruce and I ventured to the Broadmoor for dinner. We ate at the Penrose Room. Have you been?"

"I can quote the menu. Before Daddy became sick, we'd lunch there once a month."

"Breathtaking place. The history is just as fascinating. But, it pales in comparison to your abode."

Juliana smirked. "It was obtained for purpose."

Dionne burst through the side door. "Ben, may I ask for your help with this tray?"

Ben rushed to gather the tray plentiful with grilled chicken breast, salmon, mixed vegetables, and rolls.

"Thank you. You can place it on the table," Dionne said.

Ben marveled at the presentation. His habit had been to dine out. The ritual of cooking a singular meal depressed him. His only culinary joy was the luscious pecan pies he baked for Sheila and the twins.

"Ben, sorry to keep you waiting. Here you are." Mrs. DeLauer handed Ben an ivory plate with utensils wrapped in a linen napkin.

"Mrs. DeLauer, this smells and looks amazing."

"Why, thank you! You're our guest, so you can be the first to fix your plate." Ben placed samples of each item on his plate and waited for the women. Mrs. DeLauer sat to his left and Juliana to his right. Suddenly, Mrs. DeLauer screamed. Ben looked over his shoulder and discovered Bruce walking along the rose bush path near the back of the yard.

"I apologize, ma'am." Bruce halted his stroll. "I didn't mean to startle you."

"Mrs. DeLauer, this is Bruce Carter, my bodyguard."

"You nearly received a grill fork through your skull, young man," Mrs. DeLauer said, swinging the fork in her hand. She inhaled, causing a great swell in her chest. "Well, Mr. Carter, are you hungry?"

"No, ma'am. If it's all right with you, I'll take a seat here beside the waterfall."

"It's pretty warm out here. At least take some water."

"Thank you, ma'am." Bruce took the chilled bottle and sat on the wooden bench situated beside the cascading water.

"Let's bless the food." Mrs. DeLauer said a prayer of thanks and Ben marveled at her words. They seemed intimate as if she were speaking to a valued friend.

"Oh, I almost forgot," Mrs. DeLauer slapped her generous thighs. "Pastor Michael phoned. He had to reschedule the church's softball practice to Friday night."

"What happened?" Juliana nibbled on the chicken.

"It coincided with the elders' meeting."

"Tricia will not be happy. This is the second time this week I've had to bale on her. The wedding is bearing down and she's beginning to freak."

"She's one of those covenant friends. She walks in perpetual forgiveness."

"Umm." Juliana took another bite of the grilled chicken. "This is incredible, Mom. The meat is so tender."

"Thank you, baby. I marinated it for hours in my famous citrus combination."

They looked toward Ben. The actor's full attention was held by the tasty cuisine. When Ben noticed the conversation had ceased, he looked up at the women. They all burst into laughter.

"It simply is not right for the studios not to feed you, Mr. Powers."

"Mrs. DeLauer, I determined after my first bite that you could call me often and Ben all at the same time."

"Well, thank you, sweetie. If you could extend your stay, I'd invite you over for Sunday dinner. "

He groaned as if she had speared him. "Do not tempt me."

"Well, I suppose you'll simply have to visit us again in the future."

He looked directly at Juliana. "I would consider it a privilege."

Juliana lowered her eyes and forked a broccoli head.

Mrs. DeLauer asked, "Ben, I imagine your parents must be very proud. Where did you grow up?"

"A place with the population of two thousand called Crater, Idaho. It is fifty miles north of Boise."

"Did your parents also grow up there?"

"My mother, yes. My father was raised in Wyoming and went to the University of Idaho where they met."

"Do you have siblings?"

"Yes, ma'am. Two older brothers."

"Did you attend your parents' alma mater?"

"No, ma'am. I attended Northwestern in Illinois. I studied communications."

"Your plate is empty. I'll stop chatting so you can get more."

"Thank you." Ben smiled and placed more of the sumptuous food on his dish. "Juliana was beginning to tell me how you obtained your home."

With the spotlight fully upon her, Juliana blushed. "My mother is the artisan cook, but Daddy was the consummate host. The more people crowding the corners of his house—the deeper his bliss. Our place in Littleton held much potential; four bedrooms, massive backyard, and finished basement, but it wasn't designed to entertain large crowds. So, Daddy started dreaming."

A hawk, amber wings spread wide, squawked above their heads. Juliana paused to observe its masterful dance with the heated current. She placed her fork to the left side of her plate. "Whenever Daddy had been traveling across the country, preaching at various churches, he loved to treat us to a meal that took hours where the intent was to savor the food as much as our time together."

Juliana paused to sip her tea. Translucent beads bubbled against the outside of the glass. When she replaced the tumbler on the tabletop, she wiped her fingers on her napkin. "It was at one of those dinners he informed us of this place. His excitement was so contagious; we hopped in the car and trekked over. The community was so new only three homes existed and the front gate was still under construction. Daddy turned in and we saw it. Something I *still* struggle to articulate caught in my heart."

Juliana suddenly became fascinated with the crystalline waves in the turquoise pool. Dionne dabbed the linen napkin to the edges of her mouth and continued the chronicle. "Many felt we simply were caught up in greed. I mean, what family of three truly needs fourteen-thousand square feet? But, it was Quincy's purpose for the place—his vision that most still don't understand. And because of the greed insinuation, he paid for it with the proceeds from his books. Not one nickel came from the ministry."

"His vision?"

"There are nine bedrooms, and he wanted those we weren't using to be filled with boys the church had written off. He volunteered as a basketball coach at an inner-city rec center and prayed about whom to pick. Two had been homeless, four were being raised by single parents who had prayed for a man of integrity to take interest in their sons, and the other had dropped out of school and was headed straight for prison."

Juliana had found her voice. "At one point, when I returned for winter break, there were seven young men here, and my dad was beaming. The house brimming with noise, activity, life."

"Wait." Ben's frown was decorated by a slight chuckle. "How did he maintain ... order? I mean, I'd be standing guard outside of my daughter's bedroom with a loaded shotgun."

Dionne laughed, the sound as calming as wind chimes on a mountain deck in the rain. "Location, location, location. Juliana's bedroom is directly next to ours, so you have no choice but to pass us to get to her. And Quincy was six-feet-six, three hundred and twenty pounds, and a very light sleeper."

"I was also taking classes and lived in my apartment near DU. Plus, every guy was given a list of chores, had to attend high school or have a job, was required to attend Bible study and help out at the church. So, the nights were pretty sedate. Subsequently, four went on to college and two are associate pastors at the church."

"Amazing." Ben recalled the sheer rush of a dream manifested.

Dionne rubbed her hands together, her eyes suddenly taking the mask of recollecting a painful memory. "The second group of guys consisted of four. Somehow, this group seemed to tax Quincy. Don't get me wrong, he still loved every one of them, loved pouring himself into them, but something was different. That September, he went in for his annual physical and discovered he had colon cancer."

Juliana scooted the remaining carrots, cauliflower, and broccoli around her plate with her fork. "One of the hardest days of my life."

Ben shook his head, nearly tasting Juliana's grief. "That must have been a horrendous shock."

Juliana nodded and cleared her throat. "One week later, the molestation accusations hit."

Ben sighed, wishing somehow it had never occurred. Maybe he'd be sitting with the threesome, gauging his words for not only Juliana and her mother, but especially the revered cleric.

Juliana looked over her shoulder to the expanse of their property. When she faced her dining companions, Ben noticed her struggle to rail her composure.

"In the midst of the physical and emotional agony, he still believed God was not only in control, but would honor his prayers, no matter how outrageous."

Both women looked at one another then to the actor. Dionne nodded, her eyes amazed at Ben's perception. What came to Ben's mind was that the basis of Quincy's entire existence depended upon a God who would perform the miraculous. There was never a time in his life when God had failed him. It had become intrinsic. He saw the radiance in his wife's and child's eyes when they caught the passion of his dream. The pastor was convinced God wasn't about to stop being God. But God had proved the pastor and Reginald Powers wrong.

Ben and his parents had habitually connected once a week spouting details of their activities, their conversations seasoned with encouragement and laughter.

The hair on the back of Ben's neck had prickled when his father increased the frequency of the calls.

Then the call no child had wanted to receive had occurred.

He and Bruce had boarded the flight to Idaho and had witnessed the hard evidence of Reginald's devastating medical prognosis.

All before the rare genetic disease had silenced his declarations.

Before God had shifted and made it impossible for father to connect with son.

Bruce, within the expanse of Ben's inhaling and exhaling, fixed upon his charge from the pine bench beside Juliana's pool.

Juliana played with her collar, eclipsing the length of her neck. "The sexual accusations sprung from the least likely to indict. Only fifteen at the time. And he was Daddy's nephew."

"His nephew!" Ben reeled from the implications. The information Grace had provided had omitted that substantial slice of the tumult.

Juliana tugged slightly harder at the ruffles. "At the time, it simply didn't add up. Daddy maintained solid relationships with all his siblings and their children. We discovered my cousin's motive the week Daddy died. He resented his own father abandoning him. So, any man became a target for his hostility. Daddy's sincerity was more than he could fathom."

Ben wanted to divert his eyes to the hovering hawk, the tranquil waves of the pool, the soaring evergreens, anything other than their faces. Because what tinged their wound wasn't bitterness, regret, or anger. It was forgiveness. It was incomprehensible how they could tell him the story that had ripped her father's dream like steel to flesh without an undertone of detestation. Especially when it came from blood.

"We weren't fighting against my nephew. No. The battle was against an enemy far more aged and cunning. Quincy knew this, and it was what fueled his prayers for that child. He was being used to destroy something that had changed young men's lives. He was being manipulated to block us from reaching another soul for God."

"What happened to your nephew?"

"He became a runaway a few days after Quincy's funeral." Dionne dabbed at her eyes with the napkin. "He visited Quincy, his last week. Quincy had been in and out of consciousness, his strength sapped from the medication. But he sat up for him, sat up, grabbed the back of his neck, and kissed him. It was all too much for that child. He couldn't comprehend how someone he intentionally attempted to destroy could embrace him."

Ben pressed his back to the chair. For several moments, the poolside gathering heard only the sound of the waterfall as it bubbled and splashed into the edges of the pool.

Dionne looked at Ben, her eyes unrelenting. "In the end, our enemy thought he'd won because of Quincy's death. But he won nothing. Death wasn't Quincy's enemy."

Ben looked upward in the smoke-blue sky, heavy with storm clouds, internally incensed by the absurdity of her words.

Dionne gathered the dishes. Ben and Bruce carried the largest platters into the sprawling kitchen and deposited them in the sink. Ben turned to the woman whose words unnerved him. "You must have believed God would heal him."

"I did."

"But he died." Ben's tone nearly sounded juvenile.

Dionne held his hands in hers. "Ben, no one who believes in the Father and the sacrifice and gift of His Son ever truly dies. There is this life and there is eternity."

Ben looked to his black loafers, the dark gleam so glossy it appeared bottomless. He lifted his head to look at her. "You have provoked things in me."

"Just because you're leaving Denver doesn't mean our conversation has to cease. Or my desire to prepare you another meal."

"Thank you."

To Juliana she asserted, "Baby, we can take care of the dishes in the morning. For tonight, enjoy your company. I have a stack of prayer requests from the crusade that need my attention." She kissed Juliana on the cheek and lightly squeezed her shoulder. Bruce asked and received approval to linger in the den.

Juliana busied herself pouring the coffee. Ben leaned against the twelve-foot bronze granite island and gazed out at the darkening sky. He folded his arms across his broad chest and sighed lazily.

Juliana handed him a steaming cup and stood beside him. The silence wrapped around them creating an innocuous cohesion. "Do you believe death is the enemy?"

Ben looked at her, a bit taken aback. "It is the antithesis of life."

"So death, for you, is the end?"

"I certainly don't view it as the beginning."

She sipped her coffee. "Did you ever stop to consider who God is?"

"He is this silver-haired, beard down to His belly old man who sits on His throne and spends His days shaking His head at us."

"Shaking His head?"

"God thinks, 'Oh, those silly, dim-witted humans. When will they ever stop destroying themselves and the earth they inhabit?'"

"So no one has ever told you He passionately seeks after you to pursue a eternal relationship?"

"If He cares at all, He has better things to do with His time."

"He cares so much that He designed a plan to make certain you would know how profound His love is."

Ben placed the mug on the counter. "Look, I know all about Jesus dying for my sins. But if any of what you proclaim is true, then why is the human race so messed up? Why am I not seeing Christians taking a firmer stand against the atrocities that poison our society? I see you marching outside of abortion clinics, but you are not denying the enticement of prostitution, embezzlement, or domestic violence. You shout that you're better than me. I strongly beg to differ."

Juliana nodded, slowly. "You're right."

Ben stared at her, astonished.

"We're not perfect. Many of our sins are a mirror reflection of nonbelievers. What you have witnessed is our discounting the power of God's redemption."

"What?"

"Jesus never said we wouldn't fail. But we haven't accurately demonstrated the fullness of His empowerment to completely carry out redemption's plan."

"I'm lost."

Juliana smirked at the accuracy of his self-description. "God desired that our relationship with Him would reflect such intimacy that when we failed, we would immediately turn to Him fully aware we would be covered with love and grace, not shame."

Ben cupped the mug in his hands.

"We have attempted to bury, cover, or worse, dismiss our sin. Yet, none of that has ever changed how zealous He is about me or you."

He stared at the warm fluid. "Can we agree to disagree?"

"Only if we agree to revisit this conversation."

"It's a free country."

Juliana swallowed. "When we first met, it was very curious how you wrote the number."

He remained very still, taking nearly imperceptive breaths. "Yes?"

She took another sip and pondered. "At first, I thought you were toying with me. There is only one other person I've ever seen do that, and he's a mortician in South Africa."

"Go on."

She chuckled convinced her thoughts were absurd. "Anyhow, you couldn't have been too serious. I wasn't asking your assistant out for coffee."

Ben internally loathed his lack of courage to confess that the action had been calculated. "This may be too long ago for you to remember, nearly ten years, but I befriended a young actor who was so talented he mesmerized every film crew. He was only twenty, nowhere near the age that could have birthed the experiences and pain of his characters. But his ability to pull from within left us mesmerized."

"Wait," she cocked her head. "Are you talking about the guy who was cast to portray Cal Trask in the remake of *East of Eden*?"

"You do remember."

She nodded, as the memory unfolded in her mind. "They dubbed him the next James Dean. His performances left me breathless. I forgot I was watching a movie."

"He confessed he had a dread of solitude, and I thought I could help him conquer it. So he stayed with me awhile. Then my films started to take me overseas for months at a time."

"Uh-oh."

"He wasn't pleased."

"His fear began to manifest?"

"With a vengeance. I'd find him in my closet, naked, covered by my clothing."

"Ben, no."

"He said my scent calmed him." Ben concealed the shudder that time had failed to quench. "Then the pets arrived."

"Your tone doesn't indicate poodles or tabby cats."

"Piranhas in a two-hundred gallon tank he had installed in his bedroom wall."

"No way."

"Way." Ben sipped from his cup. "Then, five boa constrictors. He kept them in his tub."

"What next? Cheetahs?"

"A leopard."

"Where did he keep it?"

"He had a sanctuary built in the back yard. The property was isolated so the neighbors had no clue."

"None of this was sanctioned by you?"

"No."

"And, still, you allowed him to stay?"

"I underestimated him to be eccentric, quirky even. I never thought he was psychotic."

"I'm scared to ask how it all ended."

Ben rubbed the space above his right brow. "I took my car in for a routine check-up, and the next thing I know L.A. SWAT descended upon the dealership."

"Why?"

"The mechanic discovered a remote-controlled detonator on my gas line. He confessed and that's pretty much how it ended." Ben's cavalier tone didn't match his humorless expression.

"How that must have hurt."

"I can't say it's completely dissipated."

"But how does that tie in with the weird number trick?"

He wanted to smooth the toffee cheek beneath his hand. "You'll discover the answer. Soon. My hope, more than you know, is that you'll still be interested in this man when you do."

It was Juliana's turn to be stunned. She moved to the coffee maker and freshened her cup. When she returned to his side, she remarked, "We have more in common than I ever would have believed."

"Commonality makes for great beginnings." Ben raised his cup. "To genuine friendships."

She clinked his cup. "To genuine friendships." She touched the wrapped gift situated beneath her mother's bouquet.

"Open it."

She placed her cup on the counter and ripped open the rectangular box. "I cannot believe you did this!"

He was surprised at how exquisite her laughter made him feel. "Now you shall never be without."

She removed the Namiki pen from its black leather casing and held it up to the chandelier. "It's breathtaking."

"I was assured it is hand-wrought sterling and each pen has hand-etched Japanese design art work on the cap and barrel."

She held the luxurious handwriting tool against her chest. "Thank you."

They finished their coffee then she retrieved his jacket and walked him to the front door. Bruce moved outside, opened the passenger door to the SUV, and waited.

Juliana twirled the pen between her fingers. "If I give you my direct number, can I expect you to keep in touch?"

He nodded and removed his phone from his belt loop. She thumbed in her number and returned the phone to him. He reached for her hand, caressed her smooth knuckles, then released. "Thank you. Sleep well."

Bruce walked around the truck then joined him inside. He started the ignition, and Ben watched Juliana wave from the doorstep. He returned the wave.

"It appears as if you had a pleasant evening," Bruce commented as he exited her street.

"Much more than I ever imagined."

"Very good."

"Very good indeed."

CHAPTER EIGHT

Pastor Michael carried the wicker basket with one hand; the other escorted his grandfather toward their favored tree. It resided near the manmade lake where different varieties of foul cavorted.

Once Michael spread the thick blanket and adjusted the napkin on his grandfather's collar, he served the fried chicken, mixed greens salad, and cornbread.

"Still warm, Michael." The bishop grinned.

"Fried it this morning, Papa."

"Tell me how it went."

Papa meant to narrate the story Michael often told and re-told. Michael had no idea why it amused his papa so, but he earnestly indulged him.

Thirty-six months ago, he had arrived for an interview at Living Water. Cage had disclosed his educational credentials and professed his doctrinal beliefs to the nine men and the deceased pastor's wife.

"You obviously deeply care for your church, they reasoned. Why would I consider a move from Missouri, they wondered. I explained that your fight with Alzheimer's had stifled much of your strength. It was when I traveled here to interview the Alzheimer's center that I discovered Living Water's search for a senior pastor. I considered this a nudge from the Almighty. I explained that my main objective was to be the man Bishop Cage raised me to be. It was then I told them of what happened to me when I was three."

For a moment, the bishop's eyes clouded and Michael's chest tightened. His grandfather's memory was unreliable when it came to this point in Michael's life. The torture in his papa's eyes after Michael explained that his twenty-year-old son and eighteen-year-old daughter-in-law had died of heroin overdoses was always raw.

Papa patted his hand and Michael exhaled a raspy breath wrought with relief. It ripped to retell of his parents' demise. Not because of his tragic loss, but because sometimes it shocked Papa's core so relentlessly the man would withdraw into a soundless cocoon that no medication nor Michael's gentle coaxing could pull him out of. During those episodes, Michael prayed with such fervency he neither ate nor slept. He wasn't prepared for Papa to lapse into the afterlife.

"'Such a overwhelming affliction for such a young boy,' one of the elders nodded introspectively then added, 'We are sorry for your loss.' I thanked him and I think I touched my tie.

"I told them how you had petitioned the courts for custody. Already widowed and in your late fifties. And I was not an easy child."

"No, sir!" Papa chomped on the salad. "But I knew you would use that stubborn nature for the glory of God. Felt it from the first time I held you. You would be different than your daddy. His was for selfishness. But you I knew would be different."

Michael returned his gaze to the older man who had sacrificed solitude to nurture him. "I don't know how you put up with it, Papa. I rarely did what you told me the first, second, or even the third time."

The older man pointed a finger, stemming from a hand tremulous and heavily veined, toward a toddler playing near the water. "Couldn't blame it all on your nature. Your heart was broken—aching in a way you couldn't explain. All you knew was something was growing inside you that seemed to give you power and weaken you at the same time."

The little girl, empty of bread, decided to chase the birds. She clapped her hands and giggled as the foul retreated to their watery hermitage.

Michael removed a thigh from the basket wrapped in foil and placed it on Papa's plate. "I told them how I started as part of the janitorial crew. As a young teen, I assisted with Sunday school, and while attending the University of Missouri I ministered to the youth. It wasn't until your condition worsened that I was asked to take your position."

The bishop patted him on his shoulder, the awning of leaves casting shadows on his aged skin. Michael remembered this to be Papa's favorite part of the chronicle. "I told them how you stressed the importance of keeping your word, no matter how difficult. Despite the enormous task of rearing such a young, grieved child, I witnessed your commitment to me day after day. So I felt the best manner I could honor your love and sacrifice was to make certain you obtained the best care."

"That's when that policeman spoke up and asked how our members felt about us moving to Colorado?"

Again, Michael marveled that his grandfather could recall such detail, yet often forgot that Michael was his grandchild. "That's right. I informed they were struggling with the decision but understood the treatment you'd receive in Colorado was extraordinary."

"You couldn't conceal your resistance to leave the beloved congregation."

"Then I said, 'Despite our innermost desires, obedience to God must take precedence. Once we give our lives over to Him, we cease to be our own.'"

Michael recalled how he had looked to Mrs. DeLauer at that point. At the far end of the conference table, she had gently smiled. Unbeknownst to Michael, she was a master at concealing emotion. No one in the room had ascertained that her heart barely contained her exuberance.

Papa interjected into Michael's reflection. "It ain't always easy to do God's bidding. No, sir. But living any other way just ain't living."

Michael forked a few spinach leaves and chewed them in a brief silence. "One board member consulted his notes. 'Isn't the college campus over fifty miles away from your church?' I affirmed that it was. 'How did you accomplish such a feat and maintain a 4.0 G.P.A?'"

Both men looked to each other and spoke in union. "A definitive grasp of time management."

They chuckled and settled into the velvety comfort it provided.

"The youngest member inquired, 'A young man who shows commendable dedication to his grandparent, graduates in the top percentile of his class, volunteers his scant spare time to various charities has somehow managed to remain single. How is that possible?' I responded with 'As you can perceive, I've had little time for anything else.'"

Michael had added that his primary focus was to care for his grandfather and the ministry. He did not lack the desire to marry and raise a family. He had simply found it unwise to mix the two.

"Then they hit ya." Papa smirked, punching the air with quavering fists.

"They certainly tried. 'Have you been able to maintain sexual purity?' And you know me."

"That stubborn streak crept up and brought its friend ornery along with it. But my boy looked them straight on and answered, 'Yes.'"

The men had shared judging glances, while Mrs. DeLauer had rhythmically patted her chin. Michael had caught her eye and held her gaze. Her face was expressionless, yet her eyes had revealed affirmation.

Papa sputtered, "As if a man can't stay pure in this day and age. Once you realize His goal is to protect you, the struggle to do what's right stops being a struggle."

"But sometimes arriving at that conclusion is monumental. It seems much easier to grasp that God's commands are to keep life restrained and dull. With a thick text of sixty-six books, each denoting His desires, sometimes it's difficult to believe that God actually has our best interest at heart."

"You can think yourself right out of the truth and what's best for you, rejecting Someone who can give you what you've craved all along."

"Finally, the last question was asked. 'If you were to become our senior pastor, how would you balance such demanding responsibilities?'"

Michael had stated his complete peace with the center's ability to care for Bishop Cage and then he had took time to meet the eye of every one in the room.

He had confessed he felt daunted simply interviewing for the position. He had read Pastor DeLauer's books, studied his sermon tapes since undergrad school. It was apparent his objective was to shepherd a congregation who were convinced they were the sons and daughters of God. Any individual who accepted the position would face the monumental task to prove themselves worthy of the trust, respect, and love of the extraordinary assembly.

The birth of every new day could have ushered the imminent death of their venerated leader. What Michael knew, but didn't articulate, was that the congregation deserved only the best candidate selected by God to serve from Pastor Quincy DeLauer's pulpit. Nothing about this, from the first notion of Living Water's search to the interview, was taken capriciously.

"You still question."

Michael wiped his mouth, his plate barren, his appetite satiated. "I am humbled, Papa. It has never crossed my mind to attempt to lead without God's constant guidance. The conviction is far too great."

The older man removed his empty plate from his lap. Michael placed it in the empty grocery bag designated for trash. He removed two bottled waters and unscrewed the lid for his grandfather.

Papa leaned against the considerable maple trunk, his thoughts as mystifying as the heart of a woman. He sipped the chilled liquid in silent observation. A woman jogged behind a baby carriage, the tempo of her run lulling the infant to sleep. Geese, ducks, and pigeons vied for the chunks of bread tossed by an elderly couple.

"You can't hold onto Jeanine forever," Papa said. "Keith, there comes a time when a man has got to let go of his wife who's passed on."

Michael inhaled deeply then exhaled as he studied the bishop's profile. "Papa, it's me. Michael."

"Who?"

"Your grandson."

He ended his scrutiny of Michael with a snort. "You ain't gave me no grandchild. That's what I'm talking about. It ain't right to hang on like you do. You're too young for that. Might want to consider Miss Juliana."

Michael dropped his head, removed his sunglasses, and rubbed his eyes. "I have considered Juliana."

"Any fool could tell the woman's got feelings for you. Tell that every time she look at ya."

"She's not receptive to pushing, Papa."

"Why you keep calling me Papa? I'm your daddy. You been shooting up that stuff again?"

"No, sir," Michael answered, hating the bitter clue that their picnic was near its conclusion.

"Good. I told you, stay away from that mess. It's gone kill ya."

"Yes, sir." Michael leaned toward his grandfather and kissed his cheek. "I love you."

"I love you, Keith. Can't nothing already done or to come change that. Ya hear?"

"Yes, sir. I hear."

Again, the silence. Michael willed his grandfather's memory to return to the present, knowing once it traveled backward, it might take hours before accurate recall returned. Soon, clement snores exited his grandparent's throat. He removed the bottle from the slumbering man's grip.

Michael allowed a few moments rest before he stirred his grandfather.

Months after Michael had been chosen as senior pastor, Mrs. DeLauer informed him of what had occurred after his departure from the conference room.

The debate had raged.

Michael Cage was a keg of dynamite, they had declared.

"What happens to the care of the congregation when Bishop Cage's condition grows worse?"

"He's never been married."

"He just turned thirty."

"Did you see the way the women reacted when he entered the office?"

"He admitted to us, near strangers, that he was a virgin! Who shares that in an interview?"

Dionne had cocked her head. "You asked him."

The board member had huffed and scuttled.

"Have none of you paid any attention to my husband's prayers regarding his successor?"

They had gaped at her.

"He prays the Lord will send us a man young enough to possess the energy and drive to fight every battle thrown his way; those created before and after his arrival.

"He prays his love for people will exceed the walls of the church. He prays his integrity and character will be above reproach. He prays his successor has experienced profound pain so he can relate to those who have walked through deep, dark valleys. He prays the man to take his place will have more than a passing sense of loyalty. Do any of you remember what your senior pastor prays?"

Forty-eight hours later, Michael Cage had been hired.

Immediately, he had asked permission to visit their ailing leader.

Pastor DeLauer, although raked with pain, had offered the young man wisdom, exhortation, and encouragement. Michael's visits had become as constant as those of Mrs. DeLauer and Juliana.

Then the rumors had surfaced.

The Living Water board had allegedly hired Michael as a suitor for Juliana.

Michael understood he had been chosen because he could carry the weight of the pastoral position with compassion, integrity, and passion.

The needs of the wounded congregation were daunting. Several staff members had turned in their resignations.

Determined, he had reiterated he had no intention on altering the vision Pastor DeLauer deemed for the ministry.

For several months, the growing pains had been brutal, but in the midst of the struggle, they had grown to mutually respect, honor, and love one another. He wanted nothing more than to be their tender shepherd until his dying day, with Juliana as his wife.

As Michael's vehicle approached the center, Papa touched his shoulder. As if reading his grandson's mind, Bishop Cage assured, "Don't give up on Miss Juliana. God's working on her heart."

CHAPTER NINE

Benjamin stood with his back to the conference room door counting the floors of the building across the street. Eternity Alise was late. Nearly by an hour. He folded his arms across his chest.

Thirty-five.

This may have been just another transaction to her...

Thirty-six.

But to Ben, it made him want to come out of his skin.

Thirty-seven.

Their home had been a literal sanctuary where he had locked the door on the endless career obligations and A-list parties. Behind the ten-foot stone perimeter, he was Benjamin Luke Powers—a son born and bred in the Midwest. Here he had lingered online in photography chat rooms, raced in place for his ninety-minute treadmill regimen, became engrossed with the Sci Fi channel, played in the backyard pool with the twins, or baked his infamous pecan pies.

"They're in the elevator," Grace informed from her seat at the kidney-shaped table as she flipped her phone shut.

He turned, revealing the tense periphery of his profile, then looked back to the window.

Thirty-eight.

Thirty-nine.

"Good morning!" Eternity's cheerful greeting punctured the tense surroundings.

He turned. She was decked in lemon bright Versace, her model-thin figure taut beneath the burnished fabric. Her silky, dark hair was pulled into an elegant bun, which magnified her luminous, emerald eyes. Beside her stood her manager, Mitchell Cannon.

"Denver must have been to your liking. You look positively nectarous."

"Eternity." Ben took a seat beside Grace.

She extended a hand to the couple and her gold bracelets clinked like Baccarat crystal. "Eternity Alise."

They feebly obliged.

"Traffic, as you know, was incomprehensible. Is that de Gautier?"

The woman, attempting to remain unreceptive, blinked. Then a smug grin crossed her ruby lips. "Why, yes it is."

"It looks as if it were singularly made for you."

The woman beamed. Eternity focused on the man. "I seem to recognize you. Do you receive your facials at *Genesis*?"

The man straightened in his chair, flattered to be recognized. "Every Tuesday."

"Isn't Renard amazing? How did we ever survive without him before he moved from Chalons-en-Champagne?"

Grace interrupted. "Mrs. Loveman has a pressing engagement. We should begin."

After one hour and fifteen minutes, they completed the paperwork. Ben shook the Lovemans' hands, shielded his eyes with sunglasses, and made his exit. While he and Grace waited for the elevator, he felt denied of oxygen.

Grace touched his arm. "Ben?"

He lowered his head and breathed deeply through his nose. It was final.

In a matter of ninety minutes, their refuge possessed new guardians who hadn't painstakingly chosen its contents. Once the elevator arrived and the carriage emptied, he rushed inside.

"You look the shade of bleached parchment. Seriously, Ben, you're scaring me."

Grace handed him her handkerchief.

Ben bent from the waist, moped his brow, then placed his hands on his thighs.

"Hold the door!"

A well-jeweled man's hand blocked the elevator's closure. Ben rose gingerly and recognized the hand as Mitchell's. Ben pressed his back to the elevator wall and sharply inhaled.

"My." Eternity grinned and stood very near his side. "Where are you rushing to?"

Ben reached within his deepest reserves and exhaled. He faced Eternity. "To celebrate."

She smiled then slowly took him in from head-to-toe. "Have you met someone, Ben?"

"I meet people all the time."

She inched closer in the constricted space. "This someone has you gushing allure. And we both have grown accustomed to the press knowing whom we're dating long before we do. Anyone I know?"

"Why, Eternity, are you flirting with me?"

She wrapped her arm through his. "Would she be jealous if I were?"

Ben held his reply.

"Why don't we completely mix it up and exit arm-in-arm?"

"I don't recall us needing extra attention from the media."

The elevator doors opened to the main lobby. Ben withdrew his arm from hers and used his body to hold the door open. Eternity exited last and walked beside him.

"You don't look well. Aren't you ecstatic to be free from the financial burden of the house?"

He stopped, causing their managers to halt as well. The provocation he had been able to subdue returned. "To you it was brick and glass and mortar. To me, it sheltered everything I esteemed as sacred."

Ben walked through the doors and felt the heat press through his imported silk suit. He inhaled and the humid air felt like wool in his lungs. The gang of press rushed up the concrete steps.

Ben felt like a fattened lamb in the middle of a wolf pack. He paid little attention to the blurted questions as Grace resolutely repeated, "Mr. Powers has no comment."

They made their way to her Mercedes and quickly shut the sedan's doors.

The press leaned on the vehicle's hood as she shifted the engine in reverse.

"Ben, is it true you're still in love with Eternity?"

"Do you feel like a failure?"

"Is it true Eternity was spending her nights elsewhere long before the divorce?"

"With her latest co-star?"

"What of the rumors that you're gay?"

The reporters soon caught sight of Eternity and the swarm headed her way.

It was a judicious move on their part because Grace had no qualms in running them over. Once they hit the freeway, she turned to him. "You doing better?"

"Define better."

"Here." Grace reached behind her and miraculously produced bottled water. "Drink."

He swallowed a few tepid sips.

"Oh, by the way, those papers you requested arrived." Again, she reached to the rear. This time she combined it with a change to the left hand lane.

"Grace, how have you managed to reach your fifty-fifth birthday?"

She glared. "Forty-ninth."

Grace's age was difficult to ascertain. She maintained her enviable body with strength conditioning and Pilates, took great care to pamper her skin with luxurious spa treatments, and believed in the empowerment of Yoga. Sensational, beguiling, and stylishly feminine were the labels publications had given her.

She placed an 8x10 manila folder on his lap. "DeLauer" in red Sharpie was marked on the upper left corner.

He glanced at her. "There's more?"

"There's more."

Grace's cell chirped, and Ben opened the envelope and settled in his seat. Inside were dozens of *Denver Post*, *Charisma Magazine*, and Internet articles on Pastor Quincy DeLauer. As Ben perused each piece, he discovered DeLauer had assisted the Denver mayor in bringing many of the denominational churches together for a fundraiser to benefit inner city youth. DeLauer had won awards for his work to provide job training, shelter, and clothing for ex-inmates and the homeless. The pastor had also received honors for his dedication towards those affected by HIV/AIDS. He was named "Man of the Year" by *Time* and his motivational books had topped the *New York Times*' bestseller lists week after week.

Ben released a low whistle. Grace shot him a curious glance mid-sentence. He waved a hand to ignore him. Then he read the article of the pastor's valiant battle with colon cancer. Several political dignitaries had spoken at his subsequent funeral. Pastor Michael Cage had officiated.

He flipped the pages and stopped at the photo of Juliana at her father's graveside. The loss seemed to reverberate through her like a merciless tremor deeply etching its mark on her face.

He reached the section regarding Michael Cage. The man had moved from Missouri and taken over the pastorate at the age of thirty. He had shepherded the wounded, mourning flock and increased the numbers by several thousand in a year. Cage was handsome, scholarly, and single.

"Humph." Again, Ben held up a hand. Ben imagined the advantageous allegiance. The congregation would have the best of both worlds if the beloved daughter wed their newly appointed pastor. There would be a bit of the cherished old and expectant new. He closed the envelope and gently patted the folder on his lap.

"So," Grace ended her call and turned her attention to him. "I don't see disappointment on your face."

He shook his head as his mind produced questions only Juliana could answer. "No. I'm not disappointed."

"I do, however, see apprehension."

"You see intrigue." He faced her. "Stop the investigation."

She nearly received whiplash as her buttery-blonde bob swayed when she looked at him. "You're certain?"

"I'm certain."

He looked at the folder on his lap. During breaks on the Denver set, he had found himself searching the Internet for her articles. She was a witty, astute writer who ushered her readers into every expose she penned. She was also an extraordinary woman unmoved by his celebrity.

"It's time I looked for a place of my own."

Grace smirked. "As soon as you've found something, I'll update the confidentiality agreements of the housekeepers and the private trash removal company to include the new address."

In his earlier Hollywood days, he hadn't understood the sharp consequence of unchecked trust. Reginald and Joan raised him to extend certain graces to humankind. When the undisclosed location of his wedding had appeared in the morning edition of *Variety* and helicopters swarmed above the festive venue, the necessity to exterminate prior beliefs stung well beyond their newlywed phase.

He nodded, his eyes not concentrating on the traffic bent around the highway like a carnivorous, gleaming snake. Ben was mentally back in Denver, sharing a gratifying meal with the mesmerizing woman who had experienced more than her share of pain.

In an hour, he would be in the midst of a cover photo shoot for *GQ*. Thereafter, he would tape a *Tonight Show* segment hyping the film he completed last May and then head to its premiere. Ben couldn't count the numerous offers to escort him. None held his appeal.

Grace tapped his arm. "You still with me?"

He faced her. "I haven't thrown myself from your speeding sedan."

"I thought you handled yourself remarkably with Eternity."

He shrugged. "You've assured me how devastatingly unhealthy it is to hold onto the past."

She eyed the envelope in his lap then held his gaze. "Now, about that new house ... "

The sun dipped below the majestic Rocky Mountains creating hues of plum and indigo. The basketball team of Living Water gathered their equipment and packed it in the storage area within the gymnasium. Once all was replaced, the men headed to the locker rooms. Juliana walked down the corridor past the gym doors.

"Juliana, hang on for a moment." Pastor Michael's voice reverberated throughout the large gym. She moved to the entryway and slipped off her pumps to protect the gymnasium floor. He shut and locked the equipment door. His baseball cap was turned backward, giving him a boyish look. His muscles were exposed beneath his Nike tank and matching shorts. As he made his way toward her, Juliana couldn't resist grinning.

"What?"

"You don't walk, Pastor, you glide."

"I glide?"

"Yes." Her voice sounded off the walls of the deserted gym. "I'm certain if we looked up regal in *Webster's*, there your photo would be."

He scratched his earlobe and shook his head. "You are complimenting me, correct?"

She grinned the grin that portrayed warmth yet reservation. "Naturally."

"I hoped that was the case."

Someone who hadn't spent Saturday afternoons at ball games, jet skiing on Cherry Creek Reservoir, gorging on Dionne's Sunday dinners, and shopping at Park Meadows with him would have missed the subtle linger in his eye. "Tricia and Winston's wedding is next Friday."

Juliana rolled her eyes. "She is about to drive me crazy!"

Pastor Michael chuckled softly. "It is to be expected. Every bride desires for her special day to be perfection."

"Manmade perfection doesn't exist. I think we put entirely too much self-inflicted pressure upon ourselves. Seriously, it makes me want to take a jet to some Caribbean isle and elope."

"It's perfectly natural to want the most important day of your life to be spectacular. Someday, you'll be in her shoes."

The heat rushed to her face. "But I pray when it arrives, I don't have people lining up to fit me for a straight jacket."

"Until then, would you allow me to escort you to the wedding?"

Juliana's mind split in two separate directions. Two veins seamed—the conflicting draws to Pastor Michael and uncomplicated solitude.

"Uh," she stammered. "Well ... "

Pastor Michael cocked his handsome head.

Juliana shook her head briskly.

"Is your answer no?" Pastor Michael blinked rapidly.

"No!" She placed on hand on his well-developed arm. "I'm wondering."

"Wondering?"

"Why me?"

"Why not you? You aren't intimidated or enamored by my title. I *laugh* when I'm with you. I *unwind* when I'm with you. I trust you. I enjoy the man I am when I'm with you."

Juliana opened her mouth, then realized his answer had surprised her. He folded his muscular arms behind him and dipped his chin.

Her smile slowly danced across her lips. "Well said, Pastor."

"I still don't have an answer."

"Very well."

"Praise the Lord, woman!" He clasped his hands in prayer. "Were you going to make a man beg?"

She swatted his arm and realized it was damp from the workout. These moments sent her reeling: a man's amorous smile, his lingering gaze, his perspiring arm. They were all foreign, and Juliana had often refused them entry.

She graced his cheek with a swift kiss. "See you on Sunday, Pastor."

He jogged for the showers. Just as Juliana opened the door leading to the parking lot, she turned and looked in his direction. Pastor Michael had paused at the locker room door. For a moment, neither moved toward their destinations.

Juliana's phoned chirped. He grinned and disappeared behind the locker room door.

She pulled on her shoes and smiled hard, willing the cheerfulness to thrust through the wire. "Maid-of-Honors-R-Us!"

"Where are you?"

Juliana headed to her car. "Just leaving the church. What's up?"

"The caterer can't assure we'll have oysters!"

Juliana disarmed the alarm and opened the door. "How is that possible? They were specifically chosen because of their cast-iron connection to a reputable seafood supplier."

"A week before the wedding. Oh, Jules, this is horrible."

She slammed her car door and started the vehicle. "Are you with the caterer now?"

"Yes." Tricia sniffled. "We must have oysters! They're Winston's favorite."

"I'll be there in ten minutes." Then she added, jokingly. "Until then, ask them to serve you a double martini."

"Jules!"

"I'm joking. Don't kill anybody. I'm on my way."

An hour later, the issue resolved, Juliana ordered take-out from Tanner's and met Tricia at her DTC condo. She plated the food and joined Tricia in the bright kitchen nook.

"Cinni?" Juliana called as Tricia ignored her beloved steak salad. "What's going on?"

Tricia looked around at the bare walls, unadorned oak floors, and austere granite counters. "Nearly all of my things have been removed."

Juliana and Tricia's older brother had moved many of her belongings to Winston's downtown loft in custom with Chinese tradition in preparation of her future with him.

"They came this morning." Tricia sighed.

"Who?"

"Winston's immediate family. They arrived bearing red baskets and boxes."

Both women looked to the precise linear arrangement on Tricia's lone coffee table.

"Soon, all I'll have here are those red baskets. *Uang susu.*"

Juliana stopped her plastic fork midway—Tricia's Alain Saint-Joanis lacquered utensils had been shuttled to Winston's kitchen. "Wang sushi?"

Tricia listlessly eyed her meal. "*Uang susu.* It means milk money. It's a customary gift from the groom's family to the bride. Three days before the wedding, they'll bring more red boxes. They'll be full of personal gifts to replace the ones they moved to Winston's place. My personal belongings are probably heaped in some closet."

Juliana placed the fork beside her plate, ignoring the noisy protest from her stomach. "What's on our heart, Cinni?"

"We're supposed to reciprocate. Three days before the wedding. As if I'm not under enough pressure."

"T, it's covered. I was with you when you shopped for Winston's new shirts, shoes, and then spent the afternoon making his favorite almond cookies."

Tricia shrugged. "You know Winston's supposed to bring gifts soon for you as a consolation of letting me go."

"T, he never said I had to let you go."

"Tell me something, Jules? Who has their wedding at 6:30 in the evening?"

"You mean besides you?"

"Exactly!"

"Why is that an issue?"

Tricia shot her a look of utter exasperation. "Most people get married on the hour. Not on the *half*-hour."

"Winston explained that custom. The couple begins their life with the hands of the clock moving upward, not downward."

Silence.

"I have to share the limo with him."

"That's a bad thing?"

"I wanted to share the limo with my *father*, like most daughters. But no. I have to look at Winston's mug all the way to the church."

"I think it would be cool to snuggle up with my groom before we took the plunge. It might even soothe frayed nerves."

She picked up the crumbled napkin and waved it at Juliana. "I wanted my bridesmaids to wear champagne. Luminous, sparkling champagne. I can see it now. You all will look like a line of roosters primping for the hens."

"It will look amazing. You know his mother requested red because it symbolizes happiness, prosperity, and ultimate joy. It's her way of saying how happy she is for you."

"It will look like you're ladies of the night headed for happy hour. I hope you know the lyrics to 'Lady Marmalade.'"

Juliana's tongue probed her cheek. "What's really going on?"

Tricia looked through the nook window at the hectic Union Parkway. "Do you remember when we first drove by this place?"

"The complex was still under construction."

"As soon as I saw the layout I fell in love. We rushed over to Bed, Bath and Beyond and filled the baskets with furnishings that same afternoon."

"You had to stash everything in my basement storage area until you closed."

"That's my point. *I* closed."

"Cinni—"

"This was my first place. It was something all my own."

Juliana frowned, studying her friend through the emotion. "Has Winston made you feel as if you're intruding on his space?"

Tricia shook her head, sadly. "Just the opposite. He's gotten rid of most of his furniture to accommodate mine."

"Then what?"

"I'm saying good-bye, Jules. I hate to say good-bye."

"But, that's not where the story ends. You're beginning a whole new life with a man who equates your love to air."

"I wake up in the middle of the night, panting and willing my heart to calm. I get up, get a cup of water, and look out my bedroom window. I adore that window. It holds the best view. A few miles down the road, I can see the lights of I-25 and when I look above them, the shadows of the mountains." She paused to purse her lips. "The view out of Winston's window is of Coors Field and an industrial park."

"Many pay millions for that view. Besides, you've always raved about his place. How you love the contemporary lines and amenities."

"My commute will be murder. Right now, I'm less than five minutes from the spa."

Juliana scooted the chair back and knelt at Tricia's feet. "Look at me."

Tricia obeyed and Juliana clasped her hands. "Do you love Winston?"

"Of course, but—"

"Do you believe he loves you?"

The near bride nodded. "So much so that it makes me dizzy."

"Do you trust him with your life? With those of the unborn children I'm going to spoil?"

Tricia's lips curved in a slight smirk. "Yes."

"Do you believe he is the man God has chosen for you?"

"No doubt."

"Then face your future screaming at the top of your lungs if you have to, blazing right through the fear. Change can be daunting, I agree. But this is change beside a man who would slay a three-headed beast for you and bring you the head. He'd return for the hide if you said you wanted a new coat and matching shoes."

Tricia released a giggle, smacking Juliana's shoulder. "Oh, shut up!"

"Tell me I'm wrong? Besides, the Ong's haven't asked you to include every custom into your wedding."

"What do you mean?"

"Well," Juliana paused, tapping Tricia's knee. "Following the ceremony, the couple are led to their bridal chamber where they sit on the bed and drink wine and honey from two goblets linked by a red thread."

"There's that blasted color again."

"Listen, it gets better. Invited into the bedroom are family and friends who heckle you until midnight. So, just picture it, T: a room full of your beloved hurling insults at you and your man."

"You're making this up."

"Honest." Juliana grinned. "Because of the humiliation the couple feels compelled to perform stunts."

"Stunts!"

"Yep. The more we boo, the more you perform."

"Oh, stop. This is too much."

"Uh-huh. For hours, we would taunt and jeer. Imagine the derision."

Tricia's laughter resounded off the empty walls. "Stop. My stomach is hurting."

"Sometimes, it continues for three days." Juliana stood and kissed Tricia's forehead. "That's much better."

Tricia reached up and held Juliana in a squeeze. "You bring me joy, Jules."

"Now, can we eat?" When they separated Juliana raced to her spot at the table and munched hungrily.

"You know, someday I'll be returning the favor."

"Oh, T, please." Juliana pointed at her seared tuna. "I'm eating."

CHAPTER TEN

The following week was a blur. The extensive hair, electrolysis, and waxing treatments caused her to be unconscious before her head hit the pillow. Stress was Juliana's kryptonite, exacerbating her medical condition. Tension spiked her testosterone levels, stimulating the hair on her upper arms, lip, and face, yet aggravated scalp follicles causing extensive breakage, thus rushing Juliana to her stylist's chair to weave in hair, thickening the sparse channels.

Due to the countless speeches to calm Tricia's fears, endless trips to the airport to collect the bride's out-of-town relatives, attending Tricia's bridal and bachelorette parties and rehearsal dinner, Juliana could recite every internal mêlée and covert aspiration of Vie's personnel.

Pastor Michael was an engaging fixture, their hectic paths crossing amongst the dizzying errands. He joked with her, cooked dinner for the wedding party as they decorated the wedding chapel and church's reception hall, and even allowed her catnaps in his office. Despite the pressures and frayed nerves, Juliana judged the week priceless.

As she walked down the aisle beside the best man in her striking cranberry gown, grinning at the five hundred plus crowd, a question intruded. *Where is Ben at this very moment?* The uncertainty caused her smile to twitch.

He had called several times, yet their conversations had consistently been stifled by her schedule. Text messages had become a more effective path to communicate. However, their timing had been off. If he texted her in the morning, she hadn't been able to answer until that evening. Disappointment had crept into her emotions more often than Juliana wanted to admit. To acknowledge the dissatisfaction was to face the likelihood that she actually missed Ben. Missed the enchantment of discovery as he unveiled layers of his world. Yet, to dwell on such things was unwise. Benjamin Powers held little assurance beyond heartache. Juliana surmised his presence would have roused an exploration she wasn't ready to discover. Besides, Tricia would have seen him seated in the pews draped in garnet organza and passed out.

Pastor Michael, spectacular in the tailored dark suit, smiled at her. Juliana broadened her grin, winked at Winston, and took her place beside the four bridesmaids. When Tricia appeared through the ten-foot double doors, Juliana gasped.

She attended every fitting. Yawned as Tricia tried her umpteenth "wedding day face;" even sat beside her that morning at the salon in meticulous preparation of the anticipated day. Those images paled in comparison to the woman who sauntered down the aisle holding the arm of her father. The faint candlelight danced upon Tricia's ivory gown. The crystals, personally sewn into the glossy fabric by Mrs. Ong, shimmered like dewdrops. Juliana was gripped with overpowering joy that Tricia was on the threshold of a wonderful future with a wonderful man who held wonderful promise. She began to sob.

"*Hawph.*" Juliana omitted the vulgar sound from her throat. Her eyes widened in shock. Immediately, she drilled her attention to the lustrous carpet.

"*Mpwah.*" This time the distraction alerted the wedding party. Quickly, she looked up and wished she hadn't. Tricia shot her a probing look beneath the shimmering veil and Juliana sucked in gulps of air.

The soloist's lilt caressed every pew as she rendered lyrics of eternal, treasured love. Pastor Michael leaned in her direction and whispered, "Breathe, Juliana, breathe."

Between the tears and a spirited attempt to collect herself, she nodded in response. When Mr. Wilson and Tricia stopped at the pulpit's edge, Juliana hiccupped. Mortified, she slammed her eyes shut.

"Who gives this woman away?" Pastor Michael asked.

Tricia's father boomed, "Her mother and I do."

The mesmerizing bride handed her unglued friend the varying bouquet of flame tree, lotus blossoms, and orchids in diverse shades of red. As Winston took Tricia's hand, Juliana hiccupped again. It resonated from the vaulted ceiling to the rear of the chapel.

A ripple of laughter crested.

Juliana breathed. "Sorry."

Pastor Michael began his matrimonial declarations. "Honored guests, Tricia and Winston welcome you to the celebration of this momentous day."

"*Hiccup!*"

"In the time they have been together, their love and adoration of each other has only grown richer."

"*Hiccup!*"

"And, now they have decided to share their lives together as husband and wife."

Juliana buried her mouth in the massive array of flowers from Tricia's and her bouquets and prayed God would open up the chapel floor and swallow her whole. She pensively peered over the floral arrangements.

Pastor Michael took the bridal couple's hands. "You made it."

Tricia sang, "Thank you, Jesus!"

Winston shouted, "Halleluiah!"

"Please join me in prayer: Heavenly Father, Winston and Tricia are now about to vow their unending loyalty to each other. We ask You to accept the shared treasure of their life together, which they now create and offer to You. Grant them everything they need, that they may increase in their knowledge of You throughout their life together. In the name of Jesus. Amen."

The crowd, in near unison, cheered, "Amen!"

Michael progressed, guiding Winston and Tricia through their ardent exchange of nuptials. Mercifully, Tricia had decided on two solos as they shared communion. After Michael proclaimed them as husband and wife, Tricia swallowed her scarlet-faced friend in a smothering hug.

"At least my chagrin is in theme with your color scheme."

"Only you, my dear Jules, would I allow to steal the show. I guess it's payback for all the agony I put you through."

Michael admonished the crowd to now greet Mr. and Mrs. Winston and Tricia Ong. After the receiving line, Juliana raced to ladies' room and flopped on the chintz sofa. She had vowed God Almighty would have to manifest in the flesh to get her out of that restroom.

"Juliana Marguerite!"

Juliana moaned as if harpooned. "I'm not coming out."

"Yes, you are." Her mother appeared, iridescent in her butterscotch hued gown.

"Trust me, it's best I stay right where I am."

"Get up." Dionne didn't shout. She never had to. Her tone possessed a natural air of authority that didn't require a bellow.

Juliana removed her hands from her eyes and sat up. "You saw what occurred."

"Yes."

"Then you know what happened?"

"I did not raise you to hide. You are a DeLauer. We do not grovel, cower, or pay retail for anything. Now, get up. Your best friend needs you."

Juliana stood and slumped her shoulders. Her mother examined her daughter's face and flipped open her evening bag. "Let's get you fixed up so you can go grin and mingle and be your amazingly devastating self."

They ate heartily, danced until the women kicked off their heels, posed for dozens of photos, and celebrated well after the newly married couple's departure. It was two a.m. when Pastor Michael pulled beneath Juliana's portico. She had dozed off in the passenger seat. Pastor Michael softly called her name. Finally, he caressed the side of her cheek. She jolted.

"Whoa. It's all right."

"It has not been my day for portraying ladylike decorum."

He shrugged, his custom-made suit flowing with his movements. "Your joy was touching."

She stretched and reached for her matching evening bag. "I was not a memorable senior pastor's date."

He reached for her hand. "Oh, you made it memorable all right."

Juliana slugged him in the shoulder. "My date has morphed into a critic."

"You were beautiful, and there is not an ounce of objection in me."

She mentally recalled the moment she first felt that he stirred her emotions.

Juliana had been busy studying for senior finals and had barely paid attention to the fuss her mother was making over the new pastor. When she had opened the door, a bulky book in her hand, her hair littered with various writing instruments, she gaped at him.

She had stared at his tall, fit frame enhanced by the caramel skin and jet-black, wavy hair.

It was as if she had never before encountered him.

Michael hadn't been insulted. He surmised that her mind had been entrenched in her father's suffering and pending graduation.

Finally, he had extended his manicured hand. "Good evening, Juliana."

She had grunted a response.

"I was invited for dinner. May I come in?"

Another grunt.

He smiled.

Juliana had dropped her book. When they both dove to retrieve it, their heads crashed.

"I'm sorry. My mind is consumed with journalism commentaries."

"When is your test?"

"In two days. Friday."

"What if I come over tomorrow and walk you through what I know?"

"You have time?"

"I have time."

Juliana had marveled that his intelligence wasn't so lofty she couldn't comprehend.

Juliana had raced to his office to reveal her A, and they celebrated with double scoops of Cold Stone.

When her father had passed away, Juliana perceived the tender commonality within Michael and allowed him to witness her biting grief.

Pastor Michael Cage faced life's complexities head on, shrouded in the revelation of God's immense love. He never faltered from any commitment. He wouldn't deny her love simply because she bore a condition doctors had no cure for.

So, Juliana agonized, why couldn't she open her heart and fully welcome him in? "Still, it was a marvelous evening."

"It was."

She glanced at the clock. "Wisdom says I should exit now because you have a sermon to preach in a few hours."

He nodded, slowly. "I do."

"But I'm not quite ready for the night to end."

He touched her hand. "When you think of your future, where am I?"

Juliana's eyes widened and her jaw dropped.

"I'm trying to determine whether you and I are moving forward in the same direction."

Juliana sat back in the seat and bit her lip. "You know how I feel about you."

"What is it that I'm supposed to know?"

"You're my pastor."

"I asking how you feel about me as a man."

Juliana swallowed the boulder in her throat. "You need an answer tonight?"

"I'd like that, yes."

She inhaled heavily. "You're the kind of man I always dreamed I'd marry and welcome in every New Year. You're compassionate, giving, and your integrity is unsurpassed."

"Yet?"

"The truth is, Michael, I can't tell you where we're headed when I'm not certain where I'm headed. I am interested in becoming a wife some-day. But, I've just become interested in the possibility of dating."

He held her hand firmly. "Every precious part of you has been reserved for a very, very special man."

She smiled tenderly at him, harassed by the desire to kiss him. Insight screamed that her affection would only perplex them both.

"All I ask is you not limit your focus."

Ben, her mind called. *Ben.*

He raised her hand to his mouth and held it against his lips. An electric current scurried from the soles of her feet to the base of her skull, scuttling through her jaw and throbbing at her temples. He released her hand and exited the creamy interior of the Infiniti. As he walked around the car, Juliana battled guilt. She placed her coat around her shoulders.

He opened the car door, took her keys, and unlocked the front door.

"Thank you." She hugged him, the urgings of affection still clamoring against her nerves. The chilled night air swirled in silvery curves around them.

"Are you assisting with the children's Christmas play?"

"Absolutely. Rehearsals begin next week."

"Maybe we can grab dinner beforehand."

She nodded. "I'd like that."

He took a step behind and stood on the middle stair of the porch landing. "Goodnight, Juliana."

"Michael." She looked to the expanse of the portico roof. "I refuse to allow my emotions to lead us down a path neither of us may be prepared to walk. I care too much for you to permit that to happen."

He mounted the stairs and kissed her cheek. "I'm a very patient man."

After she had looked in on her mother, who was already in REM sleep, Juliana prepared for bed. She pulled the cool sheets to her chin and admired the twinkling lights from her neighbors' residences.

Pastor Michael was the epitome of safety, charisma, and stability. Theirs was a connection cemented by debilitating grief.

Ben was a captivating mystery she was unveiling who shared her hunger to nurture those many disregarded.

Yet, so did Michael.

There was a lucid distinction between them. It fell to Who ruled their hearts: the Father or the father of this world—the Prince of Peace or the prince of destruction.

Juliana rolled over. "I feel you, Father. Inscribing my future on every inch of my heart. Penning detail as intricate as centuries old lace. I pray I don't reject what You have prepared for me. I'm listening, Father. I'm listening."

CHAPTER ELEVEN

Juliana, Dionne, Maya, Thomas, and Pastor Michael had spent Thanksgiving at Tricia and Winston's. As they shrugged on coats at the Ong's front door, Michael tied her scarf around her neck.

"You'll be out-of-town next week?" he asked.

Juliana knew the question he was asking. "Yes. I have an interview with an orphanage in L.A."

"L.A.?"

"There's this center that shelters children whose parents have been infected with HIV or houses those who have become orphans due to the disease. It's supposed to be superior to most."

"No way to postpone it?"

"Thanks for reminding me to call if the memories of Daddy and his birthday become too much."

"I'm holding you to that."

Since her father had died, Michael had habitually diverted her focus whenever the calendar fell on her father's birthday.

The first year, they had removed the coverings from her father's paintings. Michael hung them, his fingers tracing the ornate borders.

The second, they had taken the Winter Park Ski Train through the dramatic alpine wilderness and pondered the snowy vistas.

The following Wednesday morning, she had arrived in L.A. and failed to phone Ben. They had conversed via text messages and spoken a half dozen times since Tricia's wedding. He was focused on the Vancouver production of his latest film, and she was consumed with her article surmising the ambitious pledges from the Denver HIV/AIDS Symposium. The organizations purposed to enlighten and assist communities, and their drive to educate caused Juliana to swell.

As she wheeled her suitcase from her car rental to the hotel entrance, she stopped to shrug off her jacket in the eighty-degree heat. Such a difference from her home, where December's temperatures frosted trees and lawns in the Colorado morning light.

Juliana checked into her hotel, maneuvered her rental to South Central, and parked in the rear lot of the *Kgotso Center* on Alameda Street. Above the entrance in elegant script she read,

> What does love look like? It has the hands to help others. It has the feet to hasten to the poor and needy. It has eyes to see misery and want. It has the ears to hear the sighs and sorrows of men. That is what love looks like.
>
> St. Augustine.

She gaped at the priest's words, their power inhabiting like affection. The receptionist behind an ash-paneled desk broke her reverie. Juliana introduced herself and spent the morning interviewing the facilitators, caretakers, and children.

The old textile plant had been converted into large living spaces, play areas, classrooms, administrative offices, a medical facility, two kitchens, washrooms, and enough bedrooms to accommodate several dozens of children.

By late morning, Juliana cradled a six-year-old girl with spindly legs and an impressive vocabulary upon her lap. As the child read the book about the big red dog, Juliana buried her nose in her intricate braids and inhaled. The scent lured Juliana where she hadn't dared visit for months. Soon four other children fought for her affection. She reveled in their need for refuge and held them close, whispering affirmation.

During lunch, she remarked, "It is peculiar to see the word *Kgotso* in the States."

The female director, Chansa Dijdo, punched a few romaine leaves with her fork. "Are you familiar with the Sesotho language?"

A bittersweet grin crossed her lips. "My mother's lineage is from South Africa. My family had vacationed there nearly every summer since I was a teenager. I became a nurse's aid, trained by those trained by Veronica Khosa."

"Ah, truly." The straight teeth gleamed accentuating her teak complexion. "Then you are a daughter of my soul."

Juliana found the woman's smile contagious. *"Ke a leboha, mme.* Thank you. Your blessing touches me."

The women enjoyed the chunky slices of succulent chicken and thick romaine leaves of the caesar salad. "It's peculiar that the owner chose a South African moniker ascribing peace."

Mme Dijdo pricked a slice of grilled chicken and studied it. "South Africa is a singular place for our proprietor."

"According to county records, your proprietor is a production company located here in L.A."

The director chewed, her expression indecipherable, her eyes obscure.

"Surprisingly, this center is its solitary enterprise. There isn't a history of TV shows or films under its production. A paper trail seems non-existent."

The director neither confirmed nor denied the information Juliana discovered. Juliana chewed, then pressed for more. "An awful amount of effort has been taken to remain anonymous. I'm wondering, mme."

"Why should you wonder?"

Juliana leaned in the steel-back chair. "Any reporter worth their salt would be curious about the name."

"Western thought places too much emphasis on the pursuit. Channeling the energy into the chase often blinds from the nuances as you race toward the kill."

"My sight has been sharpened out of the necessity to absorb—even the horrendous, the incomprehensible."

Mme Dijdo shrugged. "You are not the first to question."

"Such secrecy intrigues me, mme. Why has the philanthropist gone to such trouble to remain unidentified?"

The head director shrugged once more. "Here, life and faith are restored. It is returned to the hands and hearts of the hopeless. *Ka nnete!*

Truly. It is a nasty thing to destroy a dream simply because it esteems no value to you."

"My intention is not to destroy. I only desire to make others aware."

"I do not understand. During the tour, your questions were focused on the children and how the center operates. Now your concentration is on the owner's identity. Miss DeLauer, many have come through the door professing that they only want to reveal the wonders of *Kgotso*. *Tswarelo*. I beg your pardon. Few have honored their word."

Juliana's childhood friend, Jacqueline Lloyd, was a broadcast producer for the popular news program *News Today*. Last year, *NT* had investigated *Kgotso* regarding alleged health violations and the employment of illegal immigrants. *NT* had attempted to draw the owner out and hinted that failure to surface potentially confirmed guilt. In the end, none of the complaints had been substantiated, yet the allegations nearly shut down the center.

"Look at me, mme."

She leveled her uncompromising stare on Juliana.

"To expose, instead of edify, would be to betray my own."

Any outsider would have judged the next few moments as a stare down. However, neither woman sought proof to authenticate weakness. Theirs was an inspection of the heart. Mme Dijdo returned to the savory salad.

"You are astute, daughter."

"I understand my words will not convince. Therefore, I ask you reserve judgment until the article is written."

Mme Dijdo didn't acknowledge Juliana's request. "Where did you perform your nursing duties?"

"In Boptang."

Mme Dijdo's eyes clouded. "How long ago were you there?"

"A few months ago. In July."

"Then you were there when that mother was killed?"

Juliana hesitated. "How did you hear about it?"

Mme Dijdo nodded, as if the tone in Juliana's voice answered her query. "My family is predominantly from Botswana, but my mother, who is eighty, harbors the energy of an adolescent. She visits friends in Boptang bi-annually."

Juliana attempted to quiet the erratic pacing of her heart.

The director rubbed the area between her throat and breastbone. "So brutal to snatch a mother and wife from her beloved. Ah! I fail to comprehend such spite."

Juliana opened her mouth, but doubted her chords would respond. Her hands trembled beside the salad plate.

"The woman was murdered in a veld beside the village. Ah!" Mme Dijdo rubbed her chin in disbelief for several moments. "There were reports she and a friend had taken a morning walk when the men ensnared them. But something struck me as peculiar. They killed the mother and left the other woman alive."

"Tomorrow."

"Yes!" Mma Dijdo nodded. "That was her name. Did you know her?"

"I was the friend."

The director groaned. She leaned across the table and touched Juliana's arm. The crowd dwindled as the end of the lunch hour advanced. Juliana studied the ridged pattern of the tabletop. "I haven't any memory surrounding that time."

A man with hair that swept over his shoulders entered the dining hall carrying a basket full of tablecloths and dishtowels. Mme Dijdo glanced at him but swiftly returned her attention Juliana. By the time Juliana looked up, he was kicking a closet door shut with his foot, his back his only visible feature.

"I am very sorry, Miss DeLauer. Forgive my insensitivity."

"You could have only been insensitive had you been aware."

Juliana picked up both their empty plates and stood. Mme Dijdo gathered the glasses and they deposited the dishware in a tub above the enclosed trash container.

The director patted her arm and said, "In time it will return. But only when it's time."

Juliana followed as the administrator shuttled her from various classrooms to the observation area where social workers visited the children. As evening drew near, she stood in the foyer, hesitant to depart. Juliana thanked the director for allowing such intimate access beyond the walls of *Kgotso*.

Mme Dijdo patted her shoulder. "There is a proverb that states good men and women must die, but death cannot kill their names."

With great effort, Juliana exited. She climbed into the rental and pressed her forehead against the steering wheel, recalling the memory that still bore the propensity to burn.

At the burial site, the family had locked her in an apprehensive circle.

"You must never contact the children. It is for their safety."

"That's absurd." Juliana sighed, her bruised temple and shoulder pulsating beneath the skin.

"Surely, you can see this is for the best."

"I see nothing of the kind."

"You are only thinking of yourself, Palesa."

Juliana felt the heat rise in the back of her throat. "You call me by my nickname, *now*? You call me 'flower' to soften your blow, to make me believe you've actually taken my feelings into account. Whose decision was it to remove my belongings from Tomorrow's home?"

"You have always been wise. Even as a youth."

"Then allow me the chance to say goodbye to the children."

The crowd eyed one another then returned their cagey gaze to her. Juliana reminded, "Do you not remember that I witnessed every one of their births?"

"Tiro was correct. She is pigheaded."

"Tiro!" Juliana hissed and caught the attention of several mourners. She inhaled sharply, realizing she dishonored Tomorrow by adding to the spectacle. "Can we please discuss this in the village later?"

"Tiro believes it best you not return to Boptang for a season. Your commitment to the village through Living Water will be reinstated after he feels it's wise."

Juliana felt abrasive tears claw at the back of her throat. "Again, Tiro. Why is he not present?"

Juliana scanned the crowd. The answer was not only evident in their eyes but rooted in the deep customs of beloved ancestors. In the end, Tomorrow's eldest sister reluctantly handed her a large sack tied by one of Hanna's hair ribbons. As they dispersed, she yanked open the bag to discover every photo they had taken together and every letter she had written.

Did any of the relatives caring for them speak of Tomorrow? Did they share photos to remind the children they had inherited Tomorrow's phlegmatic gaze? Did they speak of the cutting submission she had tendered to save them? Had they been able to touch, caress, and savor any semblance of their life before Tomorrow was taken? Did the children believe Palesa had abandoned them?

The customary ache in her lower belly mentally transported her to the present. She felt as if she had been pummeled by Evander Holyfield. Without lifting her head, she dug through the front compartment of her purse for the meds. Deftly, she swallowed the Clomid and Spirotone capsules designed to ward off the evils of the disease she had battled since middle school.

There were splits of time when she believed her womb would rebuke the prognosis and someday create life. The experts deemed it Polycystic Ovarian Syndrome. Juliana often wondered if it were a proclamation of death to her fondest dream.

Reluctant to return to the lonely hotel room, she submitted to the day's fervor. She felt utterly absurd, wailing in her rental car outside a facility built to foster hope. She didn't doubt *if* God could perform the impossible. She speculated if she would ever be a recipient.

Juliana sat up and considered the pedestrians on the sidewalk in pursuit of mysterious destinations. A chartreuse handbill fluttered beneath her wiper. She opened the door and bent to retrieve it. From her peripheral vision, someone crossed behind the back of her vehicle and disengaged the alarm of the black Denali beside her.

The flyer advertised that a children's clothing superstore welcomed her to join their annual blowout sale and save up to 70%. Fresh tears skimmed her cheeks as she crumpled the paper and hurled it to the back seat.

"Juliana?"

She blinked rapidly at the longhaired, blonde, bearded man in faded jeans and a Van Halen t-shirt. Her vision still obstructed by the tears, she demanded, "Who are you?"

"It's Ben."

Juliana rubbed her eyes. "Ben! What are you doing here?"

"Volunteering. I didn't know you were in L.A."

"I interviewed the center for *Core*."

He walked to her. "Why are you so upset?"

She opened her mouth, but nothing exited.

"Was it something said during the interview?"

"No. It's. … I—"

"Do you have time to follow me?"

Juliana shrugged.

As they drove through the surrounding neighborhood, Juliana turned the air conditioner to its highest setting and positioned every vent toward her face. She filled her lungs and released the air in slow increments.

She retrieved her chirping cell from the passenger seat, read "Pastor Michael" on the display, and groaned. She watched until the fourth ring diverted him to voicemail. Had circumstances been different, she would have been back home celebrating her father's sixtieth birthday.

After a taxing freeway drive, Ben took the De Soto Avenue exit off Highway 101 and gained entrance into a gated community in Woodland Hills. Every street was lined with soaring oaks and phoenix palms. As the sun dipped behind the horizon, Juliana followed Ben up the steep drive of the Mediterranean-style home. Juliana parked behind Ben's SUV.

Ben opened her door; her eyes fluttered to the lush shrubbery resting at the front entrance, the young ivory colored shoots marking their seasonal appearance. Juliana's eyes studied the intricate stained glass double doors, their colors performing an elaborate dance on the pavement. Ben assisted her exit and pulled her forward. When he met no resistance, he wrapped muscular arms around her waist. Juliana contemplated pulling away, but his tenderness choked all resolve.

"Come inside."

Inside, a blast of cool air welcomed them. The living room was filled with beveled rectangular windows. Black-and-white photos of twin boys in various settings of recreation hung above the taupe colored upholstered sofa and matching love seat. A sprawling oak coffee table and matching bookcases filled the remaining space. The bookshelf held a picture of Ben picking seashells with the youngsters, their toes kissing the sea foam. A half-dozen towering plants sprouted from various corners.

Ben led her down a hall toward the spacious kitchen. "Are you thirsty?"

"Water."

Ben placed the keys on the kitchen table and handed her a tissue from the box on the island. Beside the tissue box was another photo of the handsome boys on the lap of a striking auburn-haired woman. Juliana dabbed at her nose and saw the plastic arm of a Transformer peek from behind the frame.

He opened the refrigerator door and removed two waters.

"Thank you." She took a few sips of water and savored the coolness against her throat.

"You can sit." She did and he chose the chair across from her. Ben took a gulp of his water and waited.

"I know you're wondering why I didn't call."

"I am."

"You've been so busy flying back and forth to Vancouver in preparation of your film, I didn't want to distract from that process."

"Juliana, take a hard look at me."

She did.

"Is there any sense I'm not happy to see you?"

"No." She sighed. "I'm here on an assignment. *Core* is covering a story on children who have been orphaned by parents who have AIDS." Juliana lowered her head. "I am usually able to keep my emotions on a tight rein. Not this time." She swallowed the water to usher composure.

"Do you want to talk about it?"

She leaned back and heaved a sigh. "It was agonizing."

He leaned forward and his new hair fell in golden waves over broad shoulders. "Tell me what I can do to help?"

"What can any of us do? These are children who have been orphaned by a disease that doesn't discern. They are so confused and desperate for affection. At one point, I had ten children attempting to climb in my lap. I couldn't hug them enough. I couldn't kiss them enough. I couldn't give enough of myself to make them feel secure that their world would someday be whole."

Ben didn't offer any platitudes or trite consolations.

"I am overreacting."

"I wouldn't say that."

Juliana parted her lips to speak then shut them because her words were aimed to distance him. For a few moments, she watched him stroke his beard.

"You said you were volunteering."

"Oh." He nodded, and Juliana witnessed a flicker of pride.

"Community service?"

He chuckled. "It's a commitment I've made. A way to express gratitude for a friend who received immense support from Mrs. Dijdo during his time of need."

"I didn't recognize you at all."

He rubbed his gritty beard. "This persona is Luke Bailey."

"Your new character?"

"Exactly. The principal shooting doesn't occur for another week, but because of the drastic change, I didn't want to be on set fidgeting and tugging at it."

She examined his new appearance. He reminded her of the heartbreaker who used to repair her mother's Volvo. Bobby Harland. She would sit beside her mother for countless hours in the greasy shop enduring the blaring heavy metal music just to see which color bandana he chose to tame his tresses. "Hair extensions?"

"It took hours."

"Interesting. Is Bailey a rock star?"

"A frontiersmen."

"Of course."

"Is 'interesting' an approval or disapproval?"

A rapture of laughter erupted from the den mingled with vigorous barking. Ben grinned as if this sound brought singular satisfaction. Juliana heard the click of a sliding glass door. The young woman and twin preschool boys in the photos rushed into the adjacent room with a leaping Bichon Frise. They had donned swimsuits, and the woman was playfully hitting the boys with a red beach towel.

"Uncle Ben's back!" The children tackled Ben, who scooped them up in each arm and wrestled them to the carpeted den floor. The Bichon leaned on its front paws with its rear high and pounced.

"Get him, Salty!" the woman cheered.

"Who can take an attack seriously from one named Salty?" Ben teased the four-pawed white puff. Salty hopped on Ben's chest and settled the argument with a vicious licking.

The red headed woman moved toward her. "I'm Sheila Powers. Ben's cousin."

Juliana stood and extended her empty hand. "Juliana DeLauer."

The quartet rolled from the edge of the sofa to the thick oak table legs and back again. "They'll be at that all evening. Can I get you anything?"

Juliana raised her water. "All covered."

Sheila opened the stainless steel refrigerator and removed a Diet Coke. Juliana sipped at her water and glanced at the woman who had emerged from the glistening waves of the backyard pool.

"So what do you think of Ben's new mane?"

"He reminds me of this auto mechanic I had a raging crush on in high school."

Sheila took a swallow and leaned against the Spanish-tiled countertop. "Yep. Mine was Dave Schultz. Man, I wonder how many trees I killed writing his name in my notebook?"

Juliana grinned. "I had a master plan. I'd graduate, and we would save enough money to someday purchase our own shop. I would work as the cashier slash receptionist."

Sheila raised an eyebrow and took another drink. "No kidding? So, what happened? He couldn't wait for you?"

"In order for someone to wait they must first realize you exist."

"Ouch!"

"Precisely. And what of Dave?"

"The night of our high school graduation, I got up enough nerve and pledged my undying love for him. He took my hands, looked me straight in the eye, and kindly informed me of his post-graduate future."

"He had joined the Peace Corp and was destined for the Amazon?"

"I wish. I could at least compete with the jungle. No, he was to become a priest."

"Oh my!"

"It took me all summer to recover."

Sheila dampened a paper towel from the water tap and handed it to Juliana. "You have smudges on your cheeks."

Juliana groaned softly. "I must look delightful."

"Actually, you look better than most people with a fresh face of makeup."

Sheila pointed to the mirrored art on the back kitchen wall. Sheila had been gracious in her description. The dark smudges had created dark rings beneath her eyes.

"I look like I dunked my head in a vat of ink and came out blinking fast." Juliana discarded the darkened cloth beneath the folds of a trash receptacle. "Bless you for being so kind."

Sheila folded her arms across her chest. "Are you okay? I mean, did we butt into the middle of something?"

Juliana blinked then realized the purpose of her question. "I just completed an assignment for my magazine. It's about children who have been orphaned or abandoned by parents who have AIDS and can no longer care for them or who have passed away."

"Looks like it really touched you."

"I wanted to personally adopt every last one of them."

The boys entered the kitchen underneath the powerful arms of Ben with Salty leaping at Ben's knees. The twins wiggled and protested in delightful squeals.

"Okay, you two. It's time for dinner."

Sheila informed him plates of chicken nuggets were in the warmer.

"It's my favorite!" one boy shouted.

The other exclaimed, "Mine, too!"

"Sheila, go rest. I've got this covered."

Sheila took the last swallow of her Diet Coke. "Are you dismissing me?"

He kissed Sheila's forehead and shoved her out of the kitchen with a bump from his hip. The boys rushed to her and she bombarded them goodnight kisses. Then they headed to the kitchen table with Salty nipping at their toes. She turned to Juliana. "It was great talking to you." Then she glanced at Ben. "I hope this won't be the last time."

"Not if it is up to me," Ben stated. Juliana recovered from her chagrin by bidding Sheila goodbye.

He placed the plates on the counter and added sliced carrots with

Ranch dressing from the crisper. "Sheila works the night shift as an ER nurse at Mercy Medical."

The boys were busy crashing a pair of metal airplanes head long into one another. Juliana walked to the island and stood beside him.

"Their dad died a few months before their birth. Sheila does a remarkable job caring for them."

"Who keeps them while she's at work?"

"When I'm not on location, I do."

"We don't hear about that on *Entertainment Tonight*."

"There's also the next door neighbor, Suzanne, Salty's owner. We watch him whenever she has an errand to run."

At the sound of his name, Salty ran to Ben's feet and barked. Juliana bent to rub the dog's ears. "I imagine Salty would not like it if left alone for more than a minute."

"Exactly. Trashes the entire house. It's probably due to the marked decrease in noise when Suzanne's not around."

"You lost me."

Ben handed the meal to the twins and returned to her side. "There was a study done sometime ago regarding the number of words women speak versus men."

Juliana swallowed the last sips of her water. "Right. Women equated to about 20,000 and men 7,000."

"Thanksgiving we invited her over. We lost count at 200,000."

"Stop." Juliana shook her head. "No way."

"Tell me if I'm wrong once you meet her."

"Aunt Joan says she's a Chatty-Kathy," one of the twins announced between bites.

"Aunt Joan?" Juliana stopped rubbing Salty's ears.

"My mother," Ben informed.

"I have this thing. I find it interesting to discover how people's parents met."

"It's called being a nosey romantic."

"Call it what you like."

"Mom received a full scholarship to the University of Idaho in biochemistry. The summer before she was to attend, she met my father at a church social."

"They fell madly in love?"

"He proposed in August and the rest," he patted his broad chest, "they say is history."

He leaned against the counter. "It wasn't until I graduated from high school that she returned to college. She held off her dream to stay home with us. I am perpetually grateful for my mother's sacrifice."

"I wasn't as judicious as you. I felt like my mother was hovering."

Salty whimpered lacking attention. Ben pointed and immediately Salty retreated to a fluffy cushion in a corner of the kitchen. "Really?"

"Until middle school. One day we were released at noon due to some teachers' conference. I returned to the church offices with her. I watched her maneuver her crazy schedule as head of the prayer and outreach ministry, organize and help maintain the food bank, visit the sick, and participate in a senior pastors' wives Bible study. From that moment forward, I never took for granted that she always greeted me at the front door."

Ben grinned slowly at her. "The young man in the blue trunks is Thomas."

"Tommy!" he corrected.

"The young man in the red trunks is Timothy."

"Timmy!"

"Say hello to Juliana."

They did then returned their focus to the meal. Their mannerisms, build, and features were so identical Juliana couldn't help but stare.

"What?"

"They are amazing. How on earth do you tell them apart?"

"It's subtle, but look closer."

Juliana gawked at the hungry boys with their tanned skin, deep-brown almond eyes, and coal black hair. Juliana snapped her fingers.

"Yes?" Ben grinned in anticipation of her discovery.

"The hair. Tommy has a slight wave and Timmy's hair is bone straight."

"Impressive. It takes most weeks before they realize the difference."

Juliana nodded toward the direction she imagined Sheila's bedroom. "When does Sheila's shift begin?"

"In four hours. I'll bathe them and put them down for the night."

Juliana shifted her attention to the adorable boys devouring their dinner. "How do you feel about your new look?"

"At first, it was wonderful to pump gas, take the boys to a movie, or shop and not have one soul recognize me."

"At first?"

"It didn't take long before *they* surmised it was me."

"It's kind of crazy isn't it? You've worked hard to achieve recognition. Now you're working feverishly to be unrecognizable."

His body tensed and his complexion reddened. "My mind just returned to our discourteous goodbye outside of Java Amore. I cannot fathom why my every move creates interest. A team followed me through Whole Foods last week and publicized my grocery list. Who cares that I prefer wild sockeye to north Atlantic salmon?"

"Apparently, millions."

"What I wore to work, when I departed, where I went after work, how long I stayed, who was in my company, what we ate. It's all so very inane to me."

The boys completed their meal and deposited their plates in the sink.

Juliana whistled. "Impressive."

"Sheila runs a very tight ship."

Ben scooped the boys in his arms, squinted one eye, and adopted a gravely tone. "Argh! It's off to the dunk for you two scalawags. Then, a wee bit of shut eye."

They squirmed and giggled in his grip.

"Are you able to wait?"

Juliana nodded.

She turned her attention to the dishware and loaded them in the dishwasher, then wiped down the table. The hushed voices of the boys and Ben as they prepared for bed created an ache in her heart.

Juliana removed a fresh tissue from the decorative box and wiped her eyes. She knew deep down that her father was reveling in immutable peace and joy. Even if given the opportunity, she wouldn't ask to bring him back. But...

His stubborn devotion had been instrumental in the woman she had become. Just before apartheid was abolished, the shattering reason behind her lack of menstrual periods, sudden thinning hair, embarrassing black patches on her neck, and excessive forearm hair was discovered.

When the doctors dispensed medications that failed, he bragged of her strength. When the medications finally worked, he boasted of her perseverance. When her thick curls fell from the crown of her head in alarming clumps, he trumpeted her beauty. When the doctors held dismal hope she would ever conceive children of her own, her father proclaimed her incontrovertible value.

"Juliana." A small voice stirred her from the emotive memories. Tommy was dressed in Bob the Builder pj's.

Juliana dabbed her eyes. "Hi, little one."

"Are you crying?"

Juliana nodded sadly.

"My mommy cries."

"Oh, honey, I'm sorry to hear that."

"You know what I do when she cries?"

"What, baby?"

The little boy grabbed Juliana tightly around her thighs. She bent and placed her lips to his dark, wavy hair.

"Don't cry, Juliana. It will be okay."

Ben's sandaled feet appeared. Juliana squatted so she could look into the little boy's eyes. She smoothed the dark hair that bent in gentle waves. "Tommy, I feel better already."

"My mommy says I give good hugs."

She rubbed his cheek. "The best."

Ben touched the child's shoulder and gently led him down the hall. She sat down at the table, shut her eyes, and didn't suppress the wondrous memories.

After awhile, Ben quietly joined her at the table and gently touched her hand. When she didn't resist, he placed it between both of his warm palms.

She opened her eyes. "Today would have been my father's sixtieth birthday."

Ben remained silent, yet his eyes communicated ardent solace.

"I still can't figure out how to celebrate it. I mean, you can't throw a party." Juliana attempted to suppress the sobs. "Yet, I feel it's such a betrayal to do nothing at all. I don't know what to do."

"I'm here."

"I should go. This is not the right thing to do."

"You don't have to run, Juliana."

"You don't understand."

Juliana retrieved her purse from the living room. When she faced him, he was leaning against the corridor wall.

"There are things, complicated beyond measure."

He remained positioned against the wall. "I'm right here."

Juliana headed for the front door. The moonlight bounced off the windows painting an array of diamonds across the textured walls. She turned and cautiously met his ingenuous gaze. "Nothing about this is easy."

"I wouldn't dare imagine it would be."

"You're not simple—who you are."

"If I were, would you be interested?"

"Your life, your world could be more elemental."

"You're not headed beyond that door, beyond us, because of the complexity of *my* life. You're bolting because of your resistance to face your own."

Juliana was stupefied at his brazenness and the truth he spoke. Eventually, she dropped her purse and returned to him. "Know-it-all."

"You must know it's too late."

"For?"

"Evading."

"Meaning?"

He pulled her back to the kitchen table and waited until she was seated across from him. "My father died believing God would heal him. As he lay in that hospital bed, he wasn't speaking of goodbye or admonishing his sons to care for his wife. He spoke of repairing the rotted posts of our fence and painting the den in Gambol Gold. He complained that his hospital stay thwarted his elk hunting trips with his grandchildren."

"Oh, Ben."

"The first symptom had hit long before my mother noticed the involuntary muscle spasms. My oldest brother, Samuel, is the lead fore-man for my dad's landscaping company. He noticed something affecting dad's ability to operate the equipment. After months of hounding, Dad finally acquiesced to a physical. If only he had gone in sooner, there would have been more time. Ninety percent die within three to twelve months of diagnosis."

"What did they find?"

"CJD. Creutzfeldt-Jakob Disease."

"I'm so sorry."

"You know what I'm grateful for?"

She blinked against the tears blurring his image. "Tell me."

"The disease is a slow chain reaction caused by damaged proteins in the cerebrum. Brain damage is permanent." He paused to lower his eyes not fearful of what she would see, but that the intensity would frighten her. "He was gone before his eyes would stare and not see, his limbs would twitch but not feel, he would receive a kiss and not know who was bestowing affection."

She gripped his hand. Ben found the sensation inviting. He raised his eyes, careful to temper their rue. "The loss, this grief delineates, doesn't it?"

Juliana nodded. "Sections off—partitions quarters of your soul reserved for them alone. They've been with us since our births."

"For seven years I've questioned if it were possible to *thrive* without him."

"We're still here, Ben. So I am propelled to believe it's possible."

"I told you, the evening of our first dinner, we had more in common than you realized."

"I was hoping for taste in movies, pizza toppings, or favorite artist."

"There's more still."

She held up her hand and nodded. "We take it step-by-step—in our own specialized rhythm. Besides, I'm on emotional overload."

He stared at their hands, benefiting from the sense of her touch and hating his cowardice.

CHAPTER TWELVE

Juliana drove to Ben's Bel Air home Sunday evening. After her subsequent visits to *Kgotso* to complete her research, Thursday through Saturday evenings had been a whirlwind. She had cheered for Timmy and Tommy at their t-ball games and raced them eating scoops of Cold Stone afterward.

A few yards down the street from Ben's manor crouched various cars. Beside the vehicles were men with telephoto lenses and pricey recording devices. Juliana shook her head and resisted the urge to make as goofy a face as possible. She blinked against the flash of bulbs and turned into the drive.

The camera attached to the stone pillar whirred and faced her. The gates opened and she parked behind a $500,000 sports car. Near to the front door was a Bentley. To its rear sat an extravagantly detailed Cadillac Escalade. The rented Ford Tarsus stuck out like a cat suit at a black tie dinner party.

"Welcome." Ben embraced her. "I hope you're hungry."

"I am."

"How did you spend your day?"

"I worked out at the hotel gym, visited a church, and completed my article this afternoon."

Ben admired the cobalt skirt suit and matching scarf she wore. "That color is amazing on you." Her perfume reminded him of the crispness of the air after a rain.

"Thank you. Sky blue bandana. Nice touch." Juliana complimented the accessory that concealed his tresses.

"It keeps it away from my face."

Juliana gazed at the twenty-foot ceilings, marbled floors, stone pillars, and extravagant furnishings. "Your home is beautiful."

"I can't take credit. It's rented."

"It is still gorgeous nonetheless."

"Nonetheless."

They entered the massive kitchen with double Gagganeu ovens, a sub-zero fridge, and hand-carved cabinetry. Juliana pointed to the staggering display of barbecued ribs, brats, potato salad, cheeseburgers, fried chicken, four types of chips, pecan pies, and soft drinks.

"I ... umm ... don't eat—"

Ben removed a plate from the refrigerator. "For Miss Juliana." He removed the covering with a flourish. The contents held fresh fruit and sashimi. "And for your discerning palate there is bottled water."

"I was about to excuse myself and make a beeline for the nearest Whole Foods."

"Now, I must warn you. The men you're about to meet have stood by me despite every controversy, every storm. Their conversation and manners will decline as the evening progresses."

"I have been warned."

Ben carried her plate onto the spacious patio where three men sat at a table covered with plates, drinks, and poker chips. Classic 80s' soul blared from concealed speakers. Two of the men were arguing above the heavy bass. Ben saw recognition cross Juliana's expression. "Those two legends in their own minds are movie director Marcus Jacobs, whom you may remember from our meeting at Tanner's, and Ian Knight."

The men ceased their bickering. "Good evening." Ian's British accent was as crisp as his cerulean polo and khaki shorts. He was lean, well maintained, and his honey colored hair seemed thicker than on the big screen.

Marcus stood. "Man, stand up when a lady enters the room." He was of average height, wore his hair short, and his skin reminded Juliana of roasted almonds. Jacobs had a flair for creating blockbuster action flicks, cracking jokes, and dating savvy businesswomen.

"You cannot cease telling people what to do," Ian shot back.

"And you cannot take direction."

Ben nodded at the twenty-something companion. "And the mellow, barely legal one counting all his winnings is TV sitcom gold, Hunter Green."

Hunter smiled shyly. His jet-black hair was purposefully unruly. His legs stretched far beneath the table to sizable feet. The green of his eyes compelled, yet quickly fleeted from, Juliana's gaze.

"Hello, gentleman," Juliana addressed the poolside group as Ben pulled out her seat. Juliana sat and placed the napkin in her lap. Ben deposited her tray in front of her. "Wait. Where's Bruce?"

"He insists I give him the occasional day off. I hope he's basking in it. The next won't arrive until Easter." Ben smirked.

Marcus returned to his seat. "You referred to us as gentleman. You may want to refrain from that opinion for a few hours."

"Especially of you," Ian countered.

Marcus rolled his eyes. "Who stood when Juliana entered?"

"How long are you going to beat that horse?"

"Fellas!" Ben took the seat to her right. "Play."

The men busied themselves with calling bids. Juliana munched the delectable dinner and observed the entertainment. After an hour of their affable barbing, Juliana's cheeks were sore from laughter. Marcus, Ian, and Ben left the table to reload their plates and refresh their drinks.

"Juliana, you playing?" Hunter shuffled the deck.

She pointed to her bare plate. "I came only to feast."

Hunter shyly grinned. "Ben brags that you're next in line for the Pulitzer."

"Does he?"

"No joke."

Hunter pointed to the empty chairs. "He mailed each of us a copy of your latest article—the one about the HIV/AIDS Symposium in Denver last month."

"He did not!"

"No joke."

"Nothing like putting your friends on the spot."

Hunter shook his head. "It didn't happen like that. Ben is very big into people being educated about HIV and AIDS. He sends us that kind of thing all the time. It wasn't until just a few days ago we found out you were the writer. And it wasn't because he told us."

"How did you put the two together?"

"Unfortunately, thanks to the tabloids. They named the magazine you work for..." Hunter snapped his fingers as if they held the answer.

"*Core.*"

"I knew it had something to do with your insides. Anyhow, they flashed the title of your article with your pix."

Juliana widened her eyes. "I had no idea."

"You've become a household name."

"And I haven't even won the Pulitzer yet."

"You can't get away from it. There's just no way. Not if you plan on hanging with Ben."

"I spent the other morning at *Kgotso*. Ben happened to be volunteering when we accidentally met. He's never mentioned before how he felt about the subject."

"There are certain things that aggravate him to no end. One happens to be when Hollywood elite tout a cause just to get publicity or boost their lame career."

"How often does he volunteer?"

"As often as he can. His schedule is kinda the enemy, though."

"It's been confirmed he donates enough to support a small nation."

"You seriously do your homework."

Juliana shrugged. "It's what they taught in J-school." She slid her fingers in an upward pattern to the top of her glass. "He's quite private about his involvement. None of those disclosures were sent by his publicist."

"That's what I'm saying." Hunter placed the cards on the table and spread them out in sections of three. "What's up with Mbeki?"

Juliana picked up her water; the ice cubes clinked against the sides of the glass. "How do you mean?"

"I read an article about him and the fact he believes HIV doesn't cause AIDS."

"Right."

"The president of South Africa is watching his own people die on his door step."

"You have to take into account the turbulent history. The HIV/AIDS epidemic emerged in South Africa around 1982. However, the country was torn apart from the horrors of apartheid, so the HIV issue was mostly ignored. Political unrest dominated the media and HIV began to multiply, primarily in the gay community. The disease spread beyond the gay population, and heterosexuals were being infected equivalent to the same rate as gay men. By the mid-1990s, HIV infections increased by 60%."

"Crazy, because you would think somebody in power would have caught on this thing was for real."

"I so wish." Juliana sighed. "In 2000, the SADF—South African Department of Health—drafted a five-year HIV/AIDS Plan. Thabo Mbeki gave it little support."

"Yeah, I heard about that. Didn't he get together with some scientists who believe extreme poverty is the culprit of the AIDS epidemic?"

Juliana nodded. "Without government support, the SADF plan faltered. Meanwhile, HIV infections for pregnant South African women soared to 30%."

"You think political support has got to be there for success?"

She shook her head as if she had mulled the question endlessly. "I used to. Sure, it's necessary, but I think we've put too much emphasis on laying it at the governments' feet. I think it's time for the Body to step up and make a difference."

"What body?"

She replaced the glass on the table. "The Church."

Hunter gawked at her as if she'd claimed he impregnated her. "Oh."

"Even when the South African government finally established a plan that would make HIV medications widely available, it was sluggish and deficient. HIV experts worldwide believe that political unrest, meager government support, political denial, and lack of information have fueled this disease."

The young actor's sea green eyes remained locked on the cards, dazed by her unconventional solution.

"Governments have never quite been able to forge lasting progress because they aren't the answer."

He looked to the pool. "When the news revisited the anniversary of her death, it got my head all twisted."

"Whose death?"

"Gugu Dhlamini."

Juliana shot a look at the young man; this time she was stunned. "What did you say?"

"I still can't wrap my brain around it. I just don't get how we can be so basic with each other. She was thirty-six and her village stoned her."

Juliana shuddered. "That happened in 1998."

"Yeah. My point exactly. She died because she wasn't going to hide anymore. She revealed her positive HIV status at the World Aids Conference. A village spokesman claimed she brought shame upon the community. Imagine that? She was breaking free of the shame by not hiding and she still lost her life."

After several moments, Juliana realized her eyes were riveted on him. Hunter frowned. "Hey?"

"Huh?"

"You look like you might throw up."

Hunter handed her the glass; she held it, but couldn't bring it to her mouth. Hunter leaned forward and assisted her. She took a shallow sip.

Hunter asked, "Did you know her?"

"No."

It billowed like oil to the water's surface; a memory crept from the murky edges of her subconscious then just as quickly departed. *Murder. Speaking out to destroy the shame,* she considered.

Hunter thumbed the edges of the cards. "Ben and I met on a movie set four years ago. You know, I hate to admit it, but I never gave it much thought until I met Ben."

Juliana waited quietly. He leaned forward, but kept his gaze on the deck. "I mean, I was twenty-one and making millions. Everywhere I went, everybody knew my name. I didn't have to buy much because so much was handed to me. Too much."

Juliana suddenly recognized his deep resemblance to Timmy and Tommy. But, the timing didn't add up. Ben had stated their father had died a few months before they were born. Four years ago.

"It was kind of strange, you know. Here was the infamous Ben Powers actually seeking me out for friendship."

"Strange."

He handed her the glass. "You still look like you might pass out."

The men rejoined them. Ben handed Hunter a fresh drink and placed bottled water in front of Juliana.

"What happened out here?" Marcus looked around him. "The atmosphere darkened."

"We were talking about Gugu Dhlamini," Hunter explained.

Ben squinted. "Really?"

Ian and Ben shared a tacit exchange. "Her death was rather hard to swallow."

"So, you're here interviewing at *Kgotso*?" Marcus acknowledged.

"Yes." The troubling returned, darting through the subliminal then seeping toward her heart.

"What was your impression?" Marcus asked.

Juliana held the chilled bottle against the heat of her face. "Amazing place. The mission is ambitious, but I'm impressed at how well it's executed. And I wanted to adopt them all."

Ian stated, "Well, gentlemen, I believe we have discovered a female Benjamin Powers."

"Oh, God forbid!" Marcus groaned.

"That would be so wrong on so many levels," Hunter added.

Juliana moved the bottle back and forth against her cheek. "I can't believe it."

Ben asked, "What?"

Hunter squirmed. "Oh, man. I think she's gonna heave."

"I can't believe I didn't see it sooner."

"Tell us," Ian asserted, his expression intrigued.

Juliana looked skyward. "Wow. Your intense interest in HIV and AIDS and South Africa. Gugu Dhlamini's death. Of course."

The men seemed to become sudden victims of cryogenics. She took great measure to look them in the eye. She stopped at Ben. "See, I should know better. Now I understand why journalists aren't invited to come out and play more often. We fling the cover off of things no one welcomed us to unearth."

Ben seemed to stop breathing. Marcus had begun to open his soft drink and the pressure, impatient for release, created a hiss that reverberated throughout the patio. No one paid attention to the foam curving between his fingers.

Marcus set down the bottle. "What exactly is it that you believe you've unearthed?"

"One or all of you own the production company that funds *Kgotso*."

Ben exhaled and the others pretended her words were illogical.

"I admire your diligence to remain anonymous. It seems you want the children to remain the focal point, not your celebrity."

Marcus expounded, "Curious. A few particulars emerge and you believe they are the missing pieces to the puzzle. We've been interviewed by Barbara Walters, Diane Sawyer, and Oprah Winfrey, and none of them arrived at your conclusion."

"They weren't focused on *Kgotso*. Their audiences were more interested in what designer you wore to the Academy Awards than what charities you sponsored."

"I noticed it the moment you approached the table at Tanner's." Marcus flexed his meticulously pampered fingers. "How often has this perceived intuition gotten your hand smacked?"

"My reflexes are immediate."

Ian inserted, "I suppose it hasn't been lost on you that this could be our last meeting?"

Although she wanted, she refused a glance at Ben. She had to stand on her own to prove her merit. After all, she had been a big enough girl to undo the can of worms. "Once you stop taking risks, you wither."

Ian claimed, "That makes you desirable and loathsome all at once."

"Such flattery at our first meeting."

Marcus emphasized, "You understand we came here to play poker, right?"

Juliana met their shielding gaze. "It's a free country after all, isn't it?"

Hunter spoke next. "So what happens next? You gonna print your suspicions?"

Out of the corner of her eye, Ben sipped his root beer and watched her.

"If the article were about you four, then I'd be obligated to take that slant. But that's not why I came."

Marcus leaned forward, somberly. "Understand something from this moment on."

"Tell me."

"I will teach you how to play poker and you will play on my team."

Ben smirked, his eyes never leaving Juliana during the edgy establishment of her resolve.

Marcus continued, "Seriously, Ben, the woman's got skills."

Despite the uneasiness the revelation exposed, Juliana couldn't contain her laughter. The men joined her. Ben lightly touched her hand and squeezed. "We have your word, Juliana?"

She returned the squeeze. "You have my word." She drank from her bottle. "Although, my instincts were described as both desirable and loathsome."

"Not entirely loathsome," Ian countered. "Maybe simply bloody annoying."

"That sounds much better."

The next ninety minutes the theatrical quartet charged the balmy backyard with raucous barbs. She excused herself, grasping her belly made sore from their hilarity. She discovered the powder room adjacent to the den. Upon exiting, the profusion of photographs on the grand piano caught her eye. Several were of Ben's amusing poolside crew. One print was a formal shot, every man dressed stylishly in designer suits. One hadn't been a guest that evening, his absence piercing Juliana's interest.

There were shots of Tommy and Timmy, Sheila, and two older men, with families, who shared Ben's refined traits. Dead center was that of a couple. Juliana discovered the woman had Ben's intense eyes and bone structure and the man possessed his thick hair and smile.

"Those are my parents."

Juliana jumped, riveted from her concentrated exploration.

"I'm sorry, I didn't mean to startle you."

"Don't apologize. Again, I have been caught snooping."

Ben pointed to the photos of the older men he resembled. "This is my oldest brother, Samuel. Earth, vegetation, and stone are his gift, so naturally he inherited Dad's landscaping company. His wife, Colleen, is the company's accountant. Their children are Sarah and Hannah. This," he pointed to the next photo, "is Jacob. He is a colonel in the Air Force and resides in Illinois on Whiteman Air Force Base. Those are his twin boys, puffed with adolescence, Joshua and Caleb."

"No wife?"

Ben shook his head. "Becky walked out six months after the boys were born and we haven't seen her since."

"That must have been horrible."

"Jacob never remarried and denied promotions to dedicate his time to raise his boys."

Ben plopped down on the sofa and leaned into the plush cushions.

"In the photo of you and your poker buddies, there's someone I haven't met."

"That's Kevin." Ben palmed his bandana. "He died about four years ago."

The cognitive wheels spun in her head, but she kept her thoughts concealed. Hunter bore a striking resemblance to Kevin.

Ben stared up at her.

"What?"

"You're remarkable."

She rolled her eyes. "I thought I leaned more toward 'bloody annoying.'"

He removed the hand from his head and rested it on his flat belly. "When you walk through hell with somebody, the bond is fierce. That was a test, and you passed with superlative approval."

She squinted at him playfully. "What next? Blood and urine samples."

"That's next week."

"I haven't laughed that hard in a very, very long time."

"Now you understand why we hang out and often."

She joined him on the sofa. He took her hand. "I meant what I just said. You've carried weight I've seen emotionally cripple many. Yet it doesn't seem to take much exertion for you to relax and enjoy life. I am very pleased you asked me for a cup of coffee."

Ben's free hand touched her cheek. His hand moved in subtle circles, the pattern delicate and affirming. "Juliana, there's something I have to tell you."

"Yo! Ben! Man, where are you?" Ben shut his eyes and sighed deeply.

Marcus rounded the corner and halted. "Oh! My bad."

"Your timing is appalling." Ben groaned.

"I know. That's why I'm leaving."

"Fantastic."

"Ben!" Juliana scolded.

"My mama didn't raise no fools. Well, maybe my brother Johnny, but that is a whole 'nother story."

"Out!" Ben shouted.

"I head out to D.C. to begin shooting on Tuesday. Give me a call before then."

"That should allow enough time to forgive you."

"Precisely." Marcus jogged to the sofa and touched Juliana's shoulder. "It was a pleasure to meet you. I hope we spend time together again even if you are bloody annoying."

Juliana smiled. "Have your people call my people."

The director jogged to Ben's side and planted a wet kiss on Ben's forehead. Ben flailed his arms frantically. Marcus trotted toward the entrance and waved goodbye over his head.

Ben shook his head. "It is not fair."

"What?"

"I have to suffer such abuse."

"You love every minute."

"Benjamin," Ian called.

Ben sucked his jaw, jumped up, and pulled Juliana to her feet. "Come with me to kick them out, please."

Ben and Juliana discovered Marcus, Ian, and Hunter had cleared the dishes from the patio. After all four cleaned the kitchen, Ian and Hunter wished them goodnight. She followed Ben to the garage where they carried the overflowing trash bags. Ben removed a set of tiny keys from his pocket, unlocked the large blue container, deposited the bags inside, and locked it.

"Mr. Powers?"

"Miss DeLauer."

"You lock your trash?"

He nodded, solemnly. "I do."

"Help me out here."

"Do you remember some time ago when I sued a tabloid for printing that Eternity took Cefuroxime for a sexually transmitted disease?"

Juliana shook her head. "Sorry."

"She had been prescribed Cefuroxime for a sinus infection. Neither of our doctors disclosed that info."

"How can you be certain?"

"Our doctors sign confidentiality agreements."

"Aren't they already obligated by law to keep your information private?"

"It hasn't been enough."

Juliana folded her arms across her chest. "All right."

"At that time, we placed our trash on the curb just like everyone else. This was before that tidbit blared from the headlines."

"So, you're saying someone dug through your trash, pulled out the prescription bottle, and ran to the tabloid?"

"That's precisely what I'm saying."

Juliana shivered against the humid air within the garage confines. "That's crazy, Ben."

He sighed and gazed at her as if she were a brilliant student refusing to use one iota of brain matter. "The tabloid's source ended up being a paparazzi ringleader. The police discovered old take-out menus, discarded toothpaste tubes, personal grooming products, and the infamous prescription bottle in his home."

"Ben, that's too sick to even comprehend."

"You shouldn't try."

"Maya prescribed it for me when I had a bronchial infection. Cefuroxime is used as an antibiotic for several reasons."

"Which is something the average person doesn't realize. Thus, the tabloids can spoon-feed lies and the public gobbles them up. Eternity has never been labeled virtuous. But to print that the prescription was ordered because she had contracted an STD and passed it on to me was a bit too much."

"Unbelievable."

Ben brushed by her and bounded up the stairs leading into the kitchen. Juliana followed and Ben's force to self-protect swelled around her. Juliana couldn't blame him. She merely wondered what price Ben had paid for his privacy; how many substantial parts of him had it choked?

Ben placed the dishtowel beneath the sink, and Juliana noticed it was near midnight. She sat at the kitchen table and rubbed her jaw.

"Uh-oh." Ben sat beside her. "There's that look."

"What look?"

"The one that screams 'Gee, I need to express this, but I don't know how he'll take it' look."

She ceased rubbing her jaw and tightly folded her hands. "I am very attracted to you."

"I would skip right now if your tone wasn't so reserved."

She steepled her fingers and tapped them. "I'm just going to say it."

"Please."

"Sex before marriage isn't an option."

He stared at her for several seconds then leaned back in the chair. "I see."

"I've taken serious note of how easy it would be for you to receive … affection from someone else."

"Someone else?"

"I'm not expecting you to be celibate."

"Why not?"

She shot him a look of utter disbelief. "Since your divorce, hundreds of women bought t-shirts with 'Ben, I'm yours!' emblazoned across their chest."

"And?"

"And," her voice grew stronger, "seduction wouldn't even be required. No dinner, no dancing, just here I am, take it."

"Those women are prejudiced by my professionally manufactured image."

"I mean, I have to be realistic."

"Realistic?"

"I'm not expecting you to live by my values."

Ben drew figure eights on the tabletop. For a few disconcerting moments, neither spoke. Finally, his eyes met hers. "Twenty years ago, you know what I thought was clever? The number of women I could bed in one night. After all, it was just sex, right? It was fun. If anyone got hurt, it was their problem. Never mine."

Juliana swallowed the lump budding in her throat. Ben jabbed his finger at the table. "Some men look back on their conquests with pride. Not this man."

His eyes felt like a drill through her heart. "I watched Kevin wrestle with death believing in the worth of the conquest. There was nothing I could do to stop his death or his pain."

Then, it all tumbled in her head, took shape and contoured—his abundant donations to HIV and AIDS projects, dutiful trips to teach men and women of the disease, and monogamy. Kevin's features carried character Hunter hadn't quite developed, but the resemblance was uncanny. *Had Ben struggled to release Kevin to the point Hunter had been welcomed as a replacement?*

Juliana felt her heart cave within her chest. It had seemed utterly implausible that Benjamin Powers actually had suffered profoundly and lived what he preached.

"I'm so sorry," Juliana muttered, her tone deferential.

His attention was locked on the gentle waves the night breeze stimulated in the pool. "Kevin believed he was invincible. I couldn't get him to listen. I couldn't change him."

Although Ben was only inches from her, she felt he had never been farther away. Charily, she reached for his hand. Juliana was deeply relieved when he didn't resist. They sat accompanied by the rustling of the backyard trees through the screened french doors.

"My father said people tell you who they are, if you'll only listen," Juliana offered the veiled apology. "I didn't. I'm sorry."

He squeezed her hand. "It's getting late. I don't want you falling asleep at the wheel."

She retrieved her purse from beneath the table and he escorted her to the door. He raised their hands and rested them on his muscular chest. "You cannot ever mistake me for the image you see on the screen, or a talk show, or the red carpet. Highly skilled professionals manufactured that man. This," he lightly beat their hands on his chest, "is who I am."

After he walked her to her car and she drove from his house, two of the loitering paparazzi ignited their engines and pursued her. The Bel Air security patrol pulled behind the one vehicle that remained and flashed its lights in warning. The occupant had been transfixed on the gated perimeter that safeguarded Ben Powers. On the passenger seat were copious notes transcribed on a legal pad. He shoved the state-of-the-art eavesdropping device beneath the passenger seat and started the engine. He had heard every word of the revelatory evening and his decision became clear. It was time for Ben to pay for his past transgressions.

CHAPTER THIRTEEN

Ben rose near dawn and jogged five miles through the argentine mist. After completing his morning routine, he looked at his watch and surmised Juliana was probably ambling through security at that very moment, her scheduled take-off in an hour at 8:30. As he snatched the cordless phone from its resting place on the counter, it rang.

"Powers."

"Ben..." It was Sheila. He wasn't scheduled to pick up the boys for another four hours.

The hair pricked on the back on his neck. "What's wrong?"

"I'm at the hospital."

"Were you called in early?"

"No."

"I don't understand."

She sobbed and mumbled something he couldn't comprehend.

"Sheila, what's wrong?"

"It's Tommy."

"What's happened?"

"I promised them a pancake breakfast at IHOP. They were all excited, running around the truck. It took me a while to get them corralled."

He shoved his wallet in his back denim pocket and clutched the car keys. Ben had no concept of what her next words would be, but felt that their impact would demand action.

"I was getting Timmy in the car seat. Tommy insisted on getting the newspaper near the curb. So, he opened the gate and dashed out and—"

"What, Sheila?"

Her next words contoured into a groan. "I heard it before I saw it. The wheels screeched as it turned the corner going way too fast. It headed straight toward him and jumped the curb."

"Oh, God." His grip tightened on the receiver.

"Ben," she sobbed, "he's hurt bad."

"I'm on my way."

Ben dropped the cordless. It clattered in protest against the honey colored marble. He jumped the three steps of the garage landing and snatched the car door open. He slammed the European coupe in reverse and had to screech to a halt when he realized he hadn't raised the garage door.

Ben pressed the button. "Come on!"

Ben broke every speed limit through the drenching rain, hastily parked the car in the hospital lot, and dashed into the ER. There were ten people ahead of him at the check-in counter. He looked around and discovered a small information booth to the right.

"I'm looking for Tommy Powers."

The clerk didn't look up from her romance novel. "Is he a patient here?"

"Yes. He was just brought in. He was hit." The words were a rush of jagged air burning his lungs.

She adjusted her hefty girth. "Did you check with the ER?"

Ben inhaled sharply. "Are you blind? Look at that line!"

This caused the disinterested woman to raise her abundantly teased head. She squinted and immediately erected her posture. "Oh, my god! You're Ben Powers."

"Ma'am, please. His mother stated his condition was critical."

She flipped through the printout, the tremble of her hands slowing her process. Ben nearly ripped it from her. He heard his name. Sheila stood to the left of the crowded check-in counter.

She ushered him through the hectic waiting area, through a set of massive doors marked "Emergency Room Personnel Only," and beyond a set of triage rooms. The last room on the left held Tommy.

His tiny cousin lay motionless on a bed meant for an adult. There seemed to be miles of tubing; plastic tentacles distending from machines that pierced the broken, diminutive body. Tommy's head was shrouded beneath a bulky dressing tainted by deep ruby circles. A bandage swathed the red, shredded skin from right temple to chin. Ben's hands rushed to his mouth. He folded his arms across his chest. Hot tears flooded his sight.

Sheila clung to his side. "I tried, you know. I tried to move. My mind was screaming. But, I couldn't, Ben. Oh, God. I couldn't move."

He cradled her head. "Stop."

"What's wrong with me?"

"Look at me."

"I've been an ER nurse for years. How could I just freeze?"

"Sheila." He called her name again. "No."

A nurse moved into the room. Ben slowly released her but grasped her hand. The nurse handed Sheila a tissue.

Sheila motioned to the nurse. "Ben, this is Natalie. Natalie, this is the infamous Uncle Ben."

Natalie smiled, the corners of her mouth melancholy, then turned her attention to Tommy. She took his pulse. She removed the blood pressure cuff from the wall mount and wrapped it around his heavily bruised arm.

"Where's Timmy?"

"Suzanne heard. She came blazing from next door. She thought it best he stay with her until I knew more." Her words didn't seem to register that the child was unharmed. "Ben, he's all right. Really. He was in the Explorer in his car seat."

Ben nodded, yet felt fragmented. He wanted to be there for Tommy, yet he ached to embrace Timmy. Sheila inhaled deeply. "The x-rays show he's got a broken arm, fractured ribs, and a broken leg. Our major concern is that of an epidural hematoma."

Ben gaped at her, moving his fingers across the back of her hand.

Sheila explained. "Bleeding within the skull. The blunt force trauma has caused significant swelling of the brain. Surgery is imminent."

All Ben could manage was a weak nod. The nurse approached them. "Dr. Troy is on his way to the ER. And, you know, we're all praying."

Ben looked to the left, then the right, then to his feet. His chest tightened as he attempted to fill his lungs with the air that only seemed to burn. Ben's legs grew unsteady beneath him.

"Sir?" Natalie eyed Ben. "Here, why don't you have a seat?"

"I'm fine." Ben knelt beside the bed and rested his elbows where the child lay. He touched the uninjured side of Tommy's face.

Nurse Natalie patted Sheila's arm as she departed.

"You listen to me, little man. Uncle Ben's right here. I'm not leaving until we walk out of here. Together."

A tall man appeared in the doorway. He caressed Sheila's shoulders. "Dr. Troy. Thank you for coming on your day off."

"I insisted." He moved beside Tommy's bed, perused the chart, replaced it, then extended a hand to Ben. "I'm Dr. Evan Troy."

Ben stood. "Ben Powers."

"Tommy is a remarkably strong boy."

Sheila bit her lip. "Always has been. There were two inside me, but I always knew when Tommy kicked because it was fierce, like he was proving in utero that he was the strongest."

Dr. Troy smiled, Sheila's memory seemingly created affection inside him. "Tommy's GCS screen revealed a score above twelve. That's a strong indicator the brain injury is serious, but not severe."

Sheila nodded, her lips tight. "That's real good."

Dr. Troy centered on Ben. "The CT scan delineated a epidural hematoma—a mass lesion of bleeding on the brain. Sheila can confirm that surgery is the most effective manner to deal with the bleed and decrease the intracranial pressure."

Sheila nodded, her eyes fixed on her son. "You'll take him soon?"

"In just a few minutes."

"Ben, do you have any questions?"

The questions were strung like terrorizing beads in his mind. He refused to belay Tommy's healing with immaterial queries. "No."

"Who's assisting?" Sheila probed.

"Matthews and Gransfeldt."

"Good. Real good. Their skills are impeccable."

"The surgery is scheduled to take about six hours. We'll come out in intervals to keep you updated." He touched Sheila's shoulder. "Is there anything else you need before I go?"

Sheila choked a sob. "Take care of him."

Dr. Troy pulled her into his arms. The doctor's manner of embrace lingered, seeming to test his will of professional restraint. After a few moments, Sheila pulled away, chagrin tugging at her countenance.

Troy opened the door. "I'll see you soon."

After the door shut, Ben extended his hand to Sheila. "He will pull through this."

Sheila grasped it. "He arrived fighting to be first outside of my womb, didn't he?"

Ben nodded, the twin's entrance to the world flashing across his mind. "It's comforting to know the man operating on our boy cares."

"Yeah." Sheila dabbed at her nose then glanced above his head. A look of horror contorted her features. Ben followed her gaze to the mounted TV.

The bottom of the screen held a brash yellow caption: Ben Powers' toddler cousin victim of DUI. A female reporter stood outside of Mercy's ER doors. Sheila reached for the remote settled beside the cotton swabs and throat dispensers and smashed the volume button.

"…near dawn. Sources state the boy is currently being prepped for surgery, although the severity of his injuries are unknown. Police report the vehicle driven by the intoxicated man had impacted at fifty miles an hour."

The screen split and a male anchor in the studio solemnly asked, "Do we have any word on the mother?"

"Well, that is the good news, Larry. According to police, she and the child's twin brother were unharmed."

"Indeed. Is there any indication Ben Powers has been notified?"

"Yes."

Ben exhaled and looked to Sheila. Sheila glanced at him then back at the screen. The reporter continued, "He arrived at the hospital shortly after the child was transported by ambulance."

"Well, our hearts go out to him and his family. Thank you, Kathy, for your report."

Ben punched off the power. "If I had known my being here—"

"It's been so long, but I think we should pray."

"Pray?"

"Yeah."

"What do we say?"

She shrugged. "I guess what we want God to do."

Ben's gaze lingered over the injured child before shut his eyes. "God. I don't … why? He has a lifetime ahead of him."

Images of Tommy breaking tackles, dunking championship baskets, standing beside his bride on the church altar, phoning Ben to inform him of the birth of his first child all raced through his mind.

"We haven't had time to teach him. We want to see him grow to be a man."

Sheila's sobs created an erratic swell of her chest. "Don't take that from us, God. He's just … four. Cause him to wake up and thrive."

A team of medical personnel entered the room. The cousins held hands as the gurney wheeled toward the elevator doors. Sheila bent to kiss her son. "See you soon, baby."

Several seconds after the doors shut, Ben still stood as if bolted to the floor. Sheila lightly touched his shoulder. Two policemen appeared around the corner and approached.

"Greg and Jerry, this is my cousin, Ben."

The officers nodded, somber and composed. "Sir. Sheila, we're so sorry. We were on patrol a few miles away, heard the 10–53, and came right over."

Sheila tugged the bottom of her sweat jacket. "I appreciate that, guys. He's just headed to surgery."

"Dr. Troy's the surgeon?" Greg, the dark-haired officer, asked.

"Came in on his day off."

Jerry, his red hair cropped close to his head, certified. "He's the best in this region."

"Yeah." Sheila's voice tightened around a haggard edge.

"Listen," the dark-haired cop motioned toward the door marked exit, "we can escort you upstairs to the private waiting area and hang out until the assigned blues arrive."

The officers led them up three flights to a concealed lounge.

Sheila crossed the threshold to the buttercream walls and uncomplicated furnishings. The younger officer asked, "Is there anything else we can do?"

Sheila probed. "Where is he?"

The young one frowned, failing to catch Sheila's query. The older one responded, "He's been booked and is now sulking in a holding tank at the jack."

Ben looked to Sheila. She answered, "Juvenile Hall."

"His alcohol level was above .15."

Sheila sighed. "The state limit is .08. What was it? A night binge of liquid death to his brain cells?"

"It seems. But he's shut as tight as a clam. Refusing to speak until his attorney arrives."

Sheila detected something in the older officer's eye. "What aren't you telling me?"

He looked to his younger partner then back to Sheila. "You've got enough to deal with."

Sheila stepped to Greg, her hands on hips. "It'd be a shame to add blue canary to all that I have to deal with. So, you might as well start talking."

Officer Greg sighed, chomping his gum. He rolled his shoulders. "He's lilywhite. No record. But the blues at the scene found fifteen K in a briefcase on the passenger seat."

Sheila cocked her head. "No way he made that pulling the nightshift at Wendy's."

"Not likely."

"I appreciate you sharing that. Keep me posted."

The rain slammed against the window, mirroring their anger and provocation. Ben held her in the austere room as they submitted to the forlorn wait.

Dozens of aircraft awaited clearance as the ominous clouds saturated the tarmac. She sank deeper into the unyielding chair in the gate area and sipped her Starbucks chai latte. She inhaled the luscious aroma and took another delicate sip. Juliana had headed to the airport early this morning. She felt her heart dip when the rental car shuttle halted at the airport entrance and her call to Ben was routed to voicemail.

Annoyed, she checked in at the ticket counter, crawled through security, and commandeered a seat near the window in the boarding area. The gathering beneath the terminal TV swelled. A college-age male dressed in low-rise jeans and an untucked Versace shirt seated to her left stated, "That's busted."

Juliana politely asked, "Are you referring to the TV?"

"Some drunk hit a little kid."

Juliana looked at the gathering horde then back at the youth. "Why the crowd?"

"He's related to that actor." The man snapped his fingers. "He's portrayed nearly everything."

"That doesn't narrow it for me."

He popped his fingers. "He was voted sexiest man alive over and over."

She straightened in her chair. "Benjamin Powers?"

"Right!" The man grinned at her recognition. "The truck hit him going over fifty."

The cup in her hand toppled, making a steaming stain on the carpet. She deposited the remainder in the nearby trash, shifted her purse strap on her shoulder, and her laptop carrying case on the other. She shoved her slender body through the crowd.

"…hospital sources state the boy has just entered surgery to repair numerous broken bones and diminish the swelling in his brain. His condition is critical."

The anchor stared gravely into the camera. "Powers and his family must be beside themselves. Thank you for keeping us updated, Kathy."

"What hospital!" Juliana screamed at the screen. The crowd eyed her curiously.

"Mercy." A man to her right grunted. "Why? You next of kin?"

Juliana sprinted to the airport entrance and seized a taxi. She blurted her destination to the driver. "Get me there in less than thirty minutes and I'll double your tip."

As the driver sped toward Mercy, Juliana tried Ben's cell number in dizzying succession. Juliana finally left a message that she hadn't returned to Denver and was headed to the hospital. When the taxi screeched to a halt outside the ER entrance, Juliana moaned.

The driver announced, "Looks like if you didn't arrive by ambulance, you aren't getting in."

She paid the fare and tipped him as promised. The crowd was corralled behind police tape, sheltered beneath umbrellas or rain gear. She fumbled through her bag for her press badge. At least it would provide entrance into the hospital lobby. She pressed her way through the throng singing nursery rhymes, carrying signs of "We're praying, Ben!", and clutching teddy bears. She held out her press badge. The policeman shook his head and walked away.

"Wait! I'm a journalist from *Core Magazine.*"

He faced her. "No media is allowed beyond this point, lady. I don't care where you work." He nodded to the rear of crowd. "You and your crew can set up on the perimeter."

Juliana moved toward the back of the crowd, her silk dress inadequate protection from the hard rain. To her left were several news groups feeding live shots of the scene across the country. To her right were dozens of LAPD squad cars blocking any access near the hospital. Juliana tapped her right foot and demanded her brain develop a swift resolution.

"Yes!" She dialed the number.

"Margo Bennett."

"Ms. Bennett. This is Juliana DeLauer. Ben gave me your number as a way to contact him."

"How may I help you?"

"Listen, I'm standing outside of Mercy now. Security is fierce. I've attempted his cell phone, but he's not answering. Please inform him I did not return to Denver. I'll wait outside Mercy until I hear from him."

"Certainly, Miss DeLauer."

"Thank you."

As Juliana disconnected, she tugged at the drenched material of her dress. She shut her eyes and pleaded with God to heal the wounded child, her fervent whispers bombarding heaven.

Margo raced to the production office conference room. Eternity sat at the head of the wood table, the same hue and gloss of espresso, conducting a meeting. Margo whispered the tragedy into her boss's ear.

Eternity stared incredulously at the *Purpose Films* assistant. She quickly excused herself and led Margo into her office.

Eternity shut the door, but neither woman took a seat.

"It's imperative you follow my instructions."

"Yes."

Eternity gathered her purse and leopard patterned trench. "Finish up the meeting in the conference room, then postpone my engagements for the remainder of the day."

"Yes."

"Contact the film's director, Meyer, in Vancouver and inform him of the accident. Initial shooting begins tomorrow. Ben won't be there."

"Right."

Eternity's hand was on the door handle when Margo informed, "Oh, and Miss DeLauer requested Ben contact her."

"Who?"

"Juliana DeLauer. The woman he met while filming *Slow Bullet*."

Eternity's eyes flashed. "Under no circumstances are you to inform Ben about that. Allow me. The less distractions, the better."

The twenty-one-year-old assistant realized Eternity had no intention of updating Ben. Margo didn't argue. She enjoyed the lavish perks and steady paycheck too much.

Eternity headed through the door and removed her cell phone. The local assistant director in charge of the F.B.I. answered on the second ring.

"Dad, I need a favor."

The crowd had grown. Police had set up security checkpoints at the hospital's street perimeters. Unless you were bleeding on a gurney, all vehicles were diverted to other hospitals within twenty miles.

Juliana wished she hadn't packed her jacket. The rain pelted against the bare skin of her face and legs. She fingered the dampened hair from her face and glanced at her Movado. 9:45.

Suddenly, the pain surged from her lower abdomen. She leaned against a squad car and inhaled through her nose. After a few arduous moments, she straightened her back. She vowed once this ordeal had passed, she would make an appointment with Dr. Martin. Stress increased the frequency and intensity of her habitual ache. The marked increase of pain wasn't something to be ignored.

As she raised her head, a dark car halted at the entrance. A breathtaking, dark-haired woman in a leopard-patterned trench exited. As she raced through the doors the crowd cheered, "We love you, Eternity!"

Suddenly, her cell phone beeped. Low battery. Juliana raised her fists then slammed them against her sides. Her charger was packed inside her suitcase, merrily situated inside the belly of the 767 headed for Denver.

She brushed the drenched hair from her face and squinted beyond the devoted crowd to every visible entrance. Her steps led her to the back of the crowd, to the far right, where she waited. She studied the officer's frequency of radio communication. A change of the guard had to be forthcoming.

An hour passed.

She bent at the waist from another stab of pain and the rain smacked the back of her neck. She hadn't worn a scarf. In the L.A. heat, it felt like a clammy noose. Her hand covered the nape of her neck. Slowly, she stood squinting at the hospital entrance, every movement laced with agony.

Now five officers patrolled the barrier. The younger, freckled one, his red hair plastered to his neck, eyed her with the suspicion possibly given to a terrorist. She released the grip on her belly and her cell phone sang its familiar melody. "Hello."

"Jules!"

She closed her eyes. "T..."

"Are you at the airport?"

"Not since I heard the news."

"Oh, it's just awful. How is Ben?"

"I'd imagine utterly despondent."

"You're not with him?"

"No. I'm standing outside the hospital. I've called his assistant and asked her to forward my message but haven't heard anything."

"Oh, Jules. It's raining like crazy there. You must be drenched. Did you show your press badge?"

"To no avail."

"Did you try his cell phone?"

"More times than I can count. No answer."

"What's that beeping?"

"My phone. Very low battery. I packed my charger in my suitcase."

"What can I do?"

"Pray. Often."

"Is there anyone here I can call? Any contacts?"

Juliana slammed her hand against her forehead. "Yes! Thomas. He interviewed Ben while he was in Denver. I'm sure he has Ben's agent or publicist's numbers."

Juliana disconnected with Tricia then redialed Ben's assistant's number. It connected to her voicemail. Again, her phone alerted of its diminishing charge. She noticed some of the residents headed to the coffee shop adjacent to the hospital. Juliana followed, the leather of her Jimmy Choo sandals squeaking against their forced drowning.

As she suspected, the place had a TV locked to the frightful situation. Juliana took a seat at the sprawling bar near the picture window facing the hospital entrance. It offered a decent vantage point. Her phone chimed. The display read "Restricted I.D."

"Ben?"

"Good morning! This is Ralph with Superior Mortgage. How are you today?"

Juliana slammed her hand on the counter. "You have got to be kidding."

"No, ma'am."

"This is not a good time."

"Oh, I'm sorry to hear that. When is a better time?"

She resisted the urge to scream *never*. "Later."

"Later as in this evening or—"

"I'm awaiting an urgent call."

"Very well. How about if I call you back this time tomorrow? How does that sound?"

Juliana disconnected and her phone rang again.

"You must be half out of your mind."

"Thomas. I'm so glad Tricia was able to reach you."

"Still no word from Ben?"

Juliana felt the hot sting of tears against her eyelids. "He isn't answering his cell phone. I've called his assistant, but so far nothing."

Thomas paused as if suddenly distracted then asked, "Where are you?"

"In a coffee house facing the hospital."

A collective gasp rocked the shop. Juliana turned her focus to the crowd near the TV screen.

"Juliana? Are you still there?"

"Hold on. Something's happened."

"Juliana, don't look."

She ignored him. The same reporter brushed rain from her cheeks and squinted against the biting wind. The patrons reacted.

"My God."

"Oh, how sad!"

"He was so young!"

"It can't be true."

"Sssh!"

The reporter steeled her shoulders and said, "This, I repeat, has not been confirmed by any hospital personnel."

Juliana stood from the barstool.

Thomas beckoned, "Palesa, are you still with me?"

The reporter continued, "Again, we are waiting for official word that Ben Powers' four-year-old cousin did not make it through surgery."

The breath escaped her lungs and Juliana did nothing to assist its return. The room swayed. The phone chimed a cycle of beeps, its demise near.

"Listen to me," Thomas pleaded. "I confirmed our interview with his manager, Grace Connors. I'll call you back shortly. Do not leave the coffee shop."

Her grip lessened on her phone. "My phone—the battery—is very close to—"

"What's the name of the place?"

Juliana looked around until her eyes fell on a menu. "Beginnings."

"I'll call you back directly."

"Tommy has wavy hair."

"Pardon?"

"Tommy. He has wavy hair. Timmy's hair is straighter. Like Ben's."

"Juliana, listen to me. God still works miracles. Do not give up."

Her phone chimed and automatically reverted to shut-off mode. Juliana returned to her seat and hid her face in her hands. Before long, she crumbled on the counter.

"Please, God. You are faithful and merciful. Let it be a lie."

CHAPTER FOURTEEN

"Baby." Eternity leaned forward and squeezed his hand.

Ben was far beyond the room, the hospital, and the planet. Sheila collapsed in Dr. Troy's arms.

"Ben, baby, look at me." Eternity's voice seemed baseless like the hollow of a tunnel.

Ben hesitated. "His heart stopped."

Sheila reached out for Ben; he met her in two steps. She gripped him and sobbed against his neck. Ben had no idea of the duration of their embrace.

"We did everything," Dr. Troy stated. "It's usually not standard practice, but the entire operating room arena erupted in a roar when he recovered." Dr. Troy's relief was substantial.

Sheila reluctantly pulled from Ben and smiled through tears. "Our baby pulled through!"

Eternity wrapped an arm through his. "I think Ben may very well be in shock."

Dr. Troy nodded, still in his operating room gear. "He is a remarkable boy. The swelling in his brain has already begun to decrease."

"What happens now?" Ben asked, his questions no longer a threat to Tommy's wellbeing.

"He'll be moved to recovery where we'll observe him for the next few hours. By midnight, he should be ready to be moved to I.C.U."

"Tommy is really doing well? You're not simply saying that, are you?" Ben asked.

The surgeon shook his head and smiled assuredly at Ben. "Not at all. He has to be one of the strongest kids I've seen. We will keep a tight watch on him for the next seventy-two hours, but I feel very good about his recovery."

"When can we see him?" Ben questioned.

Dr. Troy looked to Sheila and back to Ben. "Once he's out of recovery. I'll personally escort you. Please feel free to use my office for any of your needs."

Sheila thanked the doctor, who swept a hand across her cheek then disappeared down the hall. "We'd better call Idaho and Illinois. It's no telling what the media has reported since this morning."

Ben reached into his pocket feeling only his wallet. "I must have forgotten my phone at home."

Sheila turned toward the door. "Follow me."

Ben unraveled his arm from Eternity's. A glint of reproach crossed her gaze, but she swiftly recovered. Sheila informed the officers flanking the door they were on the move. They followed, seemingly accustomed to her directness. On their way to the doctor's office, a nurse positioned behind the nurse's station called to Sheila.

Ben stopped and looked to Eternity. "I appreciate you coming."

"There is no need to thank me. What a relief to know the surgery was a success."

"Relief multiplied by infinity."

She closed the space between them. "I'll stay as long as you need, Ben."

Those eyes, which once assured him every need he could ever conjure would be met without hesitancy, locked on him. Juliana's face flashed before him.

"Oh man."

She touched his arm. "What is it, baby?"

"I need a phone."

She removed a sleek number from her bag. "Use mine."

Ben hesitated. Sheila approached with a hand full of pink slips. "People have been attempting to reach us, Uncle Ben." She shuffled through the slips. "Grace Connors called several times."

"My cell must be inundated."

Sheila stuffed the notes in her pocket. "Call Crater first."

He rubbed his chin and realized none were from Juliana. "Right."

"Someone from the hospital leaked that Tommy's heart stopped beating."

"So they all think Tommy died?"

"The report was never confirmed, but the speculation must be drilling holes in their guts."

Sheila escorted the officers, Ben, and Eternity near the end of the hall into the immaculate office of Dr. Troy where they phoned loved ones relieving their anxiety. "I'll go pick up Timmy, get him dinner, and keep him with me."

Sheila raised an eyebrow. "That sounds like you're not showing up on set in Vancouver tomorrow?"

"Sheila. I'm not leaving L.A. until I'm assured Tommy is out of danger."

Sheila looked to Eternity, who shrugged. "He would be a wreck on the set anyway. Ben, I'll deal with the director."

"Thank you." Ben reached for Dr. Troy's desk phone. Grace answered on the first ring.

"It's Ben."

"I've been trying to reach you all day."

"Tommy is very much alive. The swelling has begun to decrease. Dr. Troy is incredible."

Sheila nudged him. "I think God helped just a little."

"Correction. Sheila states Tommy had divine intervention."

Grace sighed. "I was completely unglued. How is Sheila?"

"Marvelous. Glowing. Deliriously grateful."

"No way not to be."

"The doctor's are concerned about the next seventy-two hours, but his outlook is promising."

"Do you need anything?"

"Uh … yes." His voice trailed off.

Eternity smiled, those emerald eyes trained on him as if he were a mislaid treasure.

"Juliana?" Grace answered.

A rush of gratitude hit him from the crown of his head to the soles of his feet. "You deserve a raise. No matter the amount."

"That's just emotion speaking, but remember my phone records every conversation. Her editor called and said she never left L.A. Once she heard about the little guy, she left the airport and headed straight to Mercy."

Ben straightened. "Really?"

"The news crews have convened outside in record numbers. Apparently, she was blocked at every turn. Last Thomas heard she was at the coffee shop nearby. Beginnings. I drove there, searched, but she wasn't there. The wait staff said she stumbled out in the rain an hour before I arrived. She told Thomas her cell battery was dying. I tried but was immediately shuffled to voicemail."

Ben glanced at his Tag Heuer and calculated she had been dealing with the tragic ordeal, alone, for eight hours. "Again, thank you, Grace."

"If she calls me, where can I tell her to reach you?"

He recited Sheila's cell number before he affirmed it was in her possession.

Grace asked, "Do you need me to contact your director and producers?"

"No. Eternity assured me she'd speak to them."

"I see." A sense of curiosity edged her tone. "What else?"

"For the moment, that's it. Thanks, Grace."

"Not at all. Stop wasting time and go find Juliana."

As Ben disconnected the call, he noticed the sky was an eerie canopy that rammed stiff droplets against the window.

Eternity stretched. Ben's mind reversed to those lingering moments in the dawn when neither of them had any particular place to be.

Eternity surmised, "From the sounds of that call it seems as if you're headed somewhere."

Sheila answered, "Ben, I need you to get Timmy from the sitter's and bring him home with you. Spoil him rotten—do whatever is necessary to divert this nightmare from his mind."

"Will you be all right?"

Her hazel eyes flashed, as if he hadn't taken the cue, but spoke coolly.

"All there is left to do is wait. Now that things have calmed, I'll snooze over there on that swanky couch."

Eternity addressed Ben, "Do I have your solemn word you'll call me if Tommy's condition changes?"

"You do."

"Very well." She traced the length of his chin. "I'll see you first thing in the morning."

Once she exited, Sheila tossed him her cell phone. "Get a move on."

"How far is Beginnings from here?"

"Right across the street. Why?"

"Juliana's been here the whole time."

Sheila's eyes widened. "No kidding."

Ben stood and overwrought muscles protested. "I thought that was why you gave me an excuse to leave."

"Eternity was creeping me out. But this is better. Much better."

"Juliana has no idea if the rumor is true."

"Then why are you still standing there?"

"After I get Timmy, I can bring dinner back for you."

"I'm fine. The cafeteria serves light meals around the clock. Besides, I think you'll have your hands full explaining why you didn't try to reach her."

"Are you sure you'll be all right?"

"I'll stay in here—holed up in this paradise. There's the couch and a private bathroom. I want my face to be the first one Tommy sees when he awakens."

"Call if anything changes."

She kissed his cheek and shoved him toward the door. "Go!"

Ben nearly jumped down the sets of stairs to the lobby. Once he reached the ground floor, he grimaced. He couldn't leave through those doors without alerting an onslaught of attention. He sprinted up the three flights and stopped at the nurses' station.

"Yes, Mr. Powers?"

"I need a quick exit. Unseen."

"Follow me."

Juliana shivered in the back of the taxi. Her clothing clung as if slathered by adhesive.

"Lady, I ain't got all night!"

The harsh rain diminished a lucid view of the residential streets. She had no idea how much acreage the community of Woodland Hills covered.

"I'm sorry. I only visited once."

"Can you call?"

"There was an emergency. No one's home." She hated that she hadn't paid closer attention days ago when she first visited.

He slammed on the brakes and shoved the transmission in park. "I know it's raining and it's obvious you have no idea where this house is. But I can't keep circling. Where else can I take you?"

Juliana slumped against the seat. When they had arrived at the subdivision security gate, remarkably it stood open. Juliana was clueless as to how the malfunction occurred but had praised Jesus anyhow. Now, it seemed the tiny marvel was performed in vain.

"Take me to the nearest hotel."

He grumbled and shoved the cab into drive. She shut her eyes and prayed for another miracle that would somehow lead her to Ben.

She gasped when the car lurched, plowing her head into the plastic partition.

Through the hammering rain, a voice cried, "Salty, no!"

Juliana rubbed the bump on her forehead. "What happened?"

"A dog just ran out right in front of me." The cabbie grunted.

"Bad boy, Salty!"

Juliana witnessed a frantic figure stoop to retrieve a dog so drenched its fur looked pink.

The cabbie wound down the window. "I almost hit him!"

"I'm so sorry. He never does that. I opened the front door to bring in some potted flowers, and he darted out."

Juliana flung the door open and raced to the dog's owner. "Suzanne?"

The woman wiped the downpour from her eyes and squinted. "Who are you?"

"Juliana. I'm a friend of Ben's."

She considered Juliana head-to-toe. "I don't know who you're talking about."

The cabbie blew his horn and both women jumped. The Bichon growled. "I need to get paid!"

Juliana reached into the back seat for her purse. She handed him a wad of bills, then retrieved her laptop. "Thank you."

The driver wound up the window and sped down the empty street. Juliana tipped behind the woman, the leather of her three-inch heels soaked and cutting into her flesh. "Suzanne. Wait!"

The woman hastened her sneakered stride.

"I've tried to contact them all day, but Ben isn't answering and I couldn't remember Sheila's address."

The woman reached her front door and flung it open. "I'll call the police."

"Please! Can you at least tell me if it was Tommy or Timmy?"

Suzanne halted, faced Juliana, and glared. "How did you know their names? The news hasn't released their names."

"I k-nn-now B-en." Juliana's shivering became violent. The dog squirmed in Suzanne's arms and whimpered. "Please. All I want to know is if he's all right."

The woman slammed the door. Juliana dropped her head. As she turned to return to the pouring rain, the door opened and the porch light flipped on. Juliana squinted at the harsh illumination. Suzanne stepped onto the porch and held a magazine next to Juliana's face. Salty whipped circles around Juliana's feet.

"Sit!" She commanded Salty. "Do you have any I.D.?"

Juliana sniffled, pulled out her wallet, and handed it to the woman. Suzanne inspected the photo as if Juliana was requesting admittance to the Pentagon and returned it.

"Come in."

Juliana nearly wept. "Thank you."

"I cannot be too careful. Ben is crazed about their privacy. You have no idea how many reporters have come by looking for Sheila. Until today, no one had any idea Ben was even connected to that precious family. I imagine some hospital staffer tattled that he had arrived looking for Tommy."

"Tommy…" Juliana whispered.

"How long have you been out in this storm?"

"Sss-ince it began. Security at the hospital was un-bbbe-lievable."

Suzanne rushed off again. Juliana leaned into the warmth of the cushy pillows adorning the sofa and wrapped her arms around her middle. She listened as the rain thumped against the eaves and gutters; the tempo pleasant now that she was sheltered from its deluge.

Suzanne returned with a steaming cup, towel, and a thick blanket. She adjusted the covering around Juliana. Salty rested at Juliana's saturated feet. "Ttt-hank you."

"Drink. You'll end up in that hospital with Tommy if you're not careful."

"So, he's not…"

"See what happens when there's a news frenzy? No one takes the time to stop and check the facts anymore. What's most important is being the first to blab. Edward R. Murrow, Walter Cronkite, Ed Bradley, now those men checked facts before they went spouting off at the mouth."

"Tommy?"

"Oh, right. Sorry. It just gets me so fired up. He's recovering even as we speak. They think he can be moved to I.C.U. in a few hours." She reiterated the morning's events and the extent of Tommy's injuries. "Someone from the hospital called the news. It was probably the same ninny who leaked that Ben had come to see about Tommy. They snitched that Tommy's heart had stopped during his six-hour operation. Can you just imagine that dear soul under the knife for that long?"

"Sss-oo the doctors expect a fff-ull recovery?"

"Well, the next few days are critical. But they are all amazed at his resilience. Children always are, you know? They bounce right back. It took me months to recover when my hip was replaced. If only George had been here. George was my late husband. He was a scriptwriter for MGM until he retired six years ago. The poor soul just went to bed one night and never woke up. It was very peaceful. He even had a smile on his face."

"Thank you, God." Juliana closed her eyes and the tears painted warm streaks on her chilled cheeks.

"I suppose that is a blessing—to simply just slip away in your sleep. That's how I'd like to go when it's time. Just lie down and—"

"Juliana?" a small voice called. She shot up. Timmy rubbed his eyes and waddled toward her in his footed pajamas. He climbed on her lap and snuggled against her chest. Juliana buried her face in his bone-straight hair and wept, careful not to press him against her dampened clothes. Suzanne removed the cup from Juliana's hand and placed it on the table in front of her.

Timmy raised his head. "Why are you at Miss Suzanne's?"

"I came to see about you."

"Tommy got hurt."

She nodded slowly. "I know. But the doctors are taking extra special care of him."

"When's Mommy coming home?"

Juliana looked to Suzanne. Suzanne's voice altered to a soft lilt. "Real soon, honey. She wants to be there for Tommy when he wakes up."

"Can Juliana stay?"

"I'm sure she'll stay as long as you need. As long as the day is long and as long as the sky is wide."

He snuggled beneath Juliana's chin and she rocked him, the motion also soothing her nerves.

"If it's okay, we'll just stay here. I'm afraid he'll wake up if we move."

"Certainly, dear."

Juliana closed her eyes and felt the enormity of the day drain from her body inch-by-inch.

"Oh, I forgot to tell you. Ben's on his way."

Suzanne leaned closer and realized Juliana had drifted off. She patted the pair and switched off the tableside lamp.

Ben ordered a black coffee and pretended to search for a seat. He paced the length of the place twice, but Juliana was nowhere in sight. He pulled the Lakers cap lower and sipped at the scalding liquid.

"What a trooper!"

"They say the swelling is still there, but it's starting to come down."

"What a fluke. The poor kid is headed out for pancakes and this happens."

"Poor little guy has a 70% chance to fully recover."

"The driver's blood alcohol screen came back. Well over the legal limit. Dude must have been drinking for twenty-four hours straight."

Ben eyed the group adorned in hospital scrubs consuming their dinners. "Not to change the subject, but did you get a look at Eternity Alise?"

One of men emitted a low whistle. "My god! I never would have let that one go. For her, no amount of begging would have crossed the line as unreasonable."

"*You* never would have been given a chance."

Ben pulled the windbreaker tighter and headed into the storm. He dashed to his vehicle and maneuvered the five miles to Suzanne's. He rubbed his eyes attempting to relieve the dull pounding beneath them. Fatigue pulled at him, but he wouldn't unwind until he found Juliana.

As Ben had searched for her at Beginnings, he looked up and phoned every hotel near the airport and hospital on Sheila's iPhone. None had her registered.

He pulled up Suzanne's drive and parked. The wind bit through the flimsy windbreaker. Salty whimpered longingly at his approach. He shut the door against the forceful wind. Salty performed several circles for Ben's approval; he squatted and rubbed the dog's ears.

"Oh, my," Suzanne gasped.

"I know. The moustache is pathetic and the wig has definitely seen better days."

"You remind me Charlie Chaplin. Except you have a few blond strands poking out. Did you ever see a Chaplin film?"

"Not that I can recall."

"Oh, if you had you never would have forgotten. He was a genius. George used to say that all the time. He'd say, 'SuzSweet,' that's what he used to call me. He'd say. 'Chaplin has more talent in his pinkie than most have in their whole body.'" She paused to pat the ivory ruffles on her bathrobe. "Where are my manners? Can I get you anything to eat?"

It occurred to him he hadn't eaten since that morning. "No. Thank you. I'm just going to head home with Timmy."

"You be careful. That storm is vicious. It's expected to dump all night."

The throbbing in Ben's head increased. He stood and rubbed his temples. "Suzanne, I cannot tell you how much I appreciate you stepping in for us. I don't know what we would have done."

She flipped her hand at him. "Nonsense. I adore those little angels. I can't tell you how many times Sheila has stepped in for me when I had a doctor's appointment or had to grab some things from the grocer. They have been such a godsend. I'm so glad you picked this neighborhood."

He yawned. "Excuse me."

"Listen to me rambling. They're right over there."

He stared at her. "They?"

"Yes. Timmy and that pretty woman you've been photographed with."

Suzanne pointed to the sofa to his right. Ben crossed the ample room in seconds. He stared at the sleeping figures covered by a plush blanket then knelt—a smile bursting across his face.

"Juliana." He gently touched her cheek. Salty joined Ben and tapped his front paws on the blanket.

"Juliana." Ben called once more. She snorted, and Ben didn't think he'd ever heard anything so magnificent. She slowly opened her eyes and analyzed him.

"I've been looking for you, I think."

Ben removed the hat, wig, and moustache. "All day I've heard."

"I called your cell."

"In the rush, I left it at home."

"They wouldn't allow me beyond the perimeter."

"If I had known, I would have come to you."

She yawned. "I'm sure your mind was on overload. Are you taking Timmy home with you?"

"That's the plan, but not just him."

She smiled lazily. "I was thinking that due to the chaos of the day, it might be better if you two slept in his house, surrounded by smells and sounds most familiar."

"I adore how you think, Juliana DeLauer. But you're missing part of the equation."

"What?"

He leaned closer. "You."

Before seven, Juliana showered, borrowed a pair of Sheila's jeans and a t-shirt, and headed to the kitchen. To her surprise, Ben and Timmy were happily munching pancakes at the table.

"Wow!" She grinned and wished she kept more than eyeliner, mascara, and lip gloss in her purse. The storm had tightened her curls, and she felt like her head resembled a wooly mop. She had tugged and pulled, pulled and tugged to cover the dark patches on her neck. In the center of the table sat a carafe of coffee, sliced melon, and wheat toast.

"Juliana, Mommy said Tommy is getting better."

"Oh, sweetie, that is the best news I could have received this morning."

She joined them at the table. Ben filled her cup with steaming coffee. "How did you sleep?"

"Fretfully."

"Me, too. And Timmy's right hook did not help."

She grinned at the toddler clad in footed pajamas.

"Tommy's vitals have improved remarkably."

"Has he regained consciousness?"

"Not yet. Yet every passing hour becomes a demonstration of his strength." Ben's thoughtful gaze was interrupted by Timmy's attempt to shovel a forkful of pancake into his mouth. "Timmy, I think we should open our own pancake house."

"Yep." The toddler chomped merrily.

Juliana sipped her coffee and drank in the glorious scene. The thought had hit her last night and she informed Ben. She had two weeks' vacation and personal days on record. If necessary, she could research any material from her laptop and write while Timmy napped.

"Juliana has offered to stay with us this week."

"Yeah!" Timmy cheered.

Ben grinned and took another bite. In between chews, he managed, "She'll take care of you when Mommy or me are at the hospital with Tommy."

"Can we go to Disneyland?"

"Sure." Juliana nodded.

"And Legoland?"

Ben playfully grabbed the boy's shoulders. "That's in San Diego."

The child shoveled a mound of pancakes into his tiny mouth. "Yep."

Juliana laughed and shrugged. "What else have we to do, right, little guy?"

He nodded gleefully. After the plates were empty, Timmy rushed to the den to play on his Leap Pad. Ben cleared the dishes from the table; Juliana placed them in the dishwasher.

He leaned and nudged her shoulder. "You are remarkable."

"Stop it."

"You take a week off to care for a woman and child you met just four days ago. And washed their dishes, twice."

She shut the dishwasher. "I'm honored that she trusts me to assist."

For a moment, she felt as if he desperately wanted to kiss her. He took her hand and brought it to his mouth instead. Her feet tingled.

He pulled her closer. "Do you trust me?"

Her palms felt as if they held an electric charge. Ben closed the diminutive space between them. "I want you to trust me, Juliana."

A bell chimed. Juliana looked around, but Ben turned her face back toward him. "Timmy and Sheila aren't the only ones who want you to stay in L.A. I'm asking you to become a greater part of my life, Juliana."

Again, the bell sounded. Timmy raced from the den sofa toward the front door.

Ben whispered in her ear, "Do you agree?"

"Uncle Ben! Come here! It's Auntie E!"

Both adults stared at one another in disbelief. Ben rushed from the kitchen to the living room where the four-year-old had parted the shades and was waving frantically out of the window.

Ben opened the front door. Eternity stepped over the threshold in a blaze of morning sun.

"Good morning." Eternity's skin was luminous as the sun beaming through the windows in Sheila's foyer.

Ben folded his arms across his chest. "I understood we were to meet at the hospital."

"I wanted to check on this little guy." Eternity ruffled Timmy's hair.

The toddler asked, "Is that your car? It looks fast."

Eternity's laugh resembled a song of inspiration that caressed cathedral ceilings. "It's very fast."

"Timmy, can you finish playing your game while I speak with Eternity?"

"Okay. Bye." Timmy dashed to the den.

"You don't appear happy to see me." The sides of her full lips turned to an alluring angle.

"Sheila's privacy has already been compromised. Your arrival won't help."

She stared at him, skeptically. "Surely, you're joking."

"Not even a little. Our connection to them is no longer private. I wish you had been more thoughtful."

She cocked her head. "I had no intention of upsetting either of you. I tried your Bel Air place first. Then I figured you probably slept over due to the storm."

Ben rubbed the scar above his brow—a distressing souvenir of fanatical photographers. "Juliana! Please, can you come here for a moment?"

Juliana peeked around the corner, wiping her hands on a dishtowel. Ben detected the slight stiffness in her stride. Ben wrapped a hand around her waist. "Eternity Alise, Juliana DeLauer. She's a family friend who decided to help us care for Timmy."

For a brief moment, Eternity's mesmerizing eyes glinted. Recovering, she held out her hand and flashed a smile that would have disarmed Castro. Juliana shook it firmly.

"Do you live in L.A.?"

"Denver."

Eternity's dark brows rose. "You traveled from Denver simply to care for Timmy? How noble."

"Caring for him is the very least I can do."

"Well." Eternity stepped toward the door. "Ben, I'll see you at the hospital. And Juliana, have a wonderful stay."

Eternity disappeared behind the door. Juliana and Ben stood in the foyer, staring at the door.

"Did you have an opportunity to check your voicemail yesterday?"

"I checked by remote access last night after I picked you two up from Suzanne's."

She looked at him. "Any messages from Margo?"

"One. She wanted me to know her thoughts were with me and to phone if I needed anything."

Juliana looked back to the door. "That's it?"

"Yes. Why?"

"I called very shortly after I arrived at Mercy. I asked her to tell you I was waiting outside."

The revelation of her words dropped in his mind like icicles pressured by the sun. Ben removed his hand from her waist and rubbed his chin. "What was her response?"

"I believe, and I quote, 'Certainly, Miss DeLauer.'" She twirled the dishtowel. "You know, Ben, my father had an infamous saying."

Ben recited, "People always tell you who they are. If only we would take the time to listen."

She tossed the towel over her shoulder and returned to the kitchen.

CHAPTER FIFTEEN

Ben and Bruce arrived at Tommy's I.C.U bedside cradling children's books, a breakfast burrito, and coffee.

"What did you do, buy a bookstore?" Sheila teased.

"Numerous studies report that those in a coma can hear everything taking place in their surroundings," Bruce answered.

Ben added, "I've decided to read him his favorites."

After Ben coaxed Sheila to eat the burrito, she moved to Tommy's side, rested her head on his bed, and slept.

Bruce placed a hand gently on Tommy's forehead and closed his eyes. "He's stronger than you know."

Ben stared at the disturbingly still toddler. "There's a long road ahead."

Bruce moved to the window. "He's not alone."

Ben whispered the beloved tales to Tommy. Eternity entered and stood beside Bruce at the window. Ben then rehearsed lines and pretended the child corrected him whenever his delivery was flat.

"You truly deserve to be a father someday, Benjamin."

He ceased his rehearsal, shot a look to Bruce, and gawked at her. "It's startling to hear those words from you."

Eternity looked to Tommy. "What you've done—how you've stepped in when Kevin rejected them is phenomenal."

"Kevin was a child himself in many ways."

She smoothed the surface of Tommy's books that Ben had placed at the foot of the bed. "Ben, how is it possible with all the pain and regret you've walked through that you can love so dangerously?"

Bruce moved to the door. "I'll just be outside."

Ben placed the script on the edge of the bed and walked her to the window, away from the slumbering pair. "What's going on?"

"I look at that little boy, helpless and broken, and it makes me realize how fragile we all are. A split second can change everything." She leaned against the tiled windowsill. "The choice to turn left instead of right. The decision to take the morning flight instead of the train could change it all."

Ben looked to Tommy. His heart ached for the boy's challenges. Tommy would require extensive physical and potential speech therapy. Four additional surgeries were scheduled to repair the damage to his face. No one could fully ascertain until he came out of the coma how much damage had occurred to his brain.

"I have never believed in coincidence."

"Neither have I. That attribute strongly drew me to you."

"Nothing happens to us without a purpose."

She leaned closer. "I agree."

"Although I'm not certain of the reason, there was a reason."

"But we are all in control of our destiny."

"I'm no longer convinced we are. There is the possibility something greater than myself may control everything."

"You sound like Joan."

He subdued the irritation that she hadn't caught his point and mocked his mother's convictions.

"If what you say is true, then it's all been pre-planned, which means we don't have a choice?"

"Correction. It is all about choice. Every decision is a choice. I'm beginning to wonder if by submitting control, we actually gain freedom."

"To the power of the universe?"

"To something other than ourselves."

"We are responsible for our lives. The power of life is within us, above us, and through us. It doesn't dictate the how, when, or why. Nor does it dictate that there is only one way we come to it. We do. In order to receive the immense possibilities from the universe, your consciousness must be awakened to spiritual truth."

"Yet, you had no desire to conceive."

She looked to Tommy. "There are scores of children who've either faced rejection or have been orphaned. It seemed superfluous and egocentric to have children of our own."

"You've never told me you felt that way."

She peered out the window. "I was terrified."

"Terrified? Why?"

"Because of..."

And it hit him. All Ben could do was gape at her, the revelation burning the recesses of his heart.

"It was too much for me, Ben. Just the *possibility* was too much."

"Why didn't you tell me this?"

She sighed deeply. "Because after all was said and done, it felt like I was judging you. You had no idea you were infected when you passed it on to me."

Ben quieted as she struggled to compose her confession. Shock seized his movement and speech. She placed her hands above her heart.

"You were reeling from Kevin's death, the twin's birth, and your diagnosis. I was a coward and it felt grotesque. Although I professed nerve, below it all, I didn't have the guts to face the actuality someday I might have to bury our children. Or that in their childhood, they would bury us."

Pale shadows crossed the room as dogged winds corralled opaque clouds; they stood in constricted silence, absorbing hidden truths.

She raised her head and searched his eyes. "I love you, but I just couldn't overcome. I was keeping you from your greatest passion. And I knew you wouldn't move toward your freedom if my actions weren't merciless."

"Medical science has greatly improved since the eighties. We may live to be a hundred."

She gripped his hand. "And, baby, we may not."

"Children now have a 25% chance of being healthy. Look at Tommy and Timmy. They're not infected."

"Kevin was HIV positive, Sheila isn't. Their chances are much greater because only one parent was positive."

Ben kept his voice low. "Everything could have been so different had you just told me." He shook his head. "I begged you to go to counseling."

"Yes."

"Eternity, I withheld nothing from you. It was you beside me when the doctor revealed I was HIV positive. It was you who bought scores of materials educating us on how to stay healthy, studied the best medications, and fought diligently to keep the industry from discovering."

Tears formed at the edges of her eyes. "Oh, Ben. You desperately wanted children. That wasn't my truth."

"We didn't have to end."

"Ben."

"Why now?"

"What?"

"What motive do you have to tell me, now?"

"Because when I look at Tommy lying helpless in that bed, it reminds me. It reminds me that could be our child, fighting desperately for his life, infected with a disease without a cure. And we are powerless to stop it."

Her cell phone beeped. She wiped her tears and sucked in a large breath. "It's Mitchell. I'm sorry. I have to take it." She walked to the door. "Mitchell, what's up?"

Ben returned his attention to the injured child. Her disclosure quaked far beyond regions of conjecture, pledge, and debate.

She sniffled. "I'm here at the hospital right now...oh, the kid is amazing. Ben is better. A little shaken, but better. How is the production? That is precisely what I want to hear. I suppose I could leave in the morning...I must have misunderstood you. I'll call you right back."

She clipped the phone shut and turned on her heels. Ben felt her gaze from across the room. Eternity's eyes narrowed. "May I speak to you outside for a moment?"

They exited the room where they met the puzzled gazes of Bruce and the police officer standing guard at the door.

Eternity walked a few paces down the hall to distance them. "You didn't tell me you fired Margo."

"Shortly after you visited Sheila's this morning."

"Why would you do that the first day of shooting?"

"Eternity, *Margo* is what you want to discuss after what you just revealed?"

She rubbed the back of her neck. "I'm trying to fathom your justification."

"Wow. Isn't that ironic?"

"What else do you want me to say? I can't go back and change it."

His eyes fixed on her until he summoned the courage to ask, "If you could, would you?"

Her concentration fixated on her Manolo Blahnik pumps. "I don't know. Perhaps."

"Who informed you of the accident?"

Her head shot up. "It was all over the news."

"Right. But who told *you?*"

"Why does that matter?"

"Because the same person who informed you of Tommy's accident was the same person I fired this morning."

She placed a hand on her slender hip. "What would possibly constitute her dismissal? She is an exemplary assistant."

"She failed to relay an urgent message."

Eternity tossed her hair. "Neither of us has the time or patience to hire a new assistant at this point. We are already delayed on principal shooting."

"Deduct it from my salary."

"There were obligations we had trained her to take care of, Ben."

"Well, now, we will train someone else."

He allowed her to storm off, gather her belongings from Tommy's room, and return to the hall. "Eternity."

She halted and pointed her finger at him. "When we birthed this production company, we agreed to discuss every major change."

"I visited her in person. I allowed her the chance to respond honestly. She said she never received the call."

"Why is that unreasonable?"

"Because she didn't have the logic to empty the incoming database from her personal extension. I scrolled through and the individual's number was right there—more than once."

Eternity glared at Ben. "I hope the person whose message wasn't given is well worth the aggravation."

Ben rolled his eyes as he returned to the room. Sheila sat upright, smoothing Tommy's cheek. "You okay, Benny?"

He stood behind her and massaged her shoulders. "Your tone suggests you detect otherwise."

She dropped her head. "Eternity and I have never taken marriage vows, but that bomb even spattered shrapnel to my heart."

"They say confession is good for the soul."

Sheila stilled his hand. "Answer the question, Benny."

"I'm not today. Maybe not for a while. But, I will be."

She gauged whether he had spoken fiction or truth. When satisfied, she turned to caress Tommy's brow. "I was haunted by those same thoughts."

"You were?"

"When you told me Kevin was HIV positive, I was infuriated. People thought it was because he didn't have the guts to tell me himself. I was terrified of losing the boys."

"We went to the doctor's thinking we had the flu. Amazing how one diagnosis can change your life."

He and Kevin had caught colds that morphed into the flu that progressed to rigorous bronchitis. Prescribed medications hadn't helped and doctors recommended they be tested; a week later revealed the crushing results. Absorbing the wrenching blow had been gradual for Ben, but Kevin asserted full-blown denial.

"Before I became a mother I imagined unparalleled horrors. Yet every one of them withers in comparison to burying a child."

Ben pressed against her shoulder muscles that were the texture of entangled rope.

"It might be a good idea for you talk to someone. Maybe the counselor you saw after your divorce."

He nodded slowly. "Possibly."

Sheila sighed and stretched her head side-to-side. "You're going to make some woman very happy."

"I'd give my life for it."

She studied him, the heartrending reality of his pending death lurking behind her gaze. "Juliana said she'd bring Timmy by so we could eat dinner together. He wants Chili's."

"I think it should be just the two of you. He may not want to share you."

"Umm, maybe you're right. And that way you don't have to share Juliana, either."

She shoved him with her elbow, and he playfully returned the shove.

"*Ontibile*," Juliana whispered, just as Ben rounded the corner of Tommy's hospital room the following afternoon. Rules stipulated a limited number of visitors could occupy space in Tommy's room, so Bruce positioned himself outside the door. The door hadn't closed completely before Ben's eyes met Bruce's with alarm. Bruce trailed in behind Ben.

"What was that?" Sheila asked as she smoothed the cover of one of Tommy's favorite books.

"What do you mean?" Juliana asked.

"How you ended your prayer. On-tee-bill?"

Sheila motioned for her bottled water. Ben remained at the threshold.

"It was the summer before I entered high school. My parents and I were about to return from our annual holiday in Boptang."

"Boptang?" Sheila frowned.

"Boptang, South Africa."

"I'm thirsty, cousin. What's up with your legs?"

Ben moved forward and handed Sheila her water. Her hazel eyes questioned his reluctant behavior. Ben imagined the distant memories flooding Juliana's mind as her heart attempted to keep pace.

"Leaving had never been easy. Yet that summer I couldn't shake my desperation to remain. I did not want to leave Tomorrow."

"You mean you weren't ready to leave the following day?"

Juliana chuckled softly. "No. I mean I didn't want to leave my closest friend. Her name was Tomorrow."

"What an appealing name."

"She was unlike any other." Juliana inhaled solemnly. "She was getting married the September of my high school freshman year. We begged and carried on, yet to no avail. I tried to reason that a best friend's attendance was mandatory, but nothing swayed our parents."

"You were thirteen?"

"Yes."

"In retrospect can you understand why your parents were reluctant?"

"Today, certainly. I cried all the way to the States. What I just said is what Tomorrow said to me the night before I left. It's Setswane, a language predominately spoke in Botswana, for 'God is watching over me.'"

Suddenly, Sheila turned to Ben. "Wait a second. Ben speaks Setswane or something, don't you? Did you recognize that saying?"

Ben swallowed the lump in his throat. "Yes."

Juliana smirked. "I learned Ben sojourns to South Africa from Hunter Sunday night."

"He's been itching to take the twins with him. I'll feel more comfortable when they're older. Especially with what occurred on the last visit. Normally when he returns he's all fired up. He's so excited he's made a difference that we can't get him to stop talking about his trip. This time," she paused to look over at her cousin, "was very different."

"What happened?" Juliana frowned.

The innocence in which her gaze met him created nausea in his belly. "I buried a young woman."

"Not just any woman. A mother of," Sheila turned to Ben, "what did you say? Three young children?"

All he could manage was a feeble nod.

"She was falsely accused of adultery and contracting HIV. But it had really been the husband who was to blame."

Juliana scowled. "That's awful. Was she someone you helped treat at the clinic?"

Ben shook his head.

"He's helped numerous families bury their loved ones, but she was different. The disease hadn't had time to ravage her body. She was beaten to death. He and Bruce discovered her in a field."

Slowly, Juliana's eyes met his.

Sheila, taking this as confusion on Juliana's part, continued, "It was as if he couldn't shake the grief. I'd pick up the boys, he'd be there, at the kitchen table, staring at this teal handkerchief in a plastic bag."

Juliana's posture became rigid. "Ben?"

Ben held up a hand, which quivered. "Juliana."

"Say her name."

Sheila's hazel eyes trailed from Ben to Juliana and back to Ben. Bruce moved to Ben's side.

Juliana stood and every sense shouted alarm. All too suddenly, she remembered the hot wind as it caked yellow earth to her eyelids, cheeks, and mouth. The stench of hate and oppression hovered like a noose ravenous to snap a neck. There, beside her, lay Tomorrow broken, bleeding, gone. "Say her name, Ben."

"Timmy!" The cry was raspy, yet possessed unparalleled urgency.

Every eye turned toward the hospital bed. Sheila was beside Tommy in seconds. She caressed his forehead. "Baby, Mommy's here."

"Timmy!" The breathing tube in his throat cloaked the child's wail. He raised his hands and attempted to claw the tube.

Ben gently grabbed the boy's hand. "No, Tommy. Uncle Ben knows it feels uncomfortable, but it helps you breathe."

"It hurts."

"I know," Ben acknowledged, soothingly. He moved to the headboard and pressed the button for the nurses' station. "See? I'm calling for the nurse. She'll be here soon. Just hold on."

The boy nodded wearily. "Is Timmy hurt?"

Sheila vigorously shook her head. "He's fine, baby. As a matter of fact, he's waiting for you to get better and come home."

Two nurses rushed in, and Juliana moved through the door. She flopped on a bench near the end of the hallway. She pulled her knees to her chest and pressed her forehead against her kneecaps.

"Thank you, God. Thank You for hearing our prayer. Thank You..."

The tears created a hazy veil as figures rushed through Tommy's door. She turned her face from the activity and stared at the pale green wall. Juliana rocked slowly until the queasiness subsided.

A figure approached and knelt in front of her.

"You've known all along."

"It wasn't our intention to deceive you," Bruce expressed.

The remembrance of Tomorrow's blood, the bitter taste of the earth, the crush of Ben's steps as he had walked beside her through the veld emerged.

The haunting images cascaded in relentless succession; Mr. Parker's perturbed manner as he had peered through the peephole from his door.

On his porch had stood a well-dressed white man in the company of two blacks and a morgue van.

The director had guided them to a rear office that seemed as gloomy and cheerless as a tomb.

She remembered she had wanted to scream as the mortician itemized the bill for every number was written with meticulous care inside out.

Juliana stood and the hospital hallway swayed. Bruce reached for her arm. She forced her back against the wall and inhaled sharply to suppress the eruption from her belly. The dampness of her palms seeped through her khakis as she rested her hands on her thighs.

"Ben has agonized over telling you."

Out of the corner of her eye, someone exited Tommy's room. Ben hurried to her.

"Tell me." Her body began to quake. "Say it."

Ben looked to Bruce. Bruce looked to the guards flanking Tommy's door. "I'll get a nurse."

The bodyguard raced to the station and promptly returned with medical assistance. She took one look at Juliana. "Let's get her in here."

Juliana's legs refused to cooperate; Ben eventually had to carry her to the unoccupied room.

"The napkin where you wrote your assistant's number . . . "

Ben pulled her tighter against him and the immense pounding of his heart resounded. He placed her on the freshly laundered bed. Bruce hung back by the door.

The nurse hooked the BP cuff around her arm. "Juliana, I'm going to take your blood pressure, then I need you to rest for awhile. Okay?"

"Your wrote the numbers from the inside out."

Within Juliana, the war raged. She loathed him for his omission, yet his anguished stare perforated her fury. "Just like Parker. Every number, inside out."

The nurse shot them a puzzled look then took Juliana's pulse. "Juliana, when was the last time you ate something?"

Juliana shrugged. The nurse nodded. "I'm going to bring you some juice and crackers." She turned to Ben. "Dr. Troy is checking Tommy's vitals. Can you stay with her until I return?"

Ben nodded without breaking eye contact with Juliana. The nurse rushed from the room, and Bruce moved to the hall closing the door with a hush.

"Do you remember my response after dinner at your house?"

Juliana dabbed the back of her hand against the tears. "You said when I discovered why, you hoped I'd still be interested."

Ben sucked in a heavy breath. "Are you?"

She closed her eyes, from him, from the moment, from even facing the possibility of answering the question.

"It was never my intent to hide it from you this long."

Juliana opened her eyes. "You paid for it all? Internment, flowers, casket, administrative fees?"

"Yes."

"Parker refused, no matter how much I threatened, to reveal your identity. Finally, when he'd had enough of my badgering he confessed, 'the person whose identity you seek is much more capable of crushing me than you.' Now, it makes perfect sense."

"Juliana?"

"We share the same passion. We crusade against the same inconceivable injustices. Is that what has held us this long?"

"That and more."

"What did you have to gain from withholding?"

"I … I just didn't know how to tell you."

The a.m. nurse returned with the promised sustenance. "Miss Powers is aware you are just across the hall."

Ben asked, pensively. "How is Tommy?"

"Cranky. But that is what we're looking for. It means he is definitely on the mend."

"You should go to him," Juliana stated to Ben and reached for a cracker from the bedside table.

"Don't try to get up until you've finished that. I'll check on you in a few minutes." The nurse ordered then departed.

"Juliana."

"I pleaded with them."

"Who?"

"The men. They didn't want to hear me."

"Nothing would have changed their agenda. They had targeted Tomorrow."

"They knew my name."

Ben stilled, a chill disturbing the angle of his spine. *Had Juliana also been targeted after all? Had she been spared because Bruce and I erupted through the grass?*

Ben caressed her jaw. "I–"

She recoiled. "It is true. You are different than most white men."

"Stop."

"Most never would have gotten their hands dirty. Most never would have driven across the street, let alone crossed the Atlantic to aid the needy."

"You needed my help."

"Once you witness the unbearable oppression, once you smell the stench of hatred, it's nearly impossible to eradicate the blemish from your safe, tidy, pristine existence, isn't it? Unless you plan to return next year to wave around more cash."

"Be careful."

"Even now, you've warned me twice."

"I'm lost here. Are you angry that I withheld or that I assisted you and the residents?"

"Do you think me too dimwitted to reason with? I guess you'd be justified. Look at how long it took me to figure out that it was actually you." She closed her eyes, attempting to expunge every prolific memory of him. "I need you to leave."

"No."

She opened her eyes. "What *were* you doing in Boptang?"

"I was paying the water fee for the village where I was volunteering. It is an agreement I have with them."

"Naturally. *The* Benjamin Powers won't just stop at bandaging wounds."

He suppressed the sting of her accusation. "I had heard of those men. How they used their fists to destroy. The malevolence, the sadism, cloaked in the guise of justice sickened me. I wanted to stop them. Permanently."

"Bruce was armed?"

"As always."

"Why didn't he shoot?"

"We weren't certain of how much firepower would have erupted. A gun battle would have been injudicious."

"It must tear you up."

Ben stood beside the bed, preparing for and yet denying what she seemed bent to vocalize. "What?"

"The paradox to save, yet annihilate all at once."

"I get it now."

"Leave."

"You're lumping it all together. Your acrimonious frustration that they refused to hear you, refused to step outside of their aggression and reason with you. You're not only furious that I didn't tell you, but also that I didn't order Bruce to take the shot. Regardless."

"It could have all ended right there."

A mega-ton bomb couldn't have diverted his glare. "We saw movement in the veld. It had a feel that crept toward us. It was sinister and merciless. We had no idea what we'd find. It didn't matter. The danger was extraneous. What mattered was stopping them with whatever force necessary. And then we saw you."

Juliana sipped the juice, the coolness dampening her throat. She looked down at Ben's hands and realized they were red-hot against the pallid bedcovering. Juliana replaced the juice on the bedside tray.

"Bruce would have pulled the trigger in self-defense."

"But never for revenge."

"I've volunteered in clinics near Jo'Burg for years, but I've never seen that much blood. You spoke nothing and shook the entire ride to Parker's. All I could do was play out the scenario in my mind, and I didn't like it. I did not want to return you to the village. I feared they would come back for you. But how could I have communicated any of my concerns? We were near strangers."

"I wonder if we still are."

Ben tapped his fingers against the thin cloth. "I had no idea if you had the resources to pay for her funeral, so I took the initiative. I didn't do it for repayment. I did it because it was what she deserved."

She swung her legs toward the bed's edge. "You had plenty of other opportunities to just come out with it."

"Maybe you didn't hear me, so I'll repeat it." He bit out every word. "If you did not recognize me, then it was very feasible you had no recall of the details of her death."

Juliana felt the gentle nudging. It rose from her belly beseeching her to meditate on wisdom instead of indulging her ruthless emotions. Tomorrow lay dead while her killers roamed free to execute again. Her children had been forcefully uprooted and banned from Juliana. She denied the request. "I think you wanted to play hero. Therefore, when my memory returned, you would be there to catch me as I fell breathless and pathetic into your arms."

"Breathless, possibly. But I seriously doubt you've ever been pathetic."

A prideful surge empowered her ill channeled wrath. "I'll wire you the money for the entire amount first thing in the morning."

"And I'll refuse it."

Wisdom still subtly prodded against her misguided rancor. "This is not up for discussion."

He jutted out his angled jaw. "You have every right to be furious with me. But I was not willing to absolve my conscious just to thrust you into a breakdown."

She stood and immediately wavered. Ben moved to her aid and she blocked him with her right arm. "I do not need *your* help."

He leaned close so that the distance between them was only inches. "Of that, I no longer question. Now, there is one thing I must make clear. I will never regret removing either of you from danger. I will never regret whatever reason brought you to my table at Tanner's. I will never regret the time we've spent since. However, what I deeply regret is the time I've wasted debating with you when I could have been assuring Tommy, despite it all, he will be all right."

He stood so quickly Juliana fell backward upon the bed. She returned upright and watched as he stormed from the room.

After Dr. Troy had assessed her vitals, and felt certain she wasn't in danger, he escorted her to Tommy's room. His head bandage had been redressed and he attempted a smile. "Juliana."

Immediately, the tears hit her cheeks. She dabbed at them as she made her way to his bed. Sheila sat on Tommy's right side. Ben and Bruce moved toward Dr. Troy when Juliana approached.

"Do you have any idea how remarkable you are?" Juliana rubbed the damp hair on his brow.

He shook his head and winced. "If I was Superman I could have stopped that truck."

"Are you kidding me? Superman has nothing on you. And I heard that Spiderman is actually jealous."

"He is? Why?"

"You didn't hear? Well, neither of them has ever been loved as much as you."

Tommy grinned. Dr. Troy released a deep sigh of relief. Tommy still possessed his fine motor skills. His speech was clear, although raspy. Juliana almost cried out at God's profuse magnificence when the child slowly raised the cast shrouding his arm. "Uncle Ben was drawing Superman with my face. See?"

Again, she dabbed at her eyes. Sheila handed her a tissue from the nightstand. When their eyes met, although she could tell Ben had shared their dispute, Sheila's gaze wasn't adverse. Juliana bent to gain a closer view. "Wow. Very handsome and very brave."

Tommy nodded, and Juliana perceived the fatigue. "I got to talk to Timmy."

"You did? That's great. He misses you very much."

"You guys went to Disneyland and Legoland?"

There was a rustle of laughter from the room's companions. "We did. However … " Juliana paused at the prospect of making a promise she couldn't keep. An hour had changed the probability of any future with the Powers' family.

Tommy yawned. She kissed his forehead. "I'm going to stop yapping and let you rest. Okay?"

"Okay." Tommy shut his eyes.

She lingered near the window as Dr. Troy explained what the family should expect in the next weeks, month, even year. The child had surpassed every expectation and astounded the experts.

The surgeon's greatest concern was Tommy's arduous yet hopeful recovery process. Plastic surgery and physical therapy was imperative. He hoped the child wouldn't succumb to the depression most experience after a traumatic brain injury.

Ian and Hunter arrived later bearing stuffed animals. Grace brought Dodgers paraphernalia, and Marcus shipped an iPod from D.C. Sheila arranged the gifts so Tommy could easily see and reach them. She tucked the iPod in her hip pocket, explaining to him that she would take it home and program it with his favorite tunes.

After they shared a prompt dinner in the hospital cafeteria, Sheila returned to Tommy's room; Dr. Troy tackled a mountain of paperwork; Ian and Hunter departed; and she, Ben, and Bruce drove in silence to Woodland Hills.

The Denali pulled up to the ornate security gate. Six cars, telephoto lenses jutting from windows like cannons from a battleship, parked on either side of the block. The lenses flashed, expelling their fire. Sheila's haven had been officially breached.

They exited and Ben opened the front door. When he didn't follow, she turned to him.

"I need to get Timmy from Suzanne's." He turned on his heel and headed for Suzanne's.

Bruce moved toward the den, and she retreated to the guest room and stared at the newly purchased suitcase. Within were freshly purchased clothing, accessories, and a new cell phone charger.

The pain drummed above her hipbone. She tugged her purse from the floor and removed the medicine bottles. As she swallowed the pills, she reasoned her return to Denver was essential. In their conversation, Dr. Martin had been uneasy that the painful bouts had increased and insisted Juliana return to the office for a full check-up. After all, Tommy was on the mend and Sheila could soon resume her routine.

Ben passed, carrying the sleeping child. He did not attempt eye contact. She shut the guest bedroom door, climbed in bed, and shut off the bedside light. Two doors down, she heard Ben's luminous tenor as he conversed with Bruce. It held the same tenderness when he convinced her she was not safe in the veld—requested her pen so he could write down the phone number—and accepted her invitation for coffee.

He rose early and Bruce joined him in his pre-dawn jog. They returned and he showered, wrapped a towel around his waist, and stared at the black toiletry bag on the guest bathroom counter. The twice-daily routine hadn't faltered in several years. No matter where he spent the night.

Ben shoved two pieces of wheat bread in the toaster, chomped a banana while they crisped, and removed bottled water from the fridge. He munched the slices as he returned to the bathroom. He unzipped the pouch and removed the prescription bottles, the vials, and a hypodermic needle. He removed the caps from the four bottles, rested the bulky pills on the counter, and inserted the needle into the sterilized water vial. Then he removed it, inserted it into the Fuzeon powder, and carefully mixed the solution.

The Fuzeon was recently added to his HIV medicinal cocktail to help inhibit the virus from infecting healthy cells. As with the other meds, it had taken several efforts to determine the correct balance of medication and Ben's ability to accommodate them. In the beginning, he had missed several days of work due to vomiting, diarrhea, and extreme fatigue.

There were viral load tests to monitor the progress of the disease and the stringent physical conditioning to maintain quality health and the slew of pills and the battle to succumb to the despair. Some mornings, Ben stared at the ceiling and pretended this regimented existence belonged to someone else.

He unscrewed the cap from the water and poured it into a tumbler. He swallowed one pill and the conflict to self-condemn mounted.

He swallowed another pill and the ire at his hedonistic stupidity stabbed at the surface.

Another pill and another.

Every morning and evening, during this required ritual, he struggled against the desperation and austerity.

As he pinched the skin on his belly and inserted the needle, the despondency nearly won.

It hadn't helped that his doctors were concerned that the length of time he had taken the HAART—Highly Active Anti-Retroviral Therapies—drugs, coupled with aging, might eventually create irreversible effects on his system.

After he tidied the paraphernalia, he rested his palms on the counter and stared at the carpet, unable to face the man in the mirror.

"Happy birthday," Ben whispered to himself.

Eventually he dressed and walked to the den. He had no idea how long it was before he was able to pick up the group photo of his closest friends. Or the stretch of time he stared at it. After Ben's diagnosis, Ian and Marcus instantly curtailed their casual liaisons. Kevin had ignored every admonition.

Although the diagnosis had been clear, Kevin lived in denial and refused to take any meds. He discovered Sheila's pregnancy and refused to take responsibility. That had pained Ben so deeply it nearly ended their friendship. After he had been hospitalized, he summoned for Ben, still denying his illness. As the end drew closer, Kevin had begged Ben to not depart until he had fallen asleep. The final day, Kevin had succumbed to the desperation and sheer terror that a malevolent God would greet his death.

Ben hadn't known God to be necessarily malicious, but he hadn't experienced Him as compassionate either. Juliana spiraled into his thoughts with her beliefs that God was loving and just. He had learned that repentance was paramount to receive redemption. Kevin hadn't repented, only lamented that God wouldn't have forgiven him if he did.

It was torment to wonder who was correct.

Juliana's slumber had been fitful, her dreams filled with a pressing beck-oning. She sat for several minutes on the edge of the bed battling rea-sons to exit the room. She heard Bruce, Ben, and Timmy's voices and their subsequent departure. Finally, at eight, she showered and dressed. Just as she was leaving the bedroom, her phone rang.

"Good morning, Palesa."

"Mom..." Juliana felt the tears burn the edges of her eyes.

"What's wrong? Has Tommy taken a turn?"

"No. As a matter of fact, he's awake and astounding us."

"Praise God!"

"Exactly."

"That's funny. You sounded just like Ben when you said that."

Juliana searched the room for a tissue box. She removed a sheet and wiped her nose. "I suppose that means I've been here too long."

She heard the creak of her mother's office chair as she settled. "What's happening?"

She recalled the arduous disclosure. Dionne sighed. "Oh, Palesa."

"I can't believe I utterly blew it."

"It happens. Our goal is to make certain we yield to the prompting more often than not."

"It's best I apologize and pack."

"I'm not trying to run your life, but it seems that leaving should be the last thing on your mind."

"Why not?"

"Because you've never run. When you care, you seek restoration no matter the cost. And, Palesa, you care."

"But I shouldn't. Not this much."

"Who told you that?"

"It's common biblical sense, Mom."

"I'm not certain it's common or biblical."

Her mother's assistant buzzed to inform her another call was wait-ing. Dionne asked her to take a message.

The assistant cleared her throat. "I expressed that you were on another call. He requested to hold. It's Benjamin Powers."

"Did you hear that?" Dionne asked her daughter.

"I did."

"What would you like me to do?"

"Take it. He's entitled to call."

"I have a board meeting in fifteen minutes and a counseling session directly thereafter. Shall I call you after lunch?"

"Sure."

The call disconnected, she slumped into the kitchen and sipped orange juice. The waves rippled upon the pool's surface. On the kitchen table sat the keys to Sheila's Explorer. The note beneath notified that Suzanne had taken Timmy to the zoo and Ben was headed to his production office. Even in the thorny residue of their conflict, he still thought of her.

She jabbed Sheila's cell phone digits and received her voicemail, to which she informed she could bring breakfast if needed and wondered how Tommy had fared the night. She then grabbed the last breakfast bar and headed to Safeway. Three men lingered far too long in the feminine hygiene aisle to be innocuous shoppers. Juliana purposefully examined every hygiene product until they moved to another aisle.

At the check out, her picture graced the cover of three tabloids. Some included Ben as they exited the hospital. Some included her exuberant escapes with Timmy—her chin facing the ground; her eyes shielded by large designer sunglasses. The consistent theme wasn't surprising.

Ben's family discovers that Juliana's secret past isn't all sugar and spice and everything nice.

Figures exceed a million for the bridal bash!

Juliana's mom warns: Wed him and you're disowned!

Despite her exasperation, she laughed aloud. The lurking trio trailed her exit. As she deposited the groceries in the trunk, she heard the mechanical snap of a high-powered camera. She looked up, highly irritated that the sound had become customary. One lone intruder leaned against his vehicle, grinning at her as if they were best buds.

"Nice day we're having." He snapped another shot.

She slammed the trunk and closed the distance between them. "There are atrocities taking place all over the world, and yet you stand here snapping pictures of me."

He studied her behind dark lenses. His leer wasn't in the least bit sexual, but inquisitive—as if examining the innards of an extraterrestrial. "Very true, Juliana. But they don't draw six figures."

"But it is an honest living. One where you don't have to self-medicate to fall asleep at night."

Something struck Juliana as strange. There was a sense of familiarity about him—as if she'd seen him before but could not narrow the time or place.

He shot another photo. "Says you."

She returned to the Explorer.

"What are the big plans for Ben's birthday?"

She hesitated, then climbed into the SUV. He joined the path of cars following her but detoured after several miles. As she closed the garage door, Sheila called.

"Tommy required some tests and I've become quite codependent."

"Is everything all right?" Juliana set the bags on the counter.

"Oh, yeah. Just the general stuff to make certain we're not headed for any preventable hiccups. He rested through the night, and he's in great spirits this morning. Ben stopped by and Tommy asked if he would bring him a Happy Meal with Super Size fries for dinner."

"Music to my ears."

"Hey, why don't you come here for lunch? We'll eat at the Chili's down the block, say around noon."

Juliana consulted her watch and calculated that was two hours away. "You need anything?"

"Nope. The last suitcase you packed is plentiful."

"Is it true that today is Ben's birthday?"

"Yep. I tried to talk him into a small party, but he said he wanted to wait until Tommy was better."

"I'll see you soon."

She unpacked a dozen grocery bags, replenishing the food supply. Then she vacuumed, dusted, did three loads of laundry, unloaded the dishwasher, and called Thomas. After she updated him regarding Tommy's condition, he informed her latest assignment would take her to five college campuses beginning in the South then moving West. Her two-week mission was to investigate how those administrations informed students to combat HIV.

Her concentration level was that of a toddler in FAO Schwartz. The drive to the hospital did zilch to alleviate Ben from her mind. When she arrived, Tommy was wiped out from a mild physical therapy session.

The two women walked the distance to the restaurant. Soon, they had company. The questions weren't original: When had Ben popped the question? Was Sheila excited to have Juliana as an in-law? Was it to be a church wedding or civil ceremony? Was Dionne still ticked that her Christian daughter had accepted the proposal of a heathen?

As they entered the eatery, Sheila placed a hand on her hip and faced them. "This is as far as you go."

"Look, sweetheart. This is a public place."

"I'm not suggesting. I'm telling you. Do not follow us. We have a right to eat without you snapping pictures of every mouthful. Now, are you leaving, or do I have to interrupt those fine gentleman eating their lunch?" Sheila pointed at the uniformed quartet sitting near the entrance. One stood immediately from the booth and started their way.

"Whatever." The leader grunted and they exited.

"Thanks," Juliana expressed. "I just confronted one in the Safeway parking lot. They're around so much they're beginning to seem familiar."

"Whenever you need it." Sheila turned to the policeman. "Thanks, Greg. They've scattered."

The waitress positioned them at a rear booth. "How do you know those officers?"

"See the two facing us?"

"Yes."

"They were rushed into the ER one night when I was on shift. MGSW—multiple gun shot wounds—received during a fire battle with a gang. They give me credit for helping to save their lives. I was just doing my job. And screaming at them that they had no right to die on my watch."

"Your wrath does invoke fear."

"We've hung out at barbeques or carpooled to our kids' ball games. Sometimes Ben will bring the boys here and we'll have dinner. That bunch of morons must be a new crew because they normally stop at the front door."

"How often do they follow you?"

"Every time. But Ben refuses to give them any satisfaction that they've bothered him. It's like he's able to completely shut them out. But it truly irks him. Especially when they try to engage the twins in conversation. It's all done to get what the paparazzi call 'an R-shot.'"

"What is that?"

"If Ben reacts, yells at them, or loses his cool, they can sell it for boatloads. Or it goes in some electronic file and is reserved until Ben has some breakdown or gets arrested late night for a DUI." She held up her hands as if to frame her face. "Ben comes undone. Details at eleven."

After they placed their order of salads and southwestern egg rolls, Sheila leaned forward. "Do you want to talk about it?"

"You're certainly hoping I do." Juliana took a large gulp of water. "Where to begin?"

"What's going on in your heart, right now?"

"I can't stop thinking about him. Believe me, I've tried. By the way, your house is immaculate. You have enough food to feed a rugby team, and every bit of laundry is washed and folded."

"Thanks, Jules. Geez, you have got it bad. But then again, so does he."

"Why do you say that?"

"He called, first thing, and tried real hard to sound casual. But there was nothing casual in his tone. He thought you were sleeping in to avoid him."

"I couldn't drag myself out of bed. Restless night."

"If I didn't see what you two are pretending not to see, I would never say this to you. But that last trip to South Africa really changed Ben."

"How so?"

She shook her head. "It's like ... he's also grieving your friend's death, although he never knew her."

Their egg rolls arrived and Juliana blessed the meal. The young mother stated, "After we ate dinner with Evan, I was thinking."

Juliana raised an eyebrow. "Evan, is it? No more Dr. Troy?"

"We're talking about *your* love life." She placed three egg roll halves on her plate and spooned avocado dipping sauce in the corner. "Maybe this has been so hard on him because he hasn't had the opportunity to discuss her with you. You loved her; you two grew up together, so–

to-speak. Yet he wasn't able to share his grief because you couldn't remember."

Juliana dropped the egg roll on her plate. The officers had completed their meal and sent a wave in their direction. Both women waved in return. "Tell me why that would matter?"

Sheila contemplated the question for a while. "This disease isn't something Ben puts behind him once he leaves South Africa, *Kgotso*, or a symposium. He was with Kevin when his results came back positive and held him when he died. He was with me when I was tested and had the twins tested."

"Is Kevin the boys' father?"

"Yes. Although he denied it."

"What are you saying?"

"This disease you're battling has crossed your doorstep. People you love have experienced its effects firsthand. The same has happened with Ben. He watched what I went through. He has observed how countless others are doing the best they can to live responsibly. He was so close yet couldn't prevent Tomorrow's death. Feeling powerless and culpable, he immersed himself in the aftermath."

Juliana pierced the egg roll repeatedly. "I never thought of it that way."

Sheila completed her share of the egg rolls and leaned against the calico fabric of the booth seat. "It's in Ben's intricate make-up to rescue. And when he can't, it tears him apart."

Their salads arrived and Juliana stared at the appetizing bowl. Sheila munched awhile, allowing her words to penetrate Juliana's heart.

Juliana picked up her fork and took a few bites. "I don't need him to rescue me. I already have a Savior."

"I'm not saying he's supposed to. But he's basically an outsider looking into your pain that has morphed into his own. Does that make sense?"

"He wasn't there to actually witness Tomorrow's death, but that hasn't taken the edge off of his grief. He has wanted to share his sorrow all along, but he didn't want to push me."

"You should have been a shrink." Sheila swallowed. "Maybe he could have handled it differently. But what he did was not out of malice."

Juliana finished chewing and swallowed. "Thanks for revealing a different angle."

Sheila held her hands up in surrender. "I'm done. No more meddling."

"Let me ask you something."

"Anything."

"Why did you decide to interfere?"

Sheila pointed her fork at Juliana. "That's simple. Houssaye said, 'Tell me whom you love, and I will tell you who you are.'"

"You're quoting Houssaye?"

"On occasion."

"Houssaye also said, 'The more I see of dogs, the less I think of men.'" Juliana stuffed romaine leaves into her mouth and munched loudly.

"In a pinch, you can't go wrong with Ben and Jerry's Cherry Garcia."

"For?"

"An impromptu gift for Ben."

"I thought you said you were done meddling?"

Sheila playfully rolled her hazel eyes. "Eat up! Tommy should be waking up soon."

Juliana departed the hospital and entered Paradise Cove in Malibu into the GPS. Miraculously, she obtained a close spot, removed her sandals, rolled the hem of her khakis, and took a meditative stroll through the tufted sand. Scattered clouds kept the heat at bay and a gentle breeze played in her curls.

She ordered Ahi tuna to-go from the Paradise Cove Café, commandeered a spot on the beach, and munched while admiring the vibrant green grass called Mermaid's Hair swishing on the rocks.

Near evening, she parked Sheila's Explorer in the driveway and stared at the front door. Every detail of Tomorrow's murder had unfolded; the scent of gunmetal, the brutal grip of the killer drilling into her arm, his eyes unrelenting and depraved. The worst had been Tomorrow's hand. It rose not in surrender to the assassination but only in submission that the end of her purpose had arrived.

In Juliana's dreams, she had heard Tomorrow's voice asking her for greater things—things far and beyond *The Plan*. The Plan had been shrewd, efficient, and simple. It included her college education, career, salsa, Latin cuisine, and her ministry. It would have been successful if it weren't for Benjamin Powers. *When did the toe talk the foot into crossing the line? When did the foot convince the leg to take the step over? Where the heck were the warnings? Danger! Proceed with caution! Have you lost your mind? Run, you idiot!* she wondered.

Juliana loved that love was a matter of choice. What she hated was that romantic love cultivated such uncertainty. It could usher unabashed joy, mortal agony, or an indecisive mixture of both. There were no guarantees. Which is precisely what propelled her to resist it. No matter the cost. And, suddenly, the cost had become too high.

Right smack dab in an editorial meeting, the dimple in his right cheek, the way sky blue increased the gold flecks in his eyes, or the symphonic style he had called her name would surface to her mind. Somehow, her heart had chosen without her brain's consultation. It had plunged ahead, despite the persistent warning that those they served were diametrically opposed—the God of Peace and Eternal Life and the god of chaos and spiritual death.

Beads of sweat formed at her brow line. The air inside of the SUV no longer cooled since she had disengaged the engine. She pulled the keys from the ignition and opened the door. Her legs flung over the driver's seat, dangling. She took several drags of the smog-spiked air, coughed, and missed the Colorado high country. Her phone chimed. She dug it from the side pocket of her bag.

"Feeling any better?"

"I had lunch with Sheila. Tommy endured his first physical therapy session this morning. It wiped him out, Mom."

"That's promising. It means he has strength to be expended."

"You talked to Ben?"

"I did."

"How is he?"

"He sounds just as pathetic as you."

Juliana shut her eyes. Not out of conceit, but because she had used that very word to describe herself last night. Then she had wanted misery for him; however, this new day birthed clemency.

"Juliana, I want you to concentrate on purpose."

She frowned, watching gray squirrels chase one another, their bushy tails twitching in flirtation. "Purpose?"

"Sometimes, it never turns out the way we've designed."

"Why are telling me this? I've always been sensitive to my purpose."

"In your health, education, ministry and career, certainly. But not regarding your future husband."

Juliana groaned. "You cannot be saying what I think I hear you saying."

"This is what I know. I've always prayed God would make you aware of His intent in this area. I also prayed you would not reject His decision because His choice may not be what you've expected, but it has everything to do with your purpose. There are times when our purpose makes absolutely no sense."

Juliana rubbed her forehead, the sweat dampening her fingers. "So many in the Bible knew their purpose and jumped right in. Daniel. David. Solomon."

"There are just as many who fought it because it didn't line up with what they perceived God wanted for them. Esther and Hosea."

"So, you and God have been talking about me?"

"Not about you, *regarding* you. He speaks to whoever will listen. Are you ready to listen, Palesa?"

"I'm terrified, Mom. Michael terrifies me. Ben petrifies me. But Michael is at least the much wiser, secure choice."

"Perfect love casts out fear."

"Oh, Mom."

"Pray, Palesa. I'm asking you to pray and not reject when He answers."

"I love you, Mom."

"I love you more."

They disconnected the call and Juliana sat, sweating inside the vehicle.

She spoke no words with her mouth but bombarded her Savior from her heart. After she felt a slender opening in her submission, peace came like a barreling mist from the ocean.

Juliana heard the familiar chime and looked down at the phone in her hands.

B. P.

She closed her eyes and released a quick breath. "Ben."

"How are you?"

"Edgy."

"Understandable. Where are you?"

"Sitting in the Explorer outside of Sheila's house."

"Is something wrong? Have the paparazzi crossed the gate?"

"Not as far as I can see."

"Juliana, what is it?"

"Ben, are you still at your production office?"

"Yes."

"Is it far from Sheila's?"

"It's about thirty miles, but the route can be tricky. Why?"

"I'll explain it all when I arrive."

She inhaled for ten counts and exhaled for eight. Juliana felt the surge of a challenge, but unlike any she had in the past. "What's the address? I'll type it into the GPS system."

He provided the locality; she swung her legs inside, shut the door, and started the ignition.

"I'll let the guards know to expect you."

Bruce escorted Juliana beyond the arena of office assistants, mass of fax and copy machines, an editing bay, a studio where voice-overs were recorded, and a comfortable eating quarter.

Bruce stopped outside of the conference room.

"Bruce, is there a freezer I can place this?" Juliana referred to the Ben and Jerry's pint of Cherry Garcia decorated with a red bow.

"Allow me." He took the pint from her hand. "May I get you anything, Miss DeLauer?"

"No, thank you. And, Bruce, you helped save my life. I think it's time you called me Juliana."

He gathered her in with those dark, incisive eyes. Instantly, she felt as if he would gladly put his life on the line for her whenever required. "Very well."

Bruce left her to stare at the backs of Eternity and her manager, Mitchell. A striking twenty-something female flanked Ben's right and faced Juliana. Juliana noted a solitary silver band on her right hand, middle finger. Ben's profile was in clear view from his position at the head of the table. He turned.

Although there were comfortable chairs and ample reading material, Juliana paced with her head down. He picked up the blue highlighter and circled a few line items for Jessica Kimura, his new assistant, to update. Ben watched as Juliana's concentration was fixed toward the floor and her lips moved in a frantic pace.

"I see we have over 400 employees contracted. All reported on locale in Vancouver last week?" Ben asked Jessica.

She nodded and her jet-black ponytail bounced. "As you see, we were able to negotiate the rate of the construction crew by inviting them and a guest to the premiere in nine months."

"Clever." He smirked at her.

"All signed?" Eternity patted the thick folder to Ben's left. Ben nodded. It held the final contracts with the directors, co-financiers, and producers. Also included was a list of every vital individual to the film from actors, directors, artists, wardrobe, managers, set designers, technicians, drivers, caterers, and security detail.

Movement from his peripheral vision drew his attention toward the transparent barrier. Juliana's hands were now lifted heavenward and swirled in impressive circles. He pressed his lips tightly to suppress the smirk.

"The stop date has changed from January 16 to January 23. Approved?" Eternity asked, her back to the most glorious fluster of energy Ben had ever seen.

"Right on target." Ben caught Jessica's eye. She, like Ben, had witnessed Juliana's muted outburst.

Jessica pointed to the prorated figure. "One point eight million, one-fifth going to the studio, and one-sixth for the location for a period of less than a week for the principal actors."

"Right." Ben tapped the highlighter on his lips.

She shifted papers. "Here's your revised copy of the shooting schedule."

Ben scanned through detailed pages. He sighed for there was no avoiding his appearance on the Canadian set in three days. "Very well."

"Here are your copies of the first day-strip." Jessica shuffled more papers and handed Ben and Eternity individual copies of the color-coded computer print out. The 24-inch paper described whether the scenes were to be shot inside or outside, day or night based upon their color.

Ben thumbed the yellow sheet signifying a day shoot outdoors. "Shooting begins at five a.m. I should take the Saturday evening flight."

"Your trailer resembles a mini Ritz-Carlton," Eternity remarked.

"I am most appreciative. Our daily running cost is averaging three-hundred thousand. Meyer arrived when?" Ben asked, referring to the film's director.

Jessica answered, "Last Wednesday."

Ben nodded as he placed his papers in the cobalt blue folder and tapped the gold embossed company's insignia on the top right corner. *Purpose Films.* "Excellent. Tommy sends his profuse gratitude for the Lego set. Sheila said his eyes lit up when the nurse stated he could play with it this weekend."

"It was my pleasure," Jessica said.

"He must be built with strength from the Rock of Gibraltar," Eternity commented.

"I have a friend who claims it's simply from The Rock."

The trio frowned; just as he was about to explain, Mitchell asked Eternity, "Have you seen the mock-ups of your signature line?" His exuberance filled the professionally designed space.

Eternity shifted to him, wide-eyed. Mitchell—who waved heavily jeweled, manicured fingers—produced a lively artist's rendering of Eternity's recent endeavor of women's shoes.

Ben turned and met Juliana's eye. She leaned against the merlot-colored granite counter, arms folded tightly across her chest. Effortlessly, Ben winked. Even behind the shield of glass, Ben saw the acceptance of his affection.

"Jessica, thank you for your swift response to collect every signature and conduct this meeting."

"No problem, Ben. Is there anything else you need before Saturday?"

"Nothing at the moment."

"Call if that changes."

"Thank you. Eternity?"

She turned, her entire face aglow from her exchange with Mitchell. "You should look at these shoe designs. Amazing is a profound understatement."

"I'm needed elsewhere. But I wish you the best."

Ben gathered his suit jacket and case. Eternity arched a dark eyebrow and returned her interest to the smitten Mitchell. Ben smiled deeply at Jessica and nearly flew out the door.

Juliana took four steps to his two and clutched his forearms. "Ben, I'm so sorry."

"We're in mixed company," he whispered.

"Where then?"

Ben had to physically restrain himself not to pick her up and rush through the door.

"How was your meeting?" Bruce asked. Juliana jumped at the voice from behind. "Forgive me, I didn't mean to startle you."

"I'm pretty jumpy. Thanks." She took the ice cream from his hands. To Ben, "Happy birthday."

"Most productive and thank you."

"I heard it's one of your favorites."

"You heard correctly." He grinned and looked to Bruce. "What about a night off?"

"There are three teams of paparazzi near the parking lot. I wouldn't recommend it."

Ben looked to Juliana, then back to Bruce. "I'll disembark first, my arms full of the packages. Then, you'll exit a few moments later, your biceps flexed under the pressure of other cases."

Bruce nodded, the glint in his ebony eyes perceptive. "They'll follow but believe you're headed home in preparation for a trip."

"I'll drive Sheila's SUV."

"I'll pick up my lady and take her out for a protracted meal. Me and the Denali won't see you until the morning."

Ben took her hand and opened the door to a room stocked with men and women's clothing, hats, wigs, luggage, and golf club cases.

She grinned at the traveling items efficiently stacked in the corner. "I adore how you think. It fascinates, chills, and sometimes intimidates me."

"Your words have power, Miss DeLauer. A power to encourage a prince to relinquish his fortune."

"I won't require a fortune. Unsurpassed devotion, perhaps."

"Granted."

Five minutes later, Ben departed the office. Light bulbs flashed furiously. Ben lowered the rear seats and loaded a dense garment bag into the rear of the SUV. He placed the ice cream on the passenger seat, punched two on the disc console and the stylish vocals of Amel Larrieux surrounded the cooled leather. He flipped to "Weary" and grinned.

Ten minutes later, Bruce, looking purposeful, carried a suitcase and golf bag to the Denali. One of the hovering locusts buzzed, "Ben getting ready for a trip, bag boy?"

Bruce ignored them and carefully placed the items in the trunk.

Another tried, "He's moved up to suitcase detail, sons. Looks like an improvement."

This was followed by raucous laughter louder than necessary. Stone-faced, Bruce shut the trunk and adjusted his black suit jacket. The merciless sun hit the holster of his Glock sidearm. The laughter came to such an abrupt halt Bruce imagined it sounded very near that of vultures choking. He entered the vehicle and started the ignition. Today, there was no need to impress them with his astonishing aim or his fourth-degree black belt honed while at the FBI, nor his swift ability to perform CPR.

Had he wanted to perform it, that is.

CHAPTER SEVENTEEN

Ten minutes into their drive, she lay swaddled in the designer leather bag admiring the dance of treetop canopies against the mantle of the cerulean sky.

"You okay back there?"

Ben heard rustling, then the chatter of the zipper opening. There was more rustling before her head appeared on the armrest.

"I hope the load wasn't too heavy."

"You're not heavy. You're my Juliana."

"The garment bag is cozy, really. Although, I'd hate to test my new-found experience had the zipper stuck."

"I heard you groan a few times as I transported you from office to truck."

"If you carried the bag any other way, it would have been obvious you were carrying a body. Then it would have been game over."

They cleared the property gate, rounded the drive, and watched as the garage door opened.

"Are you hungry?" Ben asked, twirling a spiral curl around his finger.

She shook her head. "Parched. The bag is comfy but doesn't allow for much air."

The garage shut before they climbed out of the truck. Gathering the ice cream, spoons, and drinks from the fridge, they made a path to the backyard pool. The sun had just begun its descent behind the Sierra Mountains when they rested poolside, the air breezeless and flat. They settled on the ornate iron bench shaded by the upper deck. Ben removed his tie and opened two buttons on his shirt. Sky blue.

Juliana allowed her gaze to land on her chilled water bottle, then to Ben. "I'm sorry."

He opened the ice cream lid and scooped a hefty spoonful. "I know."

"My accusations were pretty fierce."

He offered her the spoon. "You're forgiven."

She shook her head. "It's all for you. Forgiven?"

"Yes. I never meant it to be a betrayal."

"No, I meant why did you choose the word 'forgiven' instead of 'apology accepted'?"

He spooned more into his mouth and chewed. "There is a theory that stresses parents should never argue in front of their children."

"I've heard of it."

"Reginald and Joan threw that philosophy out the window. Mind you, their fights were never vicious, but they were heated. What they showed was the breakdown of communication, the heat of the battle, and the reconciliation. Not once did they ever retire for the night without settling the quarrel."

"What was that like to observe?"

"It taught us that conflict was not the end of the world and seeking reconciliation was paramount. If someone was hurt emotionally by our words or actions, we learned to apologize and to seek forgiveness. I understood never be flippant with an apology, but to approach it with sincerity. Thus, because you apologized, I wanted you to know I had forgiven you, not just accepted your apology."

"I said some pretty foul things. I acquiesced to my rage while dismissing the destructive aftermath."

Ben hesitated. "You do realize that it is in my nature to abet if I am able?"

"So I've been told." She picked up her water and took long sips. "You called my mother."

Ben grinned. "I was wondering when you would get around to asking. I wanted to personally thank her for her prayers for Tommy. It's crazy and I don't know precisely how to explain it, but I dreamed and saw her praying for him as if he were her own."

"That is more reality than you know."

Then the dream had changed. Ben felt the blood drain from his face because the edges of the dream had deviated into his habitual nightmare of screaming, clawing at flesh, and blood-drenched hands. Contentment one moment, biting terror the next.

Ben replaced the lid on the near empty container.

"Are you all right?"

"Fine." He drank his water. "The day started very early." He asked a question that had nagged at him since morning. "Has more of your memory returned?"

Her body shuddered head-to-toe. "Yes. Everything came tumbling in after my lunch with Sheila. It's beginning, you know."

"What is?"

"Accepting there was nothing else I could have done."

Ben fought not to close the physical distance between them. He knew it was imperative for her to make the first move. "I desperately wish it had been different."

"This, I know, is true." Tears spilled from her cheeks to her shirt. "Thank you for forgiving me."

"Of course."

She removed a tissue from her pant pocket and wiped her eyes. "That day that Hunter and Marcus came by to visit Timmy, they told me how Dhlamini's death affected you. Your reaction really shook your friends."

"The Bible talks about seven things God abhors. The shedding of innocent blood is one of them. I'm not anywhere close to being God, but I can understand why it is repugnant. Her stoning, for a long while, caused me to hate with such ferocity I alienated myself from everything that mattered to me."

She dabbed her tears. "Ben, does it ever feel as if we're not making headway in this battle to alleviate this disease? Sometimes, in the middle of the night, it creeps in, like a poison. I have to combat doubt that my life is truly making a difference."

She submitted to a torrent of tears and rested her head on his chest. They remained that way until the sun yielded to the shadows of dusk.

Now, the inner churnings implored him. *Tell her now.*

"That's not all. It terrifies me to say this." She faced him. "I want so much more."

"I don't understand."

"I want more—for us to be more. But that lacks wisdom."

"Wisdom?"

"You've made it clear you're not looking for a girlfriend. You are searching for a wife."

"Yes."

"But, Ben—"

"Back at *Purpose*, I thought I heard that the struggle was over."

"What did you just say?"

"Back at my production office, I heard differently."

"*Purpose*? That's the name of your company?"

He struggled to conceal his frustration with her allure of the company's name. "Juliana, tell me why it lacks wisdom to be with me."

"Oh, man. Purpose." She shook her head as if to align her thoughts. "You and I don't serve the same God."

In a silence sharp enough to pierce emotions, delusions, and cognitive reason, Ben seethed. The night grew darker and Ben saw the soft illumination of the streetlamps. "It's rather pointless, wouldn't you agree?"

"How do you mean?"

"Us, here, this close, yet nothing has truly changed."

She sat up. "I deeply care for you."

"And what am I to do with that insightful confession?"

"Your acceptance that Jesus is genuine and absolute cannot be based upon me."

"Do you want me?"

"Ben, it's not that elementary."

"Oh, I believe it's pretty basic."

"It isn't and you know it."

He felt sapped of his energy. He released her, his arms dropping to his sides. She gripped his hand. "My motive is not to be cruel. What I feel for you terrifies me. I wrestle with it all the time. It's not what I've been taught. It's not appropriate."

He faced her. "You think I want to hear that? Do you really believe you're helping me with those words?"

She saw every bit of what he attempted to mask as he said, "There's this desperation in my soul to discover why you've penetrated me so deeply. I've examined it from so many angles. It horrifies me to recognize it may never be fulfilled."

She placed his hand over her heart. The incessant pounding nearly did some things. It nearly caused him to grasp her and to consume that pounding until they were breathless and fulfilled.

"Ben, I don't know how to love you."

He snatched his hand away. The repugnance had gripped since Eternity's confession. It pooled from his heart like blistering magma, consuming every constructive principle he had regarding women motivated by their convictions. Eternity's petrified theory had caused her abandonment of their marriage and rejection of his oath. He vowed to be sharper with Juliana and had no intention of giving her that power. And he had to distance himself from that unbearable pounding.

"It's late. Wait for me in the truck."

He climbed the staircase to his bedroom, obtained the item, and entered the garage. Behind the wheel, Ben placed the sealed turquoise kerchief on her lap. She gaped at him, speechless.

Ben turned the ignition and opened the garage door. Juliana gripped the steering wheel and whispered, "Wait." She took his hand and held it to her cheek. Her warm tears wedged into the creases of his hand.

"You are prolonging the inevitable."

"There's a reason, Ben. A reason beyond me, a reason I can't fully perceive, why I can't walk away."

"I'm not a little boy, Juliana. Either you want to be with me or you don't."

She looked as if he had slapped her. "I do, Ben. But how?"

"Let me make this simple. Go home. Soon. And forget me."

"Ben—"

"Because I assure you I have every intention to forget you."

The house was quiet as Juliana unlocked Sheila's front door. She fell into bed and buried her head in the pillow to muffle the agony.

In the morning, she arranged her belongings in the suitcase

then entered the kitchen. Sheila wiped the counter with a lemony disinfectant.

"Good morning, gorgeous." Sheila placed the towel on the hook beneath the sink.

"It's too quiet."

"Timmy called Ben near dawn begging him to take him to the beach. They departed around eight. He left the truck if you need it."

"Things may become uncomfortable for you and the boys if I stay."

"What are you saying?"

Juliana had wrestled with the appropriate words all night—words that wouldn't place Ben in an unpleasant light.

Sheila put a hand on her hip. "What did Lughead do this time?"

Juliana held up a hand. "It's not entirely his fault. We've come to an impasse. I'm not sure when it will change."

"Don't do that."

Juliana frowned. "Do what?"

"Right now, you just thought 'if ever.' I can tell I'm right by the look on your face."

"Sheila," Juliana placed her hands in the prayer position, "I'm being realistic."

"I'd call it being fatalistic." Sheila poured a fresh cup of coffee and handed the steaming cup to Juliana.

"Are you angry at *me*, Sheila?"

Sheila pressed her lips tight. "One of the things that has caused you to grow in my heart is your diehard stance on what you believe. You're so confident, so reserved about it that it intimidates and creates envy in me at the same time. It makes me wonder what the heck is inside you; makes me kinda jealous because it doesn't live in me."

"So, you're angry that my leaving may put distance between your discovery of what it is that you see in me?"

"That, mostly."

Juliana placed the cup on the counter. "But you understand why I must leave?"

"Since you've been here, something has been pulling on me—some force I can't explain. I don't fear it, really. It's just unfamiliar yet convivial all at once. Like I've never been around it and yet it's been there all the time."

"Sheila, that's God."

Sheila huffed. "Why would God be concerned about me to the point He'd allow me to *feel* Him?"

"To get your attention."

Her hazel eyes drilled. "So, why is God trying to get my attention?"

"To let you know how much He loves you."

"You say that because you don't know the things I've done. God probably hates me."

"It's not necessary for me to know, and He doesn't hate you."

"How could He not? There are things in which I am highly ashamed."

"There is already a plan to remove all of that from His memory."

"Impossible."

"Not at all. His son, Jesus, sacrificed His life to assure that would happen."

Sheila rubbed her chin, encompassed in thought. "I've tried to push it away. But it just returns. Never pushy, never aggressive, as subtle as air. Tommy pointed it out first. This same feeling is in his hospital room. He described it this way: when he's scorching with fever and I rub his forehead with a cool cloth, or when he's been caught in a drizzle and I make him hot cocoa."

"I like that."

"Despite every internal protest, I still fell in love with Kevin. It was so stupid. I didn't even argue with people who tried to get me not to love him. I knew our greatest achievement would be heartbreak. Then I got pregnant."

She put her chin on her shoulder and looked toward the ripples in the pool. "I'm a solidly educated, trained professional. So, understand I was very absolute in my decision to have them. I felt in every fiber within me the moment they were conceived. And I instantly fell madly in love with them.

"I was advised by many to abort them. I was twenty-three, single, and had a flourishing career. Babies, fathered by a man who was clearly only interested in me for amusement, was not a wise choice for such a smart woman. I cooked this amazing meal, right. My apartment was dim with candles emitting his favorite scent, and after dinner I placed the pregnancy test on the table in front of him."

Juliana sipped the hot liquid, watching and waiting.

"He stared at the test strip for a very long time. Then, his eyes fell on me. They were full of wrath as if I was forcing him to face something he had been able to habitually elude. He was out the door in a flash and he never looked back."

She faced Juliana. This time, she didn't wipe the tears. "As they grew inside me, as they were born, I wanted to be more. I wanted to give them more. So, I started going to church. I was fine until I heard about Jesus."

"What do you mean?"

"His Father gave Him over to die. He gave Him over to people who could have cared less, who despised Him. I tried to picture the twins as men, tortured, broken, and bleeding as I just stood by and watched. The pastor explained it was all about a much bigger picture than Jesus being detested. But the logic is beyond me."

She touched the young mother's hand. "You can't fathom that kind of love?"

Her lower lip trembled. "Is that love or lunacy?"

"The sacrifice of His life is the most profound love."

"It scared me so much I haven't returned." The tears flowed, dampening her chin and pooling at her throat. "But, you've made me want to know more. So, I want to discuss the belief that everyone has a purpose, a destiny set in motion before we ever exit the womb."

Juliana clutched Sheila's shaking hand. "Okay."

"I want to know how Jesus could give His life for others who wanted nothing more than for Him to die. That can't happen if you run away."

Juliana led Sheila to the kitchen table where they embarked upon the most imperative conversation of Sheila's life.

The remainder of December, Juliana attempted to hide her misery in the demands of her assignment with *Core*. Juliana covered the Southern college campuses like a Tasmanian devil. She rose at dawn to gather applicable research from several undergrads at breakfast and collapsed into her hotel bed beyond midnight after shadowing several graduate students.

Only her service knew she had deleted a dozen text messages to Ben before sending them. And God. Who also knew how desperately she missed him. As she shopped for Christmas dinner, she noticed the tabloids.

Jessica had escorted Ben to various public appearances.

The tabloid headlines screamed.

"Jules is out!"

"Don't mess with Jess."

Juliana, still hounded by the photographers, heard every taunt as they pursued.

"Good bye, Polly Anna!"

"You'd have to be nuts and delusional to think he'd pick you over Jessica. Have you seen how *hot* Miss Kimura is?"

Once, late for an appointment at the church, she had seen the trail of hunters in her rearview mirror. She had pulled into the parking lot and exited her car. Light bulbs had flashed, nearly blinding her if not for the oversized shades as she had raced to the entrance.

"Frigid Gidget!"

Juliana had halted at that one. Her virginity had become a source of mockery to strangers who knew nothing of her heart or why the conviction to remain celibate ran deep.

Juliana had turned. "What did you call me?"

More maddening flashing.

"You heard me. I'm only surprised it took Ben that long to wake up and smell the promise of absolutely nothing!"

As if she had spent hours practicing, she had deftly lifted the weighty camera from his hands and pummeled it into his face. Some tabloids had paid $150,000 for that shot. It had been looped on every infotainment show nationwide.

The police report stated she had inflicted the victim with a broken nose, shattered several teeth, and cracked his upper left cheek. After being released on bond, Juliana had made a public apology, replaced the camera, and paid for his medical bills, also agreeing to finance subsequent physical and psychological therapy.

Ben also failed to convince life was bliss. The production suspended filming the week of Christmas and resumed after New Year's Day. Ben's holiday mood had been quiet and sullen. One brisk January afternoon, Marcus and Ian visited him on the set. Hunter, who was in production for his series in L.A., repeatedly received a frosty reception whenever he called. They gathered beneath the colossal tent warmed by portable heaters.

"Either this is the role of a lifetime or you're headed for a straightjacket."

"Thanks." Ben smacked Marcus on his bulky shoulder. "It's great to see you too."

"Your eyes are beginning to bear little resemblance to those of my heroic crusader."

After an awkward silence Ian stated, "What Mr. Smooth meant to ask was, 'How is the filming?'"

Ben tugged at the leather string clasping his hair. "Stressful. But Meyer is impressed with the dailies."

"Stressful? Why?"

Ben glanced through the tent flap at the majestic meadow nestled near Blue Grouse Lake with its soaring pines and radiant blue sky. "Luke Bailey is not an effortless character to portray. His sole ambition was to be a husband and father. On the evening of his youngest son's second birthday, a gang of men with no destiny or principle came and destroyed that dream. The men tied his hands with steel wire and forced him to watch as they slaughtered his family one-by-one. Then, they left him for dead. His entire world was shattered and he was powerless to stop it."

By the end of his explanation, Ben's chest was heaving.

Marcus and Ian shared a glance.

"As if that wasn't brutal enough, the local head of the law—who wouldn't have spit on Luke if he were on fire—set out to prove Luke had something to do with their murders. He spends years in jail, plotting, after every beating he suffers at the hands of the sheriff."

"Revenge?" Marcus asked, spotting an eagle soaring and was seemingly captivated by the sight.

"Yes."

"Does he avenge the deaths of his family?"

"Yes."

Marcus met Ben's eyes. "How?"

"He proves his innocence, is released from jail, and in humiliation the sheriff loads a bullet into his own brain."

Ian folded his arms behind his blonde head, the gray of his blue eyes flickered. "I haven't read the script, but I imagine Luke's hunt is methodical. He seeks every person he's deemed as guilty one-by-one."

"In the same manner they killed his family. Once Luke extracts the reasons why—often with brutal force—he brings each of them to justice."

Ian blinked. "Justice according to whom? Luke or the law?"

"If I answer, it will ruin your desire to see the movie."

"What I see in your eyes, this desolation, profoundly concerns me," Ian asserted.

"It's why I win on award's night."

Ian glanced at Marcus. "It can be a fanatical craft, this business of drama. We relish the thrill of sinking our eyeteeth into a character, especially one who resembles nothing of our nature. It's why we read volumes, conduct interviews, and spend countless hours morphing into their temperament. Certainly, as human beings, we share elements of their greatness and elements of their darkness. The role in which you won your first Oscar, you adopted so much of that personality it took you weeks to release him. There is no doubt your talent personifies genius, but Benjamin Powers is not Luke Bailey."

"I am more of him than you know." Ben folded his hands so tightly, his fingers flushed red. "More than either of you is willing to accept."

The stillness in his voice nearly chilling, Marcus stated, "Ben, Juliana hasn't been taken from you."

Ben grunted and looked toward the crew setting up for the next scene. "This is a wasted conversation."

"Hardly," Marcus contended. "Your character, Luke, had someone to blame."

"Are you blaming Juliana?" Ian posed.

Ben shook his head and a few strands loosened from the leather band. "Not entirely."

"Then, who?" Ian asked.

"God."

Both men were taken aback. "How?"

He looked from one man to the other as if the answer were as straightforward as two plus two. "She's convinced she could never be happy with me. What a fallacy. There are plenty of people who live proper, decent lives who have never set foot in a church and their marriages have lasted a lifetime."

Marcus nodded, reflectively. "True. But, according to what you've told us, this is not what Juliana desires. She wants a church-going man."

"Christians are such hypocrites!" Ben poked his finger on the table-top. "Where is the extension of understanding in that narrow-minded thinking? She is certain we are 'unequally yoked.'"

"What does that mean?" Ian asked.

Marcus answered, "It's from the Bible. The theory is that believers of Christ have nothing in common with unbelievers. Light has nothing to do with darkness. Righteousness has nothing to do with evil."

Ben sputtered, "It's a dogmatic, antiquated principle."

"However you choose to label it, it is still her principle," Marcus surmised.

"Then answer me this: why even cross that line in the first place? Why bring me this close," he squeezed a diminutive space between his right thumb and index finger, "giving me hope, then shut it all down?" Ben's voice cracked at the last word.

Ian and Marcus sat gauging the depth of their friend's wound.

"I have a question?" Ian placed his hands on the table. "You were raised in a Christian home, correct?"

"Yes."

"When I visited for Christmas two weeks ago, we all shuffled to church on Christmas Eve, but your mom had subsequent times she attended some other services."

"My mom sings in the choir and attends weekly Bible study."

Ian snapped his fingers. "Right."

"So why is this such an issue with me? Is that your question?"

"That's precisely my question."

"Mine too," Marcus chimed in.

"I've attended church all my life. I participated in every kid's program from Easter to Christmas. I attended every picnic and bake sale. God was someone we talked to on Sundays, led by the pastor's prayer, or at the beginning of a meal, or when Grandma Mae had her stroke. He was far, far away handling things in another part of the world. I didn't feel He was ever near me."

Ian nodded. "Juliana seemed to have something very different. As if it were deeply personal. That day we dropped by to give her a break from taking care of Timmy, when she returned, she had purchased a few books. One had an interesting title so I asked about it. Truthfully, I don't remember her complete answer. What I remember is the *way* she spoke about God. It was the same way I speak of my own dad. It was as if she shared a relationship with God."

Ben kicked a pinecone near his foot and studied it. "How is it possible to feel that way about someone you've never met?"

Marcus probed, "Are you angry that pleasing God is more important to her than pleasing you?"

Ben's eyes darkened. Before he could answer, Jessica approached. "Ben, they are ready for you."

Ben stood. Jessica's alluring perfume stirred every one of his primal senses. "Marcus Jacobs, Ian Knight, this is my new assistant, Jessica Kimura."

She removed a leather glove and extended a delicate, manicured hand. "Gentlemen. Welcome to our home away from home for the next four weeks."

Marcus took another lingering look at the spectacular surroundings. "A mile away is a lake and at two hundred feet is the base of the mountain. I feel for you, truly. You must have nightmares having to stay in this dump."

Jessica asked, lightly touching Ben's arm. "Will you be joining us for dinner?"

Ian followed the caress and looked directly at Ben. "Without a doubt."

They watched as Ben and his new assistant walked toward the center of the meadow. As they strolled, her graceful shoulder nudged Ben's bicep.

"'Will you be joining us?'" Ian scowled.

"'Our home away from home?'" Marcus grunted.

"I have *Core's* number on speed dial."

"My grandmama would accuse you of meddlin'."

"I've met your grandmother. She is an astute woman who would deem this an intervention."

"Dial it."

He did. When it began to ring he asked, "What do I say?"

"You're the actor. You've never been at a loss for words."

Ian was connected to her voicemail, which informed she was out of the office on assignment, but would promptly return calls when she returned. He repeated the info to Marcus.

Ian asked, "What do we do when we don't know what to do?"

"We call Grace."

CHAPTER NINETEEN

In early January, Sheila sent photos of Tommy walking with braces and toting a cast-free arm. Another displayed the impressive Lego creation with Salty at his heel. One snowy afternoon she phoned from her desk at *Core*, as the traffic on Lincoln Avenue lulled from the corporate arena toward the suburban journey.

They updated her, with the rapidity of Speedy Gonzales, of their latest escapades. Then the inevitable occurred. They asked when they would see her again. Juliana imagined Sheila not blocking the question because she also desired an answer. Juliana sighed, stating she wasn't certain of when, but that she missed them everyday. The response satisfied, and they moved the conversation toward other topics.

When Michael dropped her off at her house after they shared a meal at Maggiano's, she turned to wave goodnight and promptly collapsed. Her next conscious moment was waking up in a scratchy hospital gown at St. Joseph's.

Dr. Martin, her trusted and beloved GYN, entered the room with deep furrows etching her forehead. She shoved transparencies of Juliana's womb on the lighted board and Juliana's eyes widened. On the right side of her uterus, circled in blue, was a mass. Dr. Martin explained the deteriorating condition to Juliana, Dionne, Tricia, and Maya. Michael waited in the corridor.

"You passed out because your insulin quantities are distressing. The stress has increased your androgen levels. Your abdominal pain has spiked, as well as hair follicle disruption."

Juliana nodded miserably. Tricia couldn't keep up with Juliana's staggering electrolysis and hair-weaving appointments. The disorder she carried had caused the hair on her upper lip and forearms to grow like weeds. Yet the hair upon her head separated from her scalp with alarming ferocity.

Polycystic Ovarian Syndrome. The overproduction of androgens in her blood pumped more testosterone through her veins than her body could handle. Every month, her ovaries enlarged, formed fluid-filled cysts, and denied the release of their fruit.

Dr. Martin took Juliana's hand. "I cannot imagine what you've endured these last few weeks. The press has stalked you from sunrise to sunset."

Juliana shook her head fiercely. "Correction. It does the media an appalling disservice to categorize the people lurking after me as press. I am press. They are paparazzi. As in the Italian name meaning a buzzing, darting, stinging, or hovering insect!"

Dr. Martin looked to the women who circled Juliana's bed, then returned her gaze to the frazzled young woman. "I have a trusted colleague and friend who resides over a medical resort out-of-town. He is one of the top specialists in his field. The center is near a lake with magnolia trees."

"That sounds nice, Jules." Tricia patted her shoulder.

Juliana rolled her eyes, but allowed the doctor to continue.

"I cannot force this upon you, Juliana. But I believe in your heart, you know this is necessary."

"So," Juliana scowled, "what happens at this medical resort? Will I be tested and poked my entire time there?"

"I wouldn't exactly describe it as such. There are various tests I've requested to discover the extent of the damage your stress has caused and—"

"I did not cause this stress, Dr. Martin!"

"That's not what I meant."

"Oh, it's exactly what you meant. I brought every bit of this on myself. What was I supposed to do? Give up every principle for a few moments I would have regretted for a lifetime?"

"Juliana Marguerite." Her mother's tone was hushed, yet firm. "Let Dr. Martin complete her sentence."

"I am concerned, deeply, that the medication has failed to stop the bleeding. I cannot examine you until the bleeding ceases. Until the bleeding ceases, I can't determine whether the mass is benign or malignant." All eyes, except Dr. Martin's, returned to the x-ray. "I've asked advice and every consultation has returned with the same conclusion."

"But we agreed!" Juliana's hands flew to cover her belly.

Dr. Martin held up a hand. "I haven't forgotten. Surgery—hysterectomy—would be our very last resort. This center is able to offer resources I cannot."

"But, Dr. Martin, you are one of the top gynecologists in the nation. How is it possible this other doctor can offer what you cannot?" Tricia asked.

"Because they specialize in endometrial disorders," Maya stated.

"Precisely." Dr. Martin answered and placed her hands inside her white coat.

"I'll go with you." Tricia squeezed Juliana's hand. "I'll make arrangements this afternoon. Winston will understand."

Juliana gaped at her. "You don't even know where this place is, T. And, I haven't agreed."

All four women looked to the doctor. "It's nestled near the base of Grouse Mountain."

Juliana's mind flashed to Mrs. Pillmeister, her sixth grade geography teacher. The realization made her feel as if a wrecking ball had assaulted her. "Are you ready for this, T?"

Tricia looked around the room, oblivious and wide-eyed. "What?"

Juliana laughed, the acrimony thick in her pitch. "Unbelievable!"

"Jules, what!"

"It was an extra credit question on my sixth grade geography test. Grouse Mountain is just north of Vancouver, British Columbia."

Ben used his despondency to fuel Luke's on-screen persona, pouring every emotion into the character. Only Bruce had heard the torment played out in Ben's habitual nightmare.

One of the film's production assistant's had delivered the day script at two a.m., surprised to find Ben fully awake, inside his trailer. This day's call sheet had a report time of 3:30 a.m. The anticipation of the day's shooting created fervor in his mind. The frenzy within wouldn't cease until he had completed the fundamental scene where Luke held his nemesis accountable.

The cast's early arrival on the set was required because the scene needed to conclude near dawn. Although the hour should lessen the number of distractions, numerous takes would be essential.

Ben tossed the third Red Bull can in the wastebasket. As he shut the trailer door, he wiped the saliva from his lips. His heart thumped as he entered the wardrobe trailer.

"It's remarkable any of us are coherent at this hour, huh, Ben?"

Inwardly, he grinned at the costume designer's reaction to the snarl he shot her. Ben Powers had normally extended such benevolence to his cast and crew that by the end of the filming, the general consensus was that he seemed like a brother. Nothing could have been further from the truth during the past few weeks. The designer precariously handed him his outfit. Luke snatched and purposefully bumped into her as he went to the dressing room.

In make-up, Ben's favorite artist attempted small talk. He responded with deafening silence. When he arrived on the set, Meyer greeted him jovially. Ben immediately climbed upon the horse he was to ride in the scene and glared down at him. Meyer exchanged a perplexed look with Luke's nemesis.

The assistant director passed on key instructions from Meyer. "Quiet on the set!" Everyone was positioned. "Roll it!"

"Speed!" Sound recording had begun. The clapper walked to the camera, clapboard or slate as it was better known in hand, and announced, "Scene one hundred and thirty, take one."

Luke's horse, Pearl, started to fidget. Luke pressed his thighs closer to the animal and whispered, without visible perception, "Settle." The horse instantly obeyed.

"Action!"

Luke gently pulled on the reins and Pearl trotted slowly around the corner of the boarding house. The sun seemed uncertain it wanted to usher in a new day as sapphire draped the mountains and edges of the sky. Luke commanded Pearl to stop beside the trough. Luke dropped to the horse's side and quickly tied the reins to the nearby post. He stood impeccably still, his eyes riveted to the front door of the boarding house. This moment had been what kept him alive. This moment had been the sole reason he purposed to heal.

Blade, his nemesis, had sliced open his family as if for sport. He came after Luke with such vigor, no surgeon could ever rid him of the scars. Melanie, the woman who had nursed him, had certainly tried. But, Luke had sealed his heart shut except for one purpose. This moment.

Suddenly, the porch light flashed and the front door opened. Luke held his breath until the light no longer cast shadows upon Blade's face. Nimbly, he dropped to the terra cotta dust, removed his boots, and traversed the space between him and the evil that had snatched away his life.

Blade removed a cigarette from his vest and customarily lit the match on the bottom of his boot heel. Luke's mind flashed to the moments he first witnessed this purposed action. Before each slaying of Luke's family members, he snubbed out the cigarette, then re-lit the match ignited from his heel.

One-by-one, Luke had discovered Blade's gang and taken vengeance. The first accomplice had determined he could beat Luke with his fists and ended up plunging to his death from a rocky cliff. The second accomplice had been in the middle of an attempted bank robbery. Luke slid the rope from the base of his ankle just as the robber turned his back from the terrified crowd. He flew through the wooden doors in a hail of gunfire. Death met him before he hit the threshold.

The match dropped to the pine porch and Luke appeared from the shadows. Instantly, Blade removed the knife from his breast pocket and aimed it at Luke. Luke leaned with graceful precision to the left, then right when the second blade raced by him. Blade was in possession of two others, yet held them. The two men stood on the dim porch as the sun marked the beginning of the day with violet and ruby.

Suddenly, Meyer yelled, "Cut!"

Trevor/Blade turned to the director. "What happened?"

Meyer pointed to the boom mike, held too low by the operator. Dozens rushed in to dab their faces with fresh make-up, adjust clothing, and offer drinks. Ben stood silent, glaring at the man in front of him.

"Hello? Earth to Ben!" Trevor waved a hand in front of his face.

Ben held his stance, as solid as granite.

"Dude, I know this is why I admire you greatly, but that stare is freaking me out. Didn't you hear Meyer call 'cut'?" Trevor asked.

Ben offered nothing. He stood, eyes rigid, fists clenched at his sides. The AD announced "back to one."

Ben returned and mounted Pearl.

The previous commands from the crew sounded.

Luke commanded Pearl to turn the corner and they began where they had originally started. Two knives soon flew past Luke and the men stood, blatant and gauging.

"Some believe God decides the date of their death." Blade shook his head and blew smoke from his twisted mouth. "No such truth. God has to ask my permission."

With the speed of a lightening bolt, Luke dove forward and the men crashed on the dusty planks. This fight had been practiced to perfection; each man knowing when to throw a punch, dive, shove, or collapse from a blow. They tousled on the porch where Luke was being pummeled. He brought a knee to his chest and knocked Blade through the white spindles with a hearty kick.

Instantly, Blade stood and charged headfirst up the steps toward Luke's gut. Luke flung himself upright, calculated, and dug his naked heels deeper into the flat timber. As Blade closed the gap, Luke's eye caught the glint of steel. He loosened his stance, but failed to divert the slice across his abdomen. He saw a horizontal crimson line cut across his suede jacket as he staggered backward into the door. This action caused a rush within Luke. He jabbed forward, landing a torrent of blows to Blade's face; two actually connecting fist to flesh. Blade's lip released real blood, and he wiped it with his black sleeve. Lights from surrounding windows illuminated the air, which took on the hue of a mossy river.

"Son," Blade grunted. "I've danced with you long enough."

"No argument out of me."

The knife from Blade's back pocket stung Luke in his left shoulder. Luke gripped the handle and ripped the dagger from his flesh. His face contorted as he glanced at the manufactured red stain on the steel. With mastered aim he had learned from Melanie, he threw the knife and watched as it landed in Blade's sternum. Luke marveled at the emotions that clouded his enemy's face—disbelief, shock, and degradation. Luke reveled in the latter. A window above opened and a woman screamed. Other windows followed suit, yet neither man paid attention.

"It's over." Luke's voice was resigned. "Where's the last one?"

"I'm not dying today, Bailey. You are."

Luke rushed toward Blade, lifted his leg in a roundhouse kick, and caused the dagger to deepen into the man's chest. Blade dropped to his knees and released an inky scarlet substance from his mouth. Luke shoved him and his back met the earth. Luke hovered over the gasping man. "Where's the last one? The one you used to carve up my wife?"

His adversary liberated a bitter laugh, clouded by an eerie gurgle. "Don't worry. You'll get it soon enough."

Pearl picked that moment to gallop into the scene.

"Cut!" Meyer groaned. "Why is Pearl in my shot?"

Trevor climbed to his knees, dusted the ginger-colored earth from his clothing, and patted Ben on the shoulder. "You are beyond intense this morning. Powers, are you feeling you don't have enough Oscars on your mantle?"

Ben turned and headed to the seats beside the director. He sat shoulders squared in the canvas chair with the film's name emblazed on the back. Wardrobe assistants arrived and cautiously handed him a new jacket. Make-up artists rushed over to wipe some of the grime from his face. The crew scurried to recreate the image the set had before Luke pitched the knife into Blade.

Trevor walked over, donning a fresh shirt, dagger liberated from his chest, and sat beside him. "Hard to believe we do all of this for eight minutes on film."

Silence.

He took a few moments to study the crew. "We've worked together on three other films. So I'm not a stranger to this intensity. But, this," he waved a hand over Ben, "downright borders on demon possession."

"You should know."

"Ben! What is going on with you? Seriously, man, I'm concerned. Marcus, Hunter, and Ian are concerned. I've heard they've called Grace and she's headed here because she cannot believe the things they've told her."

Nothing.

Trevor blew out a weighty sigh. "Have you noticed the way Eternity has been watching you over there?" He pointed and Ben refused to look. "Marcus and Ian haven't returned to L.A. There's a reason."

Ben jumped from his seat.

"At least tell someone why you've chosen to go so deep. Help us to understand."

The AD approached; the men returned to the spot where Blade hurled the knife into Luke's shoulder. Blade seemed edgier and nervous. There was pressure to wrap the scene before the sun dismissed the darkness. The scene proceeded.

———————————————

Luke hovered over Blade who gasped and spit blood. Blade vowed Luke would experience the slice of his knife.

The embittered widower clasped his hands around Blade's neck. "I'd tell you to pray. But I doubt even the Almighty has that much grace. Use these last moments to prepare to meet Him." His grip tightened. The terror in his co-star's eyes wasn't manufactured. His thrashing to escape was quite real.

"Luke!"

He stopped his crushing of Blade's larynx and turned toward the voice. "Melanie!"

She approached, cautious and looking to the spectators gendering from their windows. The hem of her yellow skirt gathered wisps of the soil. "This is not the way you want it to end. Remember? We agreed."

"We agreed he deserved to die."

"Never by your hands. I didn't teach you what I knew so you could intentionally take a man's life. It was for protection." Her wispy blonde hair caught the breeze and floated across her face. She swept it backward. "I've been watching you this whole time, and you made the first move."

Luke stood and glared at Blade. "Just like he did he six years ago."

She moved to him and touched his arm. "That wound doesn't look good. Come. We'll get him help—"

He recoiled from her as if she generated unbearable heat. "Help? Is that why you followed me here? To help *him*!"

"Hey, Bailey. She looks just like your wife," Blade mumbled from the ground. "Until she wasn't recognizable."

Luke squatted beside his rival. "You've wasted time. Before, I was simply going to snap your neck. Not anymore."

A thick trail of red flowed from Blade's mouth. His breathing grew shallower. "I took delight in every one of their deaths, Bailey. But that wife. Now, she made me tingle."

Luke's hands increased the pressure on Blade's throat. Melanie rushed to his side. Her hand on his arm didn't cease his grasp. "Listen to me. Not like this. You came here to bring him to justice." The pressure of her touch increased. She studied the sputtering man whose chest wound now seeped into the sleeves of Luke's jacket. "Let go. Luke, let go."

Everyone around him felt it; the struggle to end it swiftly or to allow the life of his enemy to slowly seep away. He sat on his heels and stared at Blade. The crew knew moment by moment what was to occur, yet they seemed to hold a collective breath as it ceased to be words on a page.

Hot tears started at the edges of Luke's eyes. Images of his family returned, except this time, they were whole and smiling at him. Luke placed trembling hands on the top of his thighs and allowed the grief to bleed from him. Melanie leaned her head upon his but kept watch over the dying man. Luke turned to bury his head in the fold of her neck. Blade's right hand moved to the concealed weapon.

Luke wept with his entire body so that it became difficult to hold him. Melanie cradled Luke's head and rocked him against her as if her arms could arrest the pain. Blade retrieved the razor from his side and with every ounce of energy raised it to the level of Luke's carotid artery.

A blast from Melanie's left hand shattered the silence. Luke jumped to see Blade gasp sharply, then stilled on the ground. A curl of smoke exited from her sidearm. Melanie trembled against him, her arm still raised. Gently, Luke lowered her arm. The boom camera rose in precision with the director's instruction above their heads, above the relieved looks from the crew, above the tops of the evergreens.

"Cut!" Meyer breathed. The crew broke into applause.

Ben retreated to his trailer to meet Grace, since he wasn't due back on set until that evening. As his foot landed on the top step, he realized he hadn't an appetite for breakfast and even less for a lecture. When he opened his trailer door, the space was empty.

He removed the costume, quickly showered, shrugged on jogging pants, and collapsed on the bed.

Eternity entered the trailer, kicked off her heels, and joined Ben in the bedroom.

As they approached the city from the northeast, Juliana discovered she was holding her breath. She marveled at the magnificent spectacle of colors—the cast of indigo upon the mountains, the lush of emerald layering the city, the rich azure of the water surrounding the land. Specks of alabaster dotted the lakes where boats were moored at the shore.

Thomas had approved her absence without argument. Michael had insisted on traveling with her. Juliana was far too drained to argue. He had ushered her to the ER; it seemed pointless to hide her secret from him any longer.

Juliana huddled in her window seat, allowing her best friend, pastor, and mother to chat excitedly during the three-hour plane ride. Somewhere, far below, was Ben. Although it would only take one phone call to connect to him, Juliana balked at the idea. Her heart had surpassed being satisfied with just the tenor of his voice. Juliana wanted so much more. And it wasn't possible.

After they cleared customs, Juliana detoured. Her mother and Michael agreed to retrieve their rental car while she ambled to Jetway Café and News and ordered a large decaf coffee. Tricia hung with her and grabbed two iced teas. As she shoved the change into her Chanel bag, a male voice called her name. Her head jerked and her eyes frantically searched the area for a familiar face. Ben's face. Tricia joined the search.

Suddenly, a raven-haired girl, near the age of six, rushed to a man standing at the entrance of Bath and Body Works. He scolded her for "rushing off without Daddy," then scooped her up and planted a kiss on her cheek.

Juliana turned and saw the photos. The blood drained from her face. Immortalized in full color was her twisted face and snarling lips as she attacked the man with his camera. Her eye panned; it graced several publications. The revulsion had followed her across the border.

Tricia wrapped her free arm around her shoulder. What should have taken her ten minutes, took twenty. Juliana felt no need to rush to her impending fate. *Why hurry to doctors' grim faces and bleak reports?*

They drove the rental car through downtown to Grouse Mountain connected by one soaring bridge to the other. Juliana ignored the striking scenery offered by Stanley Park, the Capilano Suspension Bridge, and the Cleveland Dam. She rested her head on the window from the rear passenger seat, fixated on the rippled texture of the back of the driver's seat. The two women in the front seat commentated on the beauty of the city, pointing excitedly. Juliana tipped her cup to savor the last drops of coffee.

"Juliana." Michael touched her hand and smiled tenderly.

Juliana lowered the cup. "Hmm?"

"You will make it through this. I know you will."

Juliana placed the empty cup between her knees and found it much more interesting than the optimism in his eyes. When Juliana remained quiet, Michael caressed her hand. Juliana held it limply. "You've always told me God has a purpose and a plan. Always. Remember what you quoted to me in those turbulent first months when I took over as pastor?"

Juliana nodded dully. "Jeremiah 29:11."

"'For I know the plans that I have for you, declares the Lord, plans for welfare and not for calamity to give you a future and a hope.'"

All she could manage was a weak nod. Michael squeezed her hand. "And in the moments ahead of us, when you seem to have forgotten, I'll remind you of His promise to you."

They pulled beneath the maroon colored awning of the Kennedy Center for Women's Health a few minutes after six a.m. Even at that hour, Juliana was greeted and ushered in as if she were a monarch. She completed the necessary insurance paperwork and received a tour of the facility. Although it sprawled from one end to the other, the bronze painted walls, numerous skylights, fireplaces, hearty indoor vegetation, and plush rugs covering pine floors felt inviting. Her first appointment was with the center's head, Dr. Anthony Giantanna, at seven a.m. the following morning.

Sapped, Juliana fell upon the full-sized bed. The last thing she remembered was her mother humming softly as she unpacked her daughter's suitcase.

CHAPTER TWENTY

She glided across the bed and rested inches from him. Her cool fingers caressed the sides of his face and he smelled Chanel perfume. "You're so tense."

Ben blinked slowly in a state of lulled consciousness. He instantly wished he hadn't given Bruce the morning off. She moved her hands to his back and stroked. "Let me help. Remember how I used to ease the tension?"

"Why?" Ben's voice seemed strangled.

"Why not?"

He shook his head, lightly. "Stop."

"You don't want that anymore than I do." Her hands began to move to areas that hadn't experienced a woman's touch since Aiko. Eternity remembered the precise amount of pressure and timing to awaken his every sense.

Every urge in him screamed for release. "You must leave."

"Not until it's time."

"Has there been change since Tommy's hospital room?"

"I've been soul searching."

"Are you still too frightened to create a family?"

"I'm frightened that the man I see before me is headed to a place that I'm not certain he can return."

He pulled away. "That's not what I asked."

"We can talk about that later. Right now, I want you to concentrate on the fact I'm the only one who knows what you put yourself through to portray your characters. And," she kissed his fingertips, "what it takes to bring you out."

Ben lost himself in the luxury of her lips. She looked to the call sheet on the nightstand. "You're not due back on set until late this evening."

She pressed against him and every moment of their martial bliss seeped through him. The grueling shooting schedule, absence of his family, and sheer exhaustion overcame him.

Without knocking, Marcus, Ian, and Grace entered. "Benjamin!"

Once the trio realized where the duo was, all five stared at one another as the air thickened within the sheltered confines of the trailer.

Finally Ian prodded, swinging an imaginary golf club. "Our date with the greens, remember?"

Ben stood. Eternity's voice was like silk. "Ben, we were in the middle of something crucial. Surely it's not too much to ask you to postpone your tee time?"

Her emerald eyes left no doubt that she would meet whatever physical need he had, without reserve.

He looked from Marcus to Ian to Grace. He then pulled Eternity from the bed, placed his hand on the small of her back, and pressed her toward the door. "This is for the best."

Once the amorous guest departed, Marcus asked Ian, "Do we even have a tee time?"

"No." Ian cradled his Blackberry. "At least not at the moment."

"Make it four hours from now." Ben returned to the bed. "And lock the door on your way out."

"All right then, Pinocchio, make the arrangements."

The nurse gently shook Juliana to inform her she needed to take her blood pressure. Juliana blinked and extended her arm.

"Your family went to check into their hotel. They will be back shortly."

She squinted at the nurse's nametag.

"Thanks, Vickie."

Once the sun illuminated the room beyond any possibility of sleep, she moved to the leather chair beneath the window and stared at the violet sky. She smiled, the creases of her mouth higher than they had been since her departure from L.A.

"I know You didn't just do it for me, God, but thank You for making the sunrise my favorite color." She pulled her knees to her chest and hugged them. She heard the clatter of trays as the breakfast round was being served. The scent of the center's coffee brewing crept beneath her door, and she longed for the perfected nectar at Java Amore.

Her mind immediately flashed to Ben, sitting across from her, riveted by her conversation. How that day seemed like an eternity from the days that had crept past.

She grabbed her Bible, clothed in violet leather, from the tabletop. It opened to Psalms 31. Her eyes fell to the first four verses.

> In You, O LORD, I have taken refuge. Let me never be ashamed. In Your righteousness deliver me. Incline Your ear to me, rescue me quickly. Be to me a rock of strength, a stronghold to save me. You are my rock and my fortress. For Your name's sake You will lead me and guide me. You will pull me out of the net which they have secretly laid for me. For You are my strength.

Juliana smoothed the silken pages. "'You will pull me out of the net'? What net?"

Juliana stared at the vivid sky. Her door opened. The staffer removed the tray from the cart's middle shelf and entered the room with a grin. "Did you get a gander at that sunrise? That had to be the richest purple I've ever seen."

Juliana nodded. "It made me breathless."

"Good morning. My name is Margie."

Margie settled the breakfast tray on the table beside Juliana's Bible. "Reading the Psalms, I see. Great book. I find it brings me great comfort when I'm burdened."

"Juliana DeLauer."

The salt and peppered spiky-haired woman stared at the Bible.

Juliana hadn't bothered to wipe the tears, but she suddenly wanted to be left alone.

"You don't know me from Adam, but God wants you to read John 14:27."

Juliana's attention locked on the food service employee. "What did you say?"

Margie had repeated the command with a smile radiating from her core before she departed.

Juliana didn't bother to gather her Bible. The verse had seared her soul and renewed her strength during the months following her father's death.

Juliana's thoughts returned to the tray and she unveiled the contents of her breakfast. "'Peace I leave with you. My peace I give to you; not as the world gives do I give to you. Do not let your heart be troubled, nor let it be fearful.'"

A few days later when Margie entered the room, Juliana was staring out the window and cradling her cell phone in her hand. Her fingers lingered over the letters in preparation to send text. Gingerly, she walked to table. Every placement of her foot on the taupe colored tile shot spasms through her abdomen. Although the doctors had been able to stop the bleeding, the throbbing remained.

"That scripture you told me to look up the other day was long committed to memory."

"Looks as if Someone is trying to get your attention."

"Aren't you concerned someone might report you for quoting Scripture?"

Margie shook her head. "It's all about trust. I make certain the prompting is coming from God before I ever open my mouth."

Juliana surveyed the contents of her breakfast. "My appetite hasn't returned."

"It will," Margie stated, as if Juliana had asked if the sun would rise tomorrow.

"Can I ask you something?"

"Go right ahead."

"Have you ever asked God for something and in the middle of your pleading, He interrupts and poses a question?"

Margie grinned. "Sometimes."

Juliana forked the egg white, tomato, and spinach omelet. She took a bite, swallowed, and tasted nothing. "I allowed my pride to dictate and failed to illustrate His unconditional love."

Margie released a low whistle. "Pride will do that every time. What happened? Your ego got bruised and you squeaked away?"

"Not exactly squeaked. I abandoned someone God brought into my life, someone who needed to see His love fully demonstrated."

Margie clapped her hands and started for the door, her occupational task coming to mind. "If you want to talk more about it after lunch rounds, I can take my break and we can sit by the fireplace."

Juliana mentally recalled her day's agenda. "I'm scheduled for the endometrial biopsy then. I'm guessing I won't be very talkative thereafter."

"I haven't stopped believing He's going to heal you, Juliana."

She smiled faintly. "I appreciate it."

"Keep reading those Psalms and stay encouraged. I'll check on you before I leave for the day."

Juliana forked her breakfast until it was scattered throughout the plate. Finally, she covered it and waited for her guests to arrive. When they departed for lunch, she sat at the table and bowed her head.

"Forgive me, God. Forgive me for not realizing Your plan and purpose for my meeting Ben, Sheila, and the twins. Forgive me for thinking it was all about me. Oh, Lord, forgive me for the hurt I've caused. I pray You will give me the courage to ask for forgiveness. Use me to show them the power of Your love."

She inhaled and dialed. Her hands shook as she switched the cell from one ear to the other.

"Hello." A female voice she didn't recognize answered.

"Hi." She felt her heart's pounding in her throat. "This is Juliana DeLauer. Is Sheila available?"

The female paused. "No. She's working."

"Oh." Sheila must have accepted overtime.

"Juliana, this is Joan Powers. Her aunt. Ben's mother."

"Oh." She inhaled sharply, then forgot to exhale for a few moments. "Hi."

"Hello." The woman's tone carried the same easiness and poise of her son's. "I will leave her a message informing her you called. I assume she has a number to reach you."

Suddenly, Juliana heard one of the twins scream her name. Then the subsequent staccato of questions: Is that really Juliana! Auntie, I want to talk to her. Where is she? Can I please talk to her, Auntie?

"Juliana, the boys would like to speak with you. Is that okay?"

The tears burned against her cheeks. "Absolutely."

Juliana pictured one of the twins taking the black cordless phone with his tiny hands. "Juliana!"

She reached for the tissue box and wiped her face. There was no doubt she would have to reapply her makeup. "Timmy. Hello, little man. How are you?"

"Good. Auntie was reading the paper. It's snowing in Denver a lot."

"It is?"

"Yeah. There were pictures of lots of snow."

"I'm away from Colorado."

"Are you here?"

"No, sweetie."

"When can we come visit? Mommy says there's lots of horses where you live. I want to ride the horse on the mountain. Tommy can if you or Mommy hold him."

She sighed. "Oh, baby. Let me talk to your mom about it first."

He sighed as if she had denied him of something essential. "Okay. She'll be home later. Can you call then?"

Juliana nodded. "Yes. I will. How is Tommy?"

"Tommy!" He screamed without taking the phone from his mouth. "Juliana wants to talk to you."

She heard rustling and mumbled questioning. "Juliana? When are you taking me to Disneyland? And Legoland?"

"Hi, little guy. I have to ask your mom first. How are you feeling?"

"Good. I'm walking faster. She won't mind. I just can't walk for a long time. I get real tired."

Juliana rested her head on her bent hand and tried to corral her emotions. "I am so glad to hear that, little guy. That is amazing."

"And my scars are almost gone. Mom says it's 'cause you prayed a lot and asked God to fix me."

She laughed and the tears ran into the corners of her mouth. "It wasn't just me, Tommy. There were hundreds praying for you."

"Mom and Auntie don't know this, but I was praying you would call again."

Juliana felt her body shake as she wept. "Really?"

"Yep. And, you did."

"God is marvelous, isn't He?"

"What does that mean?"

"Marvelous?"

"Yeah, marbleus."

"It means the best and the greatest."

"Yeah," then to his brother, "she said she had to talk to Mom first."

"I didn't realize how much I missed you two."

"You're not home?"

"No. I'm in Canada."

"She said Canada," he answered his brother. "Wait, that's where Uncle Ben is? Are you with Uncle Ben?"

Juliana looked out the window beyond the lake toward the eastern view of the mountain. "No, sweetie."

"Auntie said he's making a movie in—" The boy took the phone from his mouth and asked his aunt the name of the city Ben was filming. "Vancouver. Do you know where that is?"

"Yes." She traced a pattern on the tabletop and discovered the dampness her finger left behind. "I'm in Vancouver also."

Even miles away, Juliana perceived his mind twirling. "Then why aren't you with Uncle Ben? He's your friend." His observation struck Juliana deep in her heart.

She nodded. "You're absolutely right, Tommy."

Again, she heard rustling. "Auntie says we have to eat our lunch. Do you promise to call Mommy when she comes home?"

She smiled through the tears. This type of persistence from an adult would have been met with bullheaded resistance. From the twins, it caused fractures in her obstinacy. "I promise."

Joan returned to the phone. "They can be something, can't they?"

"Yes. Gloriously something."

"Are you all right, Juliana?"

Juliana cleared her throat. "I had no idea how much I missed them."

"They talk about you all the time. You made an impression that will likely last a lifetime."

"As they have in me. It's difficult to reject the unconditional love of a child."

"Working in landscaping, I've come to realize some things. When you set an impression in fertile medium, the only way to destroy the impact is to annihilate the medium."

Stunned, Juliana sat staring at her Adidas.

"Otherwise, it remains for life."

All Juliana could muster was, "Thank you for telling me."

"Take care, Juliana. I'll be certain to tell Sheila you called."

Juliana disconnected.

There was still one call she needed to make.

CHAPTER TWENTY-ONE

Ben returned to his trailer after the morning shoot and dialed Sheila's number. The twins both picked up extensions and informed him of their latest adventures. Their voices caused tenderness to prod at his soul.

"Auntie's taking us to the beach. Tommy says he ready."

"Auntie says she hasn't been to the beach in years."

"Yeah, she can get pretty busy helping Uncle Sam planting stuff."

"She needs a tan," Timmy said.

"Mom said that wasn't nice to say, Timmy."

"Sorry, but, she does."

"Oh, you two are Uncle's Ben heart."

"No, we're not."

"Mommy said your heart is in your chest. We don't live there."

Ben squeezed the tears with the tips of his fingers. He took a quick sip from his papaya juice. "Oh, but you do."

"Oh, we talked to Juliana."

Ben spit the contents on the table. "What?"

"She didn't know anything about the snow," Timmy stated.

Ben wiped up his mess with a napkin. "Did you say you talked to Juliana?"

"Yeah. But, she wasn't at home," Tommy said.

"She was away from Colorado so we can't ride horses with her," Timmy added.

"In the mountains," Tommy informed.

"In Colorado," Timmy expounded.

"When did you talk to her?"

"Today."

"But we had to go eat lunch."

"Did Auntie talk to her?"

The boys fell into a fit of giggles. "Silly."

"Of course, Uncle Ben. She answered the phone."

Ben cleared his throat, exited the trailer, and headed toward the meadow. "You said she wasn't at home."

"Nope."

"She was away," Timmy informed. "She said she'd call Mommy when she got home from work."

The air caught his Ben's throat. "Did she say where she was?"

"Yep."

Silence. Ben wasn't able to contain himself. "Can you tell me?"

"She said she didn't see you."

"I guess Bandcover is big."

He stopped mid-step. "Vancouver. She's here in Vancouver?"

"Told you it was Vancover, Timmy."

"So what, Tommy? You're not always right."

"Boys!" Ben shouted then lowered his head. "I'm sorry. I didn't mean to shout."

"Are you going to see her?" Tommy asked.

The fortress of prideful resolution began to splinter. "I'd like nothing more. Tell Auntie and Mommy I'll call them later. I love you."

Ben stood gazing at the breathtaking splendor before him. As much as it had driven his creative forces to breathe life into Luke Bailey, it also drove him to ignore the arguments and justifications not to call her.

As he dialed her number, the questions bombarded his mind. *Where, when, why was she here? Had she actually decided to mend their broken relationship?*

"Hello?"

Ben frowned and immediately his heart sank to depths unparalleled. He released the call. Wherever Juliana was in the city, she wasn't lacking companionship. The person who answered her phone was clearly a man.

Juliana's cell rang as she washed her hands. "Can somebody grab that?"

Michael, Tricia, and Dionne searched for the phone. On the fourth ring, they discovered it beneath a *Style* magazine Tricia had purchased to cheer Juliana up. Michael was nearest the phone; he picked it up and read the display. "B.P."

Fifth ring.

Juliana stumbled through the bathroom door. "Answer it before it stops ringing!"

"Hello." The pastor greeted, smiled at her, and repeated. "Hello?"

He glanced at the display. "They hung up."

Juliana sank to the bed's edge and caressed her belly. "He hung up because a man answered."

"He who?" Tricia asked from her seat beneath the mounted TV. "Oh, sweet Jesus. Ben!"

The phone rang again. Dionne took it from the pastor's grasp, pressed the answer button, and handed the phone to Juliana.

"Hello." Juliana sighed, fully expecting Ben's voice.

"They said you were alive. But, honestly, I was beginning to wonder."

"Sheila."

"Why has it been so long since we've heard from you?"

"Things have gotten complicated."

"Things are always complicated. You realize that's a lousy excuse?"

"Understood."

"The boys tell me you're in Vancouver."

"I am, although it's probably not what you think."

"What do I think?"

"I'm here to see Ben."

"It certainly is what I was hoping."

"I'm receiving treatment at the Kennedy Center for Women's Health." Juliana informed why the procedures were merited.

Sheila remained quiet for a moment. "Complicated was an understatement. You have people around you who are encouraging you, full of faith, right?"

"I do."

"Good. You still like chocolate?"

"More than ever."

"I'm sending you the most indulgent package of chocolate your taste buds will ever experience. Keep it away from the nurses. They won't be able to concentrate on their job for dreaming of the decadent parcel."

"Thanks, Sheila. Hey, what's the latest on the criminal proceedings of the accident?"

"The guy's toxicology report stated he was not only wasted on alcohol but had a hazardous amount of drugs in his system. It's a marvel he was able to insert the key into the ignition. He pled guilty on all counts."

"He did?"

"My attorney said it was just plain weird. He didn't even want to discuss a plea. It was as if he was *anxious* to get behind bars. He received the maximum amount of time—twenty years to life. The kid is only nineteen."

"What of the fifteen grand in the front seat?"

"The police believe it may be drug money. However, the kid isn't talking. He was just in a hurry to get behind prison walls. It was like he felt safer in there."

"Weird."

"That's what I'm saying."

"Okay, onto brighter conversation. How is Dr. Troy?"

"Brilliant. Determined. Persistent."

"Are you speaking personally or professionally?"

"Both. But my hands are already quite full."

"Why are you so reluctant to give him a chance?"

"Because I'm an ER surgical nurse who happens to work in the same hospital he performs most of his surgeries. It would be like fraternizing with the help."

Juliana held her belly at that one, the laughter rippling in appealing waves. "I love you, Sheila."

"How could you not? My charm is irresistible."

"Then you shouldn't deny Dr. Troy a measly date."

"Are you certain you want to discuss denying men dates?"

"You win."

"Hey, Jules?"

"Yeah."

"This cancer doesn't have the audacity to whip you. You hear me?"

"I hear you."

"Keep me informed. I love you back."

Juliana agreed, asked Sheila to explain the situation to the twins, and disconnected the call. She held the phone beneath her chin and it rang once more. Without looking at the display, she chimed, "Grand Central Station."

There was silence. After a moment he spoke and Juliana felt the quiver tickle her spine. "How are you?"

She looked at the anxious faces surrounding her. "I've been better."

"Is something wrong?"

"I'm in Vancouver receiving medical treatments."

Tricia and Dionne shot one another furtive glances. Michael leaned against the table and crossed his ankles, inspecting the sheen of his shoes.

"Treatments? For what?"

"There was a mass found on my uterus. I'm due for my biopsy in just a few moments to see if it's benign or … " Her voice dropped.

She heard Ben's irregular breathing. "I want to be there with you. May I?"

Slowly, she nodded and gave him the center's name. "I'm headed to the operating room soon. The procedure is scheduled to last only a few minutes. I may be asleep when you arrive."

"I'm on my way."

"Ben." The line was already void of connection.

Dr. Giantanna arrived, wheelchair in tow. "Your carriage awaits."

Ben had disconnected before she had the opportunity to advise him of Michael's presence.

He discovered Bruce chatting with the stunt coordinator and snapped his fingers.

"We're snapping fingers to get my attention, Jenny?" Bruce questioned.

"I said you could call me that after I falsely accused you while we were in Denver."

"I thought you meant anytime your behavior was questionable."

"Then, you should have been referring to me as 'Jenny' since our arrival."

"I wanted to keep my job. What's up?"

"Juliana is in Vancouver."

"She is?"

"I just spoke to her. She's receiving treatments at the Kennedy Center for Women's Health. I'm looking up the address now."

They drove the winding road toward the patrolled barricades and security gate. Bruce pulled off the roadside just inches from the security booth and exit. The paparazzi climbed off their hunches and sprang to action. The bulbs flashed like firecrackers.

Ben shifted in the seat to gain a clearer view of the Blackberry screen. "Here it is. That can't be." Ben looked directly ahead at the street sign.

"What did you find?"

"2393 Olive Tree Lane."

"That's the road we're facing."

They exited the lot, turned left, and discovered the address numbers of the dime store and gas station along the road increased. Bruce turned the vehicle around and aimed the car down the winding mountain road a few kilometers. In less than ten minutes, they arrived at the sprawling center cloaked by maple trees, rose bushes, and meticulously sculpted shrubs. The same lake that edged the set was within walking distance from the center.

"How may I assist you?" the guard asked from his position in the booth.

"Mr. Benjamin Powers here to visit Miss Juliana DeLauer," Bruce answered. The guard checked his list and requested photo ID's for confirmation.

The guard returned their ID's with an affable nod. "Please check in at the welcome desk."

"Thank you." Bruce passed Ben his ID. "Also, may I ask a favor?"

"Sir?"

"Do you see the navy Tahoe, white Taurus, and Honda CR-V idling on the side of the street?"

The guard glanced and nodded. "Yes?"

"It's press Mr. Powers hasn't authorized to follow him. Do you understand my meaning?"

"Absolutely."

"Your cooperation will not go unrewarded," Ben pledged.

Although Bruce stood several inches taller than Ben, it was an effort to keep up with Ben's swift strides. As they approached the desk, a toffee-skinned woman with flawless skin and womanly curves stepped in his path.

"I'm Tricia." Her voice quaked.

"Tricia." Ben extended his hand. "Pleased to meet you."

She shook it as if she had waited an eternity to do so. "Yes, you are."

He released her hand and smiled. "Is her procedure complete?"

She stared, taking him in like a sculpted masterpiece. "Who? I'm sorry. I'm just a bundle of nerves. Dr. Giantanna said it would take only a few minutes."

"I'm harmless and will probably end up boring you to tears." He noticed he had drawn the attention of several staffers. "Juliana sounded as if it's been a tough struggle."

"It's hard to read Juliana because she has a tremendous tolerance for pain. None of us knew how serious her situation had progressed. Is this Bruce, your bodyguard?"

Ben followed the direction of her beautifully manicured finger. Ben nodded and made introduction. "Forgive me."

They shook hands. "Okay. Follow me."

They walked through a dimmed corridor with bronzed walls, russet colored sconces, thick rugs, and black-and-white photos of women of all nationalities and ages. Ben paused and admired the craftsmanship and technique.

"Those are women who've been diagnosed with cancer and received treatment here."

"Are they all survivors?" Ben asked.

Tricia pointed to the silver plate beneath one of the photos. The face that peered back at him couldn't have been more than twenty. "Not everyone. As you can see she passed away last year."

Ben felt as if lead had been added to his legs. He stepped back. "She was so young."

Tricia nodded, sadly. "They nicknamed her Bull Dog because of her spirit. She gave the staff quite a challenge because even when she was very weak toward the end, she refused to lie in bed. She would insist on being brought to the fireplace to visit with the other patients."

Once they cleared the hall, the space opened to a large social area where women sat conversing on loveseats, watching movies, surfing the web, or playing board games. The massive fireplace covered the wall with blonde flagstone. Lilting sounds of classical guitar radiated throughout the quarter. They turned left and Tricia used a swipe card to open the door. It chimed and released the lock. If they had turned right, they would have passed the operating suites and recovery rooms.

Tricia entered the room three doors down, to the left. The perfume hit him before he rounded the corner. Bouquets by the dozen covered every available counter, shelf, or windowsill colored in variations of purple. Tricia opened bottled water near the small sink and gulped. She sighed and extended the offer to the men. Both declined.

She took a seat at the table beneath the picture window framed in the same flagstone that had covered the open area fireplace. Ben hoped every room had such an inspiring view. Bruce hung near the door.

"You must have rushed right over."

"May I?" Ben touched the top of the chair opposite Tricia.

She nodded, the ebony waves of her hair swirled against her high-sculpted cheeks. "Go right ahead."

He joined her at the table. "Surprisingly, our set is just a few kilometers inland."

She smiled; it felt like the first signs of spring after a bleak winter. "I see you've acclimated to the region."

"When in Rome…"

She filled in the details from the time Juliana had collapsed until he phoned her that morning.

"The procedure, the biopsy, will it be painful?"

"The doctor stated that they extract a piece of her uterus and send it off to the lab. The nurse brought her ibuprofen about an hour ago."

Ben felt dread linger at the base of his spine. "There are these thoughts that won't let go. Was she in pain while in L.A.? Was she suffering in silence because she didn't want to worry us? And, if so, why didn't I see it?"

"Dr. Martin, her GYN in Denver, said this condition has been coming on for months, even before L.A."

"So it was simply a matter of time?"

"That's my understanding."

He rubbed the hair on his chin. "I'm got some questions, and please tell me if I've gone beyond what she'd desire for you to reveal. Can you tell me what the condition is?"

"You mean what brought this on?"

"Yes."

"She experienced a marked increase in abdominal pain with bleeding when she returned from L.A. Juliana is diligent about keeping her appointments with Dr. Martin, but this erupted the day before her scheduled office visit. There's more to why this test was run, but Juliana will need to share that with you. It seems the increase of stress accelerated the pain, which turned out to be a blessing. It may have saved her from having radical surgery."

"What kind of radical surgery?"

Tricia grimaced. "Okay. Remember when you told me to stop when I needed? Well, we've reached that point."

Ben stared at the indigo hills of Grouse Mountain, its beauty failing to register in his sight.

"Ben?" Tricia called, softly.

He returned his focus to her.

Tricia's face held a patient smile. "We don't know anything for certain at this point."

Ben frowned. "Are you worried?"

Tricia's eyes answered before her mouth could. "I have faith God will heal her. I have to. No matter what those tests may claim. Besides, God knows how much I need her to be around and be my babies' auntie."

Ben glanced at Bruce whose demeanor remained solid, but his eyes harbored apprehension.

"How is filming?" Tricia asked.

Ben consciously lowered his shoulders. "This role has been very demanding. When I return to the set, I'll be begging apologies."

"Oh-oh."

"I've not been peaceable or kind."

Tricia recognized the phrase from the Bible and raised a perfectly waxed brow but kept her thoughts concealed. Ben turned at the sound of the door opening. A nurse wheeled Juliana into the room. Her eyes were closed in a grimace.

The last time he had seen her as she climbed out of Sheila's SUV, her complexion had vigor, her body perceivably healthy, her hair a mass of chunky curls. This woman who sat in the wheelchair, visibly battling pain and trepidation, caused Ben's heart to shred.

Dionne followed the chair, her expression optimistic and resolute. He stood and moved to Juliana. The nurse assisted her to the bed, watched as she settled, and tucked the chenille blanket beside her frail body. The door clicked as the nurse retreated.

Her eyes quickly scanned the room. "Wassup?"

The room filled with nervous laughter. She evenly met his gaze. "Hey."

"Hey." Ben's voice fractured; he cleared his throat.

"I'm only on Ibuprofen, but because I'm such a lightweight it causes me to be a little sleepy."

"I don't need conversation."

She smiled, tiredly. "You may change your mind once I start snoring."

Dionne walked beside the bed. "Mrs. DeLauer."

"Dionne." She corrected with a smile and embraced him. The arsenal he had fortified in the previous weeks crumbled against the force of her affection. Ben felt as if a benevolent supremacy had infiltrated his soul.

Dionne asked, "We're going to the cafeteria for lunch. Would you care to join us?"

When Ben hesitated, she offered, "Or we could bring something back for you."

"A small black coffee will be fine."

As they departed, Bruce followed. Ben lifted a chair from the table and noticed a Bible dressed in amethyst rested upon a *Style* magazine. He placed the chair at her bedside.

"You look like I feel, Powers. What kinds of unreasonable things are they making you do on set?"

Ben stroked her hand. "You look amazing."

"Liar. You'd never make it as an actor."

"I have missed you. So very much."

She weakly squeezed his hand. "Me too." She attempted to shift and winced.

"What is it?"

"Cramps."

"Pretty bad?"

"It could be much worse."

Ben wasn't ready to inquire how. "Do you want me to allow you to rest?"

"Only if you promise to stay very near my side." She inhaled through her nose then exhaled slowly. "But, Ben, I'm not alone."

He watched, as her breaths grew deeper and soon she was asleep. The realization flooded within. He could live without Juliana. Had since that cruel night weeks ago in December. But he never wanted to again. He placed her hand on the bed and gently rested his forehead on top of it, his hair spilling over the frail appendage.

Kevin. Tomorrow. And the numerous other men, women, and children infected with AIDS. Ben had experienced every one of their deaths, each one carving at the meat of him. Now Juliana was threatening an ill-conceived departure, and Ben could no longer hold his composure.

His tears pooled over her hand. "Don't take her."

CHAPTER TWENTY-TWO

His heart tightened as memories of those burials plagued him. The virus shrank his friend's professionally athletic physique to ninety-eight pounds. Although Kevin feared his faults would cost him dearly, he rebuffed Ben's advice to mend the guilt. Kevin agonized that his rejection of Sheila and the twins would be scorned in the afterlife, but he refused to reconcile his mistake.

He had asked Ben to climb into bed with him as death hovered.

Ben had and rested his friend's head on his chest. While Kevin slept, Ben had pleaded with God to delay his death and allow Kevin another opportunity to correct his mistakes.

God refused.

How can anyone love a Being who had the power to rectify, yet snubbed the request?

He determined God to be a malevolent ruler who took great pleasure in the tears of His creation, and if God took Juliana all desire to ever know Him would die with her.

"There is much to tell, Juliana," he whispered. "But, when? When do I tell you I may not grow old?"

He stared at her breathing until the women returned. Dionne encouraged him to join them at the table. Even after he sat, Ben couldn't turn his attention from Juliana.

Dionne tenderly patted his hand and handed him the coffee.

"The doctor stated the procedure went well. We should have the results by tomorrow afternoon."

"She seems to be in a lot of pain," Ben remarked.

"The procedure causes the discomfort similar to cramps. However, she's sleeping, so it means the Ibuprofen has kicked in."

Ben nodded, not at all relieved. Dionne patted his hand once more. "God has a purpose and plan for everything. His children don't suffer in vain."

Ben sipped his coffee. "I truly hope you're right."

"I can show you if you're seriously interested."

"Let's just say I find it interesting that you're convinced."

She reached for Juliana's Bible and flipped the pages. "This is the truth, not a truth or a form of the truth. But the truth."

"Dionne, with all due respect, I've studied dozens of religions. They all speak of the same goal. We are to love one another, assist one another, and live lives of integrity."

"Whose integrity?"

Ben leaned forward. "The authentic enlightenment of integrity."

"But, Ben, whose enlightenment of integrity? Mine, yours? And where does the authenticity derive?"

"From the masters who have studied and lived their lives according to what they believe. Are you trying to tell me what they taught has no validity?"

"I'm saying there is a semblance of validity because of where they derived their beliefs. If you take the time to dig in this book, you'll see most of what they profess is rooted within these pages."

Ben eyed her warily. It irritated him that Christians couldn't converse about God without shuffling to the Bible. "I'm not convinced."

"It's all right here, Ben. All you have to do is open it and see for yourself."

"You said you were going to show me something about people suffering unnecessarily."

She laughed, her eyes brimming with compassion. "I said I would show you that Juliana is not suffering in vain." She shifted the Bible so he could also see the words. "Here. Listen to this from Psalm 34 starting at verse 17. 'The righteous cry, and the Lord hears and delivers them out of all their troubles. The Lord is near to the brokenhearted and saves those who are crushed in spirit. Many are the afflictions of the righteous. But the Lord delivers him out of them all.'"

Bruce eased through the door and held his position.

"Impeccable timing, Mr. Bruce." Tricia giggled.

"What did I miss?" Bruce's expression was cool.

"We're reading in the Bible how God safeguards."

Bruce nodded. "Best bodyguard I've ever met."

Ben looked at him as if betrayed, utterly unaware of his shadow's convictions. "I had no idea."

"You didn't honestly think my flawless skill came solely from me, did you?"

"You never told me."

Bruce smirked, impishly. "All those books you've seen me reading. The titles never struck you?"

"How long?"

"Two years. After the accident in Milan."

Ben's expression changed from perplexed to exasperation. "I feel outnumbered."

Dionne grinned. "View it as being in exceptional company."

"I heard *all* of their troubles."

"You heard correctly."

"I'm wondering."

"Tell me."

Ben grinned at the shared phrase between mother and daughter. "Have you ever seen this fail? Has God ever not saved someone from their troubles?"

"Certainly."

Ben rubbed his forehead. "I'm confused."

"There's a key here. The righteous. Do you know what that means according to God?"

"Probably not."

"Those who are in right standing, which is based upon their relationship with Him. There is a passion, a hunger to become more like Him."

Ben's mind flashed to the perpetual dream and the words he cried: I thirst. "So, God is only in the business of rescuing those who have a relationship with Him?"

"No. He doesn't ban assistance from those who don't know Him. I'm sure you've supported many you've never met."

"I have."

"The beauty of God is that He doesn't only help those who love Him either. He is eager to help those who have cursed Him or consistently deny His existence. He thrives to support those who haven't ever asked for His aid. Just like you."

"But you're saying it's different for those who have this relationship with Him?"

"It's like this. How often would you deny Tommy and Timmy access to you?"

"I can't imagine I ever would."

"Why?"

"Because I love them. I love spending time with them. They hold a very special place in my heart."

"You revel in your relationship with them?"

"Yes."

"What about your agent?"

Bruce snickered. "That's probably not the best example."

"Okay. Let's say your manager."

"I adore Grace. But it's different."

"How?"

Ben rubbed his chin in thought. "The level of relationship. It's much more personal with the twins. I share much more of myself with them than with Grace. I'd give my life for them."

"Bingo." Tricia grinned.

Dionne affirmed, "God is good. Period. Although we sing praises and declare this from the pulpit and pews, many believers struggle to adhere to how exact that statement is. If we truly believed He is good that means no matter what circumstance erupts in our lives, it is for our good because He loves us, He is connected to us and always has our best interest at heart."

"Any circumstance?"

She nodded, solemnly. "Yes."

"Rape? Premature death? Murder?"

"Yes."

Ben unbuttoned his sleeves and folded them to his elbow. "Cancer?"

Dionne's answer resounded in her stare. "That's what I'm saying."

"I've seen it fail."

She frowned and leaned back in her chair. "That surprises me."

"Steven was six and his HIV had rapidly advanced. Before he became too weak, we kicked the soccer ball daily through the surrounding fields. Every afternoon, he would habitually make me join him in prayer. I did because I saw how much better it made him feel. God didn't heal him. He died two months later."

Dionne's gaze never wavered, although Ben's glowered. After a deep silence, she spoke, "Ben, I pray from the depths of my spirit that you hear my heart when I say this to you. I have never pretended to have all the answers. God has done some things that I ache to receive revelation. But, if we could figure out every facet of God, then He would no longer be God. I trust that He loves me no matter the situation."

She took another long moment to look out the window. "Do you mind my asking what you two prayed?"

"He asked God to make his pain go away."

Tricia started to beam, but kept quiet.

Dionne touched his hand. "What do you remember about heaven from what you were taught in childhood?"

He shrugged. "It's a place of inexplicable joy. There is overflowing beauty. No tears, only rejoicing."

She remained silent as the thought penetrated his brain.

Ben assailed, "That's not healing! That's death! That's the end!"

"People fear death because they're uncertain what awaits them on the other side. If you are connected with the Father there is nothing to fear. Death is only the beginning."

Ben rubbed his beard in frustrated contemplation. Her logic to trust in an unseen, capricious being was ludicrous and irresponsible to Ben. No matter how many angles he examined it with his mind, it never computed.

Dionne asked, "You still willing to dig?"

Ben shrugged again. "Sure."

"Okay." She ripped a piece of paper from the pad on the table carrying the center's logo, wrote on it, then handed it to him. "I recommend these books for you to begin your search."

Ben read the paper. She had written in confident script the Bible, *Mere Christianity* by C.S. Lewis, and *The Case for Christ* by Lee Strobel. Ben tucked it in his shirt pocket.

Juliana roused. Ben was the first to her bedside.

She covered a yawn with her hand. "Now, I'm ready for that six-mile jog."

Dionne rubbed Juliana's forehead. "Your visitor should return in about an hour. Why don't we give you and Ben some time to catch up?"

Juliana nodded tiredly. "Thanks, Mom."

Tricia kissed her cheek. "We'll see you around dinner."

Bruce retreated to the car under the pretense of returning calls.

"Are you still in pain?" Ben asked from his seat beside the bed.

"It's lessened." Juliana sighed. "I have something to say to you."

He sat straighter. "Tell me."

"You have been hanging out with me too long." Juliana yawned again. "I was so overwhelmed with my feelings for you, I agreed the best solution was to run as far as I could—emotionally and physically."

Ben reached for her hand and she gave it readily.

"I failed to show you who God truly is. He doesn't abandon simply because the situation becomes uncomfortable."

"Is that all?" Ben sighed and closed his eyes.

He felt the sudden tremble in her hand. She looked out the window at the towering maples then slowly returned her attention to him. "I didn't count on the fact I might fall in love with you."

He had to call upon every restraint to not dash around the room. "Say that again."

"I'm in love with you. But I'm also a bit appalled at myself."

"Now, that's what a guy wants to hear."

"Listen. I've been raised quite differently. I never dated boys who weren't believers. I simply knew, beyond a shadow of a doubt, it was an incredible waste of time. It would only lead to unbearable heartbreak. Yet, knowing that full well, I did it with you anyway. My heart is breaking."

Ben thought, *Tell her.* He opened his mouth, but she held up a hand.

"Please let me finish. I want to marry you and fuss over you and gorge myself on your pecan pies."

"I'd let you."

"But I can't have you."

"You already do."

"But I don't."

"I don't want to be just your friend, Juliana. Besides, you've just proposed."

She touched his cheek. "We can't expect any more, Ben. Not now."

He released her hand and stood with his back to her. He looked over his shoulder. "I'm yours, Juliana. Whenever you're ready. But there is so much more I have to tell you."

"I'll be ready the moment we're serving the same God."

He measured her conviction against his troublesome confession until the silence seemed raucous. He walked to one of the elaborate sprays and fumbled with the card. The name caught his eye. *I hope your room reminds you of your favorite garden. Purple, fragrant, and created by the One who loves you eternally. Michael.*

Ben moved to the next vase, then the next, until he had read all twenty. He shuffled the cards between his fingers. Pastor Michael had sent fifteen out of twenty dazzling arrangements. The others were from Thomas and Maya, the fellowship of Living Water, Winston, and co-workers.

"This is a bit overkill, don't you think?"

"I thought it was sweet."

"Sweet?" Ben nearly screeched.

"Yes—"

"Sweet may have been a half dozen."

"Ben—"

"What is the man trying to prove?"

"Listen—"

"Every time you look around, he's here."

"He—"

"Fifteen!"

"Already—"

"Way too extreme."

"Is."

"What?"

She leaned her head on the pillow. "Let's stop fighting."

Ben narrowed his eyes. "Oh, Juliana, this is priceless!"

"Come to me."

"Let me guess," he did a perfect pirouette with his hands raised. "Your favorite flower is the calla lily."

She flung her arm across her eyes. "This is hard enough without you throwing a fit."

Ben's thoughts gathered like ants upon a decaying insect. "*He's* the visitor expected in an hour?"

"Let's stop this. Come to me."

He stormed to her bed and leaned close. "Who answered the phone when I called?"

She removed her arm. "What? When?"

"When I called, Juliana!"

He witnessed as resolution reddened her features. "Michael."

"Oh, now, it's Michael."

She grabbed his shoulders. "I called you because I was being hypocritical. I sulked, retreated, and licked my wounds as if that was the most important issue. It wasn't. God wanted you to witness, in actual practice, the power He possesses. He touched my stubborn, broken heart to the point that I realized He wanted to use me to reveal Himself to you."

"Why would God need to use you?"

"Because that's what He does, Ben. People are His vessels, His hands, His tools. He uses us to show those who don't know what He's like. And I love Him so much I swallowed my pride and called you to ask for forgiveness. He never would have walked away from you, no matter how much it ripped Him apart. There is too much at stake."

Ben tossed the cards on her lap. He watched them rise and fall a few times then he looked her in the eye. "Do you have feelings for him?"

She released him. "Ben."

"I'm waiting."

Her pale lips tightened. "This is about God needing you to see how deeply He cares for you. What I feel for Michael is irrelevant."

He leaned closer. "Not to me."

She searched his pained eyes for several moments then blinked against the fresh tears. "I can't deny that I care about him. We're very close."

"If I never come to believe like you, he is your choice?"

"This is impossible."

"Just be honest and admit it."

The door opened and Ben looked over his shoulder. "Speak of the devil."

Ben walked to the door without acknowledging the pastor.

"Ben."

He halted his rushed exit.

"He is not the devil."

Ben rushed through the door, where he was no longer obliged to face either of them.

He completed shooting at 3:30 the following afternoon and took a swim at an exclusive health club near the set. As the water pooled over his body, he wondered exactly what had upset him so. He had dealt with competition before. But this competition possessed an upper hand inaccessible to Ben. And Ben's pathetic display yesterday had not scored him points.

He wouldn't blame Juliana if she returned to Denver and married Michael. But he sensed he would never recover. She had told him she loved him, ached that she couldn't be with him, and he had picked a fight. Their paths collided in a bitter wind, and Ben had grappled to hold onto her ever since.

Ben only instigated conflict when he refused to face the inescapable.

He had done it when Eternity pulled away, moved out of their home, and filed divorce papers. He had ranted with her about everything except the reality that she no longer wanted to be his wife.

He had picked a fight with the hospital staff when the morgue assistant arrived for Kevin's body. Ben had refused, even when Marcus, Ian, and Sheila had gently urged him.

He flipped on his back to explore the sapphire sky through the transparent dome. Juliana's convictions were stronger than any promises he could vow and more tenacious than his charm. What carved at him like a captive buried alive was that he couldn't guarantee Juliana the future she deserved. There was so much left unsaid. *Does she want children? Is she open to adoption? Is she willing to risk marriage to a dying man?*

He explored the vastness of the sky. Ben had fully embraced the appeal of free thought. It is what fueled his intrinsic acting ability. Free thought swayed into free expression and free expression melted into unhindered freedom. This freedom allowed him to access places where he could portray a corporate executive who sanctioned the deaths of innocent people for his personal gain, the Nazi general who sharpened his firearm aim on Jewish children, or the mentally disabled man who strove to raise his younger siblings despite the government's interference.

Ben turned on his belly and returned to the stairs. *What if Dionne is right? What if there is no such thing as all paths lead to God? What if there is only one truth conceived by God? Where would that leave me, as my feelings border on disgust toward that Supremacy?*

Jessica and Bruce ceased their conversation as he climbed out. If Ben were paranoid, he would have bet he was the subject of their chat.

"You must have been on the swim team?" Jessica handed Ben a towel.

He wiped off. "Four-hundred meter relay. I lettered two years in a row."

"Will the wonders ever cease?"

"I gave you the afternoon off. Why aren't you scouring the streets of Burnaby for the latest treasure?"

She tossed her dark hair and it swirled across her bare shoulders. "It's two below zero and I received a disturbing call."

He picked up the Polo shirt neatly folded on the pool chair. "That sounds ominous."

"My friend from *Rumors*."

"That's my least favorite tabloid."

"She very much enjoys food, clothing, and shelter."

"There are other ways to earn a living."

"I agree. Why don't you hire her for your production company? That way she can get away from that sleaze?"

"Slow down, Kemosabi. Let's see what she had to report."

"You're not going to like it."

"I never do."

"One of the photographers has been trying to date her for months. One of his packages was accidentally delivered to her area, so she returned it to the photo department. He was promising her a night of unbridled bliss when her eyes fell on some photos. They were photos of Juliana."

Ben shrugged and walked toward the exit. "Pictures of her are everywhere."

Jessica followed her Stuart Weitzman heels clacking on the tile. "She was sitting beneath a large maple tree conversing with a doctor."

"How do you know it was a doctor?"

"The insignia on his coat was enlarged. A Dr. Giantanna of the Kennedy Center."

Ben stopped, stared down at her, and cursed. He entered the locker room, shrugged off the wet trunks, and tugged on his warm up suit. When he exited, Jessica continued.

"She said it's due to run in next week's edition. It doesn't seem as if they have any other details, except that it's a place where women with cancer receive treatment."

He cursed again, and after a moment of pounding his fist into his palm, he apologized. "I have to warn Juliana."

"I thought this was something you wanted to do in person, so I made the arrangements. Frontier has a flight that departs in ninety minutes and arrives at eight p.m. Your call sheet states you're not due on the set until noon tomorrow."

"She's not in Denver."

Jessica twisted her ruby colored mouth. "I don't understand."

"It's only a few kilometers from here." Ben shrugged on his down jacket. "She was trying to get away from the press in the U.S. for this very reason."

"Ben, I'm so sorry. I wish there was more I could do. Even if my friend somehow destroyed the photos, the digital files are still on the photographer's hard drive."

"You've done plenty. I truly appreciate it, Jessica. Tell your friend to forward me her resumé."

"Thanks, Ben. At least she'll be able to sleep tonight."

They returned to the lot and parted when the men entered his bungalow. Ben picked up his phone from the table.

"You're calling her?" Bruce's bass seemed to plunge deeper.

"She has to be warned."

"In a phone call?"

"After yesterday I don't think she wants to see me."

"Gee, Boss, forget the phone call. Why don't you just text her?"

Ben rolled his eyes. "You don't understand."

"You are too afraid to face her and all the implications that might bring."

"Is your resumé updated?"

Bruce unbuttoned his coat and sat on the bench near the door. "You can't fire me. We're in too thick—like Mafia."

"So, my only option is to kill you?"

Bruce, for the first time since the slaying in Boptang, grinned.

Oblivious to the duo, Jessica shivered from a concealed spot as Ben and Bruce raced to their car. She pressed number two on her speed dial.

"Grace Connors."

"He knows. Everything is in motion."

CHAPTER TWENTY-THREE

Dr. Giantanna sat next to her at the table in her room. "The endometrial biopsy was inconclusive."

Juliana rubbed her forehead. Tricia caressed her hand. Her mother rubbed her shoulder blades. Michael exhaled as if he had just surfaced from the water's skin.

"So, what's next?"

"I'm thrilled the bleeding has stopped, but I'm very concerned the pain hasn't receded. According to the blood test, your CA 125 levels are very low. That means if the mass is malignant, the cancer hasn't moved beyond the uterus. The next course of action is dilation and curettage."

"Why is that?"

"Because the biopsy suggests, but did not diagnose, cancer. With the D&C, I'll dilate your cervix and with a special instrument remove some tissue from the uterus. I will also perform a hysteroscopy where I'll insert saline into the uterus and examine the uterine lining and the mass. It should take about an hour and requires general anesthesia. This test will confirm what we're dealing with and how we should proceed."

"Will she be in pain?" Michael's eyes brimmed with trepidation.

"There may be marked tenderness, but we'll provide stringent medication as necessary."

"When?" Juliana asked.

"Two days from now on Friday morning." When she failed to look at him, he looked to Michael and teased, "Do you need to cancel a hot date?"

Juliana offered him a feeble chuckle. "Friday is my birthday. Doesn't sound like I'd be much fun."

"I'll contact Dr. Martin before I leave today with the results. Do you have any questions?"

"Thousands," she stretched her eyes, "but none you can answer."

"I know what I just told you can be discouraging. Let's not torment ourselves with what it could be. If it is malignant, then we'll face it once that's revealed." He patted the top of her Bible. "I see you are a woman of faith."

She nodded, feeling the throb in her temples swell. He looked to her cheerleaders. "And your support system is phenomenal. Take her out shopping; go see a play, movie, concert, or visit an art museum. Do something outside of these four walls."

When he departed, Juliana walked to the window. "Margie came in this morning with a chocolate croissant not part of the menu. As she handed it to me, she said that sometimes even treasures can be discovered inside something flaky."

Tricia groaned and put her hand to her mouth. "No, she didn't!"

"Oh, but she did. As grumpy as I was, I couldn't help but laugh. She said God told her to repeat it in that exact manner."

"He'll do whatever is necessary to get our attention," her mother commented.

"Speaking of getting my attention." Juliana turned her back to the window and leaned her palms on the stone ledge. "Last night, Maya called."

Dionne asked, "What did she say?"

"She suggested I read the book of Esther."

Although Dionne remained quiet, her eyes glimmered.

"Here was this young woman, orphaned and living in the house of her cousin. She is chosen to become part of the king's harem, where he changes her destiny from concubine to queen. God gave the influence and the power for a distinct purpose. All to save a nation."

"Purpose holds the weight of eternity."

"All right, ladies," Michael called. "Let's follow doctor's orders. I even picked out this amazing place for dinner."

"Sushi?" Juliana teased as she tied the scarf around her head.

Tricia made a face. "If God had intended on me eating raw fish, He never would have created tartar sauce."

When they pulled up, geese maneuvered through the frosted grass, their steps depositing forked prints. Snow speckled from the gray blanket above. Mist clung to the atmosphere above the lake like a lover reluctant to separate.

"Mr. Powers. You just missed her. They left about ten minutes ago," the front desk clerk informed.

"Did she say where they were going?"

"No, sir. I'd be happy to leave her a message."

Ben thanked her and trailed Bruce to the sedan.

"Now what?" Ben asked Bruce once they were inside the vehicle.

"You could call her and tell her you need to speak with her right away."

"And they said you were just another pretty face."

Bruce eyed the parking lot as Ben waited for Juliana to pick up. After the fourth ring it went to voicemail. He stated that he needed to speak with her and to call him as soon as she could.

"You hungry?" Bruce asked.

"Not really."

"The other day I discovered this great place. We'll go there and you can watch me eat."

"It'll be like a dream come true."

Bruce parked at Abigail's Party off West First and Yew Street. The hostess seated them near the far wall where they would receive the most privacy.

When their waitress arrived, Bruce ordered a medium rare steak with sweet potato fries accompanied by truffle butter. Bottles of lemon and orange flavored Pellegrino arrived and Ben filled their glasses.

He looked around the active place. "I've been reading in John chapter four."

"Was that about Jesus visiting the Samaritans?"

Ben sipped the citrus flavored liquid. "Exactly."

"What was your impression?"

"I was taught to believe in God, Jesus, the Bible, heaven, and hell. Yet…"

He looked beyond Bruce to the gleaming water of English Bay. "It never became real for me. You would think after the hundreds of Sunday school lessons and summer Bible camps I would be at a different place in my life. I would have a different belief system. I questioned then and I'm still questioning."

"Questioning can lead to the discovery of truth," Bruce stated. "Jesus went to this well where a Samaritan woman was gathering water. He speaks to her. During this time, it was unheard of for a Jewish man to socialize with a Samaritan, let alone one who was a woman. Jesus asks her for a drink, she reminds him of this very custom. He describes living water. Living water? What does that mean? Jesus explains to her this living water will cause her to never thirst again."

Bruce took a drink and Ben stared at his glass long after he replaced it on the table. "What?"

"How much water do you drink per day?"

"A minimum of ten of these."

Ben picked up his glass and turned it around in his hand. "I'd estimate this to be about eight fluid ounces. After ten, do you ever drink more?"

"Remember, I said minimum."

"So you are thirsty again?" Ben asked.

Bruce nodded. "Sure."

"Jesus told the Samaritan woman the water he was offering would cause her to never thirst again."

"Why did that part interest you?"

He put down the glass. "I've had the same nightmare since college. I depart from my bedroom immaculately dressed; skip down stairs covered by luxurious carpet to my seven-car garage. I start the ignition of my outrageously priced sports car and relish the purr of the engine. I cruise through my opulent neighborhood, and the ache begins in my throat. The longer I drive, the worse the ache becomes until I am viciously clawing at my throat. I pull my hands away. They are covered in blood. Suddenly, the car will not allow me to steer, no matter how I struggle to regain control. Then my throat is completely exposed. Just before I lose consciousness, my head crashes onto the armrest."

Bruce released a solemn breath. "You've dreamt that since college?"

"From the first freshman night in Kemper House. That's not all. My voice, raw from the exposure, whispers the same two words over and over."

"I thirst."

Ben frowned. "How did you know?"

"Whenever we sleep in the same vicinity you mumble it just before you wake up. I've noticed the frequency increases as your level of stress increases."

"Tommy."

"Now Juliana."

They watched as the meal arrived. Bruce bowed his head but kept his eyes open.

After Bruce blessed the meal, Ben continued, "Last night, I was wound too tight to fade into sleep. So, I tried a shower."

"I heard."

"Then I attempted deep breathing and after ten minutes was even more restless."

Bruce sprinkled pepper on his steak. "I noticed. The walls are pretty thin."

"So, I switched on the T.V. The station was turned to BET. They were airing a gospel celebration."

"I believe I've seen it. Hosted by the comedian Steve Harvey?" He piled his fork high with the fragrant beef.

"Right. Despite my frustration, I couldn't resist his humor. Anyhow, he introduced a woman by the name of Tamia. I was strangely captured by the presence in her voice."

Bruce chewed and swallowed. "What do you mean? 'The presence in her voice.'"

"That steak looks flawlessly prepared."

"It is. Have you changed your mind and want to order?"

Ben shook his head. "I know this may sound completely insane, but it seemed as if there was literally a presence in her voice. The best way I can explain it is to say it was pulling on me, drawing me."

"Toward?"

He leaned back in the chair. "I'm not sure. Sheila is questioning too. She describes it as feeling foreign yet familiar all at once."

Bruce bit into the sweet potato fries. "Something age old, yet refreshingly new."

"Tamia sang a song entitled 'Tomorrow.' It's about Jesus asking this person to welcome Him into their life. Their constant response is tomorrow."

"Tomorrow isn't promised."

"That is exactly what the song warned."

Bruce slathered truffle butter on the crispy fries and munched as Ben's thoughts structured.

"Jesus said to the Samaritan woman, starting in verse thirteen I think, 'Everyone who drinks this water will be thirsty again, but whoever drinks the water I give him will never thirst. Indeed, the water I give him will become in him a spring of water welling up to eternal life.'"

"You remembered that verbatim. Now I see why they pay you the big bucks." Bruce positioned more steak on his fork.

"It's a gift. Do those potatoes have roasted garlic?"

"I can get you a menu."

Ben, again, shook his head and rubbed his beard. "Could it be that God has been speaking to me? All this time?"

"Why not?" Bruce rested his fork beside the plate. "Where you spend eternity is paramount to Him. Is it so inconceivable that He would use whatever He believed would capture your attention? He told the woman to go get her husband. There was no logical way for Jesus to know not only that she had been married five times, but also the man currently living with her wasn't her husband. He read her mail, so to speak." Bruce returned the fork to his hand. "So it seems you aren't marking this as coincidence."

"I don't believe in coincidence."

"I picked up on that."

"However, I struggle with it being that simple. Just surrender to divinity that I can't grasp with my hands?"

"In your dream, you had everything, driving along basking in it all and it hit you. Your life lacked something essential."

"True."

"What do you believe that is?"

Ben shook his head and shrugged.

"I believe once you discern the truth, no debate can ever threaten or intimidate you. The truth is, I am a man."

"Quite a large one, I might add."

"No matter who would approach me to prove otherwise, I am still a man."

"But, Bruce, I could cut you open and see and touch organs which prove your masculinity. The books I'm reading, I can hold them. I can't experience that with God. I also struggle that if He exists, then why does He allow such horror?"

"Trust isn't simple, yet it is essential in any relationship. Remember the latter part of that passage? What else occurs?"

Ben shut his eyes, mentally recalling the scene. "At first, the Samaritan people believed in Jesus based on what the woman told them of her experience. I suppose out of curiosity and a bit of awe, they asked Jesus to stay. Which I'm certain His friends shunned. After all, wasn't it enough insult for Him to speak to the woman at the well? Now, He was going to hang out with those people? It was as if His reputation meant nothing compared to His concern for them. It also says that because of His words, many more became believers. They no longer believed based on someone else's personal account of Jesus. They experienced Him firsthand."

"Like your parents' experience with Him. Or mine. It's essential to encounter Him personally."

"How? Jesus isn't walking around today? We can't go to lunch."

"He's so amazing He doesn't have to been seen for you to *encounter* Him."

When the waitress arrived to remove Bruce's plate, he said, "The gentlemen will take Al's burger, medium rare, no onions with the sweet chili coleslaw to go, please."

Juliana changed into yoga pants and a matching shirt. Michael tucked the blanket around her, then removed the gift from the glittery bag.

She ripped at the wrapping with trembling hands, weakened by exertion and throbbing abdominal aches. "My birthday isn't until Friday."

"What?" He feigned surprise.

She looked down at the shredded paper. "Sneaky little man."

"I'm crafty that way."

She grinned and continued unveiling the gift. She snickered at the bear in a purple jogging suit with lavender fur. "Keep on Truckin'?" She pointed to the printing on the bear's chest.

Michael shrugged. "It's to remind you not to give up."

Juliana caught him in an enduring embrace. "Thank you." She leaned on the pillow, clutched the bear to her side, and yawned. "I'll call her Violet."

"You get some sleep." He kissed her forehead. Michael wasn't certain how long he sat staring at her, taking in every freckle, the full curve of her mouth, mesmerized by the measured cadence of her breathing.

Tricia walked in, retrieved her purse, and placed it on her shoulder. "Hey, Pastor."

"Hey."

He scooped the wrapping and empty box in his arms and tossed them in the trash.

"You bought her a gift?"

He pointed. "The purple bear. She named it Violet."

"How sweet. Is that a prelude to Friday?"

"You guessed it."

"Yep. The big two-five." Tricia shrugged. "Who knows? Maybe God intends on giving her a special gift that day."

Preoccupied by his aggravation, he responded with a shrug.

"Hey, Dionne and I are going to downtown Vancouver. We're shopping for presents, sweet treats, and decorations. Why don't you join us?"

Michael looked to the slumbering woman cradling the bear. "I don't want her to wake up and not have me here."

"The nurse said our little outing probably taxed her, and she just took an Ibuprofen. I think we have a couple of hours."

They traipsed from shop to shop. Michael felt at complete ease with them, even if he was asked to carry most of the bags. An hour and a half later, Michael phoned the nurses' station to check on Juliana. The nurse assured she was still sleeping.

Ben and Bruce arrived an hour later and discovered her in the main area, shrouded in a blanket, caressing a purple bear.

Bruce seated himself a few feet away near the main walkway.

"How are you feeling?" Ben asked as he sat on the plush seat across from her.

"Tired."

"Did you receive the test results?"

"Inconclusive. I'm headed for another test tomorrow morning."

Ben ached to reach for her but realized it would slash if she pulled away. "That must be frustrating."

Juliana didn't respond. Ben's mind flashed to that time in the veld and remembered the fierce wind that pulled at them. "I've got some distressing news."

Juliana stared at him for a moment. "Regarding?"

"Some photos that were taken."

She stood, wrapped the blanket around her shoulders, and led him to her room. Bruce remained in the Great Room.

They sat at the table. "I called and left you a voicemail."

"I left my phone behind when we went sightseeing." She rested the purple bear on her lap. "You said some photos were taken?"

"They were of you, outside, with Dr. Giantanna."

Juliana blinked as the realization hit her. "How? When?"

"I'm not certain. They're to be published in next week's edition of *Rumors*."

"*Rumors*? How did you find this out?"

"Jessica has a friend who works there. She saw the photos on the desk of the photographer who took them."

"All they have to do is google Dr. Giantanna to discover he's a top specialist in endometrial cancer." She rubbed the space between her eyes. "I don't even know how serious my condition is yet. The news will hit the stands under the stench of innuendo and speculation."

"I never meant to expose you."

She eyed him for a bit. "None of this is your fault. They would have found out eventually since they shadow us everywhere."

"They shadow you because of me."

"They shadow us because they're revolting." She fingered the jogging suit on the teddy bear. "Is that all?"

He paused to look out the window. *No! I'd be a fool to let you walk away. But, I'm just as trapped as you. I want nothing more than to spend the remainder of my days baking you pecan pies, but I have no idea how much time remains.*

Instead, he said, "Let me know if I can help."

As she led him to the door, he commented, "Cute bear."

"It's a birthday gift."

"Today's your birthday?"

"Tomorrow." She opened the door. "Oh, and tell Jessica I said thank you. It's comforting to know not everyone is looking to dig in a dagger."

He shut the door and the words rushed from his mouth like staccato notes in a concerto. "Your problem, Juliana DeLauer, is your complete lack of tack. You simply do not know when to relinquish, to cease. You continue to push and press and prod until no life remains."

"That comment was directed at my enemy. Not you."

His genuine feelings were too fragile to articulate, so he instigated the battle. "Aren't we one in the same?"

"You believe that?"

Ben's despair mounted, so he pressed. "Let me ask you something. When you bow your head, are you just like everyone else beseeching something that has never been proven real? How can you depend on something that had the power to heal your father but allowed him to die in unbearable pain? How, Juliana?"

She gripped the door handle and he placed his hand upon hers.

"Your best friend was beaten to death and left in a field as if her life mattered no more than dung. How is it humanely possible you could still believe?"

"You don't think I haven't questioned God?"

"Never."

She dipped her chin and shook her head. "My father was the first man to love me without compromise or restraint. No one could have ever convinced me there was anything I could have spoken or did that would have caused that to change. He battled the accusations, the court, and the cancer. Then he was gone. Suddenly he was completely unreachable. The gentle nudging whenever fear froze my path, the unquestioning exhortation in his eye when I wanted to give in … were gone, Ben. Gone."

She moved to the window. "So, I traveled to Boptang where my heart has always sensed liberty. Tomorrow was there, affirming that I had the strength to persevere. Then she was gone."

The surge of Ben's hopelessness dissipated like crankiness upon a slumbering toddler. The last thing he wanted to do was face her, yet the grief in her admission yanked on him. Ben shuffled to her, but held his thoughts.

Tears brimmed her eyes. "So your notion that I don't question Him is desperately ill-conceived. Just because He doesn't respond in the manner I believe He should does not lessen the irrefutable fact He is still God. Nor does it diminish His astounding love for me and—yes, Ben—for you."

Ben searched the lush panoramic view and wished he could escape. Yet he was the one who shot the questions at her like bullets from an assassin.

Ben's pitch seemed to erupt from a child. "Is Kevin in hell?"

"Oh, Ben."

He tightened his fists. "Just tell me."

Juliana caressed his bitter tears. "I don't know where Kevin is spending eternity. Neither of us may know until we, ourselves, are faced with it."

Ben grunted. "He is the one in charge, is He not? Isn't He in command of who enters heaven or hell?"

"It is a misconception that God sends anyone to hell."

"How?"

She gently unraveled his fists. "Think of it in these terms. I invite you to an elaborate celebration. You arrive and I present you with a gift. You have the choice to either accept the gift or decline. However, I make it clear your decision will linger with you throughout infinity. In order to receive the gift, you must receive it completely, without reserve. You see others who have also been invited mulling around. Some have studied the gift and been astounded at its magnificence and feel unworthy. Some have rejected the gift, outright convinced nothing *that* astonishing is given without significant strings attached. Some cradle the gift, terrified to open it for fear of its contents. And some have opened the gift and been humbled by its indescribable supremacy."

"Whether I receive or reject the gift, my life will reflect my selection?"

"The celebration I've invited you to is life. The gift is Jesus, offered the moment we're born and lingering with us, following us throughout our days. Once opened and entirely received, the effect is absolute. Forgotten, dismissed, or rejected, just as absolute."

Her gaze so hallow it pierced him far beyond his skin, muscle, and tissue. For a moment, he wondered if he was looking into her eyes or that of a deity.

He gripped her tightly. "I can't do it."

Although her prayer was voiceless, her petition permeated the boundary of his resistance and apprehension.

"Fight this thing. Fight it as if it were pursuing the lives of Hanna, Lorato, and Kendrick. Understand?"

"You're telling me goodbye."

He faced her. "Happy birthday, Juliana. *Sala hantle.*"

She increased her grip when he attempted to pull away. "Ben."

Ben forcibly withdrew and rushed through the door.

Juliana dropped to her knees and wept. Her entreating for Ben was broken and anguished. Suddenly, an inexplicable peace swept over her until her tears transformed from mourning to thanksgiving. She had been so entrenched in prayer that she was oblivious when her companions returned. They witnessed her fervency and quietly departed.

Eventually, Juliana staggered to the bed—the pervading effects of God's presence still upon her. Dinner arrived and Juliana's appetite was squelched by the dominant promptings to proceed offensively. She picked up her phone and dialed the number.

Jaki Lloyd, *News Today's* broadcast producer, answered on the second ring. Juliana sketched her plan and Jaki agreed to help execute it.

Caroline, the surgical nurse, wheeled Juliana into Operating Suite C. She scratched at the collar of the hospital gown and counted the tiles each wheel crossed. The sequential pattern lulled her mind, intercepting the shriek of despondency. Operating Suite C was dim, and Spanish guitar played softly from the Bose system, shaving more of the edge from her nerves.

Upon the operating table, she held Violet by her side. Caroline swabbed her arm and administered the general anesthesia. Juliana's breathing slowed, and Caroline stated Dr. Giantanna would arrive shortly. *Inhale for eight, exhale for ten*, she reminded her brain. Had she been at home, Dr. Martin would have deemed the procedure fit the criteria as outpatient and sent her home to rest. Nothing about it felt simple to Juliana. The magnitude that it would either preserve or banish her dream of motherhood struck every nerve like a chisel.

Dr. Giantanna entered the softly lit room. "Good morning, Juliana."

"Morning." Her voice was thick from the medication.

He washed his hands then came to her side and touched her shoulder. "How are you doing?"

"I feel like I'm standing on my tiptoes on the edge of a cliff in a wind storm."

"Are you cliff diving or parasailing?"

"Diving."

"What's at the bottom?"

"I can't tell. It's cloaked by clouds and it's hard to keep my eyes open."

"I'll explain every step of the procedure as I proceed. We've administered the general anesthesia, but at any time if you feel significant discomfort, just kick me."

"Be careful what you ask for."

He patted her shoulder. "All right. Shall we get started?" He pulled on a pair of rubber gloves and, with his right foot, rolled a stool toward the foot of the table. He adjusted her legs in the stirrups and flipped on the light mounted to the end of the bed.

Caroline switched on the 19" monitor and studied a tray full of surgical instruments. "I heard you enjoy Spanish guitar. Was I well-informed, or do I need to fire my source?"

"Next to gospel, it's my favorite. I long for the day I can salsa dance with my husband. On the dance floor near the beaches of Puerto Rico."

The doctor asked, "What date should I block off to attend the ceremony?"

"May 23 of two-thousand-happily-ever-after."

His salt and pepper head dipped as he applied the antiseptic. He inserted the speculum. Once inserted, Caroline handed him a series of metal rods, ranging from straw-size to that of a thumb. "Juliana, you're going to feel pressure as I dilate your cervix."

She did, but the discomfort was minimal.

"You all right?"

She nodded, then realized his eyes weren't on her face. "Yeah."

"Good. Let me know if that changes."

"Mmm-hmm."

After a few moments, he informed, "Now, I'm inserting the curette, which will scrap the inner lining of your uterus."

The seams of reality started to blend into the subconscious. Before long, Juliana was walking a white-sanded beach, the humidity dampening her skin. A salsa band serenaded beneath a lilac colored tent. She heard her name, turned, and discovered Ben. The sight of him, decked out in white, caused her heart to pound.

"Juliana, you're doing great."

She shielded her eyes from the bright sun and Ben walked closer.

"Ben."

"What was that, Juliana?" Dr. Giantanna asked, eyeing her.

Ben smiled. "Look behind me."

When she did, her eyes took in hundreds of alabaster chairs full of friends and family members. There were masses of calla lilies and shimmering tulle on the chair backs. He took her hand and began leading her toward the crowd. "They're here to celebrate us, baby. Our special day."

Juliana looked down at her ivory silk dress and halted. "Ben?"

Caroline touched Juliana's shoulder. "Dr. Giantanna just inserted the hysteroscope. There may be slight cramping as he injects the saline."

Ben tucked his hand beneath her chin. "Juliana, I've never wanted someone more. Tell me you don't love me."

"Of course I love you. But ... to be your wife ... "

Dr. Giantanna studied the magnified image of Juliana's uterus on the monitor through the hysteroscope. She felt Caroline squeeze her shoulder. "We're nearly done, Juliana."

"Everything is ready. All you have to say is 'yes.'"

Juliana searched the smiling crowd, exorbitant and brimming with expectancy. Then she saw it. The baby cradle adorned with yellow ribbon; the contents bare.

"No, Ben. Not everything."

Gradually, elements of the conscious world seeped into the subliminal vision and it faded. Dr. Giantanna removed the instruments, gently rested Juliana's legs on the table, and pulled the blanket to her collarbone. "Very well done, Juliana. We should have the results on Monday."

He tossed the gloves in the trash. Then he joined Caroline beside the table. Tenderly, he stroked her forehead. "You'll feel more cramping and soreness through the next few days, and they'll be some bleeding, which should lessen in forty-eight hours."

She slowly opened her eyes. "On a scale from one to ten, ten being the greatest, what are my chances of conceiving a child? More than one inquiring mind wants to know."

Dr. Giantanna exchanged a glance with Caroline. "Let's discuss that after we receive the results. For today, you have a birthday to celebrate."

Caroline assisted her into the wheelchair and aided her into her bed. The entire space was decorated with banners and balloons. A tray of cupcakes was placed in the center of the table. Juliana rubbed Violet's chenille fur against her cheek.

"Palesa." Her mother stood on the opposite bedside. "Happy birthday."

Juliana rested her head on the pillow and shut her eyes against the swell of tears. Caroline explained that Juliana would experience cramping, soreness, and bleeding for the next few days. Before she departed, she gave Juliana a pill to ward off infection.

Tricia sat on the edge of the bed. "Wait until you see what I got you! I'm so excited."

"Michael?" She snuggled deeper beneath the covers. "I need some girl time. Do you mind?"

He kissed her forehead. "Understood. I'll see you in the morning. Promise me you'll call me if you need me."

She agreed. Once he was through the door, she asked Tricia, "Would you have married Winston if you knew he wasn't able to help you produce a child?"

Tricia scowled. "Jules, why are you asking that question?"

"Because I want to know. Would you?"

Tricia looked to Dionne, out the window, then back at her friend. "We've only been married twelve weeks, and it's as if he's always been a part of me. As if he's always been connected to who I am. He doesn't complete me. He isn't half of my whole. It's like we are two complete separates fused together to become one exquisite, unique entity."

"Would you?"

"I want to have babies, Jules, no doubt about that. I want the house filled with noise and laughter. But, now listen close. He is what is most important to me. Our life, the life we build, is what I cannot imagine living without."

She paused, staring at Juliana until her own eyes began to water. Then she nodded. "Yes. I still would have married him. Because, I believe with all my heart, God put us together. And if in that plan children were not meant to be, then I have to trust God has a very good reason why."

Juliana turned her head and wept into the pillow. The wrenching despair seemed to descend and crush her chest. "Every test seems to point to the same inevitability. No children. I'll end up with a husband who'll eventually give me that look."

She spoke, hands thrashing. "Oh, God, help me. I wouldn't be able to bear it. As far back as I can recall, I've longed for the day I would become a wife and mother. The relentless threat has grown to realism. I try to look under it, or around it, and still it will not move."

Dionne lowered the side rail, rested her hip on the bed, and leaned close to her daughter. "Baby, look at me." Her mother grabbed Juliana's hands and held tight. "The doctors are not the final authority, nor the final word. God is. Period. And, just as we have your entire life, we are holding fast to what He says, despite what we see."

"Mom, you've seen my latest medical reports."

"I have."

"The test results could confirm my greatest fear."

"They may, baby. But, they very well may not. You have faced obstacles in which all looked impossible and God changed everything."

"I don't believe I've ever been so terrified."

"So was I."

Juliana stared at her mother.

"Top specialists from coast-to-coast told me I'd never have children. That's right. They gave me less than a 20% chance I would conceive, and even less that I would carry a child full term and give birth."

"You never told me that, Mom."

"Your daddy and I always called you our miracle child. It never seemed strange to you that you didn't come along until we had been married for twelve years?"

"Our photo albums are full of your missions' trips. I always assumed it was because of the ministry."

"I graduated from Spellman, met, and married your father, and immediately we tried to start a family. With every passing month, every year, pieces of me died. Until, one day, in the greatest depths of me, I believed I was shackling him to an unmerited future."

"So what did you do?"

"I asked your father for a divorce."

Juliana stared up at her, the amazement producing ruddiness to her complexion. Dionne smoothed the curls pulled into a sparse ponytail on her daughter's head. "It had nothing to do with him. Every year, his adoration and commitment never waned. It all had to do with me. My disappointment had eroded pieces of my heart."

"What did Daddy say?"

Dionne raised her eyebrows and pursed her lips. "I'll never forget it. He didn't shout or berate or argue."

"Yes?" Juliana wiped her nose with the tissue Tricia provided.

"We were eating Saturday night dinner, pepper steak. He wiped his mouth, got up, and pulled me to my feet."

Juliana's eyes widened. Tricia leaned in closer, eyes glued to the older woman.

"He pulled me to my feet and kissed me until I was breathless. Then—"

Juliana held up a hand. "I've got the picture."

"No. You haven't. Because you believe what you're feeling is God's will. It's not."

Juliana looked to Violet. "I don't know if I have the faith, Mom."

Dionne continued, "As I was saying, in every possible way your father proved nothing mattered more to him than our love. Do you understand me?"

"Mmm-hmm." Tricia breathed. "My, oh, my do I."

Juliana groaned. "But you didn't know you would have trouble conceiving before you married. It would be cruel to marry, Mom."

She inched Violet closer to Juliana. "That's your end of the story. You have no idea what God has planned. And, just to let you know, that was the night you were conceived."

She inhaled and smelled Michael's cologne on the bear. "I think I'm going to sleep now. The room looks fantastic. Thank you."

Dionne kissed her daughter's cheek. "We'll celebrate after your nap. I love you, baby." She stroked Juliana's cheek. "Oh, and Jacqueline from *News Today* called. She said Monday morning is all set."

Soon after, Juliana surrendered to the fatigue.

CHAPTER TWENTY-FOUR

Early evening the following day, Michael arrived in a chauffeured limousine. He assisted her into the lengthy vehicle.

"You look stunning."

Juliana had sat patiently, dozing at times, as Tricia had concealed the patchy spots on her scalp, polished nails, pampered feet, and applied flawless make-up.

She touched Tricia's gift—a necklace of diamond-encrusted women caught in an embrace and smiled for two reasons. Their center—a shared ruby heart—linked them in perpetual union. She also smiled at her brevity to finally don an open collar.

"Happy belated birthday, Juliana. May this year astound you with expectations far greater than you've imagined."

"Thanks, Michael."

"How are you feeling?"

"Sore and a little tired."

"I missed you."

"Did you now?"

His eyes fell to her neck. "More than somewhat. Your neckline is beautiful."

"See how you're completely enthralled by it? It was best to have kept it concealed all those years. It would have created too much havoc. Traffic accidents, lava eruptions, war."

"Indeed."

First, his thumb rested on the vein nearest her middle finger. Then, it traced downward to the division between thumb and index finger.

"Where are you taking me?"

His gaze held. "Time will tell."

They cruised the lush landscape toward downtown Vancouver. The destination still a mystery, she relaxed against the seat.

They dined at a quiet spot with a magnificent view of Coal Harbor. The pair chatted amongst candlelight and Spanish guitar, enclosed in a concealed space perfumed by violet calla lilies.

To assist with their hefty digestion, they strolled through Queen Elizabeth Park. The night air was chilled, but not frigid. Juliana wrapped her arm through his as they meandered toward the observatory. The massive dome filled with a plethora of flora glowed against the inky backdrop of the Vancouver sky. Michael led her to a bench where he stretched his legs.

His hand played with a curly tendril as she gathered the courage to speak. Juliana then took the hand playing in her hair and held it.

"Those books you've been reading on PCOS, have they helped you understand?"

"Yes. I wanted to learn as much as I could without seeming to badger you."

"I don't mind you asking."

"I thought you had enough to deal with without me badgering you."

She placed his hand on the dark patches on her neck. As if touching a healing scar, he tenderly discovered what had been revealed to only a few.

She was utterly unprepared for the immeasurable compassion in his eyes. He raised the hair covering the back of her neck. An exquisite shiver ran up her spine as Michael's lips kissed the leathery patches. He continued his sensitive exploration and moved toward her shoulder. Juliana shuddered from the ethereal concerto his mouth composed. She touched his thigh to still his progress. Michael maneuvered her body so they were facing.

"Open your eyes." Her eyelids opened as if she were just roused from a profound slumber.

His finger traced delicate designs on her cheek and chin. "I love you."

"Michael."

"I love you, Juliana DeLauer."

Michael pulled her closer. Juliana battled the rising quiver in her belly and the sheer determination to pull away from Michael. It was chaos and harmony. Turmoil and serenity. Pandemonium and tranquility. The glorious mixture of his declaration and physical affirmation birthed an unmarked sensation within Juliana. The floral breeze stirred around them and Juliana shuddered against the chilled air.

"Michael, I can't promise you—"

"Tonight, I'm not asking for a promise." He looked at her with such intensity she felt it difficult to turn away. "Tonight, let's just celebrate being alive."

They sat beneath the oak, its leaves shivering from the wind. Although he had walked away, Ben was still very much alive in her heart.

"Celebrate being alive." She glanced at her watch. Her hand flew to her mouth. "You'll never believe what time it is!"

"Do we really care?"

"You have kept me out way beyond my curfew."

He ceased his jousting, yet held her close. "Juliana, you know very well what you are and are not capable of. And so do I."

She touched his chin. "Michael, I can't promise you a future. Do you understand?"

"I do. All I've asked for is a chance, Juliana."

Monday morning arrived, and Juliana finally felt the strength to workout. She took a brisk walk around the grounds and lifted lightweights in the center's gym. Margie had placed her breakfast tray on the bed accompanied by an emboldening note.

Juliana was placing the last touches on her makeup when her visitors arrived. After breakfast, they drove to the NBC affiliate where they were ushered to a chilly room with a newsroom for a backdrop.

A producer guided her to the chair facing the sole camera and educated her on the format. Dionne, Tricia, and Michael positioned themselves behind the camera. Juliana adjusted the earpiece. The sound technician asked her to perform a sound check. Then Jaki Lloyd picked up a mic, looked into the camera, and greeted her from New York.

"Jaki, thanks for sacrificing your weekend to pull this all together on such short notice."

"For you, anytime. But I should be thanking you. I'm likely to make senior broadcast producer after this succulent exclusive."

"Invite me to the party."

The main theme blossomed as the show's co-hosts Caren Foster and Lyle Kennedy opened the broadcast. They cut to the newly hired newsreader, Alexander McIntyre, who rambled through the latest headlines.

Juliana looked at the monitor and smoothed the lapel of her lilac silk blouse. The overhead lights created a lustrous sheen on the alabaster of Juliana's pantsuit.

The floor director held up five fingers.

The countdown began.

Ben entered the tent, ignored the roasting pans filled with luscious breakfast fare, snagged a bagel and coffee, and took a seat beside his co-star.

Trevor, a.k.a. Blade, sipped coffee and stared at the TV screen. Ben recognized the theme from *News Today*. He blew the fragrant steam before taking a sip.

Trevor glanced at him then turned back to the screen. "That all you're eating?"

Ben nodded and bit into the chewy bread. "Not much of an appetite."

"Our food is free, you know. It's all part of the package."

"Are you referring to the extravagant crew lunch where you feigned lightheadedness as you handed me the bill?"

Trevor smirked. "It was delicious, by the way."

"Worth every penny."

Ben munched and sipped until Juliana's name was mentioned as part

of the morning line-up. Lyle Kennedy started the piece with stock photos and V-roll of Juliana and Ben accumulated from autumn through
winter. Kennedy performed a voiceover highlighting her outburst with
the cameraman.

The screen split.

"Juliana DeLauer joins us from our Canadian affiliate in Vancouver,
British Columbia. Good morning."

"Good morning."

Her hair was fuller and her complexion less shallow. Her blouse
shone like a lilac gloss against her skin.

"It has been an interesting year, has it not?"

"You've just said a mouthful."

"You are currently receiving medical treatment at The Kennedy
Center for Women's Health in Vancouver?"

"Yes, Lyle. I was diagnosed with Polycystic Ovarian Syndrome as
a teen. My condition is often tragically misdiagnosed. Women shuf-
fle from doctor to doctor in agony, disappointment, and frustration.
Researchers report one-in-ten women of childbearing age have PCOS.
Symptoms can occur as early as eleven. This syndrome alters a woman's
menstrual cycle, her ability to have children, hormones, and physical
appearance."

"Is there a cure?"

"Sadly, no. However, it is treatable by medications, changes in diet,
and exercise."

"Your condition makes it complicated to conceive, does it not?"

"Yes, but not impossible. PCOS is one of the leading causes of infer-
tility in women. But with specialized medical assistance, it can be possible to conceive."

"Gynecological experts state PCOS, also known as Stein-Leventhal
Syndrome, has been identified for seventy-five years and still they
aren't certain what causes it. It is also known to affect more than just
reproduction."

"There are weight problems and excessive amounts or effects of androgenic, or masculinizing hormones, which cause excessive hair growth or loss. While the causes are unknown, insulin resistance, diabetes, and obesity are all strongly correlated with PCOS. The symptoms and severity of the syndrome vary greatly between women, and it crosses all nationalities."

"Juliana, how is your treatment?"

She raised her hands and clasped them. "I want to thank the entire staff of The Kennedy Center. They have made my stay remarkable. I am blessed to say that my surgeon, Dr. Anthony Giantanna, is confident I will be around to give you plenty more tittle-tattle."

"The Kennedy Center specializes in diagnosing and treating cancers. Is your condition cancer related?"

"That is part of the reason I'm here and nothing has been determined."

"Why reveal this?"

Ben placed the cup on the table and leaned forward.

"It was brought to my attention a tabloid believed they had the exclusive. I did not authorize any photos that were taken. My condition is not to be ashamed of. I urge every woman who has suspicion that this condition has affected her to consult her doctor immediately. Although diagnosis can be difficult, don't give up. Treatment is available."

"Your spirits seem very high. Are you concerned?"

"I do not believe in coincidence. I was created for a purpose much greater than this five foot, eight-inch woman. I have every intention of fulfilling it."

"Are you also receiving fertility treatments at the center?"

Juliana smiled politely. "No."

"Can our viewers expect a wedding announcement in the near future?"

Juliana shrugged then grinned.

"Juliana DeLauer, the best to you."

"Thank you for the opportunity to share, Lyle."

The shot altered to Lyle in the studio with an infamous OB-GYN on set. They discussed symptoms, possible treatments, and even encouraged the viewers to take their website's online quiz.

Trevor blew a low whistle. "Powers, how did you ever charm that woman?"

Ben picked up his cup and drank.

Trevor stood and patted Ben's shoulder. "Warning: if you mess up, I'm right there, buddy. I'm just saying."

Juliana and Michael scuffled for the last piece of chocolate Sheila sent.

Tricia asked, "What's the day's plan?"

"To play Scattergories until Juliana realizes how awful she is at it," Michael teased.

"I beg to differ," Juliana countered. "Who won the last series?"

"Dionne." Both Tricia and Michael chimed.

"By one measly point. And you wimps conceded in your challenge to her."

Tricia shrugged. "Who knew paprika is considered a condiment in some cultures?"

They moved to the open area and played as teams; Michael and Dionne against Tricia and Juliana. After two hours, Michael and Dionne emerged the victors.

As they returned the elements of the game to the box, Dr. Giantanna approached. Juliana's eyes locked on the manila folder he carried.

"Well," the doctor began after they returned to her room. "I have the results from your biopsy."

Juliana waited for him to open the folder, but it remained close to his chest. Still, her eyes were riveted to the report instead of meeting his gaze.

Her mother took her right hand, which drew Juliana's focus from the file. Dionne winked and looked to the physician.

"Endometrial cancer is categorized by types and stages. Stage I through stage IV. Stage I means the cancer is in the earliest form and limited to the inner lining of the uterus. Stage IV means the cancer has spread to the mucosa, or inner surface of the bladder or lower part of the large intestine, lymph nodes in the groin, or lungs and bones."

Juliana stared at the specialist, not certain she was still breathing. He cleared his throat, rocked on his heels, and broke out into a magnificent smile. "That little lesson was so you could impress your friends back in the States. You, Miss DeLauer, are cancer free."

There were raucous screams and shouts from everyone in the room. She leapt and grabbed Dr. Giantanna.

"Thank you!" Juliana jumped up and down several times, holding his forearms, and he didn't resist in joining her. Eventually, everyone was pulling one another into exorbitant hugs. Dr. Giantanna seemed in no hurry to stifle their enthusiasm. Juliana reveled in the delicious sensation of laughter and tears bestowed by her God.

CHAPTER TWENTY-FIVE

Mid-February arrived with a blizzard forecasted for Denver. Juliana and Michael blissfully landed on the tarmac at LAX and grinned at the heated swells of translucent wings beating against the taxiway.

At the hotel, in the expansive closet, were three evening gowns; one platinum, one candy-apple red, one sky blue. After she dressed, a gentle knock rapped on the door. She peered through the peephole, gauging the identity.

She had become especially cautious since a menacing note turned up on her nightstand two weeks ago. The house alarm hadn't been tripped and the intruder had failed to make a sound as she slept. Then last week, another threatening message had appeared on her driver's seat while at work. Thereafter, appalling e-mails had arrived. That morning, a naked mulatto Barbie doused in pig's blood had been deposited upon her doorstep.

"Bruce!" Juliana embraced him.

When they parted he studied her. "You're looking very well, Juliana. What was the final conclusion of your test results?"

She beamed. "Cancer free!"

Bruce shut the door and grinned, which was something Juliana had never witnessed. He placed a briefcase on the bed. "That is wonderful news, isn't it?"

She giggled. "You seem happier than I was when I heard."

Juliana placed her ID, room key, and lip gloss in her evening bag. "What's in the briefcase?"

Bruce unlatched the knobs and removed the weapon. Juliana, her eyes focused on smoothing her curls in the mirror, didn't notice as Bruce handled the revolver.

She looked to him and froze. Her eyes fixed on the cavernous hole in the muzzle. "Put that away."

"You only have Michael to blame."

The gun gripped her, unblinking and pitiless. "Michael? Why?"

"He chose this for you." Bruce turned the gun away and pulled the sensitive trigger. The lethal click resounded throughout the luxurious room. For a moment, it seemed louder and more deadly than a tank.

The burning in her throat wasn't hindered, even though her hand caressed. Her voice, husky from the fiery pain sealing her esophagus, said, "Unbelievable."

His eyes weren't on her. He was admiring the deadly instrument. As Juliana's fingers attempted to quench the constriction to her throat, Bruce rambled the qualifications, assets, and limitations of the revolver. He smoothed the algid surface, satisfied it would not disappoint.

Juliana's fingers abandoned the massage. When she coughed, it gathered his attention. "What's the matter?"

"Help," she gagged.

Bruce scrambled for a glass and filled it with water. He handed it to her and instructed, "Don't gulp it or you'll choke."

She sat on the upholstered chair, sipped, and composed herself. "I despise guns. Just the sight of them, well, you saw what happened."

"It's for your protection."

"It's hideous."

"You'll feel differently once you've mastered it. It's a Ruger P89 DC. Nine millimeter, double action with decocker. It's a direct descendent from the P85."

"What's wrong with the one I currently use at the firing range with my instructor?"

"The P85 has design flaws."

"So it wasn't simply my deficient skill?"

"You feeling better?"

"Will you make that thing disappear if I say yes?"

"Michael would ask too many questions and you're a horrible liar."

She groaned. "Very well."

Bruce replaced the weapon in the dark case. "If I could be there to teach you, I would, you know?"

"I do." She nodded, slowly. "Gary's current assignment doesn't end until next week, but he travels to the range with me and offers encouragement."

"So, you feel comfortable having a bodyguard?"

"I like Gary—hate the fact I need armed protection." Juliana shuddered and stared at the locked case. "It's oiled metal that operates on mechanisms and firing pins. Metal that can shred a life."

"I'll store it in the hotel safe tonight."

A knock rapped at the door and Bruce answered. He and Michael greeted one another amiably. As they headed to elevator, after Juliana checked the lock twice, her walk slowed.

Michael asked, "What is it?"

"That gun seems pretty powerful."

"The fact this psychopath was able to leave a death threat in your bedroom and car and deposit a blood-soaked doll on your doorstep undetected has heightened my apprehension."

On that morning, she had flipped off her alarm and her wrist had scraped against a piece of paper. It had fallen to the floor. Her hand shook as she had raced to her mother's bedroom. It was signed "Love, God."

She informed Bruce, "I'm in my second week of martial arts training."

They stopped near the elevator doors. Bruce pressed the down button. "Paparazzi still hanging around?"

"Not as much. I asked Gary if he planned to interview them, to discover if they saw anything. But he didn't think it wise to alert the media of the threat."

"I agree. Everyone's a suspect until proven otherwise."

The elevator arrived and they stepped inside.

Michael commented, "It's infuriating. There weren't any prints, or fibers, nothing. It's like this person is a vapor appearing at will. And, he doesn't lack audacity in the manner he signs the notes."

Hard lines etched Bruce's ebony features. "That's just what's going to get him caught."

They entered the lobby and she hugged Bruce tightly. "Call if you have any questions regarding the weapon or simply crave my dazzling personality."

"Take care of yourself, Bruce."

"You as well, Juliana."

They headed to their rental and for the NAACP Image Awards. One of Michael's high school pals had been nominated as Best Gospel Artist.

"You chose the platinum gown. It makes your skin glow."

"Thank you." She looked out the window at the glorious weather. "This beats shoveling snow any day."

Bruce picked Ben up from his interview with a reporter from *Entertainment Weekly*. Ben didn't prod of his meeting with Juliana and Bruce didn't divulge. They dropped by Jessica's town home.

As Ben held open the door, he stated, "I'd be surprised if anyone pays me any attention at all. You're mesmerizing."

"Likewise."

They arrived on the red carpet for the movie premiere of *Slow Bullet* with dozens of voices vying for Ben's attention. Behind concrete barriers fervent fans, their bodies blocked but their enthusiasm unbridled, screamed for him.

"Good evening!" Ben waved.

Their screams amplified. Security detail descended to escort the couple to the theater entrance. Bruce hung back, but only by inches. They stood, smiling into the flashing lights and avid crowd for a few moments. Someone called Jessica's name. She turned toward the direction of the voice. Then froze.

In the throng of reporters, photographers, and fans, he stood amongst the assembly and grinned. Her accomplice must have followed Juliana to L.A. to witness if his threats vexed her. He and Jessica had agreed to meet only when necessary. Otherwise, Ben might grow suspect.

Her smile diminished into an apprehensive frown. It wasn't required for him to be here, snapping pictures of the celebrities. His presence completely unnerved her.

Ben looked down at her. "It's a piece of cake. Just smile as if you're amongst friends."

Jessica trembled.

"Why did the cowboy buy a Dachshund?"

She turned to him. "What?"

He repeated the question. She shrugged.

"Because he was told to get a long little doggy."

Incredulous, she looked up at him surprised he imparted the ridiculous joke.

"What kind of a horse goes out after dark?"

Jessica replied, "One with a mean night owl streak."

"Nightmares."

"Stop."

"Speaking of stopping—how do you stop a charging rhinoceros?"

"Ben, was your brain deprived of oxygen today?"

"Take away his credit card. I saved the best one for last. Why did the pig become an actor?"

"I enjoy my job too much to touch that one."

He playfully glowered at her. "He was a big ham."

Ben shook fan's hands, signed autographs, and took photos. Jessica felt their frenzied adoration and wondered that it didn't seem to faze him. For Jessica, it was suffocating. And the man nestled in the crowd unnerved her even more.

Sitting beside him and watching him on the screen seemed surreal. His ability to adopt the persona of a hard-nosed, ex-drug addicted cop astonished her. He portrayed the role with such graceful fluency; Jessica wondered what regions of his soul had been tapped.

The after-party gala recalled the days of Hollywood glamour. The men wore tailored, ebony tuxedos that shone like oil on skin. The women were adorned in glittery jewels, stiletto heels, and gowns painted in lavish shades.

Ben excused himself from the entertaining banter between the director and Jessica. He walked through the elegant crowd, down the hotel corridor, and through terrace doors. The February sun had conceded hours prior to the alabaster moon. Ben inhaled the salty air rising from the Pacific.

It had nagged and denied him sleep. There was a maniac stalking the woman he loved and he wasn't in a position to stop it. Bruce hadn't advised him, and it hadn't come from Dionne. It had been Tricia through guarded text messages admitting the risk, although she felt he should be informed.

This stalking fueled his habitual nightmare toward lurid detail; the sheen of the marble floor blinding; the roar of the engine grating; the ache in his throat excruciating; the blood on his hands garish.

The nightmares about Kevin surfaced.

Where is he?

Is there life, then death, then nothing?

Had the church teachings been true?

The trio pulled from the parking lot near two a.m. He hadn't shown affection to Jessica other than the occasional hug. However, he discerned she wanted him to usher in the morning with her.

She commented, "At the party, you didn't seem yourself."

"Meaning?"

"You enamored me tonight with your jokes. Then it turned."

Ben contemplated her words, allowing them to descend upon him like snowflakes on stark branches. "I'm just tired."

He walked her to her door. She unlocked the bolt, shock registering when he didn't follow her inside. "You're not coming in?"

"I'm really tired, Jess." He kissed her cheek. "Thanks for being such an amazing date."

"Spend it well."

Just before three a.m., he briefly showered. Even after, the haunting still clung to him. He reclined on the plush chaise on his deck, tightened the belt of his robe against the chill, and stared at the striking canvas of the sky. The heavens seemed to be in a skirmish with the crescent moon denying it opportunity to illuminate the diamonds of the sky. Ben shut his eyes and the gloom shrouded like a cloak.

"You see me, don't You?"

Nothing.

"Hiding in my skin. Masking my frailty. But You see it all, don't You?"

The wind, damp from the Pacific, caressed his face. Its richness per-fumed by salt and seaweed.

"I've made a mess of my existence. All the money and accolades were achieved because of my imperfections. What a grand production I've created."

Ben swiped at the tears before they reached his cheeks. "I have foundations clamoring for me to reside on their boards. Talk shows bidding top dollar for my appearance. Studio heads not even blinking at my $30 million salary."

The current of air swirled around him stirring his hair and creating ripples on his silk robe.

"But in the end, it's all tattered and rotten beneath."

Ben opened his eyes and this time allowed every tear to fall.

"I've become addicted to the song and dance. But I'm tired. So tired of the hollowness inside."

The current no longer felt like wind or even a breeze. It seemed to still directly above him, possessing the presence of a demonstrative shield. Ben struggled to close his eyes, to diminish the acute sensation, yet he could not. The Presence amplified to the point that Ben scanned the deck for a human being. Then It penetrated his heart. Hands of indescribable benevolence were massaging every disappointment, every heartbreak, every regret, banishing their sting.

"Forgive me. Forgive me for what I've done to destroy the life You intended me to live."

The hands extended deeper, their function intentional and direct. Ben felt no threat, no danger, only unadulterated veneration. Decades he had constructed to conceal his spirit were no match for these exquisite instruments fervent in their task.

"I don't want to do this alone anymore. I need You. I need You to heal me and turn my life into what You've always wanted. Please, change me into the man You meant for me to become."

The lengthening seemed to withdraw, unhurriedly as to not cause panic, and then serenity resided. A peace Ben had never experienced permeated so profoundly, he fell against the chair and shut his eyes. The peace seemed destined, as if it had waited all his life to reside within. The tears didn't cease, but they no longer tasted bitter on his tongue.

In the morning, the sun warmed his consciousness and alerted his awakening. He blinked at his surroundings and realized his unchanged position on the chaise. The sun beamed from the brilliant azure sky on the first day of his rebirth. He stretched and glanced at his watch.

Sheila and the twins would arrive at church in an hour. He hopped from the chaise and prepared to join them.

Juliana grasped her empty ticket wallet in one hand and her cell phone in the other.

"Since I arrived last night, the storm has dumped twenty-four inches," Michael informed.

Juliana groaned. "I hate to say you were right, but it looks as if I should have listened and taken off with you last night."

"What's your plan?"

"Last I heard, all flights were cancelled today and the majority of tomorrow."

Juliana scanned the cramped boarding area. The quarter was packed with passengers whose flights had been cancelled since early that morning. Lines to concessions and the women's bathrooms were staggering.

"News reports state the roads are treacherous. It's the first time since I arrived I canceled Sunday service."

Well." She sighed. "At least you're home in case you're needed. Make a snowman for me, will you?"

"Is that before or after I shovel the four feet predicted?"

"I'll keep you posted."

She retrieved her ticket from the gate agent and exited the boarding arena. Standing in line for a latte, she considered the waving palms and sunlit sky. Juliana decided to remain in L.A. until the storm bypassed Colorado.

The church's exterior was russet brick. As Ben moved through the glass doors, people in the lobby greeted him. Ben couldn't subdue the smile that had commandeered his face. He heartily shook the hands of the greeters, and they escorted him to the sanctuary.

Inside, he felt as if he had stepped into a glorious embrace. He took a seat near the back and searched for Sheila. The music seemed to encase and rock the congregants in sweet accord. Ben felt the Presence so strongly, he tried to be as still as possible. Not out of fear because the Presence wasn't malevolent. No. It harbored such appeal, he worried it would lift him if he moved. It was delight and peace and comfort and bliss and unspeakable love.

The minister admonished the congregation to remember that true freedom, true liberty, resided only in the Father, was constantly demonstrated in Jesus, and encouraged through the Holy Spirit.

Ben stood after the ending prayer. Sheila recognized him, her steps slowing. She stared at him searching; her heart hoping what her eyes relayed was truth.

She rushed to him. "Benny, oh, Benny."

He wrapped his arms around her.

She stood in baggage claim eyeing the display of nearby hotels when her cell phone rang. "Hello."

Timmy chimed. "It's snowing real bad, there, huh?"

Juliana grinned. "How is it that you manage to call me whenever I'm away from Colorado and the weather is terrible?"

"I don't know."

"I'm actually here in L.A."

"Can you come over?"

Juliana hesitated. "I'd love to. Is your mom home?"

"She won't mind. We went to church today."

"You did? What was your favorite part?"

"Umm, I liked when we built Noah's Ark out of Lego's."

"Very cool."

"And I was the one who put the horses inside. Here's my mom."

There was a bit of rustling and the choppy words of "Uncle Ben" and "church."

"Let it snow, let it snow, let it snow," Sheila sang.

"Not funny."

"We are at poolside gobbling down ice cream from Cold Stone and soaking up some sun."

"That would actually sting if I were in Denver."

"What do you mean?"

"I'm stuck here at least for the next forty-eight hours."

"You don't say. You said you had a quick turnaround."

"I figured since my flight left at six a.m. I had plenty of time to make Sunday service."

"There's this saying. 'God watches as we make plans and laughs.' Where are you staying?"

"I was just about to call a hotel when Timmy phoned."

"Is there a saint for bad weather? You know one who looks after those trapped in it?"

"I have no idea."

"If there isn't, I think he just might fit the bill. Anyhow, why don't you save your money and stay with us?"

"Seriously, I don't want to impose."

"It would be an imposition had I not offered."

The Explorer picked her up outside of baggage claim. She tossed her carry-on into the trunk.

"I don't want you to be shocked, but Ben's at my house."

Juliana fastened her seatbelt. "All right?"

"He met us at church. Since I don't have to work this afternoon, he decided to hang out."

Juliana shrugged. "Sure." She tried not to presume anything about his church trip.

The twins bombarded her with swift talk, and by the time they pulled into Sheila's garage, her cheeks ached from smiling.

Sheila hopped out and gathered Juliana's carry-on. They entered the laundry room and crossed into the den.

"You hungry?" Sheila asked as she headed to the guest bedroom.

"Yes."

Juliana saw movement on the patio. His hair was cropped and he appeared thinner, but undoubtedly it was Ben. He entered through the sliding door.

Tommy climbed on her lap as she sat at the kitchen table. Timmy brought a pail of Lego's and dumped them in front of her.

"Wow." Juliana whispered. "Where are the flowing locks, moustache, and beard?"

He grinned, taking a moment to study her as well. "Luke Bailey has been put to rest. At least until the sequel."

"I had nearly forgotten what you looked like when we first met."

"Had you?"

"Nearly."

Sheila fed them lunch and talked the boys into a movie. They protested once they discovered Ben and Juliana would not be joining them but calmed once they realized Uncle Ben would order pizza for dinner and Juliana was spending the night.

Once they were alone, Ben refilled her water glass and an awkward silence descended. "First, I owe you an apology. I didn't want to hear what you had to say because it hurt. It hurt that God was more important to you than I was."

"That's not likely to change, Ben."

"I understand that now, but then it made me want to curse."

The corners of her mouth turned upward. "What changed?"

"Me." His entire demeanor seemed grounded in benevolent strength. "You were incredible on *News Today*."

"You saw that, huh?"

"Self-assured in the face of chaos." Ben's eyes fell to her open neckline. "Your necklace is stunning."

She touched it. "A birthday gift from T." She drank some water.

"How's Dionne?"

"Wonderful. At a pastor's convention in Dallas." She fiddled with the necklace. "How is your family? Marcus, Ian, and Hunter?"

"Great. Really great. Super busy." He studied his hands.

"Good."

Ben nodded and studied his hands again. "You came along, and I started to believe in promises I never knew I could receive. I wanted to live out those promises with you, but I wanted them on my terms."

"I see."

"I've finally concluded which is greater. My truth or the Truth."

"And?"

"The Truth. And I honestly don't know how I ever lived without it."

She took a moment; the emotive memories and fervent prayers congregating like wispy filament in the corner of her mind. Her smile broadened.

The tears edged at her eyes. "I'm deeply happy for you, Ben. More than I could ever express with words."

"Juliana, there's something I've wanted to tell you for awhile."

"Although a relationship with God doesn't block pain, isn't it amazing to know you'll never face it alone?"

He nodded. "It is. Especially in light of what I have to say."

"Tell me."

"I'm not exactly sure how to tell you."

She shrugged. "Just tell me."

He took a deep breath. "I'm HIV positive."

She stared at him, her eyes a fusion of shock and denial. "What?"

"I've lived with this disease for nearly five years. It probably puts my paranoia of trash removal and medical privacy in a whole new perspective."

For several moments, she surveyed him, silently pleading that he was playing a colossal joke. "Oh, Ben."

They sat in silence as the revelation hit her.

"Is that why your marriage failed?"

Ben rubbed his hands together and sighed. His shoulders seemed to curve into his chest. "In a manner of sorts. I didn't know I was HIV positive when we married. I have no idea how, but she wasn't bitter that I infected her. She left because she had a dogged fear that she might not just bury me but our children."

Juliana attempted to tame the slicing of her heart as the silence lingered. Scores of health reports, optimistic statistics, and medical journals on HIV flashed before her eyes. There was tremendous advancement in the medical industry and HIV patients were living longer than ever. Yet it all seemed superficial as she absorbed that Ben was dying.

Finally, Ben said, "We are now serving the same God, Juliana. Yet—"

Juliana stood abruptly. "Excuse me."

Ben designed figure eights on the table until his finger ached. Then he smacked the tabletop violently with his palms. Her bottle teetered and rolled onto the tile.

She rushed to the bathroom and shut the door. She paced, perched on the tub's edge, then paced more. Before long, she was an anguished heap on the floor. Her mind screamed thousands of questions beseeching God for every answer. She knew, in this frame of mind, even if He replied she was too raw to listen.

A knock tapped the door. "Juliana, may I come in?"

When she didn't respond, the door cracked and Ben peeked in. "I'm concerned."

He shut the door, spooled tissue around his hand and sat beside her.

Juliana couldn't control the internal crushing. She felt as if her breathing would cease and she would be powerless to revive it.

"When I was at Kennedy, I read about Esther and Hosea."

"Yeah?"

"It didn't truly sink in then. The intent just kind of lingered on the edge. Their purpose created tremendous agony within, but was intricate to God's plan for a nation."

He handed her more tissue and she crumpled it in her fist.

"Purpose." She pulled her knees to her chest and gripped them. She succumbed to another wave of fright and incredulity.

Ben pulled her closer, burying his mouth in her tousled curls. "I've entered a new chapter in my life where my purpose has taken front stage and refuses to budge. I have no idea how God will work this out, but I've retired my boxing gloves. I'm not calling the shots anymore. Now I sit at His feet and listen as He nudges, guides, and directs."

Juliana's head shook back and forth, as the struggle between reality and denial raged.

"Juliana, I'm fairly new at this, but I realized something. You question whether God can be trusted because this plan seems to lack logic. But, in the middle of the night as I dragged through the Scriptures, I kept coming to the same conclusion. He never turns His back on those who trust in Him. Never."

"But, you may die."

"I may. But, now that I've found Life, I can't live as if I haven't."

She leaned into him and Ben pulled her tighter.

"You need time?"

"Am I insolent to even think I have it?"

Then he kissed her, and she realized God had no intention of not empowering her with the strength to fulfill His plan.

She caressed his face. "I love you, Benjamin Luke."

"Truly? I couldn't tell."

"I am overwhelmed and terrified and awestruck."

"I wish I could promise you more."

"Tell me again what you discovered in the Scriptures."

"That He never turns His back on those who trust in Him."

"I don't want to bury you."

"You may not."

"I'm so afraid."

"You're not alone."

CHAPTER TWENTY-SIX

He met Grace Connors at her business office. He had merely arrived in L.A. three days prior. Already he missed the aromatic breezes from his veranda in the Mediterranean. Deftly, he removed the silk hanky from his right breast pocket and dabbed at the perspiration along his thick hairline.

Grace's associate escorted him through the contemporary office. He didn't care for the use of steel and tinted glass. Grace must have succumbed to some quirky interior designer because her personal tastes leaned toward cheerier hues with lightened woods.

The assistant left the door open. Grace looked from her paperwork. The chic reading glasses added distinction to her angled features.

She reached into her purse and handed him the set of keys. "Do you remember what to do?"

"Have I ever forgotten?"

She did not seem amused by his response. "I leave this afternoon and return Monday morning."

"Yes, ma'am." He looked to the open office door and played along with her professional manner. "Are there any special instructions of which I should be aware?"

"No." She shut the folder upon the mound of papers. "Simply what's been previously established."

He considered lingering, but her sullen mood alerted a swift departure.

He drove the rented sedan toward her house in Pacific Palisades. Stalled in traffic, he flipped on the CD player. The infinite bellow of Miles Davis's sax filled the cabin.

His cell chirped. "Yes?"

"It's Jessica. Have you left Grace's office?"

It annoyed him when she pushed. To show her who possessed control, he tormented her with frosty silence.

After a few moments, the atypically jittery assistant offered, "I'm sorry. I wasn't expecting you in town so soon."

"Did you enjoy the premiere?"

"It didn't end as planned. What prompted your early arrival?"

"There's a thrill to be that close to Juliana when she has no idea what's coming."

"We don't have much time. When should I call you again?"

"You shouldn't. I'll call you." He disconnected.

The traffic crawled for another hour. Gridlock only agitated when time pressed on him like a vise. Already, he hungrily anticipated the next advance of his plan.

After four days, and numerous conversations about his new faith and their fears, Juliana returned home and Ben joined her. One morning, before she departed for work, she gasped as he fastened the platinum and diamond bracelet on her wrist he purchased in L.A. Each stone was suspended like a row of icicles caressed by moonlight. Ben had also purchased an engagement ring, but he was saving that for a carefully crafted evening in the future.

"Happy belated Valentine's Day."

As she entered the car, Dionne reminded they had dinner reservations with the Elliotts at six. Gary, Juliana's bodyguard, opened the door and moved to the driver's seat. Ben, Dionne, and Bruce watched as the silver sedan trailed down the winding driveway.

Bruce drove Ben and Dionne, clothed in denim and lined jackets, to Lowe's. They watched as the employee hauled the flatbed of flagstone and sand in Ben's rental truck bed then returned to the residence. Ben transported the wheeled table saw from the garage and placed it at the foot of the gazebo. He poured the sand on the moist earth of the pathway Dionne had previously plotted. Then he lifted stone pieces from the truck and placed them in the wheelbarrow. Bruce paced the vast yard, alert for trouble.

Ben knelt beside Dionne, admiring her meticulous layout. "This prep work would have impressed my father."

She grinned. "Juliana bragged about the numerous awards your family's landscaping company received."

"She did?"

Dionne cocked her head. "Benjamin, never forget she is a journalist. Digging beyond the surface comes naturally for her."

The wooden stakes lined the ground at every corner. String had marked the dug out perimeter of the path beginning at the side vegetable garden to the stamped concrete of the walkout patio the length of about fifty feet.

Dionne reached for the 2x4 to screen the gritty surface. "You take that 2x4, begin at the concrete, and we'll meet in the middle."

Ben obeyed, loving the lilt of her voice as she offered lustrous praise toward the Savior. "You must have a passion for Him, Benjamin."

Ben looked over his shoulder. "What do you mean?"

"Like when you're filming or when you're speaking about HIV awareness. There's a passion there that consumes you."

"Yes."

"Except He's carried it deeper, furnishing it with a greater substance than you've ever dreamed."

"He's done so much more than I would have believed this time last year."

"Oh, just hold. He's not done."

"Dionne." He turned and faced her. "I'm not sure how much time I have."

She stopped grazing the sand and her stare bore into him. "None of us do. That's why we better be busy doing what He told us to do. Right?"

Juliana vowed she would allow him to tell Dionne, but somehow, he believed she already knew he was HIV positive.

She continued her grazing. "The nightmare has ceased, hasn't it?"

"It has."

"The passion you have for God will keep you during the darkest moments. Never, ever forget He is in control and will always be there for you."

Ben was certain she was aware of his precarious health status. Ben pondered her words as the wood pressed over the sand.

After they met at the mid-point, she patted his hand and said, "Look at that, son. Even when something begins a certain way, it can always change."

"Juliana!" Thomas called, making his way toward her, coat and briefcase in hand.

She held up a finger and pointed to her desk phone. "Congratulations, again, Jaki. Too bad I can't make your promotion party."

"No problem. I'll record every negative comment I say about you and forward it your way."

"I appreciate you."

"Have a great weekend."

She disconnected and looked at her boss. "You headed home?"

He looked around the empty office, then at his watch. "As you should be. This is half-day Friday, remember? It's four p.m. and we are the last two souls remaining."

"I'm just going to polish my last few paragraphs, and I'll see you at dinner."

He bent to pat her head, knowing it irritated her. "Don't linger, Palesa. I'm seriously craving more and dim sum."

"Don't quit your day job, Thomas."

"Never!" He kicked his heels together Gene Kelly style and headed to the elevator.

An hour later, she summoned Gary from the conference room and they headed to the garage.

Once inside the car, Gary asked, "Did you complete your article?"

She placed her purse and briefcase near her feet. "Finally."

He started the ignition. "This one seemed tougher than last month's."

She nodded. "My topic is what role faith-based organizations play in providing healthcare to those living with HIV/AIDS and whether there are differences between the secular organizations."

He placed his hand on the gearshift. "You sound discouraged."

The gunfire immediately punctured the front set of tires. Juliana screamed and Gary shoved her head near her knees.

"Stay down." Gary demanded and removed his weapon from the shoulder holster. Swiftly, he exited the vehicle and crouched beside the driver's panel.

Another round of ammunition flattened the rear tires. She fumbled for her purse to seize her gun and discovered the strap was twisted around her ankle. She had no idea where Gary was or even if he was still alive. Her heart beat violently in her chest and the shudder of her hands didn't aid her pursuit of the weapon.

Then Gary stood, his weapon discharging rapidly. Defensive gunfire shoved him into the concrete wall and within seconds, he crumbled to the ground. Juliana twisted her body over the gearshift and squirmed toward the driver's door.

And, then he was there—his face covered in a black knitted mask, the rifle aimed at her head.

"Hello, Juliana. It's God."

———————————

They installed the edging, their hands working diligently beneath the work gloves. Dionne handed him a thermos of her spiced tea and Ben gulped. She handed him pieces of the stone she desired cut to fit her design. He placed the goggles over his eyes and switched on the saw. He replaced the pieces in the wheelbarrow and they headed to the patio. Bruce moved with them. They sat at the iron and scalloped glass table, munching on roast beef sandwiches and carrot chips dipped in Ranch dressing.

"You didn't come here to help me complete my path," Dionne ascertained, a twinkle in her dark brown eyes.

"Actually, your sandwiches are infamous. Did you cure the meat yourself?"

Bruce shook his head, a slight grin decorating his mouth. They all watched as a dark Mercedes cruised the street, creeping toward the house. No one spoke until it quickened and drove on the neighbor's circular drive across the street.

"You called me son earlier."

"I did."

"It seems you have a hint as to why I'm here, besides to help you with the path."

She popped a carrot chip in her mouth and chewed. When it was on its way to her stomach, she said, "People always say this, but I mean it. I knew it was you the first time you arrived for dinner."

"How? I wasn't the same man then."

"No. But you were on your way. I saw you kicking and screaming internally, but coming down that vein nonetheless."

"Vein?"

"Straight to the Father's heart."

He looked to the other half of his sandwich then met her eyes. "Do you doubt my ability to be the husband Juliana deserves?"

"If I did, you wouldn't have to ask. You would know."

"I will do whatever is necessary to make certain she is loved."

"I know."

"Then, Dionne, I ask for your blessing to marry your daughter."

She took painstaking care to wipe her hands then she sipped the tea. Ben looked to Bruce, who shrugged with his eyes.

"Let's see how you complete my path first."

Ben nearly choked.

"Get over here, son!"

After their embrace, they placed their dishes in the service dishwasher in the basement. They continued their work, placing flagstone upon compacted sand, adjusting the height wherever necessary by adding or removing the gritty earth. As the sun began its descent, Ben and Dionne stood arm and arm admiring the picturesque stone walkway.

"You know the grandchildren you give me will make this pathway look dreary in comparison." She nodded, convinced of her words.

Ben grinned, relishing the fact they had constructed something enduring together.

"Don't ever forget you're a mighty oak, planted by the streams of water, which yields its fruit in season and whose leaf does not wither."

"I won't forget."

She patted his arm. "This day will always be treasured in my heart. Thank you."

"With pleasure."

They cleared the tools and excess materials, placing them into the storage arena of the garage. Then moved to separate rooms, preparing for the evening out with Thomas and Maya.

In the living room, Ben was surprised to find only Bruce and Dionne seated there.

"She's still not home?"

Dionne shook her head. The mantle clock displayed 5:50. Bruce flipped open his phone and dialed.

"Who's he calling now?"

"Local enforcement. He's tried both Juliana's cell and Gary's. No answer."

"We can't wait, Dionne."

She discerned his brooding thoughts. "Let's go."

They arrived at the *Core* lot and Ben nearly jumped from the vehicle. Dozens of police cars lined the street outside of *Core's* offices. Before Bruce brought the truck to a halt, Ben was out of the door. He raced to the parking lot creeping with officers. Ben counted one ambulance.

Shaking, he ducked beneath the barrier and an officer blocked him. "There's no access, sir. There's an investigation going on. No public access is allowed."

Ben tried to break from the policeman's block and failed. "I'm not *public*. I'm her fiancé."

Bruce and Dionne flanked him. The ex-FBI agent was instantly recognized. He and the officer had shared numerous backyard bar-beques with Gary.

He leaned toward Bruce and whispered. Bruce nodded solemnly. Then the officer slightly relaxed. "These two are your responsibility. Any mistakes and it's on your head."

They headed up the concrete staircase of the garage. Dionne lacked traction due to her heels. Ben grabbed her hand and they crossed level three. Bruce opened the door, and headed toward the blue line of men. They allowed him entrance because of his highly acclaimed bureau credentials and his close connection with Gary. He informed them of the identity of his companions and that they would remain by the door.

On the driver's side of Juliana's car was Gary—face down and bleeding. A photographer busily flashed pictures of the quiescent corpse.

Bruce touched Ben's shoulder. "Wait here. I'll see where she is."

Although Ben realized the wisdom of Bruce's request, he still trembled to personally discover if Juliana was safe. Bruce talked to some of the policemen then moved to the back of the ambulance. A uniformed medic obstructed the view inside.

Dionne's hand shook in the expanse of his. He pulled her closer. "Do you remember what you told me earlier? That no matter how bleak it looked, to stand firm and remember I am an oak planted by streams of water."

She nodded, not taking her eyes from the ambulance. "I remember."

"I'm not producing fruit alone. She'll be right by my side."

A screech of tires erupted behind them. A black official van filled the empty space of the tunneled garage. The FBI representatives eyed Ben and Dionne cautiously then moved about their business to determine who had gunned down one of their esteemed colleagues.

The ambulance chirped, flashed its lights, and descended toward the exit. Behind it was Juliana wrapped in a blanket and walking toward them. Ben forgot he was comforting his future mother-in-law and raced to her. It didn't matter, for Dionne nearly beat him to her. They shrouded her, grasping and searching for injury. There was a cut on her left cheek, which mingled into a vicious bruise.

"I'm not hurt."

Ben held her, smoothing the tousled curls upon her head. "Oh, God."

Juliana's body trembled as if near frozen. "He wanted my bracelet."

Both near-husband and mother stared at the frightened woman. She held up her wrist, no longer decorated by Ben's Valentine's Day gift. The nausea grew within his belly. He inhaled to detour its eruption.

"He shot Gary," she whispered. "He didn't have a chance."

Dionne kissed the bruise then pulled her daughter close. Ben loathed this war—hunt down the man who had attacked Juliana or remain and comfort?

"He said, 'Hello, Juliana. It's God.' He said he wouldn't hurt me if I handed it over. I refused. That's when he started to drag me from the car. My shoulders and hips were banging against the gearshift and armrest. Neither yielded. I bit him."

Ben saw remnants of the killer's blood on her lower lip.

"I couldn't get to my gun, so I did what you taught me, Bruce."

Everyone's eyes fell on the bodyguard. Bruce touched her arm and spoke as if rousing a child from a nightmare. "To gather evidence of either blood or skin."

"Yeah." She sighed and Ben wanted her to stop talking so he could just take her home—usher her far from this horror. "That's when he hit me. I woke up, sprawled on the front seat."

Soon the agents closed in and requested Juliana for a statement. Bruce was the only one allowed into one of *Core's* conference spaces during the examination.

Ben and Dionne held hands in Thomas' office as they endured the lengthy interrogation. Agents moved in and out of the room like bees obsessed with the livelihood of the hive.

Thomas and Maya rushed through the door. They hugged Ben and Dionne, and Thomas asked, "Is Juliana all right?"

Dionne answered, "She's safe. The police are questioning her now."

"Oh, thank God!" Thomas exclaimed. "What happened?"

Ben retold the horror to the shaken couple.

"He actually said he was God?" Maya asked.

"Just like in his notes," Ben uttered.

Bruce emerged, gripping Juliana's shoulders. A large peach bandage covered her left cheek and her tremble seemed less visible.

She grasped Thomas and Maya in a tight embrace. "I suppose dim sum will have to wait."

Maya fervently kissed the cheek not bruised. "Palesa, we were so afraid."

Then Ben noticed it.

He stared as the officials escorted them to the elevator and to the rental truck. They converged in the expansive DeLauer kitchen where the picture windows framed the half moon and blinking stars. Juliana sipped the tea her mother brewed while Bruce, Dionne, Ben, Maya, and Thomas tried not to stare at her.

Law enforcement foot-patrolled the five-acre property.

Juliana placed the cup on the table and pulled her sweatshirt closer. "You would think his voice would have been strained or agitated."

No one responded verbally, waiting.

"It was the most serene voice I've ever heard. And polite. He even said please when he asked for the bracelet."

Again, they waited.

"None of the officers believed me, but I'm telling you his objective was not to hurt me."

They exchanged looks.

"Neither do any of you."

She sipped more of the tea. When she placed the cup on the table, Dionne patted her hand. "Why do you say that?"

"Gary pushed my head down and jumped out of the car. He killed Gary methodically, without hesitation. I recognized the sound of his gun as a semi-automatic rifle. It was so loud, much louder than I ever expected. It discharged bullets in a flash. So very quickly that Gary didn't have a chance."

Ben rubbed his chin, praying God would soon erase this nightmare from her memory.

"He didn't shoot through the rear window to get to Gary. He waited. As if he *needed* him out of the car. It was as if he seemed concerned he would hit me in the exchange of gunfire."

She sipped more. "My purse was on the floor by my feet. Before I could reach for the gun inside, he was right *there*. He told me he was God."

Another sip. "He sat on the driver's seat and stared at me through those cut out eyes. That's when he asked for the bracelet. '*Please*,' he said."

She stared at her cup. "His eyes weren't like the eyes of the men in the veld with Tomorrow. Their eyes were crazed, full of fury. His were almost...envious. As if I had something he desperately wanted."

Ben took the opportunity to examine what he'd been studying back at the *Core* offices. She finished the tea and yawned. "The tea is working, Mom."

"Good, baby."

Juliana looked at Bruce. "Gary talked about you all the time. Whenever we were stuck in traffic, I begged him to tell about your days in Semper Fi. He wouldn't. But he loved to convey about all the women who chased you at the Bureau."

"Gary's admirers far outnumbered mine. He broke all their hearts when he married Abby."

No one spoke, wondering how the wife of nearly twenty years had taken the news.

"He shouldn't have died like that, Bruce."

"I know, Juliana." Although Bruce didn't speak it, he knew according to her statement and ballistic reports that Gary hadn't suffered very long. The assassin halted Gary's life with two bullets through the heart. There was a silent smoldering behind Bruce's mahogany eyes.

"His eyes were so serene—so focused."

Dionne shivered, Bruce clasped his hands on the table, and Ben diverted his glance from the object of his curiosity. Maya reached for her husband's hand and he cried out.

Juliana stared at the cloth bandage shrouding Thomas' hand. "What happened to your hand?"

He lifted up the injured appendage. "Oh, that. I was removing my dry cleaning from my trunk and a hanger nagged me. I didn't realize the bag was trapped beneath a set of free weights."

"Ouch," Juliana replied.

"It sliced pretty deep," Maya attached. "It was a jagged wound, like the hanger got caught on his skin and as he tugged, it ripped deeper. I told you that a pair of slacks was beneath that free weights set."

Ben glanced swiftly at Bruce, who mentally affirmed Ben's deduction.

Juliana smirked. "You still haven't returned those? Thomas, it's been nearly a year. Sports Authority may refuse you."

"I know." He groaned. "Now I truly have incentive, don't I?"

Juliana yawned again. "I'm tired."

Bruce stated, "For safety, I should sleep very near you."

Juliana stretched. "I'm sleeping in Mom's room."

Dionne replied, "There's a chaise in my room where you can sleep. It's nearly six and a half feet."

"If it's all right, I'd also like to be near," Ben said.

The room looked to him.

"How near?" Dionne smirked.

"Is there an air mattress I can place on the floor?"

Dionne said, "I'll grab the pillows and blankets from the linen closet."

They bid the Elliotts goodnight and moved upstairs. The men waited at the threshold as the women readied for bed.

"I've made the necessary calls. Everything will be ready by morning," Bruce stated.

"Is James available for personal security?"

"Yes. His latest detail just ended."

"Anything on Elliott?"

"Witnesses claim he drove from *Core's* lot shortly after four p.m. No one remembers him returning. I have a couple of guys trailing him."

"Thanks, Bruce. Now we'll have to see if Juliana will agree with our plan."

The women climbed into bed and the men obtained their designated spots. The air mattress rested beside the right side of the bed, where Ben could easily reach Juliana.

Ben's mind was ruled by emotion and consumed with the dreadful possibilities. *Why would a skilled executioner rip away a life for a bracelet?*

The bracelet was luxurious but not overly extravagant. Its greater value was deemed by the sentimentality of the reunion between he and Juliana. *Why would this appeal to a stranger?*

It was like trying to solve a puzzle where the pieces were chipped and warped; nothing was as it truly appeared. Just before dawn, his mind finally rested. It didn't last, however. The images of Juliana struggling in her car with the assailant surfaced.

Ben shot up and flung away the blanket. Bruce wasn't on the chaise and the bed was empty. He sprinted down the cherry staircase, tucking his shirt into slacks, searching the marble foyer. When he reached the bottom of the last stair, he stood behind the wall separating the foyer from the den, listening. Ben cocked his head gauging the direction of the voices. They seemed to come from the basement patio. Deftly, he raced through the den and down the flight of stairs leading to the basement.

The staircase curved, as did the wall containing it. Suddenly, Ben realized he lacked a weapon. If the killer met him in the basement, Ben would be a vulnerable target. He stopped at the second to last step and listened. After a few moments of formulating if the corner held peril or wellbeing, he peered around the masterfully crafted wall.

On the deck, seated at the dining table, were his bedroom companions. He sighed and rubbed the dampness accumulating on his forehead and upper lip. Before he reached the door, Bruce saw him. Ben opened the French doors and joined them.

"You all right?" Bruce no doubt perceived the panic on Ben's face.

"Fine."

Juliana touched his hand. "You're trembling."

"I'm fine."

"Tricia just called. She and Winston are on their way over. I don't think I'll turn on the TV today."

"Probably a good idea," Bruce commented.

"Your cell's been ringing off the hook." Juliana handed Ben his phone.

He glanced through the call history: Sheila, his mother, Grace, and friends.

Ben sighed. "It must have made the national media."

"It did," Bruce confirmed, scrolling through his Blackberry.

"What's been said?"

"Juliana and her bodyguard were ambushed in *Core's* parking garage. They've confirmed that Gary was killed, she survived, but haven't disclosed her location."

Ben rubbed his chin. "Juliana, there's something I want you to consider."

"Tell me."

"I think it's imperative to move you to a safe haven."

"What?"

"After last night, I can't see that we have an alternative."

Juliana looked to her mother in exasperation then back to Ben. "Where would I go?"

"Far away."

"I've never run."

"You're not running. You're protecting your well being."

"Isn't that for me to decide?"

"Juliana, don't do this."

"Palesa, I think Ben makes a valid point. The man has gotten brazen. If we don't act defensively, I'm not sure what he'll attempt next."

"I'm not thrilled with having to be away from home."

Ben asserted, "Prayerfully, it won't be for long."

"Mom?"

"I think Ben's deduction is legitimate, baby. I'm not crazy about the idea, but there's wisdom in getting you to a place of safety."

Juliana sighed, the tension catching in her throat. She willed for logic to overrule her frayed emotions. Juliana stared at the newly assembled flagstone path. "I've never been apart from the people I love, Ben."

"Baby, if there were a better solution, I would be the first to offer it."

"Ben, perhaps you should enlighten Juliana of the question you asked me yesterday."

Ben nodded and took Juliana's hand. "I am highly motivated to see this nightmare come to a swift end. I'm not enthused to have our wedding indefinitely postponed."

Juliana looked to her mother then back to Ben, speechless.

"Dionne consented. What about you?"

"Like that was a real issue." Juliana grinned.

"This isn't the manner I wanted to propose."

"I was hoping for candlelight and Spanish guitar." Juliana rubbed her knuckles across her lips. A FedEx truck ambled down the street. As the driver rounded the curve of the cul-de-sac, he glanced their way.

"Yes!" Moments passed in earnest celebration.

"I am not going to leave you alone," Ben assured.

"What happens next?"

"I've hired a new bodyguard. He should arrive shortly. Then we move you to the safe house."

"If it's possible, Bruce, I'd like to go with you when you visit Gary's family."

Bruce's eyes flickered as he measured his response. "I think it would be wise to wait. I'm not even certain what I'll face."

The cordless phone on the table rang. Dionne checked the caller ID, stood, and moved through the French doors. "Hello, Pastor Michael."

"You should call everyone," Juliana coaxed. "Dispel any innuendo."

"I know this isn't ideal. But, you *do* understand the urgency?"

Juliana nodded. "I do."

Ben hugged her and returned the phone calls. Dionne returned to the patio, holding the phone to her daughter.

Juliana moved toward the retaining wall encompassing columbines, Blackfoot daisies, and Indian paintbrush plants about ten feet away. She faced the field, her back to those at the table. "Michael."

"Your mom filled in the details as to what happened. It sounds so stupid to ask you how you're doing, but I don't know any other way to ask."

"I'm all right."

"Juliana, what can I do?"

"This morning, we prayed he wouldn't kill again. We prayed he'd be captured very soon. We prayed for Gary's family. I'd ask you to pray the same."

"Do the police have any ideas as to who this guy is?"

She shook her head. "Not a clue. I'm just as stupefied. I've written things that have angered people, but this is the first time I've ever received death threats."

An official looking van arrived and pulled up the driveway. Her mother departed to meet them.

"Did Mom tell you our conversation might be taped?"

"Yes."

"I can't state everything, but some things have changed and I need to talk to you."

"Whenever you're ready."

"I would have told you sooner, but you've been out-of-town since my return from L.A."

"My old congregation threw a massive birthday party for Papa. He was utterly beside himself. Then I took him to Hawaii. It's always been his dream to go there."

She heard it in his voice. "Is he getting close, Michael?"

"I think so, Jules."

"I'm sorry."

"I appreciate that."

"I'm very glad you called."

"I wish I could do more."

"You already have, Michael. You always do."

Silence fell across the line. Juliana shut her eyes. The young cleric never failed to demonstrate faultless integrity. Michael prayed for her safety and they ended the call.

Ben said, "Everyone sends their love. Mom even offered to have you stay with her. She's pretty lethal with a shovel."

Juliana smiled, slowly. "I'll call her."

Bruce enlightened, "The special agents have arrived."

"Special agents?"

"They did a tour with Gary in Vietnam. It's a special favor for him."

Just then, the whoosh of rotor blades sounded nearby. Before the news copter could spot Juliana, Bruce moved them inside. Men in uniform occupied the basement. They moved room to room in search of covert details to aid in the executioner's capture. Two stood in the servant's kitchen, waiting while the Cuisinart brewed a fresh pot of coffee. Two in dark suits approached her.

"Miss DeLauer, I'm Special Agent Northern and this is my partner, Special Agent Blake. A package was discovered in the back seat of your vehicle."

"What kind of package?"

They moved toward the small walnut table with beet colored chairs. Ben and Bruce hung by the fireplace. Dionne sat beside her daughter.

"An overnight delivery to Gary Winters." Northern placed the package on the table.

"I don't understand. Why is that significant?" Juliana asked.

"It's from him," Northern answered.

Ben moved to the table. "What does it contain?"

Northern leaned forward, his hands clasped. "A typed letter that states Gary was simply a pawn who needed to be eliminated. He also stated that you're alive because patience is a highly valued virtue."

Juliana scowled. "Gary didn't mention it."

"Was there an air bill?" Ben asked.

"No. Local authorities opened it and seized it as evidence. There was an air bill but no tracking number, which means it wasn't delivered by a FedEx employee."

"Meaning he's not finished," Juliana said.

"Let's not think in those terms."

Dionne signified, "There was more, wasn't there, Agent Northern?"

A wisp of surprise passed over Northern's features. It had been imperceptible to everyone else, except Blake who had known him for two decades. "The bracelet. Who gave it to you?"

"Ben. As a Valentine's gift."

"That was known."

"He said that?"

"The note made mention of it, yes."

Juliana shook her head. "He's coming back. His performance isn't complete."

Although the agent had been seasoned by horrors most would never witness, his eyes nearly wavered. He cleared his throat. "The note also said, 'In every noteworthy tragedy, the heroine must die.'"

Ben and Dionne reacted, but Juliana remained as still as a python eyeing forthcoming prey. "He thinks he can take my life."

"This will end long before then. It's my job to make certain it does."

"Special Agent Northern, it's not his to take."

Northern measured her words. Suddenly, Juliana rose from the table. "There's research I need to complete for work. I'll be in my room if you need me."

Ben followed. She crossed the expansive rug and led him to the area holding her desk, computer, and bookcases. Ben sat in the plum colored suede-like chair by the window. An official lurked near the bedroom door.

He watched as she performed her research. When she faced him, Ben summoned the courage to ask the question burning within his belly.

"Why did you say he couldn't take your life?"

Juliana's stare pierced deeper than any blade. "He didn't give me life, therefore he can't take it from me. There's only One who has that power."

Ben's mind raced. He wasn't convinced the deranged man wouldn't cease until his goal was complete. Ben's skin crawled that the deranged note writer knew the gift was given as a belated Valentine's Day present.

Ben had purchased the bracelet through a reputable vendor in Beverly Hills. He did not disclose the identity of the recipient nor the purpose for the gift. Only Bruce had been privy to those details. Ben wasn't able to mask the shudder. His paranoia was escalating to lunacy. Just as quickly, the words from Psalm 91 rushed to mind.

Ben whispered, his faith tentative. "God did save you."

"He did."

"But evil got close to you and got through your door."

"But it did not consume me. It cannot. Can you see?"

Ben desperately wanted to seize her unfathomable revelation. Juliana had been developing her relationship with God since childhood. Ben's journey was new. He sighed, realizing this too would take time.

Bruce appeared. "Those messages on your e-mail were traced to a local IP address."

Juliana asked, "Where?"

"Penrose Library."

"From Denver University?"

"Isn't that where you graduated?" Ben asked.

"Yes. The library is accessible to the public, but it's restricted to mainly Colorado higher education institutions like University of Northern Colorado or CU and CU's numerous branches. Every transaction is coded and to check out books, surf the web, or access e-mail that code is provided by the university either through institution ID or special permission."

"They've just dispatched a unit to investigate."

Ben's inspection lingered on the ex-FBI agent who had become more than a human shield. Again, he shuddered.

Bruce caught it. "What's on your mind?"

"Later." Ben meditated on the promises from Psalm 91.

CHAPTER TWENTY-SEVEN

Juliana looked to the downtown skyline as the thoughts fell like erratic pieces in a Tetris game. She and Ben had decided to invite friends to a black tie dinner at the L.A. Four Seasons. After the guests would arrive, oblivious that they were actually attending a wedding, the couple would enter the noble ballroom in their nuptial attire. Every vendor would be required to sign confidentiality agreements threatening severe legal penalties if broken. She wondered if the stalker would appear.

In the garage, before her departure, Dionne assured, "Ben wouldn't have suggested this if he wasn't certain it was absolutely necessary."

Juliana clenched her mother, drawing strength from her limitless well.

"You are strong, Palesa. It's all going to work out."

She gripped Ben who whispered potent affections in her ear.

Tricia and Winston's visit was shortened by Juliana's prep work to depart town. Juliana wondered how many events she would miss; Easter in March, Dionne's birthday in April, Living Waters' Memorial Day Picnic, and on and on. With two suitcases in tow, she and her new protector, James Walker, entered the unmarked vehicle and slouched in the rear. In the driver and passenger seats were Personal Protection Specialists Miller and Cox. To all appearances, it seemed as if two bodyguards were in pursuit of a diner for a late supper.

Eventually she dozed and woke near dawn, the scenery unfamiliar.

They had traveled all night, the gloom keening toward the first stirring of daylight. They drove until nightfall canvassed the horizon again.

As she unpacked, the contemplation dominating her mind birthed a frenzied irritation. *If the stalker is someone close, every move is futile. Any advancement would be calculated and revealed before we could counter.*

James tapped on her open bedroom door. "Miss DeLauer, Mr. Powers is on the secure line."

She took the receiver, which resembled a bulky desk calculator, and turned her back to him. "Ben."

"Hey, baby. How are you holding up?"

Internally, she pouted. "A bit out of sorts. I could really go for a Starbucks' latte right about now."

"You have no idea how much I wish I could get one for you."

"You didn't figure the studio would release their leading man the first week of production?"

"Manny the Manatee holds some serious clout," Ben said, referring to his latest animated character role.

"Besides, we shouldn't overlook that he/they are watching you. You would lead them right to me."

"I'm believing that God is busy resolving so I can take you to Puerto Rico at least twice a year."

"Where I'll dance with you every night."

They reveled in the poignant images for a few moments. A PA signaled to him. "It looks as if they're ready for me. What are your plans for the day?"

"After I finish research for this article, I'll scan websites plotting the ridiculous amount of money I'll eventually spend on my new godson or daughter."

"What?"

She smacked her forehead. "In the rush I forgot to tell you that T and Winston are expecting a baby. They're due in December."

"That is wonderful. I'll call them and congratulate." Ben sighed. "This isn't permanent, Juliana. Please keep that in mind."

"I will. Listen, I'm keeping you."

"I'll call you later. I love you."

"I love you, Baby Blue."

The FedEx truck stopped in the Wal-Mart parking lot, ten minutes from DIA. He looked at his image in the rearview mirror. Every angle of his face blended seamlessly into the other. His complexion was the inner flesh of a golden peach. He removed the brown contacts and placed them in the case. Tomorrow, he would rinse the dowdy tint from his hair.

His fingers, the texture of butter, pulsed an allegro beat on the nametag.

Mitch.

He had studied Mitch and his routine. Mitch had erred by stopping at the McDonald's five miles from the FedEx main station at DIA. He had climbed into the truck unaware he wasn't alone. He had studied Mitch and his routine.

They shared the same build and distinguishing appearance. He had donned brown lenses, darkened the shade of his hair, and grew a moustache for the momentous occasion. The Texan accent had been effortless.

In elementary, he had been deemed a genius—his IQ higher than most who taught him the rudimentary basics. On the playground, he had been taunted relentlessly. As they shoved him into the fence, his face imprinted by the stiff wire, they had called him "Moldy Mattie." Because of his erratic home life, musty fumes clung to his clothing.

The craving to detach from the older, bigger tormentors had fueled him to complete high school in two years, his GPA the highest in school history. The taunts had grown to nasty pranks when he was offered a ride home and thrown from the moving vehicle. Or held upside down by his ankles from the roof until he had wet his pants.

He had never complained to the administrators for he knew evil feasted on fear. He never told his alcoholic father either.

He had watched his father beat his mother to death with a tire iron because she arrived home much later than his father had reasoned innocuous. Then the man, half-covered in blood, had wrapped the body in painter's tarp.

He had demanded his son climb into the trunk with the bludgeoned woman. The hour drive had birthed things him, tapped into alien tastes. His mother's body hadn't remained stationary. At every corner, she rolled against him.

He was repulsed and drawn to her all at once. He knew she was dead, but still he desired to somehow connect with her. Honor her.

When they had arrived in the desolate field, his father made him dig the grave and deposit her inside.

The following morning, his father had filed a missing person's report. Cops swarmed, searched for two weeks, and dropped the case for a missing three-year-old. His mother had been eclipsed as if her life never mattered.

He had never forgotten.

But patience was a highly valued virtue. He realized the cunning mastery of the wait. It was sheer rapture when the youthful tormentors had moved on, long dismissing their brutality. Until, in delightful succession, he had brought the revelation to their remembrance. Every one of them had died, their eyes screaming shock until the scream was soundless. Each execution had been more exhilarating than the next.

Some began with animals, perfecting the art of slaughter. Animals bored him. Their cries for mercy lacked the quality he desired.

He moved to the back of the FedEx van, removed the uniform, and deposited the items in his suitcase. He shrugged on the double-breasted designer suit and pricey shoes. He wanted to look the part as he traveled first-class to L.A.

He had mastered disguises, fooling those considered experts—such as thirty minutes ago at the DeLauer mansion. Not one of them paid close attention. That was the problem with creatures these days. No one took the time to terminate the noise and glimpse into what was authentic. One of the inhabitants even knew him but feigned him a stranger.

The house was skulking with law enforcement, some of which he remembered from the Academy. He had been commonplace then in every area except his intellect and the psychological evaluation. The instructors had dubbed him "too unstable" to carry a badge and revolver. He had been quite stable as he snapped Mitch's neck and stuffed his body where the "experts" wouldn't discover it for months.

After takeoff, he sipped the champagne, for leisure was in order. His

Colorado return had already been scheduled. Only he and those of his inner circle knew the time and place.

Once the captain granted permission to rise from their seats, he leaned the chair back and stretched his lanky limbs, the majestic Rocky Mountains below. A grin crept to his face as he anticipated the luscious method in which he would seize Juliana DeLauer's life.

The morning after, the security film arrived from Gary's assassination. James and the other two personal guards analyzed it for hours. Juliana considered coaxing him into a walk, but after she'd browsed the Internet for baby clothes, withholding any purchases, an intense thunderstorm descended. She gazed out the window and dreamed of Puerto Rico and salsa dancing with Ben.

The following morning, the storm persisted and Juliana paced like a caged panther envisioning the hunt. James reminded of the vast collection of DVDs, but she shrugged. She didn't desire electronic amusement and some the movies featured Ben. Viewing him would only intensify the fact that he was too distant to touch.

She phoned her mother, Tricia, and Maya, but kept the conversations cryptic in case their lines were tapped. After dinner, she removed a paperback thriller from the bookcase. The author's first line drew her in, but distraction reigned. She retired to her room early. By the time Ben phoned, James had found her asleep.

The next morning was dazzling, promising warmth. After breakfast, Juliana bolted to the wraparound porch with James tracking. She plopped on the swing, careful not to spill the contents of her glass. The cornfields seemed to extend as far as the horizon. The fields were barren and dark, awaiting the first sprouts of life.

"This is certainly going to take a bite out of my wedding budget."

James, sipping hot coffee from a russet mug, shrugged. "But, look at that view. Priceless."

She studied him instead of the bleak field. His voice in the morning sounded gravely and by midday, the edges had smoothed into a melodic baritone. He looked no more than thirty, carried the build of an Olympic weightlifter, and was clean-shaven. His facial structure was chunky, as if God had been in a hurry to conceptualize him for a burning purpose. His eyes, nearly black, had the power to intimidate a raging, seven-foot grizzly. Just like Juliana, his ethnicity seemed buried beneath layers of multiple nationalities.

"Do any of you guys have hair? I look around and all I see is bald, bald, bald."

"Hair slows us down when in chase. Clean shaven is more aerodynamic."

Despite the disturbing burden of her precarious state, Juliana chuckled. "Maybe this forced sequester won't be such a dreaded bore after all."

"You didn't eat much breakfast."

She had listlessly observed as he placed the papaya, milk, limejuice, ice, and vanilla extract in the blender and crushed it all. The cookbook was open to a labor-intensive sancocho recipe.

"Wasn't really hungry. I suppose you salsa?"

"What?"

She held up her glass. "You make these amazing Caribbean drinks. Are fluent in Spanish. Actually know how to prepare sancocho. I figured salsa dancing must be somewhere in your repertoire."

"I prefer the merengue. And my grandmother taught me all those things. I used to visit her in the DR."

"I love the Dominican Republic, although I haven't visited there as much as I'd like to." She paused. "You are an obscurity, Mr. Walker. Can we take a walk?"

They stepped from the porch and crunched the gravel beneath their feet as they made the journey from the expansive front yard to the dirt road. The sun warmed their faces.

"I need to keep up with my marksmanship and martial arts."

"There's a barn behind the property where you can do both."

"How were you able to hammer down the details so quickly? I mean, I'm not a dignitary or personality."

"Mr. Powers is not only sharp, but heavily connected."

They walked a few yards down the dirt road, the buffalo berry shrubs whispering in the wind. Juliana liked the fact he didn't press conversation.

"Any idea how long this will be my primary residence?"

"I'm unable to answer that."

She rolled her eyes. "Don't clam up on me, James."

"Miss DeLauer, that decision is not up to me. It's based upon the level this perp decides to take this. He could back off for months or hit us with another note tomorrow."

She shoved her hands in the back pockets of her jeans. "Warning! I'm about to whine. I want to be at home, on my sofa, watching Dr. Phil administer tough love."

They strolled amongst the murmured serenade of the pasture. She longed for the reassurance of Ben's touch. This need to have him near was so bright it felt glorious and irksome all at once.

"So, what made you decide to place your life in danger for near strangers?"

"My uncle was a top recruit for the Bureau when I was a kid. Whenever he'd visit, he'd spend hours telling me stories of his experiences. I was immediately hooked."

"So, you thought it would be cool to work for the Bureau?"

"I couldn't wait to join the Academy."

"Let me guess. You graduated top of your class?"

"I love what I do."

"What led you to the vocation of human shield?"

"Some very bad men were involved in a very bad drug deal. I tried to stop them."

"It sounds as if not many were left standing."

"Including me. But, I made it out alive."

They rounded the fenced perimeter of the property and headed north toward the backside of the land. Juliana eyed his dark gun enclosed in the shoulder holster.

"Did you meet Bruce at the Bureau?"

"Bruce is a close friend of my uncle's. When I was in elementary, sometimes he'd pick me up after school. Everyone of my enemies converted."

"Tell me something? Have you studied stalkers?"

"It's required to understand how they operate."

"Why do you think he's chosen me?"

James paused to consider his answer. "Either you've become an object of infatuation or someone very close to you has. He's become violent because it masks the shame, and he believes he can control through harassing behavior."

"You are thorough, Mr. Walker."

"You've got a theory as to who he is?"

"An inkling is more like it. And maybe I've been shortsighted about the fact he's working alone. I mean, this creep was able to enter my car and home without detection. You have to know both the front gate and home access codes before you can gain entrance."

"Obviously he is quite familiar with security systems. His use of weaponry is articulate and merciless. He ambushed a seasoned professional."

The pain of Gary's death pierced, and his wife's refusal to forgive Juliana seared like a rancher's branding iron. They ambled, their footprints marked in the damp earth. It wasn't until they hedged the area near the barn when she spoke.

"What if he's truly after Ben?"

"We're looking into that angle."

"Which unnerves me because that means Ben is in danger."

"We're not ruling out any possibilities."

Northern phoned to state he'd hit a dead end after searching the login records at the DU library. Every login must be authenticated by the DU student manifest or its academic partners. Every single student was accounted for. The most they had was a guy Juliana refused to date because he had a reputation for bedding anything that moved.

"I'm glad the sun came out. I was losing myself in speculation and probabilities that nearly made me come undone."

"This stopped being an ordinary detail when he gunned down Gary. You don't have to worry that our interest may waver."

They headed toward the barn. Juliana unlatched the door and walked into the sprawling dust. The barn had once housed horses, pigs, and chickens based upon the various partitions. All that greeted them was murky swirls of disrupted air particles.

"My gun and ammunition are in my purse back at the house."

"You ready to work on your self-defense technique?"

"My other option being returning to the house and staring at the backs of your heads as you huddle near the computer equipment?"

"More or less."

"I'd rather practice evading choke holds."

A sliver of a grin cracked the gravity of his expression. "Then let's get started."

Monday morning, out of sheer boredom, Juliana joined James for a predawn jog. He reversed his course, returning her to the house after two-miles. She inhaled ragged breaths, grasping the porch railing as he pursued the completion of his workout. When he returned, she had showered and prepared breakfast. Her watchdog crew devoured the meal and thanked her profusely.

The following week was consumed with target practice, laundry, and beating James in backgammon three times. Miller and Cox took turns guarding the perimeter or replenishing groceries.

Juliana and James moved to the cozy kitchen, grabbed bottled waters, and reclined at the dining table.

"The DNA results are back."

Her bottle stopped mid-air. "And?"

"It's too unbelievable."

"What?"

"We cross matched until there was no room for error. The samples were from an ex-recruit at the Academy."

She scowled. "Not funny, James."

"I'm serious."

She stared at him. "That's insane."

"The FedEx package also held a partial finger print. We knew it was only a matter of time before the perp got sloppy."

"Thank you, Jesus." Juliana sighed with fervent exultation. "So, who is he?"

"A Matthias Kingston. His intellect was superior, yet he failed the battery of psychological evaluations."

"Matthias Kingston?"

"We've got APB's out nationwide. What is it?"

"That name sounds familiar."

"He had a short stint as an actor. Starred in a re-make of 'East of Eden.'"

"No!" Juliana rose from the table and paced.

"He's familiar with law enforcement. He knows FBI protocol. No wonder he's been able to anticipate our next move."

Soon she closed her eyes and James saw her lips silently moving. After, she returned to the table.

"Miss DeLauer? Is everything—"

"What was Ben's reaction?"

"Bruce stated that he's recording at the studio."

She shot up again. "Can you get Bruce on the phone?"

James did, then handed her the receiver.

"Bruce, James told you the news?"

"He did. How are you?"

"Terrified for Ben."

"I'm sitting in the lounge outside the recording studio. Nothing is obstructing my view of him."

"I've calculated. Matthias still had five years before his scheduled release."

"I checked. Early parole."

"He's not done, Bruce. He said Gary was a pawn to be eliminated. I'm probably also a pawn. His real target, all along, has been Ben."

"Devastate the enemy by harming those he loves." Bruce paused. "I'm in mixed company, so I need you to do me a favor."

"Anything."

"Pray."

She entreated for God's protection, guidance, and power to defeat the enemy.

"Stay calm, Juliana. I'll have Ben call you during his break."

She thanked him, disconnected the call, and stared at the receiver. Across the table, her bodyguard's expression was peculiar.

"Who was Kingston to Mr. Powers?"

"A guy who roomed with him for awhile." Juliana stared into his dark eyes. "He hated to be alone. But, Ben's work often took him away. Ben doesn't know why, but something in Matthias snapped. He strapped a bomb to Ben's gas line."

James retrieved a lengthy fax from the machine. As he studied it, Juliana's mind whirled. He neatly replaced the pages regarding Kingston and examined her.

"I'm the next elimination."

"That won't occur."

"I hate that I'm not closer to Ben."

"When it's safe you will be."

She enclosed herself in silence as moments passed. "Gary said everyone gets a nickname at the Academy. What was yours?"

"Sangfroid."

Juliana recited the definition. "To consistently show great coolness and presence of mind in dangerous circumstances."

"Hopefully that builds your confidence in me."

Again, she was consumed by her thoughts.

"That can be our code word."

"This guy isn't getting anywhere near you, Miss DeLauer."

"On the off chance he eludes you, I'll say that word and you'll know I'm in danger without my giving anything away."

He reflected for a moment. "Agreed."

"It seems she's disappeared off the face of the earth," Jessica asserted, as she entered his hotel room.

He resisted the urge to say "not yet." Instead, he uttered, "I have every intention on finding out where. There hasn't been a response to her e-mails, no cell phone usage, nor credit card purchases in two weeks."

She tugged her wheeled suitcase to the foot of the bed. "Ben has a luncheon appointment with Eternity in four weeks at Sarriette."

"Where is he now?"

"In San Fran performing a voice recording for a movie."

"When do you leave to meet him?"

"In two weeks."

"You're certain you can stomach the results?"

She gaffed. "It is a means to an end." She plopped her suitcase on the bed, removed her toiletry bag, and kissed his chin. "I'll only be a minute."

Once the bathroom door closed, he removed the items from the bureau and began his work. Jessica was a creature of habit that rarely detoured from routine. The red bag was her favorite, and he was assured it would accompany her to San Francisco.

Two weeks had passed, and Juliana had finally been able to keep pace with James for two and a half miles. Her marksmanship sharpened to pointed accuracy. James altered their self-defense drills beneath the black pitch of night.

Submerged in the shadows of the sighing cornfield, he would come at her until she became proficient in eluding him. There were moments, in bitter hopelessness and raw vulnerability, where she would crumble beneath his force. He never pushed beyond her limits. Never once hurt her. But the realization she was mastering these skills to save her life created a profound shock.

"You're coming to terms with your immortality and taking possession of the power you possess to fight to preserve it."

"No. James. I'm ticked that we have DNA and a name, and this lunatic still hasn't been captured."

Patiently, he would allow her to sob into the sandy earth. When she stood, he asked if she were ready to continue. Some nights, she did. Once, her aggression resulted in deep claw markings on his neck and heavy bruising on his chest. In the bathroom he shared with the other agents, she administered first aid.

"Sorry. I seemed to have lost control."

He tossed the tainted cotton balls into the trashcan. "I was coming at you pretty strong. I've had men crack long before now."

"Are you saying women aren't as emotionally strong as men?"

"There you go again, Scarecrow."

They walked to the main living area. Because it annoyed her when he always preached of her strength, she compromised and said it would take the edge off if he would call her Scarecrow.

The other watchdoggers called to him. They motioned for him to move outside to the porch.

Bruce had enlightened that once Ben had realized the architect of their nightmare was Matthias, depression had descended. Ben couldn't fathom why Matthias despised him enough to endanger Juliana. Although Juliana understood the requirement for separation, her distress still escalated.

She picked up the secure line and phoned Ben. After five rings, it went to voicemail.

"Baby Blue, it's me." She bit back the emotion that threatened to crack her tenacity. It would only increase his misery.

"I'm just wondering how your day went. What's it feel like to eat up to nine percent of your body weight as a manatee? How are you dealing with the fact you don't get to shoot or blow up anything? Just call me when you get this."

The trio entered the living room, looking more grave than usual.

James joined her on the sofa. "We found a match for the print on the FedEx envelope."

"Matthias?"

James shook his head. "You were correct about it being someone close."

Juliana closed her eyes. "Tell me."

"How well do you know Grace Connors?"

Northern and Blake followed Ben as he walked into Grace's trendy lobby.

"Mr. Powers! I didn't see your name on the list today."

"She's not expecting me."

Grace's receptionist frowned and curiously eyed the men flanking Ben. "Is everything all right?"

"Stacy, please let her know it's urgent that I see her."

Stacy did and upon Grace's command, ushered them to her office near the end of the hall. The men entered and Ben closed the door. Grace was distracted by a file on her desk and took a moment to discover Ben wasn't alone.

She frowned. "Is something wrong?"

"Grace, these are Special Agents Northern and Blake. They have assisted with Juliana's case."

She stood and shook their hands. "Please, have a seat."

They declined. Northern said, "We've finally gotten a break in the case."

Grace smiled at Ben. "That's terrific news."

"A partial print was discovered on the FedEx envelope left in Juliana's car the night of her attack."

Grace moved to the side of her desk. "Yes."

"Miss Connors, have you ever visited Denver?"

Grace pursed her lips. "Special Agent Northern, why would you ask that?"

"We ran the print through our national database including DMV systems."

She shrugged. "What does any of this have to do with me?"

"Well, ma'am, as it turns out, the print belongs to you."

She folded her arms across her chest. "That's impossible."

"I'm afraid it is true, Miss Connors. We checked and re-checked with the same result."

She looked to Ben. "You don't believe I have anything to do with this?"

Northern injected, "We're going to have to ask you to come with us."

Ben admired her perfect caliber of disbelief and horror. He would have given her an Oscar.

She rushed to him. "Ben, there is no way you can believe that is true."

When he failed to respond, she turned to the agents and said, "Ben told me the package didn't have a completed air bill. Anyone could have recovered that envelope from this office."

"True." Northern rubbed his jaw. "But two FedEx employees from the DIA branch described you perfectly."

"No."

"And we have security tape showing you entering, sending other mail, and leaving with an empty envelope."

She grasped the edge of her desk. For several moments, the men allowed her to regain her composure. "I have one request. I employ numerous single parents who will be adversely affected if I'm seen leaving through the front door in handcuffs."

They waited. She looked to Ben. "Please, let them escort me to the back."

Ben considered and found compassion—for the employees. He nodded.

She called in Stacy, informed her of the vexing news, gave instructions, and gathered her purse.

She passed Ben. "I will prove to you that I've never betrayed you."

Ben stood staring at the photos taken when he first became her client. There were also candid shots of him feasting at one of her famous house parties. Ben realized smashing the pictures would do nothing to absolve the staggering wound.

"I don't believe it."

"They arrested her this morning."

"Ben must be devastated." She shot up from the sofa. "First Matthias and now Grace. I have to be with him."

James stood. "Hold on. You're not completely out of danger."

She placed a hand on her hip. "What are you saying?"

"These things, to be precise, take time. We still haven't apprehended Matthias—"

"You're telling me about time?"

"I need you to calm down."

"Maybe that's been the problem all this time, James. Maybe I've been too calm."

Cox and Miller shared a look.

James said, "I realize your nerves have been stretched to drastic lengths. But this is not helping. You're stronger than this."

"Would you quit telling me how strong I am? It's starting to make me want to choke you." She stomped passed him, beyond the living area, and to the front door. A few seconds later, James was through the door and beside her, his steps weighty and purposed.

"I didn't finish my sentence," he persisted.

"Funny, I pretty much thought the conversation was over."

"I told you to never underestimate my dedication to this case."

"Yeah, you told me a lot of things."

"Stop."

"Shove off, James. I need some alone time."

"Alone time could get you killed."

Because she had no other response, she bolted into a full sprint. Easily his stride matched hers, his more practiced and perfected.

"Stop!"

She grabbed the handle to the barn door and flung it open. Juliana didn't bother to try to close the heavy entry because James was too near and it merely would have bounced off his brawny mass like a paper clip on a rhinoceros. Inside, she climbed the uneven steps to the hayloft, her pace fueled by rage that wasn't certain where to land.

She attempted to cross the open space, but James held firm to her arm. Unsuccessfully, she tried to free herself.

"Ask me why I'm so dedicated to finding this guy."

"What?"

"Ask me!"

"Let go of me!"

"You have this egomaniacal conception that you're the only one whose life has been irrevocably altered by Gary's death. My uncle, remember the one I told you was my hero, died in that merciless slaughter."

She stopped tugging from him. Her head spun as his revelation took form. "Gary?"

"My aunt hasn't spoken to me since I agreed to take you on as a charge. And, Juliana, I love her like a mother. So, do us all a favor and quit broadcasting that you've experienced the greatest loss."

Juliana covered her mouth with a hand. The tears dampened the creases between her fingers. Everything seemed to spin. Her past, present, and future swirled in the loft like a tempest. Its pattern of birth predicted, yet the present and future obscured in frenzied, uncontrollable haze.

This psycho, who appeared and disappeared with the fluency of vapor, made a point of disruption. No security measures had been able to detect Matthias' movements, including those in her home.

"I'm so sorry. Please forgive me."

"I don't ever do this. Do you understand?"

She craned her head so she could clearly read his potent stare. "Yes."

Gary's widow had taken the death exceptionally hard. At every turn, she blasted Juliana on talk shows and in the press. Juliana's prayers included the woman more often than her own petitions.

James created a cosset of safety by empowering her in moments of raw limitation. She looked at her bare wrist and stilled her shaky hand by covering it with the other. The killer wanted her. But he wanted her alive until he could make a spectacle of her death. Somehow, for the time being, her living was more important than her death.

"We'd better return."

"James, Grace is just another pawn."

"What?"

"I know you guys feel it too. It's like Grace is too easy. Her culpability would cure an adequate amount of suspicion because she is powerful, shrewd, and heavily connected. But it isn't quite right. Matthias is using her alleged betrayal to cut Ben deeper."

He patted her back. "When we get back to the house, we'll call Agent Northern. You can tell him your thoughts and see what he has to say."

CHAPTER TWENTY-EIGHT

Jessica tossed the Louis Vuitton suitcase in the trunk of her convertible. She backed out of her town home driveway and headed north to LAX. The contents of her suitcase held promise of the weekend and her future.

She was meeting Ben in San Fran to regroup since Grace's arrest. Jessica vowed to be more than an employee before the Monday sunrise.

She checked in at the ticket counter and entered security. Loathing delays, every bottle containing liquid was the required ounces and enclosed in plastic. As she waited for her bag to clear the belt, one of the TSA agents called for assistance. And a female security check.

Jessica frowned. "Is there a problem?"

"Please step over here, ma'am."

When Jessica stepped aside, her carry-on was moved behind a plastic partition where security officers tugged on plastic gloves and gripped metal wands.

"I don't understand."

"Ma'am, would you prefer a hand or wand search?"

"Pardon?"

"There have been suspicious elements discovered on your bag. A body search is required."

"Wand."

The officer trailed the baton over her body. "Please step over here, ma'am."

Jessica obeyed and sat in a stiff chair. Every item of her bag was removed and analyzed. One of the security personnel waved over a man who appeared to be a supervisor.

Jessica inhaled slowly and glanced at her watch. If they didn't tarry, she could grab a Chai tea before her flight. Soon, the supervisor motioned to a set of police officers. The supervisor held a bundle of letters he had retrieved from her carry on.

"What are those?" Jessica murmured, baffled by their existence.

She didn't have to wonder for long. Instantly, LAPD descended, read her Miranda rights, and handcuffed her.

As they escorted her from the main terminal, Jessica was dumbfounded. Her bag had contained traces of TNT, gunpowder, and letters concealed within the suitcase lining charting the death of Juliana DeLauer.

Cox met Juliana and James at the front gate as they completed their morning jog.

He handed her the phone. "It's Mr. Powers."

Juliana grabbed the receiver. "Are you okay?"

"I've been up all night."

"What's going on?"

He relayed the details of the latest arrest.

She glanced at James. "Oh, Ben. No."

"How could I have been so blind?"

Cox quietly informed James of the latest development.

Juliana turned her back to them. "Baby, this isn't your fault."

"All of my perceived instincts and intuition failed. The police discovered evidence that she and Grace were partners."

"How?"

"Letters in Grace's handwriting documenting a time line of the past events. Dates of when to place the threatening notes, the bloody doll, all of it. Security camera surveillance captured Jessica leaving Grace's home very late several times. I was their sole connection. There was no reason for them to be meeting outside of business hours."

Juliana heard the emotional wrenching in his voice and wondered how it affected his health. "Ben, I want to be there with you."

"No," he groaned. "If he got to you..."

"All I want to do is hold you."

"I just don't get how Matthias talked Grace and Jessica into this."

Juliana didn't voice her refute that Matthias used those closest to Ben as pawns to destroy him. "I feel so helpless. What can I do?"

"Exactly as James tells you. And pray."

"Always. I love you."

"I love you."

Juliana showered and remained in her room praying for most of the day. When she emerged, James was cleaning the dinner dishes. Cox and Miller were analyzing documents on the computer.

She sat at the table, her features pallid and her eyes fixed on the tabletop. "I'm sickened by this thought."

James placed the towel on the counter and joined her. "What?"

"What was the first incident?"

"The ambush."

She shook her head. "Tommy."

"What makes you think that?"

"Sheila said the driver had $15,000 on the passenger seat. He refused a plea. He didn't even protest the extensive sentence."

"How does that point to Tommy?"

She faced him with troubled eyes. "One by one, Tommy, me, Gary, Grace, and Jessica."

He mulled her disturbing supposition as he walked to the window and stared as the darkness banished the daylight. "What would make this guy hate Mr. Powers that much?"

"Tommy wasn't supposed to survive. The driver's alcohol and drug levels were excessive. He wanted everyone to believe he was on a binge. However, he over consumed because he couldn't do it. He couldn't kill a little boy. According to Matthias, he failed. No wonder he rushed off to prison. It was safer than being free."

"You asked me if I was familiar with stalkers' behavior. I never thought of this guy as a stalker before."

"He's demonstrated that behavior all over the place."

"No." James faced her. "I mean before he moved in with Ben."

Juliana joined him at the window, her arms hugging her middle.

"He was fixated long ago. *Before* he even met Ben. They became close. Later, he perceived that Ben rejected him. Then the behaviors erupted."

Juliana rushed from the room. "I think I'm going to be sick."

He parked at the curb of the West Hollywood apartment and walked up the iron stairs to the residence. Two taps on the robin's egg blue door with his knuckles and the woman, an aspiring actress, opened the unit of 9E.

"Robert Lyons?"

"Good evening."

She stepped aside allowing him entry into the sparse room. It appeared as if her interior design was solely motivated by Goodwill. He placed the briefcase, purchased in Venice, beneath the aluminum coffee table. She plopped beside him on the tattered loveseat.

"Can I offer you anything?"

Robert, the name he was using this week, realized the photos from her portfolio were deficient in depicting her attractiveness.

"Thank you, no." He wasn't in the mood for chitchat. "You'll receive five grand upfront. The remaining five thereafter. Understood?"

Her lively brown eyes widened. "I understand."

If she were a year out of high school, he would have been stunned.

"You'll play the part of a newly engaged woman seeking a venue for your reception. Your wedding date isn't until late next year, allowing plenty of booking time. Places like Sarriette are notoriously booked years in advance."

She giggled and he repressed the urge to cringe. He picked up the black velvet box and handed it to her. The actress opened it with great aplomb. "It's huge and it looks so real."

"If you perform this well, I'll give it to you."

"Really?"

He shot her his practiced smile. Generally, he felt smiling was for circus act performers and morons. "Now. You must memorize the particulars. It's best not to leave a paper trail."

"I agree. Besides, I'm a whiz at memorization. After I consult with the caterer, I'll—"

"Let's not waste time." He placed the manila envelope containing the cash on the table. "Remember what I said about his face?"

"Yeah." She crinkled her nose. "Who would have believed he was into stuff like that?" She opened the manila envelope. "Will it be on the news?"

"Most likely."

"And he's promised not to press charges?"

"Why would he when he revels in this sort of thing?"

"And I won't be blacklisted?"

"Think of it as the audition of a lifetime."

She shook her head. "He seems so even."

"Even?"

"He's always seen around town with those twin boys and traveling to Africa to help those poor orphans. He supposedly attends church. Freaky."

"There's a gift card in the envelope for Neiman's. The outfit, stockings, jewelry, and shoes are waiting for you in the Roberto Cavalli section."

"Wow! I feel like I've hit the lottery."

"This is crucial." He handed her the business card. "This is the address where you'll have your manicure. Your appointment is with Justine. She already knows the brand name and color of Ben's favorite nail polish. You must have your manicure the morning of the meeting at Sarriette. Is that clear?"

"Crystal."

He smiled again and stood. She was dangerously lovely and much too optimistic. She would be delectable dead. The sooner he left her presence the better. He needed her alive to fulfill the task. The thrill that Juliana's demise was so near taunted his restraint.

She opened the door for him.

He promised, "I'll be in touch."

James handed her the yellow envelope precisely after they returned from their morning jog. "Here you are, Scarecrow."

Inside was a note with Ben's blocky script. *I await your arrival. Every necessity has been arranged. All that's needed is you. B.*

"How can this be?"

"All arranged. Mr. Powers' double is traveling to Oregon by car as we speak."

"What changed? He was resolute that we not meet until—"

"Scarecrow, you've waited for this for weeks. Now you argue?"

After she swiftly showered and packed. The men loaded suitcases, computer equipment, and security devices in the back of the Tahoe. As the truck maneuvered down the dusty drive, Juliana turned to survey the place that had been home for nearly two months. James flipped in a CD and Spanish guitar stroked her like silky plumes. She faced forward and James handed her a cranberry juice brightened with lime.

"Are you going to miss that place?" she asked.

"Some aspects, yes."

They entered a section of the road where they were encased by towering yellow grasses. Juliana sighed.

"What?"

"Reminds me of Boptang. The way the wind cries and how the grasses beat against it."

James glanced at her then refocused on the road. "I've never been to South Africa."

"Doesn't the wind seem beseeching?"

James kept his eyes ahead, but he questioned if the sequester was playing tricks on Juliana's psyche. "Maybe we could test your remarkable self defense on an enraged lion."

Juliana rested her head on the support. "If you go first."

The Tahoe continued its furtive mission as Juliana hummed her favored tunes. The wind raged, the fields waved, and with every mile, Ben felt closer.

Thirty minutes later, Cox deposited them at the base of a gleaming private jet on the tarmac of a regional airport. She eyed James as he opened her door.

"Is there a problem?"

"That seems to be quite an impressive aircraft for just us."

"It's not a trip you're likely to forget."

"What happens if I fail to climb those stairs?"

"Then Lisa and I will have to shove."

"Lisa?"

James nodded in the direction of the aircraft stairs. A trim, striking brunette descended the stairs, her stride purposeful and confident yet amicable. She donned a tailored navy suit. Once she faced Juliana, she extended a hand.

"Miss DeLauer, I'm Lisa Mendes. I'll be your attendant during your flight."

"No chance you're likely to disclose our destination."

She smiled, her brown eyes speckled with gold and russet. "I'm afraid not."

Juliana watched as James finalized orders with Cox and Miller then returned to the aircraft. The afternoon sun shot dazzling rays off the pristine, angled wings.

"I'm shaking."

Lisa gently touched Juliana's back. "Welcome aboard, Miss DeLauer."

Juliana chose the second row, window seat. Directly facing her were two adjacent seats draped in supple leather the hue of her mother's biscuits. James sat beside her. Ahead, was the cockpit. A woman, whose dark hair was pulled into a neat bun, commandeered the captain's chair. A man sat in the right. The captain shifted in her seat and nodded at Juliana.

Juliana rested her purse at her feet and immediately recognized the tune floating through the cabin.

"'Inspiration.'"

"Pardon?" The attendant returned, extending a glass of water with three plump lime wedges.

"The song that's playing. It happens to be—"

"One of your favorites by the Gipsy Kings."

"Lisa, do you have anything stronger than water?"

Lisa folded her hands in front of her belly. "I'm sorry. I was informed you wouldn't desire alcohol."

"I may not desire it, but I may seriously require it."

"Yes, Miss DeLauer." Lisa started to turn on her heel.

"Lisa, hold on. This has to be the most exhilarating experience of my life and it's only begun. Once I catch my breath and stop cursing everyone for keeping me in the dark, I'll be fine."

Lisa visibly relaxed. "Is there anything else I may get you before takeoff?"

"No. Thank you."

As Lisa explained the emergency procedures, Juliana felt as if her head were underwater. Every moment seemed to be accelerated and slothful all at once.

She stole a glance at James who was mentally canvassing the tarmac. "Paris will be teeming with tourists this time of year."

His expression was perfectly noncommittal. "You don't say."

"It's April. Monterey is having its annual wildflower festival."

"Hmm."

"I've heard the Catalan cuisine in Barcelona is outstanding."

"Truly?"

She rolled her eyes. As the jet approached six thousand feet, she dug her phone from her blazer pocket. The plastic felt slick against her damp palm. For several moments her trembling thumb hovered over the numbers. She chuckled softly, returned the phone to her pocket, and sunk into the sinuous leather. Whatever her destination, she decided to enjoy the ride.

———————————————

By the time the jet refueled in Miami, she had beaten James in backgammon twice. In concession, he taught her a few merengue moves. Four hours later, they landed in San Juan, Puerto Rico. Juliana profusely thanked the crew, who wished her a magnificent evening, before she descended the narrow staircase.

Her eyes widened when she recognized the man standing at the base of the aircraft stairway.

"*Buenos noches*, Juliana."

Juliana searched Bruce's eyes. "This is serious, huh?"

Bruce and James escorted her through customs and walked her to the well-appointed SUV with windows so deeply tinted she couldn't view the interior.

"Holey rusted metal, James, it's the Blackmobile."

"Quick! To the Batcave!"

Juliana fell against him in laughter. When they noticed Bruce, not amused and glaring, they parted.

The vivid sunset painted the lush Caribbean harbor. The truck cruised through Old San Juan with its centuries old plazas, James unfolding the copious history. Just as the sky blended into the most acute sapphire Juliana had ever witnessed, the vehicle turned onto a cobbled drive.

Bruce pressed a button on the console and the wrought iron gates opened. They climbed until Bruce parked near the door of the stucco dwelling, gleaming like iridescent pearls from the pathway lights. He switched off the ignition, climbed out of the vehicle, and opened her door.

Juliana walked up the stone pathway to the front entrance. James unlatched the door and she gasped as the inner dwelling came into view.

James said, "This is where we part."

He placed her suitcases to the right of the door.

"James."

"Yeah, Scarecrow."

She kissed his cheek. "Thanks."

He nodded and closed the door. The marble and thickly paned windows gleamed against the pathway of flickering votives. A cathedral ceiling the same shade as the exterior held copper beams that started at the walls' edge and reached across the expanse of the roofline as if the center of the home were its lover.

The back of the home seemed to blend flawlessly into the deep sapphire of the night, exposed through the wall of glass. A guitar strummed, luring, enticing her to seek out the conclusion of the illuminated course and her future. Through the marble foyer, the living room, and dining area, she trembled at the fact she would soon discover Ben.

Her feet left the marble and met the teak deck. She inhaled, the taste of ocean invigorating against her throat. Palms whispered as the balmy breeze provoked their rhythmic dance. Juliana touched the deck railing, its expanse covering the entire length of the house. She closed her eyes and her body swayed to the lilting strum of the guitar.

"Are you hungry?"

Ben stood beside a table, dressed in a dark dress shirt and slacks. More candlelight bounced off the tabletop and the blossoms of plum colored calla lilies.

"My stomach has battled me since take off."

He crossed the distance and held her. Juliana felt tremors across his shoulders. He took her hand and led her to the table. Ben sat across from her and poured sparkling liquid from one of the two pitchers into the crystal flutes.

Juliana sipped, the salty bubbles bursting against her lips. "Pellegrino."

"Just in case my stomach wasn't the only one in need of settling."

She smiled and studied him, the blue of his eyes cloaked by dark pupils but still intense. "I've missed you."

"Not nearly as much as I've missed you."

"You prepared dinner?"

He took a drink from his glass. "I *arranged* for dinner."

Ben moved to the elegantly adorned table with an assortment of calla lilies and dense silver candleholders. The ivory silk cloth whipped teasingly against the gentle wind. He opened several elaborately etched silver dishes. The smell was intoxicating, rising on the crest of the breeze and enveloping her.

He placed her plate in front of her. Her tears started.

"Oh, Ben."

"Compliments of Java Amore."

Juliana touched the linen napkin to her blissful tears. "Everything is here from the first time we ate there together. The Moroccan chicken bundles, baked mushrooms with Brazilian nut stuffing, carrot dip, orange-chocolate parfait, and koeksisters."

"Has your appetite awakened?"

"Has it!"

Ben reached for her hand and bowed his head. "Father, thank You for this night. Thank You for this amazing woman who enraptured me and as I grew to know her, impelled me to long for more. Thank You for this woman who has led me to the true meaning of abundant life. Bless this night. Amen."

With each bite, the tension of the taxing ordeal subsided. As she placed her fork in the middle of her barren dish, every sense was satiated, every nerve contented. Ben, however, had barely touched the luscious cuisine.

She moved to his side. "Dance with me."

He cleared his throat, placed his napkin on the table, and joined her on an unobstructed area of the deck. Gently, like the palms rooted in the yard, they swayed. The Latin pulse of the guitar strings and an enchanted language between their hearts dictated their movements. Juliana cherished these moments most with him; when clocks ceased to tick, mastered by the caprice of Ben and Juliana.

"Our first dance," Ben remarked lazily in her hair.

"A prelude to many more."

"Do you mean that?"

"How often do I speak things I don't?"

"I've tried to encapsulate my love for you. Take it from my heart and examine it so I can give it greater depth."

"Why?"

"So when I asked you tonight to be my wife you could stroke it from every angle, taste its texture, feel its unequivocal power."

Juliana studied his eyes, more prevailing than she had ever witnessed. He pulled her back toward the dining table. Tugging the largest blossom from the center, he placed it in her hand. When she bent to savor its mesmerizing scent, a sharp glimmer caught her eye. Within the lush, purple folds perched a breathtaking platinum setting encompassing a sizeable princess cut stone. The flower shook in her grasp.

Ben took the lily from her quivering hand and removed the ring. "Juliana DeLauer, I've dreamed my entire life. But never did I aspire to have a woman like you completely summon me, enthrall me, love me. Marry me, Juliana."

He placed the tasteful setting on her left hand and seemed to hold his breath. "Absolutely."

He exhaled and grabbed her, lifting her high. When he replaced her on the conditioned planks, his hands caressed the sides of her face and kissed her.

Juliana lost herself in the enchanting lure of heat and promise. Ben pulled away before the temptation became too great. They blew out the candles and moved the food into the kitchen. Just as Juliana spotted the dish soap, Ben touched her hand. "Tonight, you do not clean. I've hired help to take care of this."

"Did you?"

"Yes." He touched her waist. "Your bedroom is the last one at the end of the hall. It's getting late, and I don't trust myself to remain here much longer."

"Where are you staying?"

"In the bungalow less than one hundred yards away."

Juliana traced the outline of his lips. "Did I tell you one of the reasons I love you is because of your wisdom?"

He kissed her, this time more succinctly, yet still with rousing passion. "Good night, Juliana."

"It most certainly is."

"Use that phone. It's secure. Your mother's, Tricia's, and Maya's numbers have been programmed." He pointed to a unit that resembled the one she used during her sequester.

She walked him to the deck and watched as he crossed the darkened yard until he disappeared into the shadows of the adjacent house. Then she jumped until her calves ached and her ankles threatened not to support her exuberant bounce.

James climbed the deck stairs.

"Thank you for keeping the secret." She grinned.

He smiled, slowly. "Congratulations, Juliana."

She embraced him. "Promise to merengue with me at the reception."

He pulled away, his movements hesitant. "I promise."

They entered the den and James secured the sliding door. He said goodnight and disappeared through a bedroom doorway. Juliana raced across the room to retrieve the phone. She pressed one on the dial and squealed into her mother's ear, relaying every exhilarating detail of the day. Then she pressed two where Tricia's squeals woke Winston.

Juliana stretched in the chair, her bare feet propped on the edge of the ottoman. "What do you think of scarlet for the bridesmaids?"

Ben rose early, eager to begin the day with Juliana. He and Bruce jogged on the graveled roads three miles from the house as the dawn summoned pending promise. After he showered and dressed, he walked to the kitchen to exit through the sliding door.

"Morning," he called to Bruce and James.

They returned the greeting, munching and sipping their breakfast. Ben grabbed a glass from the dish rack on the counter and through the window caught a flash of violet. On the balcony was Juliana revolving in a salsa dance. Ben observed her, the guilt of being a voyeur overpowered by his absolute delight. Her moves were like a stream's rush over stones—perpetual and smooth. She seemed to give her entire being over to the splendor of the dance. Her hair shielded her face, her back dipped, and her legs obeyed the command of the spirited beat.

Although salsa was notoriously erotic, Juliana's moves were subdued. Her dance was exuberant and lush, yet distinctively incomplete. As if she reserved the abandon for her husband, for he alone had permission to consummate the dance. She concluded the compelling choreography. Ben sighed, the end coming far too soon.

"How long have you two watched her dance?" Ben asked the burly duo.

Bruce sipped his coffee. "If you want to keep your job, I advise you not to answer that."

Ben opened the door. She raced down the steps to meet him.

They stood in the morning sun, relishing the richness of another kiss.

"I've prepared breakfast."

"That's nice." He pulled her to him, savoring her lips once more.

She pulled away and led him up the steps. They feasted on fried plantains, Pan de Aqua, and coffee.

Juliana buttered another piece of the crunchy yeast bread and handed it to him. "Do you approve?"

"Isn't this my fourth slice?"

"Si, Novio."

"What time did you get up to make this?"

"Early. The bread needed over two hours to rise. It was less taxing to prepare because James helped."

Ben's chewing slowed. "Did he?"

"Besides, I couldn't sleep. I was too excited to see you."

He leaned across the table and kissed her once more. When she playfully shoved him, he asked, "Maya's recipe?"

"Actually it was handed down from James' grandmother."

Ben looked to the empty plate. He bit back the disturbing thoughts. "Can I trust you with a secret?"

"Eternally."

"I'm a horrible dancer."

She playfully cocked her head. "How can that be? I've seen you dance in a few of your movies."

"No," he adamantly shook his head, "you saw my body double dance. I was in my trailer."

"You're teasing me."

"What you saw were headshots during the simplest moves. The rest is movie magic."

"I'm appalled." She grinned and rested her chin on her hand.

"Perhaps, and breathtaking."

Her eyes widened. "You saw me?"

"I didn't want you to stop."

"It's a form of praise. My partner is ageless and eternal. I honestly try to put David to shame."

"David?"

"King David from Bethlehem. It was reported that he danced before the Lord with all his might, with sweet abandon, using his body to reveal how deeply he cherished the Lord."

"So his dance became worship."

"And his worship became a dance."

"Is the salsa reserved only for Him or can anyone cut in?"

"For now. However, a very distinctive man chosen by Him has the right to become my new partner. You may know him."

"I certainly hope so."

They finished breakfast and toured old San Juan. Juliana wore a floppy hat to shroud her face and Ben wore Levis, a gray t-shirt, and matching cap. Bruce and James offered privacy, strolling nearby.

They returned to the house and prepared dinner. She put on a Gipsy Kings CD and assigned tasks to her sous chefs. Ben chopped Spanish onions and tomatoes; James sliced garlic and green pepper; and Bruce sliced okra, hot chiles, and more garlic for the stewed okra dish. Juliana prepared the fresh cod.

She picked up a small green herb Ben didn't recognize.

"What is that?"

"Recao or culantro."

Ben stared at the aromatic plant. "It looks very much like a weed, Juliana."

"It's not, Benjamin. It's kind of like cilantro except more flavorful."

When she began to chop a small green pepper that resembled a habanero pepper, Bruce balked. "I'll be up all night if you add that to the dish."

She shook her head and nudged James. "Help me out, here. Scarecrow needs you."

Ben and Bruce shared a look.

"This is called aji dulce. It doesn't carry the same kick as a habanero. But without it, the sofrito would not taste like sofrito should taste."

Ben added the chopped vegetables to the olive oil and sautéed in preparation of the dinner. Juliana took over by adding the tomato sauce, cod, and sofrito. The colorful kitchen smelled glorious.

The sun cast dazzling shades of ginger and tangerine as they devoured the Bacalao Guisado and okra stew. Bruce and James retired to the bungalow after the kitchen was immaculate. The newly engaged couple lounged on the deck. Soon, their lips found each other, delighted in the contact, and pushed the perimeter of exploration.

He pushed away. "Juliana."

Breathless, she held a hand to her chest. "Ben."

"I'd better leave."

She pondered, allowing her heart to return to a resting pace. "You think?"

"I most emphatically think."

"We could go watch a movie."

"We won't be watching it for long. Besides, Winston warned me."

"Warned?"

"I asked him how he was able to wait until the wedding night with Tricia."

"Yeah?"

"Without skipping a beat, he said he was never alone with her."

Juliana nodded and pursed her lips. "True. There was always some brother, sister, or gun-toting parent."

"The man is a genius."

She rose to her tiptoes and kissed his nose. "Goodnight, my-husband-to-be."

As he walked across the grass, he lingered in the effect of the kiss. James met him at the bungalow door.

"Good evening, Mr. Powers."

"Good night, James."

Ben watched as he mounted the steps. He secured the lock on the sliding glass door. Ben stared at the darkened windows long after James had distinguished the lights.

Juliana woke to voices and the clanking of pots. She grabbed her robe and padded to the kitchen.

"*Buenos dias*," a woman preparing breakfast greeted.

"*Buena, senora. Me llamo* Juliana." Juliana wiped sleep from her eyes.

The cook introduced herself as Rosa and then pointed out the other three servants Blanca, Inez, and Doncia. James stood beside Rosa, carefully inspecting her cooking technique.

"How did you sleep?" he asked.

"Like someone hit me over the head with a two by four."

"Rosa's headed to the market. Any special requests?"

"I spied a recipe for cream cheese flan from the cookbook. Think you can help me make it?"

James hesitated. "Juliana—"

"You were a spectacular sous chef last night."

"If you insist."

Juliana returned to her room where she shut the door and dressed.

When she returned, James was gone and Ben sat at the kitchen table sipping juice.

She kissed the top of his head. "Morning."

"You met the Fantastic Four?"

"You mean Rosa, Blanca, Inez, and Donica?"

"The very same."

"I did." Rosa and Blanca placed the perfumed breakfast before them.

"They'll remain to cook, clean, and beat me off of you if warranted."

She sipped her juice. "*Aye caramba.*"

That night she and James volunteered to help Rosa prepare dinner. Juliana watched, enthralled by James' technique and expertise.

The remainder of their visit, they toured an art gallery in the evening where they purchased a piece and vowed to hang it above the mantle in their new home.

On the drive to the airport, they sulked.

"When can we return?"

"What about for our honeymoon?"

She grinned and rested her head on his chest. "Sounds perfect."

After they cleared customs and headed toward their respective flights, paparazzi emerged like a ravenous pack. Juliana kept her cool, forcing her mind to return to the waterfalls, the walks on the pristine beach, the breathtaking view from El Morro, and the cream cheese flan James taught her to prepare.

In Miami, they parted, Juliana battling the ache of missing him so soon. Because his flight was delayed, he phoned her cell and left ardent messages that would make her grin once she landed.

CHAPTER TWENTY-NINE

A fellow inmate snatched bread from Jessica's tray.

Jessica glared at the burly woman.

"Put it back."

"Make me." The inmate bit off a huge chunk.

Jessica charged and wrapped her hands around the woman's neck, sealing the bread in her esophagus. The woman gagged and Jessica's grip tightened. She hadn't heard the taunts to end the woman's life or the guards' pursuit. By the time they pulled her off, the woman's coloring was blue.

Her attack cost her morning outdoor privileges. By lunch, her reputation had escalated. As the inmates gathered to boost her ego, she saw Grace staring at the dismal plate of food. She moved closer and those sitting with Grace moved aside.

"Grace."

The woman stared, her eyes slightly glazed.

"Grace!"

She looked up, stunned, and scanned the lunchroom. "What are you doing here?"

"The same thing you're doing here."

"I didn't do it."

"He's pinned us together, you know."

"He?"

"Matthias Kingston. We need to stop him."

"Ben's old roommate?" Grace sat back and folded her hands on the table. "Why?"

"Because he's the one who planted that FedEx envelope in Juliana's car with your print on it."

"How did he get surveillance footage in Denver at the FedEx facility of someone who looked like me?"

"We hired an actress. I personally picked her."

Grace pressed her clasped hands onto her mouth. "Who bankrolled all of this?"

"Matthias is heavily connected. Because his reputation is unflappable and ruthless, he hasn't lacked work; break-ins, computer hacking, and other sordid crimes. It pays substantially well."

"Why is he so fixated with Juliana?"

"Because Ben is willing to give his life for her."

Grace glanced around the overcrowded, humid room. "How do you know him?"

She told Grace of meeting Matthias at a nightclub. How she had felt meeting him was a provocation dropped from the stars. She was mesmerized by his intellect and intrigued with his criminal connections. He hated Ben. She hated Ben. Nothing else truly mattered.

"We studied Ben and memorized his schedule. We set the plan into action."

"Tommy?"

"Matthias took a homeless teen off the streets. Set him up in a decent place and bought him a truck. Then Matthias asked for a favor. He never takes 'no' for an answer."

"Gary?"

"Eliminated to stress a point."

"That he's crazed beyond belief?"

"That no one could stop him if he wanted to get to Juliana."

The lunch hour concluded, and they were shuffled outside. This time, Grace found Jessica. They moved away from the crowd toward the fence.

"He had a stint with the FBI Academy. Didn't cut it," Jessica started. "He knew all about Gary and Bruce's backgrounds. He's proficient with Bureau procedure, security systems, and disguises."

Grace folded her arms across her chest. "He is supposed to be behind bars for rigging Ben's engine to blow up."

"Early parole." Jessica surveyed the group of women headed their way. She didn't resume until they passed. "He even charmed you."

"What?"

"The guy who has been house-sitting for you for over a year."

"Unbelievable!" Grace wrapped her arms around her middle. "His appearance has completely changed."

"He's a master of disguise."

"I don't feel well."

"You keep a set of Ben's house keys in your kitchen drawer. He copied them. Let himself in and disarmed the security system. It's how he found out about Juliana's bracelet."

"I think I might be sick."

Jessica shook her head. "You look like an easy target. Keep your arms to your sides just in case you need them quickly."

Grace complied. "So, what do you have to gain?"

"Matthias betrayed me. He placed traces of gunpowder, TNT, and doctored correspondence between you and me in my suitcase."

"Correspondence?"

"Plans to kill Juliana."

"Incredible!"

"You meet with your lawyer today?"

"Yes?"

"Tell him. If Matthias hasn't changed the plan, he'll kidnap Juliana in two days and kill her."

"Why Ben?"

Jessica fell silent. Then she grunted. "I was broke when I moved from San Fran to L.A. I did some things to survive. You would have deemed my colleagues unsavory. Matthias was different. He looked beyond basic survival. Every time I looked up, he was studying something new—computers, security systems, languages, pharmaceuticals, and especially weapons."

"Why Ben?" Grace asked, firmly.

"He refused to talk about it. So, I did some research on his background. His mother disappeared. She was never found."

"What does that have to do—"

"You've been Ben's manager for how long?"

"Over twenty years."

"Think back, Grace. You hired a housekeeper who wasn't referred by the agency."

Grace turned from Jessica to gather her thoughts. Then it hit her. She faced Jessica. "Ben had interviewed her and immediately liked her. He felt she needed the break more than any of the other applicants."

"Dorothy—"

"Kingston."

They studied the yard of listless women crushed by the strain of a limited future.

"One night I threw Ben a surprise birthday party. Dorothy needed the extra money and agreed to stay over. We ended pretty late."

Everything spun and spiraled and plummeted into an austere void.

"And she didn't show up the following morning for work."

"Or ever," Jessica affirmed. "According to police reports, there were several calls from neighbors to the Kingston household for domestic violence. There aren't any records of Kingston's dad ever being arrested. But, I get the feeling he wasn't pleased with her getting home late."

Grace ran her fingers through her hair, the thoughts descending like crashing hailstones. "Ben hired you as well."

Jessica smirked. "If you were to fill a room with the crème de la crème and one underdog, Ben will pick the underdog every time."

"What do you have to gain by revealing this?"

"Two things: If my obtuse attorney will listen, the state may be willing to accept my plea for a lesser charge. I'll confess it all."

"And?"

"I cheat him out of the one thing he's planned and invested so heavily for."

"That's it? A woman's life is on the line."

"Tell your lawyer. If he listens, and is willing to cut a deal, then I'll tell him exactly where Matthias is taking her for her execution."

Grace grunted and stepped from the fence. "Aren't you noble?"

Jessica walked away and then turned back. "Keep that attitude, sweetie. It just may keep you alive."

He and Juliana closed on their Malibu property. They celebrated by gorging on pecan pie and consuming large quantities of the Sci Fi channel. Ben was precarious about public appearances of Juliana, so they huddled indoors.

The following morning, he tapped on his guest bedroom door. When she didn't respond, he called out her name. Still, she didn't respond. He leaned his ear to the door and heard violent gagging.

He entered the bedroom and discovered her huddled over the commode. "Baby, are all right?"

Her response was more coughing, then miserable vomiting. He dampened a washcloth with cool water. She flushed the bowl and rolled onto her back on the tile.

He bent beside her and pressed the cloth to her heated forehead. "I think you may need a doctor."

She groaned and placed her hands on her belly. "The room is spinning. Make it stop."

"Can you sit up?"

He helped her to her feet; half way to the bed, she rushed from his grip to wretch more into the toilet. He rubbed her back. When she straightened, he placed a hand to her forehead.

"Juliana, you're really hot."

"This is no time to try to seduce me."

"Let me call my doctor."

He assisted her to the bed, placed the cool cloth on her forehead, and phoned his physician. "He can see you in an hour. I'll take a quick shower and we'll head over."

"You have to be on the set in two hours."

"Don't worry about that. You rest and I'll be right back."

He showered and dressed, grateful he had shaved the night before. She visited the restroom twice before she was able to pull on her pink Juicy Couture tracksuit.

After a series of tests, the doctor concluded that Juliana had contracted the flu. He sent her home with orders to down plenty of liquids and take the Tamiflu he prescribed.

As Ben tucked her in, James arrived. Ben informed him of Juliana's illness and advised she needed as much rest as possible.

Ben kissed his fiancée's flushed face. "I'm headed to the set, but I'll call you on my first break."

"Don't do that." She moaned. "I don't want you catching this dreaded thing."

"I love you, baby."

Her response was another restless moan. James retreated in the office adjacent to the bedroom.

The front gate chimed. James checked the security monitors on the console to his right and saw a delivery truck. He met Ben in the kitchen.

"Has Bruce contacted you?"

"No, sir. You haven't heard from him either?"

"No." Ben rubbed his chin. "Maybe he misunderstood that I wanted him to meet me on the set."

Neither of them had ever experienced Bruce misunderstanding a thing.

"I'm expecting a script today."

"There's a delivery truck at the front gate now."

"I'll get it on my way out. Please, call me if she worsens."

"Certainly, sir. Have a good day."

Ben's morning was consumed with the shoot. When he phoned, James informed that Juliana hadn't stirred since he had departed for the set. It heavily disturbed that Bruce had seemingly disappeared. As requested, Northern checked Bruce's residence and discovered it locked, tranquil, and Ben's Denali parked in the driveway. He awaited the sheriff's arrival to obtain entry.

In the afternoon, he met Eternity at Sarriette, forgetting the package in the backseat that had been delivered before he left the house. The sender's name: Tiro Lesaba, Johannesburg, South Africa.

After finalizing several business plans, she said, "You truly look happy, Ben."

"I truly am, Eternity." He placed his credit card in the fold.

She scrutinized him for a few moments. "If your engagement is any indication of the solidity of the marriage, then your bond should be like concrete."

"It wasn't just the two of us. I highly recommend having God in the mix."

"So you too have found religion?"

The waiter retrieved the bill and disappeared to charge the account.

"God found me. And, seriously, I have no idea how I lived without Him for so long."

"I've missed seeing you at the parties. Does your religion forbid them?"

"That's the thing most people don't understand, Eternity. When God enters your life, it isn't as if every good thing is revoked. So much more is added, multiplied. I was designed, created to love Him. In that love, everything I need is fully given."

Suddenly, a dark-haired woman who had passed him to exit touched his shoulder. "Ben?"

A dramatic engagement setting graced her left hand. "May I help you?"

She swung a lean leg across his thighs. Before Ben could object, she was on his lap. "Miss, please get up."

She smiled, her teeth perfectly spaced and white. Her arms snaked around his neck. "Now, you and I both know you want nothing of the sort."

The staff caterer stood examining the scene, torn between the immaculate appearance of the brazen brunette and Ben's dismay. Unfortunately, this type of drama wasn't bizarre in L.A. Many of the affluent patrons had mistresses who performed in such a manner during business deals. Somehow, it sparked envy in the hearts of those morally challenged.

"I need security," Ben stated.

He deduced that if he stood, the girl would end up sprawled across the contents of the table, evoking more awkward attention. The staffer snapped her fingers and immediately two robust men descended, grasped the woman's shoulders, and tugged. Unfortunately her nails, which dug into Ben's cheeks like talons, did not easily release. By the time they had liberated her from his lap, Eternity screamed.

The clawing, lap-climbing woman blared, "Juliana forced the abortion! I know you wanted our baby! It was all Juliana!"

The caterer and several other staffers stuffed napkins in his hand. Eternity busily dabbed at the bloody slashes. Ben did not like the amount of blood dampening the thick linen. He stood. "I need a private room."

"Yes, sir." The caterer tucked her dossier beneath her arm and ushered them from the riveted room. In her office, tucked far beyond the public, Ben held the napkins to his cheeks, the sting fierce and escalating.

"Ben, I think you'll need medical attention." Eternity's eyes filled with alarm.

Ben turned toward the full-length mirror on the back of the door. Eternity stopped his progression by placing a hand on his shoulder. "Let's just get you to a doctor. All right?"

"I have to call Juliana. She's home. Very sick."

A stern-looking man, gray-haired and trim, burst into the tense office. "Mr. Powers, may I say on behalf of the entire Sarriette team, we are most sorry. Sir, I assure, I have no idea how something of this nature could have occurred."

Ben shuddered when he removed the coverings and saw his image in the mirror. The wounds would indisputably require stitching. Extensive stitching. Ben's hands shook as Eternity removed the bloodied napkins, shoved them in her purse, and replaced them with fresh cloths.

Eternity scolded. "This is a travesty. I want answers!"

"Of course. Mr. Powers, Sarriette will cover every medical expense."

Ben's vision blurred. His wounds felt as if they had been saturated with a brackish solution. He held Eternity's hand to his cheek. "We'd better get to a doctor. This burning feels abnormal."

They rushed him to his sports car waiting at the curb. Across the avenue, paparazzi, already curious by the slew of LAPD, sprung into action when they spotted him bordered by Sarriette security. Eternity climbed behind the wheel. Ben leaned against the gray leather, suddenly unable to focus.

"Ben, what's wrong?"

"I don't know. I'm having trouble breathing."

"Oh, God." Eternity blasted the horn, catching the attention of the officers. Two rushed to the driver's window.

"I'm going to need an escort. He's not able to breathe."

Instantly, they jumped into the official vehicle, flicking on the siren and flashing lights. Ben attempted to inhale deeply, but his lungs were constricted. Everything dipped and he felt submerged beneath forcible waters.

"E!" Ben's voice sounded as if his vocal chords have been doused with brine. "If I pass out, promise me you'll call Juliana."

"Don't worry, Ben. I will."

The darkness surrounded and Ben found it alluring. The darkness would shepherd serenity and quench the blaze along his jaw line. Then, he roused. *If Juliana's condition worsens, I need to be alert and capable of getting to her.* "What's that noise?"

Eternity barely heard him above the din of the siren. "What noise?"

"It's a constant moan."

She eyed him with distress. "That's coming from you, Ben."

He blinked and nothing focused. "What did she have on those nails? Venom?"

Eternity answered, but her voice faded as Ben fought the persistent urge to submit to the luring blackness.

Blinding lights rushed passed in dizzying succession.

Voices were calling to him, but he couldn't decipher the words. Hands pressed, tugged, and probed. When a doctor examined the facial wounds, Ben cried out with such force he felt as if his bones rattled.

Other words—a burning pierce—then silence.

James added chilled water to Juliana's glass. She dozed, moaning in her sleep. He removed the empty pitcher and headed to the spacious kitchen. As he replenished the water, he heard the distant ringing of Juliana's cell. It rested beside her purse on the kitchen table.

"This is James. How may I help you?"

"I'm sorry," the woman's voice quivered, "who is this?"

"James Walker. What can I do for you?"

She stammered. "I need to speak to Juliana."

James heard the familiar page for a doctor to the ER stat. "Who's calling, please?"

"Eternity Alise. It's an emergency."

James frowned. "She's not available. What type of emergency?"

"I know." Her voice seemed to fade beneath the muffle of a hand.

"Miss Alise, what is the emergency?"

"Oh, God."

James did not rattle easily. But something in the woman's tone accelerated his heart. "What's happened, Miss Alise?"

"It's Ben. He was attacked."

Suddenly, the front gate notified of a visitor. James trotted to the display of security cameras beside the kitchen computer. A white van idled behind the gate.

"Miss Alise, please hold on for just a moment."

She sniffled. "I will."

James pressed the intercom. "Yes?"

"I have a script delivery for Mr. Powers."

James pushed in the code to unlock the gate. The van waited as the heavy iron swung open, then proceeded to the front door.

"Miss Alise, are you still there?"

"Yes."

"Tell me what's happened."

The van rounded the circular drive. James opened the front door and stood on the top step. The driver hopped out with a white envelope tucked beneath his arm; the mirrored sunglasses concealed his eyes.

"Out of nowhere this woman climbed onto Ben's lap at Sarriette."

The driver climbed the steps to James. "Just need a signature, sir."

James took the signature pallet and signed.

"Ben didn't know her. So, he called for security. It was awful. Before they could pull her off, she clawed at his face. He'll need extensive surgery."

James returned the pallet to the courier. The sign embossed against the side of the van read Alpha and Omega Couriers.

"There was some type of chemical on her nails. Ben's face was severely swollen and raw."

The white envelope rose, concealing the needle.

His eyes narrowed, again baffled at the fact Bruce was nowhere to be found. The uneasiness in his gut churned with vigor. The only way Bruce would have left Ben unattended was if someone had debilitated him or he was dead. James didn't like either option. He took the packet and turned his back on the deliveryman.

"Thank you for calling, Miss Alise. Try to stay off this line. I'll be in contact very soon."

The needle plunged into his neck without leniency. First his knees cracked against the tawny stone of the step. Then his right jaw. He lay motionless, yet fully conscious. He was fully aware, yet paralyzed to cease the pending horror.

The bogus messenger scanned the isolated surroundings. The gardeners had planted dense shrubbery since his last visit, which blocked the view from the street to the front door. The gate remained open. He hefted the inert protector beyond the threshold. Once inside, he plopped him face up on the glistening limestone. James followed him with blazing eyes. He picked up the phone and envelope from the porch landing, removed the electronic equipment from the van, and kicked the door shut.

"Now, we're going to play nice, James, or Juliana will pay."

He moved to the area in the kitchen that displayed the security cameras, tugged on rubber gloves, opened the casing that held the PC units, and plugged in his laptop. After a few moments of fervent typing, he had accessed the mainframe of the security company. He typed more and the steady feed of the front door popped up. Also any household activity that occurred an hour before looped through the company's processors.

The assassin pulled on the refrigerator door and opened a water. He admired the photos Ben had taken of the twins, Sheila, the candid shots of his family. *Ben always did have such a perceptive eye.* He removed the one of Juliana in Puerto Rico, a waterfall as her backdrop, and smashed it beneath his boot.

Matthias returned to the foyer and stared at the paralyzed watchdog. He aligned the toes of his work boots beside the immobile man's ribs. He turned the bottle upside down and flooded James' face. He didn't find many things humorous, but the man's pathetic reaction of ferocious blinking caused his belly to ache. Matthias wiped the tears from his eyes.

"Understand I'll have her in everyway I desire. And you are powerless to stop me."

James made a gurgling noise in protest. He responded with a robust kick to the man's ribs. The man's gurgle increased to ardent proportions.

"I have all kinds of plans for today."

He looked to James, who studied him intently. Matthias knew he was committing every detail to memory. But in a few minutes, he would seep into unconsciousness and awake with profound amnesia.

"Plans not to prosper Juliana. Plans that definitely involve calamity to take away her future and hope."

Out of the corner of his eye, he saw pink.

"James." Juliana rubbed her eyes. "I heard glass shattering."

Although disheveled, absent of make-up, the sight of her made his pulse surge. She was finally so very near. And every obstacle had been eliminated.

"James?" She removed her hands from her face.

"No." Matthias answered. "James isn't available."

She spotted her bodyguard on the floor and sprinted in the opposite direction. She dashed through rooms and Matthias marveled at her agility around corners. He removed the needle reserved for her and caught her on the steps. She kicked at him with ferocity; he had clearly underestimated her strength. Her right fist pounded against his throat and he gagged. In an instant, she came at him with a vicious head butt. Stunned, yet still gripping the needle, he plunged it into her shoulder.

"You've hurt Ben haven't you?" Juliana whispered, the tonic infiltrating her nervous system.

"Yes. Badly."

Matthias removed another needle with an attached tube. He inserted it in her arm and grinned as her blood flowed from vein to vial.

"Do you have a gun?"

Puzzled, he frowned. "I won't be using it on you. I have other plans."

"A knife?"

He caressed her cheek. "You are going to be a fun playmate."

"You realize," Juliana sighed as she slipped into oblivion, "I'll just have to destroy you with my bare hands."

Matthias removed his laptop but left the electronic attachment that scrambled the signal presenting a steady feed. He carried her to the front door and peered through the transparent slats. The bodyguard's body had submitted to the potent drug; he lay with his eyes shut, slack-jawed. The yard was still vacant. He placed her in the rear of the van and dropped the envelope and cordless phone beside her.

He returned to James, popped open the tube, and smeared traces of Juliana's blood beneath the bodyguard's fingers, belt loop, and the bottoms of his boots. Then he locked the door with the procured house keys.

Easily he pulled through the gate, propelling them toward the future he had meticulously planned.

Sesotho Translations

Sesotho is a language spoken by the Basotho people in the Republic of South Africa and the Kingdom of Lesotho. The language is also commonly known as Southern Sotho or South Sotho and is part of the Ntu (Bantu) language family.

Ako–Please
Dumela–Good day
Ka nnete–Truly!
Ke a leboha–Thank you
Ke phela hantle, wena o phela jwang?–I'm living fine, how are you living?
Kgotso–Peace
Kombi–Taxi or bus
Palesa–Flower
Papa–Porridge
Polata–Flat roof house
Mme–Mother, Ma'am
Sala hantle–Goodbye (Go well) to the person staying
Shebeen–local bar
Tsamaya hantle–Goodbye (Go well) to the person leaving
Tshwarela–Forgive
Tshwarelo–pardon

Spanish words or phrases

Hola! - hello
Mi hija–my daughter
Novia–love (female)
Novio–love (male)
Que is la verdad?–What is the truth?

Soul Cages

In the much-anticipated sequel of Tomorrow, Ben and Juliana fight to regain their lives, their assailer lurking behind the corners.

Juliana seeks to adopt Tomorrow's children, but any attempt is blocked by governmental resistance.

Her friend, Jaki Lloyd, leads a life most envy. Tormented by paralyzing panic attacks, Jaki must face suppressed memories and Alexander McIntyre's desire to salvage their broken romance.

Alexander, meanwhile, is caught in his own paradox as the politics of news reporting threaten his integrity.

Ben spends his time pursuing justice for the havoc his former trusted friends wreaked upon his life and loved ones ... but will Ben lose sight of what matters most?

And Juliana grows suspiciously close to her bodyguard, James Walker, as Ben slips away from her.

All four lives intertwine on one fateful day leaving them wondering what price will be required to liberate them from their Soul Cages.

Coming in 2009.